SHA DAA
TOYS

CREATED BY:

MICHAEL H. HANSON

EDITED BY:

EDWARD F. MCKEOWN

MoonDream PRESS

AN IMPRINT OF COPPER DOG PUBLISHING, LLC

The Sha'Daa Series

Published by Moondream Press, an imprint of Copper Dog Publishing, LLC

537 Leader Circle

Louisville, CO 80027

Visit our Web site: www.copperdogpublishing.com

Credits:

Cover and Interior Design: Helen Harrison

Edited by Edward F. McKeown

Sha'Daa™: Toys created by Michael H. Hanson

Library of Congress Control Number: 2018905727

ISBN: 978-1-943690-24-4 print

ISBN: 978-1-943690-25-1 Kindle

First Edition: May 2018

Printed in the United States of America

Table of Contents

This book is dedicated to:

Those who love us and have given us the space and time to write and dream.

ACKNOWLEDGMENTS

No man is an island, entire of itself.
–John Donne

Unity is strength…when there is teamwork and collaboration, wonderful things can be achieved.
–Mattie Stepanek

I'D LIKE TO TAKE THIS OPPORTUNITY TO THANK the small army of individuals who are responsible for this shared-world series making it into print:

ALL of the wonderful authors who have appeared in the current six published Sha'Daa anthologies.

Schelly Beth Keefer for being the First Reader of Toys.

Catherine Kovacs Van Sciver for her work on initial formatting of Toys.

Edward F. McKeown, Sha'Daa Editor/Co-Writer, whose fierce drive and professionalism has kept this project on track through some very tough times.

Graphic Artist Helen Harrison for another one of her excellent Sha'Daa covers.

The late C.J. Henderson, who two weeks before passing away, as he and I sat in his second floor den in Brooklyn, NY, off the top of his head narrated to me (sitting directly across from him) the entirety of "Langbarðr's Storm," an amazing act of spontaneous creation that I transcribed from memory later that night, and which has become the second to last chapter of this anthology, and quite possibly the last complete short story C.J. left to posterity.

From the depths of my heart, I thank you all.

Michael H. Hanson
Sha'Daa Creator/Co-Author
Piscataway, NJ
2018

INTRODUCTION

SHA'DAA: TOYS IS THE SIXTH SHARED-world short story anthology in the Sha'daa Series to date. It is also, I'm afraid I now have to tell you, the last Sha'Daa shared-world short story anthology that will probably ever see print.

No, this rollicking weird series has not met an unnatural, or natural, end, nor is it taking a major leave of absence... it is, however, morphing, changing, and altering, much like the audacious and brave Sha'Daa characters have been forced to do in these exciting and strange books when constantly confronted with monstrous, out-of-this-world creatures and demi-gods from a multitude of horrifying hell dimensions.

So, what is the future going to bring? At present, we are working on an idea for a 4-author novella anthology that is still in development. Our hope is that the project under consideration, tentatively titled SHA'DAA: ZOMBIE PARK (and set in New York City's Central Park) might attract the attention of some big-named authors.

Another project in development is a reprint anthology of Johnny the Salesman short stories penned by Sha'Daa Creator Michael H. Hanson (stories that appeared in various magazines, anthologies, and even a webzine over the years but were never included in the main six Sha'Daa shared-world anthologies). This is about three-quarters finished and will be titled, SHA'DAA: SALESMAN.

And so we come to the eventual new direction this macabre and supernatural series is taking. *Novels*. It is MoonDream Press's hope that the Sha'Daa series will continue on as a group of novels that, yes, will follow the tradition of the first six anthologies, by all taking place during the apocalyptic event known as The Sha'Daa, set in the near future over the course of the same forty-hours. Some novels will be written by a single author, while others may very well be penned by two or three authors.

One Sha'Daa book concept being considered at the moment is a terrifying apocalyptic sky journey taken by the multinational crew of a state-of-the-art and largest rigid airship ever built, tentatively titled, SHA'DAA: AERONAUTS. Other ideas are being considered.

The Sha'Daa Series debuted in February 2009 with the publication of its first shared-world anthology, SHA'DAA: TALES OF THE APOCALYPSE, and from then 'til now, over the course of six anthologies and almost a decade, we have published 116 Sha'Daa short stories penned by 60 authors (several of them making their very first professional short story sales in this series).

It has been a rough ride. I conceived and wrote the Sha'Daa writers bible (and wrote four short Sha'Daa stories that were published in various webzines) between 2003 and 2004. I then started pitching the series as a shared-world to various up-and-coming authors I found surfing the worldwide web, and it took five full years to move from compiling the first draft of TALES OF THE APOCALYPSE to gaining a permanent and talented Editor in the form of Edward McKeown, acquiring an agent, getting picked up by a publisher, and finally seeing it in print. To date, my Sha'Daa journey has spread across fifteen long, challenging, and ultimately fulfilling years.

For a decade and a half The Sha'Daa series has kept pace with the beginning of the second Gulf war, the Columbia Space Shuttle disaster, the big blackout, Michael Phelps winning a host of medals over three consecutive Olympics, the Boston Red Sox winning the world series for the first time since 1918, Natalee Holloway's disappearance on a class trip in Aruba, Terri Schiavo getting taken off life support, Michael Jackson's acquittal of child molestation charges, Pluto's downgrade to a dwarf planet, the housing bubble burst, African-American Barack Obama's election as the 44th U.S. President, Michael Jackson dying of overdose at 50, miracle on the Hudson passenger jet safely making a water landing, Kung Fu's David Carradine being found dead in a closet in Bangkok, the BP oil spill, arrival of the iPad, the Arab Spring, U.S. Navy Seals killing Osama Bin Laden, Nelson Mandela's death, the Boston marathon bombing, Robin Williams' suicide, Robotic Lander Philae touching down on a comet, the European/Syrian refugee crisis, Donald Trump defeating Hilary Clinton to become 45th president of the USA, the crypto-currency Bitcoin explosion, and oh so much more.

Sadly, three (possibly four as one old friend has been incognito for many years) published Sha'Daa authors have passed away during this time, and their presence and comradery is sorely missed. Over the course of six anthologies many authors have jumped on then left the Sha'Daa series, appearing in anywhere from one to three of the volumes, with only four authors (C.J. Henderson, Edward McKeown, Arthur Sanchez, and myself) having actually been published in *all* of the Sha'Daa series to date.

Still, I consider all fifty-nine of the women and men who I have shared Sha'Daa covers with as family. They are my brothers, sisters, and cousins of the strange. The same eldritch and spooky blood flows through all our veins. We are bound by a glamour only understood and appreciated by those who have walked the gauntlet of The Sha'Daa, have felt its bite, have tasted its wicked pleasures, and have entered and traveled it in their darkest dreams. We are bound by the same unbreakable, mystical, literary chains.

I have been blest to share the current six Sha'Daa covers with these many talented and exceptional authors, and I take this moment to offer them all of my most heart-felt and pure gratitude for following me on this magical journey.

In the end, I only ask that the world remembers… The Sha'Daa is Coming. Are You Ready?

Michael H. Hanson
Sha'Daa Creator
Spring 2018

The Toy Shop

"There are toys for all ages."

–Old French Proverb

THE DAY WAS OFF TO AN UNUSUALLY BENE-
ficial start. A line of customers stretching around the block greeted
Whirligig's owner and proprietor Willy Carroll when he arrived at
four forty-five o'clock am, jumping out of one of Chicago's new self-driving taxis.

Usually he didn't get an early crowd like this until days before Christmas,
and here it was only a hot July morning on the edge of Chicago's Oz Park. Willy
stepped up to his wide, frosted-glass double doors underneath the large store
sign. On it, the words *Whirligigs* glowed in pink neon letters superimposed
over a big Dutch windmill. He placed his naked right palm in the etched-glass
hand outline next to the teddy-bear shaped doorknob, and a quick flicker of
blue light and several beeping sounds betrayed the retreat of large titanium
bolts and rods that secured all entrances to this store.

Considering the panicked looks on everyone's faces Willy decided to open
right then instead of waiting until the official start time of nine o'clock am. Funny
thing was that he almost didn't make it into work today. The unusually loud
thunderstorm last night and troubled dreams left the toy store owner exhausted,
dragging himself from bed. It felt like the world was trying to communicate
something of import to him, but he had been too distracted to take notice.

Flanking everybody in the front foyer were a beautifully detailed, life-size
nickel-chromium steel statue of the Robot Maria from the movie *Metropolis* on
the left, and a one-of-a-kind, hand-made, eight-foot tall, classic jointed, Steiff
Teddy Bear on the right, sitting on its haunches.

Willy quickly phoned his backup staff of six part-time employees and
got to work turning on lights, activating displays. He confirmed his 'Midnight
Laborers' were hard at work in the back assembly and shipping room.

A muzak version of Jim Henson's song, *Rubber Ducky*, began playing out
of all the store's overhead speakers.

It only took minutes for the purchase line to start forming at the main
cash register.

"Quick," a middle-aged Asian woman said, "I need to get this Gojira Chia-Pet back to my neighborhood immediately…it comes with the Chia seeds, right?"

"Just like the box says, ma'am," Willy smiled and replied in a thick Australian accent, "that'll be twenty dollars, tax included."

"This Magic 8 Ball," an elderly bald Catholic priest said, "a dream told me I needed it to make decisions during communion this afternoon."

"Always happy to be of service to the church, Father," Willy said jovially, "that's ten dollars even, tax included."

"I want both of these glow in the dark yo-yos," a cute Hispanic girl in a blue dress said, "but I only got a dollar."

"Well," Willy rubbed his chin dramatically with his right hand, "I normally charge five bucks plus tax for those two gems…"

The little girl's eyes grew wide and threatened to start leaking tears when Willy's mouth split into a wide smile, revealing a large shiny diamond embedded into his right lateral incisor.

"Yeah," Willy said, "I think we can call it even-Steven at one hundred cents. Let me just bag it up aaaaaaand here is your receipt. Now a little piece of advice, little girl, rumor has it these yo-yos are just fantastic when it comes to spinning wishes. Have a good one!"

"Business looks great today, Willy."

The resonance and power of the speaker snapped Willy's head up and away from the cash register. His mouth dropped in surprise.

"Johnny," Willy said, "is that really you? Crikey, it's been way too many years. I wasn't sure I'd ever see you again."

Standing on the other side of the counter was a wide-shouldered man well over six feet in height. Belying the temperature that was already topping eighty degrees just minutes after sunrise, Johnny wore a finely-tailored, dark suit, adorned with a long, black trench coat. A fedora rested slightly off balance on his head and cast a dark shadow over half of his lean, clean-cut face.

"I made it out of the auction tent at the state fair in Syracuse," Willy said, "just moments before it caught on fire. You were fighting that giant, and getting sucked into that black hole, I mean damn, I know you're one tough hombre, but I thought you were a goner. You just stopped appearing at my doorstep, which isn't like you at all. So, of course after all of the seasons that kept rolling by, I just, well, started assuming the worst…"

Johnny pulled a hand from inside his jacket and set several large toys on the sales counter with all the alacrity of a stage musician or a savior performing a minor miracle.

"No time to talk shop, Willy," Johnny said, "I'd like to trade off this mint condition and still in its original box nineteen fifties Linemar robot with lighted eyes and smoking action."

Willy did a double take.

"This rare Kali Barbie," Johnny continued, "with twenty-four carat spun gold pants suit, emerald eyes, real ruby lips, diamond shoes, and of course four arms."

Willy leaned forward to give the items a long, slow look.

"The third piece," Johnny went on, "is a rare Princess Diana Beanie Baby Bear, and the last offering is a mint condition Matchbox Number Thirty Crane Truck, and all I want in return is on this list."

Willy snapped up the slip of paper from Johnny's hand and scowled.

"You're asking for some real expensive treasures here, Salesman," Willy murmured.

"And you're getting even bigger ones in trade," Johnny said. "We got a deal, Toyman?"

Johnny's deep tone clawed at Willy's attention.

"What's the rush, Johnny?" Willy asked, "I don't remember you ever being in such a hurry before."

Johnny leaned forward and whispered a single word.

"Sha'Daa."

Willy's face lost all of its animation and managed somehow to grow paler beneath his head of thick, carrot-colored locks.

"Ohhhhh, bugger me for a bogan."

CHAPTER ONE

A Very Bad Bear

Edward F. McKeown

"Wake in the deepest dark of night and hear the driving rain. Reach out a hand and take a paw and go to sleep again."

–Charlotte Gray

THE FIRST THING YOU MUST UNDERSTAND is that I am a very bad bear.

I do not know when I came into being. Time has no meaning where I come from, a place of pain and combat. I am not sure if I was born. One moment I was not there and the next I was and aware, in a world of tooth of claw. At first, I ate only the small and weaker creatures that wandered through the torn rocks and stinking rivers of that world.

Nor can I tell where that world lies relative to Earth. I am only a bear. Perhaps it is best to use the human expression, "You can't get there from here." And you do not want to.

I grew stronger, bigger and ate more and better. My awareness sharpened, I became cunning. I began to think and wonder. My first great realization came when I finally understood that no matter how strong I became, I was only a bear and there would always be someone stronger. It was necessary to ingratiate myself with the more powerful. So I became a wily bear.

Time passed but I could not say how much. I no longer lived like a beast in the wild, but belonged to something new, an army. In a way it was like a beast, it rolled across the world, eating, killing, mating as it wished; leaving a trail of filth and waste behind it.

In the army, I learned and observed, avoiding those who sought to increase their power by killing the weak, as I curried the favor of the strong. This gave me access to better food, mates and captives. I lived only for myself. There was no other form of existence. It never occurred to me to wonder what the army was for, or why it existed.

Then one day, a being appeared. He said his name was Willy Carroll, an uncouth and meaningless sound to me. He favored me with a strange and unpleasant grin. "Bear, you are cunning and strong for an animal." His eyes were deep pools and I could read nothing in them. I knew that his presence in the heart of the army meant he had power, and I had no choices. "But you are also cautious and thoughtful. More than you let on."

"No, no, my Master," I groveled. "I am only a humble servant."

"And proving my point," Carroll said. He smiled, if something that chilled the heart of a fierce bear could be called a smile. "You have the intelligence to mind orders and to wait for an opportunity to strike. I am the Toymaker and need one such as you."

"Yes, Master," I answered, with a stab of fear. I had heard of terrible rumors of the Toymaker. While I have no concept of toys as such, I knew him as a maker of strange and deadly devices.

"So," he continued, with the false heartiness practiced by the powerful. "You and I will soldier together in a great event that is coming, the Sha'Daa. Will you serve me?"

"Oh yes, gladly," I said, knowing that any other response would end with me as a rug or garment.

He smiled his bone-chilling smile again. "I will make a new body for you. It will seem small and powerless but it will allow you to journey to a place called Earth. There you will await the call to war."

Φ Φ Φ

So I find myself now in the window of a store called Whirligigs, with a pleasant, yellow sun beaming down on me and all sorts of food wandering by and looking in on me. My essence is now contained in a ridiculous caricature of a bear, with large, button eyes and soft, short fur. Many a child would stop in and say I am "cute" or "adorable" but I am also expensive. So I remain in the window until an adult man and woman come in, trailed by a wan, little girl who seems tired, even listless.

The Toymaker greets them and even I marvel at the change in him. He is no longer the oily, frightening creature who drafted me, but urbane and charming. I listen as the male says how he has been told that Carroll's toys are special. His little girl suffers from night terrors, something which, to me, seems quite sensible. Terror has been with me night and day since I became aware.

I look at the child who looks at me and I feel something electric pass between us. She walks past her parents and scoops me up in a hug. "Hello Teddy," she says. "You will be my new friend."

I am bewildered by this. No one has ever touched me, save to strike me. I have never had a friend, only temporary allies who I would betray, or who would sacrifice me, as needs dictated. But there is no guile in the wide, blue-eyes that look into mine. I am so confused by what has happened that I barely pay attention to the transaction where I am sold to the family.

The Toymaker takes me to the back to place me in a box. "So now you know your targets," he says, his manner is enigmatic and subdued. "Those above have decreed this family is special, though the humans themselves do not know it. They present a danger sufficient for them to be targeted at great expense by the powers. What will you do when the call comes, I wonder?" The lid comes down.

I take up my life with the Wendelyn family. They live in a small, pleasant village outside the Chicago. I do not learn much about the parents, Michael and Theresa. My time is spent with Jenny, their child.

My first night I spend on her bed. Night falls and the parents put the little girl to sleep, leaving on a night light. They have an intercom as well. I assume that this was to spy on their child. I am wrong.

Jenny cries out in the early morning hours and her parents rush to her side. Her eyes are wide and staring and to my shock, I realize that she is seeing through the veil between dimensions. She senses the dark army lairing in the space between the worlds. Perhaps my mission is to stop this?

When the child finally sleeps again, I move closer. In the shadow between the dimensions, some small and evil spirits have sensed the girl. They hover over her in the night time, when our kinds are strongest, nipping at her dreams. While I am confined to this ridiculous form, I remain a very bad bear and in the twilight world I still have power. I seize the small spirits and shred them.

Jenny sleeps. In the morning, her parents seem relieved. She has slept better than before. She has more energy. The next night I make sure nothing troubles her. Her parents greet the sun with joy, and Jenny will not be parted with me, carrying me everywhere and telling everyone at preschool that I am there to protect her. Her friends are envious and the adults indulgent.

Something curious has happened to me. I feel a queer thrill of pride when she praises me. I enjoy the feel of her arms around me, her little face pressed against me. Night falls again and I destroy any that comes near her dreams, ripping it asunder. In the morning, I am praised by both mother and father for my "valiant defense of Jenny."

The child begins to strengthen. She has energy and an appetite and plays outside far more often. Sometimes I catch her mother weeping at the sight, not tears of pain, but of joy, something I had neither seen nor imagined before.

The weekend comes and the family holds a yard sale. Jenny is in the fenced backyard playing, while her parents sell things in the front. I sit beside a tree as she plays on her swing. The sun is up and its rays fall on my face. I am drowsy.

And thus, I nearly fail in my duty. The sound of a growl wakes me and I am confused, the night vermin cannot be here under the light of the yellow sun.

They are not. A large dog has wandered into the yard. How, I am not certain, but it is there, only yards from Jenny who stands frozen looking at the growling beast. As an animal, I know barking is one thing, but a growl means attack. She stares at the advancing dog, blue eyes wide with terror. I know her parents are too far away and unaware.

The dog and I spring at the same moment. If we were closer to the Sha'Daa, I would have struck the beast down in a moment, but that time is too far in the future. Still, the dog is surprised and thrown on its side by my weight. I wrap my arms about its neck and grapple. He must not reach Jenny!

Jenny's screams rouse her parents to the danger and she flees. The dog turns on me as I batter ineffectually at it. Its paws and teeth tear at my cloth and stuffing. I am being disemboweled.

Suddenly the dog is struck and sent sprawling. Jenny's father has run out of the garage and holds a metal garden rake. He shoves it at the dog which backs away. More people are running. The neighbors at the yard sale fling things at the dog. Men charge forward as the women encircle Jenny and her mother. The dog flees the field. The battle is ours.

I lie there wondering what death will be for me. I know I am badly damaged and that the magic that holds my spirit to this toy will fade now. My fate is a strange one. I was sent here to kill this family and spread disruption. What moved me to fight for them?

Jenny has broken free of her mother and skirted the other adults to run to my side. Her blue eyes are over me and her tears drip on my face. Her father and mother kneel by my side. Well, I will not die alone. This is a better fate than my kind usually meets.

"I'm sorry, Honey," her mother says.

"God," her father adds, "in our own yard. Whose damn dog was that?"

"I don't think it was rabid," another man says. "No foaming. Just a bad dog."

"Someone call the police," a woman demands.

"Teddie stopped him," Jenny says. "He jumped on him. He's hurt."

"Honey, he's just a toy," her father says, still shaking with reaction to the encounter. A good man, but no warrior, clearly.

Jenny's mother gives him a warning glance. "I'm sure he did Jenny; he's a very brave bear. But he's all tore up now. We'll get you a new one."

"No!" Jenny says. "We have to fix Teddy."

"Darling he's been in a dog's mouth. It might have had diseases—" Jenny's mother reaches for my torn body but Jenny throws herself across my chest.

"No," she cries. "He saved me. We can't just throw him away. That's disloyal."

The parents both freeze. I am startled and afraid for Jenny. She defies their power. I don't want her beaten for protecting me. Instead her parents look with approval at the child. The mother nods.

"Ok Jenny. I'll gather him up and wash him. Then we will see if they can sew him up at Sue's."

I am carried to the sink and washed in soap and water. The next day, Jenny's mother takes me to a store. It is filled with Asian women who listen to the story of how I was so torn. They cluck over me and clean me further and refill all my stuffing and add more. It feels good in a way—giving a clean feeling to me. One woman wonders if I might be possessed by a spirit. She is closer than she realizes. Despite their best work I know I do not look like I did before. There is ugliness to me now and I fear the look in Jenny's eyes when she sees me, especially after Jenny's mom sighs when she picks me up and the Asian lady apologizes that the work was not better.

But my fears evaporate when Jenny sees me and her face is like the sun shining out from behind a cloud. She rushes to take me from her mother's hands. "Teddy, you're back! I was so worried."

What is the name for this feeling spreading through me? This moment could last forever and I would be…I would be happy. She holds me tight and takes me up to her room. There, the other toys are carefully moved aside as she makes a place of honor for me.

The days resume their peaceful march, but a cloud sits on my heart. Time ticks down to the Sha'Daa. I spend my days playing with Jenny. At night, I sit on her bed. The night terrors that I was purchased to combat, do not trouble her, but she is still a child and sometimes wakes in a fright. I am always there—the first thing she sees. Often, she falls back asleep without fully waking. This pleases me a great deal.

The awful duty I was sent to do, preys on my mind. The day before the Sha'Daa, I am an agony of indecision. Jenny has a troubling day as if she somehow senses that something is wrong. Her parents are similarly subdued: fearful of wars and rumors of war in their world. Night falls and her father leaves all the outside lights burning. Jenny goes to bed and sleeps fitfully at first before dropping off.

Strength flows into me. It is hours to midnight, but the forces of darkness stir already. We are readying for our moment, but I can feel no certainty in my purpose, only despair as I have never known, fighting in the tooth and claw world of my birth. Tooth and claw, yes, we are seeking to turn this place of yard sales and mowed lawns into what I was born into. Can that be right?

A tap at the window brings my head up. On the other side is a goblin that has shinnied up to the second story window. The small creature is a messenger. It gestures at me to open the window. I fight a second's battle with myself before going over and slipping the window open.

"Orders," it croaks in its hideous voice. "You are to eliminate this family then move down the block. Many of the people on this block have powers that they do not even know. You must take them all, but take this family first."

"I understand my orders," I say. I have not spoken aloud since I arrived here. My own voice sounds terrible to me.

"Gah," it repeats, "all this caution and planning. Night has come; it is our time. Why wait? Let me help you with the slaughter."

I seek refuge in the orders. "Wait till midnight."

The goblin looks past me at the little girl sleeping in her bed. "Come on," it wheedles. "I know that the Sha'Daa is hours away but what's the harm? Just rip off a few toes. Ah, the fresh blood, the screams." The goblin slips one leg over the window sill, its wicked teeth showing.

What happens next; happens in an instant. I seize the goblin's filthy face in one paw, grab its shoulder with the other and give a mighty heave. The goblin's neck snaps and I shove it out the window before its bowels can let go, increasing the reek of it. It falls into the shrubs below.

I turn but Jenny has not stirred. I thank….God. Yes, I thank God that she has not awoken to see the goblin at her window. I stand there shaking. Not with reaction, but with shame. I opened the window. I should never have done that. Disgrace. How can a bear atone for such a sin?

The toymaker's face comes to me unbidden. Did he know that I would do this? Did he hope I would? Whose side is he truly on?

No matter. I shut the window and walk to the foot of her bed. There I sit legs akimbo and paws on my knees. I settle my spirit for the battle to come, where quarter will neither be asked or granted. This house and family, where I have been granted love and kindness, I will defend as best I can. But Jenny must be my unconditional priority. I stare at the door. The Sha'Daa will cross that threshold only over my dead body.

And I am a very bad bear.

The Toyman Cometh

IT WAS THE YEAR SEVENTEEN EIGHTY-NINE AND well over twelve months since the founding of Sydney Cove where eighteen-year-old, William Thomas Carrolton, found himself facing the looped end of a hangman's noose. One of the original seven-hundred-thirty-six convicts carried by Captain Arthur Phillip's eleven-ship fleet to land at Botany Bay, Australia, William was a convicted London thief, who now stood accused, falsely so he claimed, of assault on one of King George the Third's soldier's teenage-daughter.

More of a drumhead trial than any kind of fair court, William didn't have legal representation of any kind as a current convict, and was not even allowed to call a single witness in his favor, of which there were actually many, as the so-called assault occurred in the settlement's public tavern where Mary Stirling, the supposed victim, was drinking up a storm and holding court as the prettiest white lass in a thousand miles. Her boyfriend Arthur, the son of the colony's Sergeant of Marines was none too pleased with Mary aggressively swapping spit with the good-looking and younger, red-maned William. A fight ensued. William knocked out the shorter, pugnacious Arthur and was arrested. Afterwards to save face, Arthur browbeat Mary into giving a false accusation.

In a matter of hours, the colony's magistrate condemned William on the outskirts of the settlement a mere hundred yards from the ocean. An impromptu gallows had been thrown together from gathered driftwood strung over a narrow shoreline rock crevasse that appeared at low tide. A crude noose was tossed over William's head. He was lifted upwards by four stalwart Marines. The other end of the rope was secured, and he was unceremoniously shoved off of the colonists' shoulders, where he fell almost a full body length before the rope went slack, stretched, and immediately, but all too slowly, began to choke the life out of him.

"And may God have mercy on your worthless soul," the Pastor of Sydney Cove spat out before closing his bible and striding away with the crowd. In moments, William, hands and feet bound together and his face turning dark, was left all alone to slowly choke to death.

Bag of Tricks

Benjamin Tyler Smith

"He who dies with the most toys wins."

–Anonymous Saying

"INTERESTING PIECES YOU BROUGHT TODAY," GINA said as we left Kutztown University's Sharadin Art Building. She looked up at me, her brown eyes glittering in the evening sun.

I slid my backpack over one broad shoulder and shoved my hands into my leather jacket's pockets. The pack was filled with prints of hex signs found on barns, farmhouses, and covered bridges around Pennsylvania Dutch country: from bright floral patterns to complex star designs—or *blumme* and *schtanne* in the old dialect. "The Folk Festival's in two weeks. Figured the out-of-staters would get a kick out it."

"Well, I was hoping you'd bring some of your real artwork in your bag of tricks."

I glanced about. "Not so loud," I whispered. Everyone knew I created and restored hex signs, but the public saw them as harmless artwork from a bygone age. Only a fellow mage like Gina would understand the true use for them, even if her magic flowed in different ways.

She laughed. "Don't worry, no one's nearby." Then she leaned close. "Or is this an excuse to get me within arm's reach?"

Damn, she was pretty. Tan skin, dark hair, curves where they counted, and a mischievous grin that promised much to its recipient. That our magical affinities matched, only added to the attraction, and my discomfort. I scratched my short, brown hair and opened my mouth.

"Mr. Wishman!" a reedy voice called.

The doors to the art building had been thrown wide. A thin man with permanently hunched shoulders and thick-framed glasses stood there, studying us both with a dispassionate gaze; Dr. Drew Moyer, head of the Ancient-to-

Modern Folk Art program at the university. A group of his students hovered close behind him.

"We are leaving to examine some ancient artwork found in the area," Drew said. He pointed at a van parked on the sidewalk and smiled. "We could use your expertise."

I clenched my jaw. Something about Drew rubbed me the wrong way, though I couldn't pin down why. He was professional to me. Maybe it was how his students hung on his every word. They practically worshipped the guy, and I couldn't see the appeal. "Sorry, Drew," I said, turning away. "It's late, and I'm beat. Another time!"

"You're certainly popular today," Gina said after we left them behind.

"Not the kind of popularity I'd like."

Gina's answering giggle was short-lived. "I haven't had a single vision over the last few days."

That caught me off guard. "Really?" Gina was a fortune-teller, one with a spotless track record. Like me, she did her best to stay low-key, and instead earned her bread teaching craft jewelry classes at KU. "Has this happened before?"

"Never." She pressed a hand to her head. "It's like the future's shut off to me."

"That makes you mortal like the rest of us," I teased.

She didn't laugh. "I'm frightened, Jim. I need protection."

"Get a gun."

"From evil spirits! Can't you give me a hex sign?"

Most of my hex signs were designed to protect entryways and enclosed spaces, but I did carry one that hid my presence from demons. My family isn't liked in the world of darkness. I really didn't want to part with it. "Well–"

She clasped her hands together. "Please?"

Gah, what a face! "Fine, you win!" I reached into my leather jacket and removed a small circle of wood, painted on both sides with a black four-pointed star surrounded by white spiraling teardrops. They looked like ghosts bouncing off a shield. "Take it. I'll paint another when I get home."

"You are such a dear!" She threw her arms around my neck. "I'll pay you back sometime."

"The thanks are payment enough," I assured her, my face heating. Damn her body, and her magic, they were enough to drive a man wild, even one who could ill afford it.

She squeezed harder, and I gently disengaged from her. Last thing I needed was her to feel the Smith & Wesson 686 revolver hanging from my shoulder. "I better get going. Long night ahead."

"Call me later." She winked. "I'll be up."

She disappeared from view, but not from my thoughts. Those followed me all the way back to my station wagon, a white, wood-grained Buick Roadmaster. It didn't look like much, but it was my pride and joy. Lots of cargo space, a relatively powerful motor, and a comfortable ride.

I bet Gina would be a comfortable—I squelched the thought. Focus, Jim. Dump the hex photos in the back, get in the car, drive. All you need tonight are ribs and beer.

And maybe a cold shower. Or three.

Twenty minutes later I walked out of the Giant supermarket, a package of pre-cooked ribs in my hand. I set this next to a six-pack of beer I'd scored at the Tavern.

A shadow fell across the parking lot, and I looked up. The sun hung low in the western sky, obscured by trees below, clouds above, and a pillar of bright green smoke in-between.

Wait, green smoke?

Shit, my house!

My Roadmaster kicked up a cloud of dust as I roared up the curved, tree-lined driveway. Even through the low, thick canopy of the maple trees I could see red-orange flames licking the sky. Green smoke poured from broken windows and the chimney.

Shit, shit, shit. Green smoke meant my reagents were on fire: my unicorn urine, my emulsified mermaid cartilage, even my stock of virgin blood.

A figure in black sat in the shade of the maple tree closest to the house. I slammed on my brakes and jumped out of the car. "Johnny? Is that you?"

"In the flesh!" Johnny the Salesman waved. "How's it going, James?"

"How do you think? My house is on fire!"

"Hmm?" Johnny looked to his left, his eyes widening. "Why, so it is! Imagine that."

"My supplies are in there!" That, plus years' worth of pre-made hex signs and carved sigils. The veil between worlds is thin in this area, and my family's always been ready. Until now. "My palette, too!" Without it, my art was useless.

"I believe you are right on that count, too." Johnny grinned, his single gold tooth gleaming even in the shade. "I have something that can help. Want it?"

The last time I'd seen Johnny, I'd found his aloof flippancy amusing, if a little creepy. Now it just pissed me off. "Yes! Quickly!"

"That's the spirit! I like a motivated sale." Johnny chuckled as he reached into his coat and withdrew a fireman's cap. "Why wait for the fire department when you can *be* the fire department?"

He held it up for me to inspect. It was a plastic kid's toy, and it hummed with magic. "Is this from Whirligigs?" I waved a hand. "Wait, we'll worry about that later. How much?"

Johnny said nothing, merely smiled and looked past me. I turned my head, my stomach fluttering. "You want my car?" My pride and joy!

"And everything in it. There's someone who needs it far more than you this night."

My jaw went slack. "You don't mean…"

He laughed and clicked his heels together. "Yes, yes! The Sha'Daa is here, as of forty-five minutes ago, though this area's Hellgate has yet to open." He pointed at me, his expression suddenly serious. "You must keep it from opening, James Wishman. Uphold your family's legacy."

Johnny had never steered anyone in my family wrong, nor had I ever known him to lie. Shit, if the Sha'Daa was here I needed my palette more than ever. If it was lost, it'd be months before I could get a replacement. And I didn't have months. "All right, deal." I tossed him the keys.

He handed over the cap. "A pleasure doing business with you!"

I crammed the little cap on my too-big head; a tingling sensation swept across my skin, and I shivered. I hoped it was protective magic, but I had no time to worry. I ran for the nearest opening, a shattered sliding glass door. No sooner had I entered the home, then the fire around me began to sputter and die out, throwing up gouts of black smoke and steam. The walls glistened, and I realized the cap was spraying water everywhere, except I wasn't getting wet.

I moved from room to room, dousing the flames that consumed my home. This was great! Heat didn't affect me; flames couldn't exist near me, and the smoke—

A searing pain shot through my throat and touched my lungs. I broke into a coughing fit. Ok, so it didn't do shit for smoke, but I could work with that.

I stumbled out of the smoldering doorway a few minutes later and hacked until my lunch came up. I wiped my mouth and grimaced. Mexican doesn't taste so good the second time around.

My other hand clutched a dark-stained, wooden palette, slightly scorched, but very much intact. It was fashioned from cedar of Lebanon, a wood known for its protective qualities against evil. Small sigils carved along the oval perimeter only enhanced those properties and extended them to my paints. The reagents were only part of the equation.

I had expected Johnny to be gone, but he was inspecting his new ride. He popped the Roadmaster's hatch and rummaged through the trunk's contents, checking off his ever-present list. I yanked the fireman's cap off my head. "This could've worked on you, too! Why didn't you save my equipment?"

"Ah, but that would make me Johnny the Fireman!" A business card floated in front of my face. "Is that how the card reads? I could've sworn I put 'Salesman.'"

"Funny. Do you charge for the comedy routine?"

Johnny shut the hatch and bowed. "The japes are my only form of charity, my friend."

I rolled my eyes and leaned against the wagon. Puffs of green smoke continued to rise from somewhere in the middle of the ruined house. "Shit, what a day."

"It's about to get worse, but fear not! I've got something to help you through it." Johnny set a bag on the hood of the car. It bore the name, Whirligigs, over a windmill logo that spun with every gust of wind that touched the plastic surface.

That answered my question about the toy hat, and brought back some memories. When I was a kid, my old man took me to Chicago for some underground magician meet-up. One day we all went on a tour of the city and found our way to Oz Park, where Whirligigs is located. Being a brat, I wanted to get my hands on all the gadgets and gizmos in the toy shop, but Dad warned me not to touch anything. Nothing in Whirligigs is at is seems, especially not its Aussie owner, Willy. I don't remember much about him, other than his boisterous laugh and how one of his teeth glinted strangely. That, and his repeated statements of "Remember, if the brat breaks it, you buy it!" followed by "Here, boy, check this one out."

The fireman's cap was tame in comparison to some of the other items there. I studied the bag. "What's this one do?"

"It will provide more of what you need, when you need it most."

Cryptic, as always. "You don't want another car, do you? Because this baby's all I've got." I patted the Roadmaster.

Johnny slapped my hand away. "All you had, and no. All I require is a single .357 Magnum cartridge, one of your special ones." He pointed at my jacket pocket, where I carried a speedloader of extra rounds. An eight-pointed star had been painted on the bottom of each casing, with a Maltese cross on the primer. No demon wanted to get hit with that. "There's someone who–"

"Will need it far more than me this night, I get it." I frowned. A single cartridge? That didn't sound like a good ending for Johnny's intended buyer. I tossed him the speedloader. "Take all seven. Maybe that'll bring better luck."

Johnny's smile broadened. "Very well, but I must return the favor. Extra for extra." He held up two fingers. "For a pair of rounds, a pair of tidbits: first, you will find the Hellgate beneath Kutztown, in a place where some looked up and others looked down. It should have opened by now, but your family's past actions have strengthened the weak veil about this place."

The sealing of Crystal Cave in 1871, and the Hawk Mountain Incident of 1934, I thought.

"Only a few demons have been released," Johnny continued, "but they have many human thralls. They need something to open the Hellgate. The same something we need to seal it."

"Do you enjoy being this obscure?" I demanded.

Johnny laughed. "Second, and more clearly: the fire company is on the way. Don't be found by them."

Far off, a siren wailed. Icy fear pricked my chest. "What's going on?"

"You'll see." Johnny shoved me toward the tree line. "Go on, shoo!"

"Hey, what about the other four rounds?" I called. "Don't I get extra for those?"

"You'll see!" he repeated.

Somehow, I was not reassured.

Johnny hopped into my Roadmaster and vanished a moment later, right as the volunteer fire company pulled into the driveway. I hid in a thicket of blackberries on the edge of my property. The thorns reminded me why I wear leather, stylish and practical.

The fire engine stopped where the wagon had just been. I frowned. Where was the tanker truck? I wasn't on public water, which meant no fire hydrant. They should've known that.

Doors flew open and firemen spilled out of the truck. A pair of them jogged the perimeter of my home, while the rest gathered about someone wearing the chief's hat, except it wasn't the chief. The other firemen looked familiar, yet not. Maybe I'd seen them out of uniform somewhere. Kutztown's a small community, after all.

The pair quickly returned. "His vehicle's not here!" one of them called. "Maybe he never came home!"

Fake Chief dug at the ground with a boot heel and growled. I couldn't understand the words, but they stung my ears and brought bile to my throat. He looked around, head twitching this way and that. "I smell him. He's been here, and recently!"

I shrank back into the thicket. How the hell–?

"Search again!" Fake Chief squawked. "Find the Obstructer!"

They spread across the property, peering up into maple trees, or poking through the smoking remains of my house. One made a beeline for the black-berry patch. I reached for my revolver, but didn't draw. Maybe giving Johnny those extra rounds hadn't been such a good idea after all.

Fake Chief's radio crackled to life and the nauseating language trumpeted from it in a wash of static. Everyone froze. The one close to me stared straight ahead, eyes unblinking, until Fake Chief yelled, "Mount up! The female's at the airport!"

Female? My chest constricted. *Gina!* I resisted the urge to jump up and run. I didn't move until Fake Chief and his lackeys piled into the fire truck. As they backed down the driveway, I fumbled for my cell phone, then cursed. I'd left it on the charger this morning. It was probably still on what was left of my nightstand, a puddle a molten plastic. I could run to my neighbor's house, but I didn't even have Gina's number memorized. Stupid modern conveniences!

Fake Chief had mentioned the airport. In this immediate area that meant two places: the tiny Kutztown Airport, or the creatively named Airport Diner right next door. I couldn't imagine why she would be at the actual airport, so that left–

Wait, the airport! A place where those taking off look up and those landing look down. It hadn't been in use since 2009, when a minor earthquake damaged some of the buildings in the area and shifted the land beneath the runway. A giant boulder had pushed its way through the middle of the tarmac, and nothing could dislodge it. The township closed the airport, and that was that.

If the Hellgate really was under there, it was Crystal Cave all over again. And it was going to take a Wishman to deal with it.

I crawled out of the thicket and ran for my shed on the far side of the property. I opened the door and jumped on my small ATV. I fired it up and rifled through my backpack while the engine was warming.

My palette was there, along with the fireman's cap and the Whirligigs bag. Inside that bag was a miniature yellow dump truck, the pull-back-and-race kind. It was just wide enough for my thumb and fingers to grasp either side of the bed's walls. What was I supposed to do with this? No wonder Johnny only wanted one bullet for it.

But, it had come from Whirligigs, and Willy didn't fly halfway 'round the world for additions to his inventory if he didn't think they were useful. I shrugged and put it back. My bag of tricks was getting weirder by the minute

As I zipped up the backpack, the palette shifted and revealed another item: my rack of ribs from Giant, still cold to the touch.

Why the hell am I carrying ribs? A note had been taped to the front of the sealed packaging: This wasn't on my list, so I return it to you. Consider it a lagniappe: something extra as the Creole would say.

That wasn't on his list, but the beer was? Johnny, you bastard.

The sun had set when I pulled into the field behind the Airport Diner, a squat, wide building with a stone façade and a red roof. The fire company hadn't arrived yet, but I could see flashing lights in the distance. I'd need to be quick. I pulled open the glass door and stepped inside.

A long counter and stools ran the length of one wall, while booths filled the windowed sides. It looked much like you'd expect from a 1950's roadside diner, minus the addition of a dining room off to the left. Despite the full parking lot, no one was here, not even staff behind the counter. The hairs on the back of my neck rose. That wasn't good.

Gina sat at one of the tables in the empty dining room, stirring her iced tea with a straw. She looked up at my approach. "Jim, are you all right? You're covered in soot!"

"Long story," I said. Why was she alone here? No time for that. I hauled her to her feet. "We've gotta go."

Tires squealed outside, and the fire engine's red lights strobed through the diner's windows. Firemen bailed out and snatched up axes, helmets, oxygen tanks, anything heavy. They were joined by a large group of twenty-somethings, who spread out around the entire building. Many wore KU maroon and gold. Students?

Fake Chief pointed at the diner. "He's inside! Get the Obstructer!"

The firemen hurled their heavy objects through the windows in a cascade of broken glass. The students flooded in through these openings, heedless of shards cutting into their clothes and flesh. They surrounded us, their eyes dull and unseeing.

"Get behind me," I said, pushing Gina back as the students drew closer. I flexed my fingers and started to reach for my jacket.

Something cold and sharp touched my neck. A knife, held by Gina. "Sorry about this," she said as she slipped the backpack off my shoulder.

"That makes two of us." My heart sank. I never imagined Gina would be involved, and willingly. The students were clearly under some sort of influence, but not her. "Why?"

"Why?" she shrugged. "They said they'd spare me if I brought you in. Something about payback?"

"We've been a thorn in Hell's side for a few centuries now," I said, feeling a foolish sense of pride.

Fake Chief jumped in through a window. He cocked his head at an odd angle and studied me. "This him?"

"It is," Gina said, stepping back.

The chief nodded and barked a command.

A muscle-bound jock stepped forward and grabbed the back of my jacket. "Come along," he said in a monotone. "Dr. Moyer wants to see you."

Drew? Son of a bitch, he's involved, too? At least that explained where I'd seen Fake Chief's men before: in Drew's class earlier today, along with the rest of these students.

A procession of students and faux firemen followed us out of the diner and across the parking lot. *Why didn't they search me?* Then again, these were brainwashed college kids, not cops or soldiers. Why would they expect someone who made quaint folk art to be armed? And what could I do with it, surrounded as I was? They'd just pile onto me and take it. No, I needed to wait for the right moment.

I was shoved past the airport's single-story office building and led down the runway. My boots crushed grass and weeds pushing up through the broken asphalt. Ahead, a dome of solid rock jutted from the ground. A hole had been dug at the base, and an extension ladder rose up from the bottom.

Fake Chief and Gina went first, followed by the students. I climbed down next, Jock only a rung behind. Long stalactites greeted me on either side of the ladder. Below, a pair of students aimed flashlights to illuminate a crude painting on one of the cave walls, above an opening to another chamber. The painting depicted stick figures bowing toward a doorway of deepest blue.

The same color as the light pulsing from the adjacent chamber.

My legs were trembling with fear by the time I reached the bottom of the ladder. Jock pushed me through the opening into a wide, domed chamber. Stalagmites and stalactites jutted from the floor and ceiling like fangs and teeth in a beast's maw. Students danced and hopped around the stalagmites in complicated patterns, chanting and singing softly. Others prostrated themselves before the far wall, where a shimmering blue portal lay. The Hellgate pulsed with bright blue light every five seconds or so.

"Beautiful, isn't it?" a reedy voice called.

Drew stood in front of the Hellgate, flanked by a pair of towering bipedal beasts, one in the shape of a bull, the other a pig. Even across the room I could smell the brimstone. Demons.

As Jock led me closer, I saw two piles of charred corpses on either side of the Hellgate. The real firemen and the diner's patrons, if I had to take a guess. I balled my shaking hands into fists.

Drew smiled, as if we were in his office back at KU. "What do you think of the artwork?" He glanced at the Hellgate. "Pales in comparison to the real thing, eh?"

I said nothing.

"Come, don't be like that." He checked his watch. "We have a couple minutes before Lord Hrolgth demands your execution. We should chat. Oh, you've met one of my associates, I believe."

Fake Chief took up position next to the pig-demon. He shuddered violently, and his skin sloughed off. Gone was the human form, replaced with a feathered body and a rooster's head.

I admit I was scared, but I couldn't help chuckling. "A cow, a pig, and a chicken? The farmer's market isn't until the weekend, Drew!"

The demons snarled and hissed, but Drew quieted them with a raised hand. "Don't take these lesser demons lightly. They may be the weakest of their brethren, but look at how they've enthralled my class."

"Charming." Damn, how was I going to get out of this one? I needed to take out Drew and his demons, then seal the Hellgate. "How'd you find out about this place?" I asked, hoping to stall for time.

"As your family serves the Light, mine serves the Dark." Drew reached into his coat and removed a wooden wand. "Long have we have prepared for this day, and now all is ready."

A mage. Of course. That explained my instinctive dislike for the man. Magic can attract, but it can also repulse.

"The life of a powerful mage is needed to open this portal." Drew grinned, the expression ghastly on his skeletal face. "All the better that it's you, Obstructer."

I sagged against Jock, who shifted his weight to hold me upright.

Drew muttered a few words and the wand's tip glowed with yellow light. "Lord Hrolgth asked me to present you to his feast table. He prefers extra crispy." He shouted a trigger word and loosed a crackling bolt of energy.

I rolled to the side, slipping my arms up and out of the jacket as I did. Jock had a half-second to realize he was holding an empty jacket before he was struck by the magical bolt. He shrieked as his skin blistered and blackened.

I jumped to my feet and unsnapped my holster's thumb-break. I cleared leather, aimed at Drew, and squeezed the trigger. The muzzle-flash half-blinded me, and when my vision cleared I saw the rooster-demon standing in front of Drew, blue blood gushing from its stomach and staining its white feathers.

"A gun?" Drew dove behind a stalagmite. "Why didn't you idiots search him?"

"Hire better help!" I shouted back.

"Kill him!"

The trio of demons charged at me, the wounded rooster leading the way. I aimed and fired again. This second round tore through its beak, and it fell with a gurgle.

Behind me, the chanting and singing faltered. I risked a glance back and saw the fake firemen looking around in confusion. Kill the possessor, free the possessed. Made sense to me.

Then the other two demons were on me, and there was no time for anyone else. The bull-demon roared and threw powerful punches my way. I ducked and weaved, then jumped back when it tried to gore me. That sent me right into the pig-demon's flying dropkick. I landed hard on my ass, my gun skittering across the floor. I scrambled for it.

The pig-demon stamped a foot on the revolver. It snorted a purple cloud and flashed blackened teeth. "Gotchya now, hoo-man." Behind me, the bull demon bellowed a laugh.

"Jim, take this!" Gina cried.

My backpack soared through the air, and I caught it.

"Gina, you traitor!" Drew shouted from behind his stalagmite.

"What makes you think I was ever on your side?" Gina spat.

The pig-demon stepped forward. I'd worry about Gina's change of heart later. I shoved my hand into the bag and yanked out the first thing I grabbed. The ribs? "Hey, Little Piggy!" I shouted as I threw. "Here's a glimpse at your future!"

The package bounced off the pig-demon's chest and struck the floor. The demon leaned over, then jumped back with a squeal. "You monster! You eat my terrestrial kind?"

I dove for the revolver, raised it, and squeezed once, twice, again.

Purple blood and offal spilled all over the package of ribs as the pig-demon collapsed. *Yuck. Veganism's looking better and better by the minute.*

Nah, screw that. I like my ribs.

The bull-demon roared and charged as I clambered to my feet. My sixth round shattered its skull and jellied its brain.

Drew jumped up then, his wand raised. He had been counting my shots. Lucky me. I fired.

My seventh round punched through Drew's sternum, heart, and back. Blood spattered against the walls. He looked down as the glow of his wand faded, a look of utter shock on his face. "How–?"

I opened the revolver and dumped the expended brass. "Didn't you ever see 'The Villain?' Schwarzenegger's not the only one with a seven-shot revolver."

Drew fell against the Hellgate and screamed as the blue light flowed into his mouth, nostrils, and chest wound. His skin charred, and blood boiled out of his body in foamy puddles. The portal sucked these fluids up with a loud slurp. Drew struck the ground a moment later, drained completely dry.

The Hellgate's pulsing quickened. Any mage would do, and Drew had fit that bill. It wouldn't be long before it opened and disgorged God only knew how many barnyard freaks into Kutztown. And I was all out of bullets.

I dropped to one knee and opened up the bag of tricks. Everything was still in there, with the addition of a robot claw. Where had that come from? It had been repaired with duct tape at some point, and it buzzed with magical energy. Willy must've had his crazy hands on it, then.

Something told me I needed the dump truck. I set it on the ground, then snatched up my palette. Johnny had said it would provide me with more of what I needed, and what I needed now was a hex sign, one that only required a single reagent. I felt my pockets. Shit, had I left my multi-tool at home, too? "Where's your knife?" I yelled to Gina.

She fumbled in her bag as she ran over. Behind her, the now-awakened students scrambled up the ladder. Good.

"What do you need it for?" Gina asked, handing over her knife. At least she didn't put it to my neck this time.

I flicked it open. "I need virgin's blood."

She glanced over her shoulder. "I could go ask them– wait, what are you doing?"

I sliced along an old scar on my left arm and let the blood dribble onto my palette. Each additional droplet flowed along the smooth wood to where the first landed.

"You're a *virgin*?"

"As a matter of fact," I hissed as I stretched the sliced skin apart to let more blood dribble out. The palette would hold any I didn't use, for days if need be.

Gina looked at me, her mouth agape. "Really?"

"You try finding a reliable source of virgin blood," I snapped, "especially in this day and age.

"Tend to this," I said, holding out my arm to her. "There are bandages in my jacket."

While she patched me up, I dipped my finger into the blood and drew what looked like a snowflake, but was actually a star fort pattern. When my ancestors came to the New World, they built these to protect their brand of civilization from a wild, untamed land. The pattern was one of absolute protection.

Close by, the Hellgate hummed and pulsed ever faster.

Gina finished taping my arm. "Hurry up, Jim!"

I drew a circle around the design and spoke the trigger word. The hex sign sparked to life and burned bright red. At its current size it would only create a barrier a few feet in diameter, but if we could get more of it…

I dragged the dump truck backwards along the ground, heard its wheels winding up. "I hope Johnny's right about this," I muttered. Otherwise I was going to look like the biggest dumbass when the hordes of hell burst through and saw me playing with a toy truck.

I let go. As the truck rolled forward, the deep-throated roar of a powerful engine shook the cave walls. The truck quickly grew in size to match the sound, until a full-sized vehicle rolled towards the Hellgate. And even then, it continued to expand.

I could no longer see inside the bed, but as the truck had grown so had the hex sign. As big as it was now, an entire province of hell was about to get evicted.

The Hellgate expelled several demons, but they were blown back in by the hex sign's invisible field. The dump truck blared its horn and crashed through, tearing the Hellgate's edges. The blue surface warped and bubbled out.

I donned the fireman's cap and grabbed Gina's hand. "That's our cue to leave!"

We ran as blue and white flames shot out of the ruptured gate. Gina pointed ahead. "The ladder's down! We need to get it back up!"

No time for that. The flames couldn't hurt us, but if the Hellgate exploded we'd be turned to pulp. I reached into the backpack again and withdrew the robot claw of dubious durability. Now or never! I threw the pack around one shoulder and pulled Gina close. "Hold on!" I pointed the claw at the opening and squeezed the trigger.

The claw shot out like a grappling hook and embedded itself into the rock. Once secured, the rope automatically retracted and pulled us to the top. I thumbed the locking mechanism and pushed Gina out of the hole. Then I climbed out and bent to retrieve the claw. A loud boom echoed up from the cave, followed by a whoosh. We rolled away just as blue flames shot out of the hole, rising a full thirty feet.

We lay there for a few moments, clinging to one another and gasping for air. I could feel her heart hammering away beneath her breasts, and I knew mine was pounding a similar tattoo. I examined the robot claw. The duct tape had been partially melted, but it seemed just as sturdy as ever. "You know, this thing's not half bad. Where'd you get it?"

Gina looked up, confused at the question. Then she saw the claw and said, "Oh, that. Some weirdo dressed up like a noir detective. Scared the shit out of me when he showed up in the girl's room at the diner, right before I got nabbed. Said he knew you."

"He does. Name's Johnny."

"Johnny, that's right! He said you'd have greater need for it than what I was carrying around."

"What did you trade for it?"

"The hex sign you gave me."

My stomach lurched. "The one to protect against demons? Good Lord, why'd you trade that? You could've been killed tonight!"

She said nothing, and then it hit me. "Wait, Johnny said I needed the claw, not you?"

"His exact words, if I recall, were 'you both.'" She flashed that mischievous grin that promised much to its recipient. "I guess even he sees us as a package deal."

I couldn't help but return the grin. "I guess so."

We hopped onto my ATV and drove back to my place. It wasn't until I pulled into the driveway that I remembered: "Shit, I don't have a house."

She had been clinging tight to me during the ride. Now her hands reached up to my hair and face. "I don't mind camping beneath the stars."

I looked over my shoulder at her. "Yeah, but your place isn't far–"

Her lips met mine, and we slid off the ATV into the grass.

Maybe it was our magic out of control. Maybe it was the adrenaline high. Maybe it was just two souls desperate for the assurance of the here and now. Whatever it was, once we hit the ground we didn't stop. I don't know how we'll fare through this whole Sha'Daa thing, but one thing's certain: my apocalypse is off to a great start. Except that I now need a new supply of virgin blood. *But, we can't have everything, can we?*

Toys Are For Sharing

"**S**HA'DAA," WILLY SPAT OUT, "THE END OF times…you're not kidding are you, Salesman?"

Johnny's mouth slowly split into an alarmingly wide, shark-like grin that exposed a full set of perfect white teeth with the exception of a glistening gold left lateral incisor.

"I rarely kid," Johnny said, "Kid…now about my list?"

Willy swallowed and took a moment to take in a deep breath and let it out slowly. For over two centuries, he'd been expecting this mother of all apocalypses. Now it was here.

"Right," Willy snapped back into focus, "Sunita."

A smartly dressed woman of East Indian descent walking through the front doors smiled at hearing her voice and hurried over to the main cash register where Willy handed her Johnny's list.

"You'll find these items in the main safe in my office," Willy said. "Bloody hell! Get a move on, girl."

A few heartbeats later Willy concluded his business with Johnny.

"Always a pleasure, Salesman," Willy said.

Johnny paused for a moment before leaving, freezing Willy with two eyes that were bottomless pools of darkness.

"I've never quite seen all the way into your soul, Willy Carroll," Johnny said softly, "and so I don't truly know whether your ultimate instincts will be to embrace resistance, or destruction."

"If I said it once, I said it a thousand times, Johnny," Willy said, "Whirligigs is neutral territory. I sell my wares to everyone and anyone…how they use my toys, is none of my concern. *Bob's your uncle,* is my take on your Sha'Daa."

"A fine speech," Johnny said, as he turned to walk out the exit, "pray that your noble stance leaves you enough room to maneuver through the next two days."

Johnny disappeared in the rush of people filing into Whirligigs. The muzak version of David Bowie's *Come And Buy My Toys* began playing from the ceiling speakers.

"Sunita," Willy said, "take charge of the register for a few minutes."

Willy turned and stepped up to a 1938, oak phone booth, that had a Stromberg-Carlson antique hand-cranked wall telephone. He picked up the receiver and gave the phone box three quick cranks.

"Hello," a lazy Midwest male sounded, "this is Kvasir the Interface."

"Of course it is," Willy said, sounding annoyed, "who else would it be?"

"How may I help you, Mister Carroll?" Kvasir asked.

"Inform the Midnight Laborers immediately that we're about to have record sales beyond imagination at Whirligigs," Willy said. "I'm offering double-overtime with a guaranteed bonus at the end of the extended shift."

"So," Kvasir said with a noticeable smirk in his voice, "double-work, twice a pittance, and low-end SkyMall swag. Got it, sir."

Willy frowned at the click and hung the earpiece on its hook before returning to the cash register.

Sunita swallowed and unsuccessfully tried to keep a quaver out of her voice. "Does this mean we'll be open later than usual today?"

"Actually," Willy said, "we're open non-stop all day today and tomorrow, all night long. Spread the word. I'm paying triple-overtime to all employees who can stay the course."

Between Boy and Man

Gustavo Bondoni

*"Everything man sees he takes for a toy.
Thus is he always, forever a boy"*

–Jessie Burton

THIS PLACE LOOKS LIKE YOU LIFTED IT OUT of a documentary about Victorian smoking rooms," Tim said.

"When your parents saddle you with a name like St. John, there are certain expectations that need to be met," his friend replied, with a smile and a fake British accent. Tim noted that he'd pronounced it the correct English way, *Sinjin,* even though all his friends called him Saint. "Do you like it?"

"I love it, but you must have paid a fortune for the wood paneling."

"Money is not presently one of my concerns."

That much was true. A rich uncle had left him a pile and a castle, which the man had immediately sold in order to buy his Massachusetts dream house. It had come as a surprise to everyone, since St. John Lewis-Evans, despite his name, had been born in Cuba and had lived most of his life in Florida, never knowing that he had a Baronet for an uncle.

The upside for Tim was that, completely out of the blue, he'd received an invitation from one of his oldest childhood friends to visit him at his new home in New England. The place was on the outskirts of Petersham, just a few miles down the road from Tim's place in Barre. He'd been delighted and had popped in as soon as he'd been able to make time.

"Even so, it's a long way from your folks' condo in Miami." Tim remembered that house as welcoming but very small.

"Isn't it? Have a look at this." Saint bounced up from his chair, all pretense to serious maturity gone, and began pulling stuff off of the shelves that lined three of the four walls in the enormous room—the fourth, of course, was the one with the wood paneling.

The first thing he handed was Tim a small, square object with a handle on the side. "That's a prototype for a miniature version of the Regina music box. They built it in 1904, but never managed to make it cost effective enough to sell to actual buyers. Seems making them that small was really expensive. Go on, try it."

Tim turned the handle, while he watched Saint bounce around. The box eventually produced a tinny sound that seemed to be some half-remembered classical piece.

A couple of books were quickly added to the growing pile in front of him and described as first editions of Newton's *Principia* and another title that Tim couldn't quite catch. "Can you believe all of this? This is just the stuff I decided to keep from my uncle's stash. I sold whole bunches just like this, stuff that was expensive but not as interesting."

Even though Saint was casually tossing around items that were worth many people's yearly salary, it was hard to feel any resentment. Tim had known him when he was a boy, and this was the same way he'd describe a lizard that he'd caught without losing the tail, or a fork-shaped stick perfect to create a slingshot around. It wasn't the price of the objects, but the fact that they were neat, that called to the boy inside the middle-aged man. And that made Tim feel like a boy again as well.

"And what about that?" Tim asked, pointing to a large chess set, sitting on a round table between two leather chairs. "Louis XVI's chess set?"

"Hah. He would have wished to have this set!" Saint replied. "That is the Trastámara fragment."

"Strange name for a chess set."

"It's from fifteenth century Spain, it's supposed to be the set with which the first games of modern chess were played. Before that, the pieces moved in a different way, especially the queen."

"Impressive." The pieces were square-based, carved of some kind of solid rock, and looked utterly ancient, with rectangular faces and features. The kings were about eight inches high.

"And that's not even counting the riddle. There's an inscription in Latin on the bottom of the board which translates to: 'Truly dark is the lady of night, but hidden among the white of royal blood is her portal.'"

"Really? That is totally amazing."

Saint snorted. "Yeah, it's also probably fake, something an auctioneer carved into it at some point to drive up the price. I've had every piece on that set scanned and x-rayed till they glowed, and haven't found any signs of secret compartments. But it's still a cool set; it belonged to a famous player called, Fernán Valdemar de Jaén. He was an advisor to the court of Castille." Saint waggled his eyebrows. "But the truly interesting bit, is that he was found murdered one day, with a game in progress. They never found his head, and they also never found the black queen. That's why they call this a fragment—it's not a complete set."

"Beheaded? That's pretty gross. Why do you even have this in here?"

He shrugged. "It's an important piece of history, even without the queen, maybe especially without the queen. And Bobby's already asked me for it. He thinks the story is cool...probably because it's gross. And he's also really into chess.

"Wow, I haven't seen Bobby in ages. What is he now, twelve, thirteen?"

"He's twelve. Give me a sec." Saint skipped to the door and hollered the kid's name a couple of times. The boy himself appeared a few moments later. He'd grown from a pudgy squirt, to a lanky pre-teen, with braces and shoulder-length brown hair.

"Bobby, you remember Tim, don't you?"

Tim expected to be yet another forgotten adult in a world of them, but the kid surprised him. "Of course. You always used to bring me comic books. It used to drive Dad nuts. You were cool."

"I'm still cool."

"Oh, yeah? I don't see any comic books."

Tim blushed. He'd completely forgotten about Saint's kid. "Not my fault. Your Dad didn't tell me you'd be here." Tim regretted the words as soon as they left his mouth. The kid had never gotten over the death of his mother, who'd died of cancer when he was seven, and he had no living grandparents. Where else was he going to be? "But I'll make it up to you. Let's pop into town and see what we can get you, and we can catch up. If it's OK with the old man, of course."

"Sure, it's a beautiful day, and it'll be good to get him out of the house a while. He still doesn't know the neighborhood boys yet, so he's spending way too much time online."

Bobby rolled his eyes at his father, but grinned at Tim. "That's my Dad, completely clueless, yet caring."

"Sounds about right. We'll see you in a bit, Saint."

"Have fun."

The drive into Barre was uneventful. Bobby told him that the major news outlets were reporting unusual incidents around the world, and that witnesses were saying that they'd been attacked by demons.

"C'mon kid, stop pulling my leg."

"It's real, here, look, it's on CNN!"

Tim just shook his head and parked the car in the lot in front of the pizza and seafood place on South Street. "Let's grab something to eat and then have a look around. There's a shop that sells some cool stuff on Cat Alley."

"Sure, whatever," the kid said, submerged once again in the world of his cell phone.

Lunch went about how Tim expected. Forty-five-year-old men didn't have all that much in common with twelve-year-old boys, so the conversation went almost nowhere, with Tim questioning the boy about school and receiving curt responses. It wasn't that the boy didn't like him, he concluded, but that whatever was happening on the phone was just that much more interesting.

"All right, show me," Tim said.

The boy pushed the phone across the table and, sure enough, there was a live video showing a column of National Guard troops advancing towards what seemed to be an army of hairy men about ten feet tall. Despite their size and clearly aggressive nature, as well as some very large clubs, the big creatures were getting massacred. Clubs and size were not much use against modern ordnance.

"What is that, some kind of game?"

"That's the video currently streaming on NBC's home page. CNN has some similar stuff, and so does everyone else. This is really happening."

"Huh," Tim said, studying the screen. What the kid said checked out—right URL, right logos, everything. "Glad we're not caught in the middle of that. Where is this?"

"That's in Ohio, but weird shit like this seems to be happening everywhere. New York, LA, I saw some stuff from England, too, but that was earlier this morning."

"Language, Bobby."

The kid seemed about to retort, and even Tim himself felt a bit lame, concentrating on something like that in the face of the news they were watching. But he felt responsible for Saint's kid, especially because the boy had no mother to keep his language in line. His father, Tim knew from long experience, wouldn't even realize the kid was cursing.

Then Bobby relaxed and smirked. "Yeah, whatever," he replied. "Are you going to show me this cool place you promised?"

"Sure, let me get the check and we'll go."

Tim had spotted the place the previous weekend, walking around with his girlfriend. They'd visited the antique store on Cat Alley, right behind the pizza place, when Cathy said they should check out the new place next door… which had turned out to be a toy and hobby shop with an unusual mix of old and antique stuff on the shelves.

They stopped at the door and told Bobby, "I think you'll love this."

He was right. The kid took one look at the wares in the window and charged in, leaving a chuckling Tim to follow in his wake.

Bobby made a bee-line for a shelf of model rockets. "Look at these," he exclaimed. "Multi-stagers. You can get like 700 feet with rockets like this."

Tim let the kid bounce from shelf to shelf, while he looked around the store. It consisted of essentially a single room in which every surface was crammed with shiny new boxes or with used toys. Everything was spotlessly clean, but, somehow, the light coming in through the windows didn't quite reach the areas further away from it, giving the sensation that the overflowing shelves were piled with mysterious dusty treasure.

There were some dog-eared boxes filled with action figures from both science fiction and military movie franchises next to a stack of antique video game cartridges from all kinds of systems, from the late seventies all the way to the mid-nineties. He would have to come back with Saint. They used to ride their bikes over to another friend's house, all the way across the US 1, to play some of these games back when they were kids.

There was some much older stuff, too. A tin-plated car looked like it was from the fifties, while some of the wooden figures and a rocking horse in a corner, looked even older. On one shadowed shelf were some houses that actually looked carved. Tim walked over to have a closer look and found himself converging with Bobby.

"Oh. My. God!" Bobby breathed as only a pre-teen from the twenty-first century could. "There she is!" He pointed.

Tim looked around for a blowup doll, or a pile of inappropriate magazines, but instead, saw something that took his own breath away.

Jammed right into the very corner, half hidden by a carved dog, stood an ebony figure eight inches high, her square face carved into a solid-looking stone.

"It's the black queen!" Bobby said, eagerly reaching into the nook and pulling on the piece, attempting to get it free of the other toys.

"It can't be, Tim answered. "You know the story—that piece was lost almost six hundred years ago. It's not just going to appear in a random toy store in New England."

"Actually, sir, the queen was never lost. It was the rest of the set that was lost." This last came from behind the counter where the shop's shadows were deepest. Tim and Bobby jumped and turned to look for the source of the sound.

The white-haired head of the shop's owner popped into view. He looked, to Tim's eyes, to be about a million years old. But he moved like a much younger man as he came around the counter and helped Bobby pull the piece down. Although, like everything else in the shop, it was perfectly clean, the old man blew on it anyway.

"The set was taken out of Spain by an emissary of the British crown, who claimed that Valdemar had given it to him as a gift. But he left before the queen was located. I suppose it's not surprising, given the circumstances."

"What circumstances?" Bobby demanded.

"Well, by all accounts, the man had been Valdemar's opponent the night he was murdered. And they only had his own word that he wasn't in the room it happened. So, he left Spain rather quickly, the following day."

"How do you know all this?" Tim said. "I've been speaking to the set's owner and he doesn't have a clue about it."

"Oh, I heard it from Will Carroll when I bought this from him, along with a bunch of other stuff. He has a shop, a place called Whirligigs, which has any toy your heart could desire, old or new. And he knows the story of every single one." The old man inspected the shelf. "Of course, I'll have to go back to talk to him again. That there queen is nearly the last thing I have of all the stuff he sold me. It's been flying off the shelves over the past two weeks."

"Probably because of the summer vacation. Kids love stuff like this."

The old man looked them over. "It wasn't kids buying them. A couple of them were old guys who looked creepy as hell. Then there were a group of people who looked like they'd been living on the street, and one guy that I was sure was gonna try and rob me. But they all paid good money for the stuff, and made no fuss. You're the only normal-looking folks who've even touched one of those things. I wanna ask Will a couple of very pointed questions about the stuff he sold me, but there's no way I'm gonna buy any more of his stock."

"We've got to take this back to Dad. How much are you selling it for?" Bobby blurted.

Tim sighed inwardly. Unlike normal retailers, one had to haggle in this kind of place. You couldn't show how much you wanted the stuff.

"Thirty dollars," the old man said.

"For a single chess piece?" Tim replied. "I could buy two decent sets for that money."

"Are you serious?" the old man asked. "That piece is probably worth ten grand if it comes up at auction. I'm only selling it at thirty because that's what Carroll sold it to me for, and I want it out of my shop."

Tim knew he'd taken the haggling a little too far. Even Bobby was looking at him like he was an idiot. He sighed. "All right. Fair enough."

The old man's eyes gleamed, and Tim suspected he's made at least a little on the deal.

"And for the boy?"

"This is for the boy."

"No, it's not. That piece has a history that's way too dark for a simple boy. I think the boy would prefer the last thing I have from Whirligigs."

Tim was about to walk out, but the man said, "Just a second," and went back behind the counter. It would have been too rude to leave, so they waited. After rummaging a bit under a shelf, their host reappeared.

"Now this is something for a boy. Carroll didn't want to sell, but I talked him into it. And I'll sell it to you guys for well under its real value. Just ten bucks."

"Wow, utterly cool, totally retro!" Bobby said, and Tim rolled his eyes again. He was just happy that the old guy had already named his price. "But what is it?"

Tim knew that one. "That's a GI action figure," he said. "Don't know the brand, probably not one of the real ones."

"Ah, a connoisseur," the old man beamed, turning the twelve-inch doll around and pulling the clothing aside to show lettering stamped in the plastic. "You're right. This one is really rare. It's a Soldier of Valor from Brown Toy Corporation. They only produced them for a few months in 1979. How could you tell?"

"I had dozens of these guys, well of the real ones, anyway. They were some of my favorite toys. The smaller figures that came later always seemed so crappy after these." He looked over at Bobby. "I thought kids these days hated them."

The kid shrugged. "Living with my Dad means that I grew up weird. Ask anyone."

"You're gonna make me buy you this as well, aren't you?"

And just like that, Bobby went shy, as if remembering his place. "Oh, God, I'm sorry. You don't need to buy me anything."

And Tim, once again, found himself tap-dancing to fix a verbal blunder. "Think of it as repayment for forgetting the comic books."

"OK, then."

They paid the owner, who seemed more relieved than happy that Bobby had taken the action figure, and the kid became a bundle of enthusiasm. He forgot about the Soldier of Valor for a moment and returned to the chess piece. "Even if it's fake, Dad will go insane when he sees this. It looks just like the rest of them. We have to surprise him."

"I thought he was going to give that set to you."

"He will, but he won't really give it to me. It will be mine, but it's always going to be in his library, as part of the collection. That it's mine just means that I can have it when he kicks the bucket." He paused and looked around. "You keep it for a few days. I want him to be totally caught off guard. Come by next week or something and we'll give it to him. No, no. Even better, you could just leave it on the chessboard and see what he does when he realizes it's there. Yeah, let's do that."

"Okay, okay. I'll do that. Just calm down."

"You rock, Tim! Thanks so much. Dad's gonna freak!"

Tim chuckled, vaguely wondering if he'd ever really been that young, and enjoying how much this kid really loved his Dad. He wondered if he'd been born that way, or the lack of his mother had affected him. If that was so, it was a sad story with a wonderful ending.

⊕ ⊕ ⊕

That night, Tim sat alone in a darkened house with the window open, enjoying the summer breeze that washed over him. Cathy was off in the mountains somewhere, enjoying time with her kids. He'd been watching the news all afternoon, garbled reports of strange stuff happening all over the world. Looking across the lawn and into the trees at the bottom of his property, he found it hard to believe that he lived in the same world. Demons and monsters had no place in that warm deer-infested countryside.

He smirked. The people on Fifth Avenue had probably thought the same thing, though.

A rustle behind him made him jump. His wife had left him years ago, and kids had never been on the agenda. When his last dog died, he simply hadn't had the energy to house train another puppy. So, with Cathy gone, there really shouldn't have been any noises in the house.

He walked towards the kitchen, stabbing at the light switch and missing. In the dark, he thought he saw an even darker patch flitting out the door.

Why would anyone be in his kitchen?

Then he remembered: the chess piece. The guy in the shop had said that it was worth a bundle, but Tim hadn't been particularly careful with it, he'd just popped it on the countertop when he came in, exchanging its mass and weight for that of a beer bottle from the fridge—possibly less valuable, but much more suited to his mood in that moment.

He rushed in, attempting to close on the shadow, but only managed to hit a bar stool and drop onto the floor in a heap, falling onto a wet patch on the floor. Eventually, he got his legs untangled and turned on the light.

Tim looked at the place where he'd placed the black queen. Then he rushed to the sink and threw up. The beer, his dinner, most of the pizza he'd had with Bobby. All of it landed in a thick soup in the basin.

When he was done heaving, he looked back at what lay on the counter. The severed head of a man lay in a pool of half-congealed blood. It had shoulder-length curled black hair, a sallow complexion and a three-day stubble. The head had been removed from the neck at a steep angle, and the flat brown eyes stared at the roof.

Tim looked down at his arm, crimson from shoulder to wrist. The pool of liquid he'd landed in had been the man's blood. He retched again, and this time got nothing for his pain but a little bit of yellow spit.

Screw this.

Tim ran out of the kitchen in the direction he'd seen the shadow go. He hit the back door running and headed toward the stairs.

"You really, really don't want to go after her in the dark. She's in the woods by now. You wouldn't last five minutes."

Tim skidded to a halt and nearly dislocated his neck when he turned. A man in a dark coat and fedora leaned against the wall of his house. He stepped forward, into the light coming out of the kitchen, and smiled. A glint of light came from his mouth, as if from a metallic tooth cap.

"You took the piece," Tim said.

"If I did, are you sure you want to accuse me? I mean that head had to have been removed somehow, right? How do you know I'm not carrying a big, ugly sword?"

Tim backed away, and the other man's laugh floated to him on the breeze. "If I intended harm, you'd be dead already. You never saw me when you passed."

"What do you want?"

"Me? I guess I want what everyone wants. I want to make a trade."

"Huh?"

"A trade. I give you something that you need, and you give me something that I want."

"What are you talking about? What would you know about what I need?"

"Let me put it this way. Do you know what you're chasing?"

"Some scumbag who took a valuable chess piece."

This time, the chuckle was louder, had more of an edge to it. "If you really believe that, you're going to end up like the guy in your kitchen. You're chasing a demon…and a particularly nasty one at that. The only reason you're alive at all, is that it needs to be somewhere else in a hurry."

"Don't be ridicul…" and then Tim remembered the news stories. In a more measured tone, he continued, "what would a demon want with a chess piece?"

"Wrong question. And even if you ask the right one, I'm pretty sure you wouldn't like the answer." The guy removed the hat and ran the back of his hand across his forehead. "I'm pressed for time, so I'll give you a hint: a better question might be what I have for you, and what I want for it."

Tim stuttered, unable to believe the situation.

"That's better," the guy said. "I'm willing to trade this." He held up a flat square about twenty inches to a side. It looked a bit like a chess board, but there were no black and white squares, only a series of lines to create a grid. There were crosses in a few of the squares.

"What is that?"

"It's something you need. It's called an *Ashtāpada*."

"Why in the world would I need that?"

"Now that would be telling, wouldn't it?" The guy in the fedora pulled a pack of cigarettes out of his trench and lit one. "Perhaps what you meant to ask is what I want in exchange." Another pause. "And the answer to that is that I want the head of Fernán Valdemar de Jaén."

"Fernán…oh, the Spanish guy. That's stupid. How would I know where his head is? In Spain, I'd guess." Tim realized he was babbling. He didn't know why he was still talking to this guy when a thief was running away with something valuable that wasn't Tim's to lose. But there was something about the man's even tone that kept him planted, even as he said one insane thing after another. Something told Tim that what this weirdo had to say was important. "Who are you, anyway?"

"That's his head in the kitchen. And most people call me, Johnny."

"His head…" Tim decided he didn't even want to know. "You're saying you'll take the head away if I agree to take that board?"

"That's not how I'd put it, but yeah."

"OK, it's a deal. Give me the board."

Johnny handed it over solemnly. "Did you ever wonder why the queen is the most powerful piece on a chessboard?" he asked.

"Not once."

"It wasn't always that way. They changed the rules in Spain, in the late fifteenth century. Before that, the queen was actually the weakest piece of all. Makes you think, doesn't it?"

"Not really."

The other man sighed. "Just take the board with you when you go after her, will you?"

"I don't think I'll catch the guy now, and I have no idea where he'll be going."

"If you know where the piece belongs, you're still in time." Johnny asked.

"Belongs? What does that matter? They've taken it out there somewhere." He turned to the woods.

When Tim turned back, Johnny was gone. He shook his head and walked into the kitchen.

The head was gone as well.

Unfortunately, the crazy bastard hadn't thought to take the blood with him.

⊕ ⊕ ⊕

Tim began to clean up in a daze, but Johnny's last words haunted him. *Belong,* he thought. *What did he mean by belong?*

Then it hit him. Whoever the thief had been knew exactly what he'd come there to look for, and where in his house it could be found. A well-informed thief like that would know precisely where to find the rest of the set.

And, strange allusions to long-dead Spaniards aside, the man had shown a willingness to kill for it.

So, to the best of Tim's knowledge, a murderer bent on robbery was on his way towards the house of one of his best friends, and only Tim could warn him of the danger. He grabbed his cell phone.

Ten minutes of frustration followed, with Tim being informed time and again that only emergency calls to the proper authorities were being routed at that time. He thought about calling 911, but knew they'd take forever to get to Saint's place.

The easiest thing to do would be to drive out himself. So, pausing only to grab the Mossberg .410 pump-action shotgun he kept as safety against rabid animals, a handful of shells and the *Ashtāpada* board, which he took because it felt right, Tim powered down his drive and onto the darkened two-lane main road.

Anxiety had him moving along the wooded road at over ninety, praying that neither cops nor deer would interfere, but there was no real need to worry. The road was completely deserted, much more than he'd have expected for a midsummer Saturday. Only once did he encounter traffic: a column of Humvees moving almost as fast as he was, but in the opposite direction. They ignored him.

He arrived at Saint's exit, stormed up the road and onto the man's driveway, cursing the fact that his now rich friend had decided to buy a place with seemingly endless grounds. Eventually, the brightly illuminated main grounds came into view.

Tim skidded to a halt.

The house looked like it had been hit by an air strike. The right side was a ruin. One of the ornamental towers had collapsed into the yard, while every window on that end was gone. Even the sturdy brick construction was riddled with holes, looking like a big Swiss cheese on the verge of complete collapse.

"What the..."

His thoughts were interrupted by a chunk of masonry that shot from house and landed about ten feet from his car. Shrapnel pinged off the panels.

His heart fell as he thought of his friends trapped inside, perhaps torn to pieces. Whatever was happening here would need a regiment to stop it. He was fumbling for reverse, aiming to get the hell out of Dodge, when he saw movement through one of the windows. It passed quickly, and it was hard to be certain, but it sure looked like Saint and Bobby had crossed that room into one further down a hall.

The sight galvanized Tim. He couldn't just run off and leave them, which meant that he had to find some way to get them out. He picked up the shotgun and, after a single moment's curse, the ridiculous board and ran for the left of the house. There wasn't really much choice: the right side looked as if it was being pulled apart by an invisible tornado.

Looking into the window through which he'd seen his friends, he realized that the room they'd retreated into was Saint's Library. He knew the paneled wall had a window leading into the yard, so he set out around the house. He sprinted towards the corner of the house.

Suddenly, every light, inside the house and in the yard, went out. Tim managed a few more steps before becoming entangled in a bush and flying head over heels. He landed on the grass and could continue on his hands and knees, occasionally placing one hand in front of his face to avoid running into things.

As his eyes became accustomed to the starlight, he began to see shapes in the gloom, and soon identified the window he was looking for. A dim white light shone from his objective, probably a cell phone light. Tim saw Saint and Bobby inside in the glow. He tapped on the glass.

The figures inside turned towards him and Tim barely managed to get out of the way as the window flew outward from a gunshot. While Tim limited himself to a single pest-control shotgun which he never fired, he imagined that a house like this one probably had a well-stocked gun room.

"Wait! Don't shoot! It's me!"

"Who?" Saint's voice came from inside.

"It's me, Tim."

"What the hell are you doing here?"

"I wish I knew," he replied. "I thought I was trying to stop a thief, but things have gotten really strange. You wouldn't believe half of the stuff that happened to me tonight."

Saint's face came to the window. "After tonight, I'm ready to believe just about anything. "Are you coming in?"

"Come out. I've got my car on the driveway, we can run for it."

"No way. That thing destroyed my house, and I'm gonna blow it back to wherever it came."

"Thing? What thing?"

"Just get in here. Watch the glass."

Tim took the proffered hand and felt his shoulder pop as his friend pulled him inside.

The source of the light was a tablet that Bobby was using to illuminate the room. The boy looked scared out of his wits, and was clutching the soldier doll they'd bought earlier. Tim didn't criticize him—after all, he was still holding an antique game board like some kind of talisman.

A huge crash came from the doorway on the opposite wall. Books fell from the shelves.

"OK, you bastard," Saint roared. He brandished what looked like a 19th century double-barreled elephant gun, probably another relic that he'd saved because it looked cool. "You have well and truly asked for it." He reloaded in a well-practiced motion, and then ran across the darkened room, pulling Tim along in his wake, and yanked the door open. There was nothing in the hall but darkness.

"Give me the light," he told his son. All traces of the sassy, back-talking pre-teen had disappeared.

The light revealed nothing but a hallway littered with shards of broken decorations. Dirt from a mangled dwarf palm, formerly potted, was piled in a neat line where the door opened, as if it had been blown against the wood by a strong wind.

Tim peered deep into the shadows and thought he saw movement. He shook his head and dismissed it as an optical illusion. But then he saw it again, and there could be no doubt. A wall of pure black was advancing towards them through the hall, moving slowly but gaining speed.

"Look out!" he shouted, and pushed Saint away, but it was too late, the blackness was cannoning through the corridor and there was no time to close the door.

The whole house shook with the impact. Books from the top shelves pelted the prone figures of Tim and Saint as dust dropped from the roof. A crash from elsewhere indicated that the house had suffered yet more structural damage.

"How come it didn't get in?" Tim asked, brushing himself off and feeling for bruises.

"I don't know," Saint replied.

"Mark says he stopped her." The third voice, barely more than a whisper, belonged to Bobby. The two adults turned to the boy.

"What?"

"This is Mark," Bobby said, standing the toy soldier on the ground in front of him. "He calls that thing the Black Queen, and he says she's a very powerful demon."

"Bobby, this isn't the time for this kind of..."

Saint's voice faded as he watched the action figure. It had begun to walk, with no outside assistance towards the door. It turned back to them, waving them on.

"He wants you to come to the door with him."

"You can talk to him?"

"I hear his voice in my head. He says he can save us."

"I can't hear anything."

Bobby cocked his head for a moment. "That's because I'm still innocent. Certain beings can talk to me directly. Your brains have learned to filter outside voices."

Saint shrugged. "We're being attacked by a black shade which can tear down big brick houses, and apparently our only defense against that is a plastic soldier with a hero complex. What's a little telepathy to top that off?" He sighed. "I wonder if this night can get any weirder."

"Well, I traded a guy a severed head for a game board which he said could save me."

"That one you've got there."

"Yeah."

"If my house hadn't just been knocked down by something I can't even see, I'd probably laugh at you for that."

"You would, but when a guy trades it for a head, then claims the head belongs to the Spaniard that owned that chess set, and then proceeds to disappear, you become superstitious about stuff."

The action figure had stopped short, hands on its hips. It was really hard to tell in the dull glow from the tablet, but Tim could have sworn that it was looking at them with a scornful expression.

"Mark wants to know if you're quite finished. And he also wants to look at that board when you have a minute."

"And now we're taking orders from a doll. Definitely a strange night."

"It just got stranger," Tim said, pointing.

The action figure standing by the door had lifted its arms, and a soft, rippling light began to emanate from them. It wasn't a ray or a flash, but a series of expanding waves of slightly illuminated space that reminded Tim of ripples in a pond.

As they watched, the darkness beyond the door took another run at them, gaining speed as it progressed down the hall. But as soon as it hit the first of the ripples, its movement was arrested, and the shadow barely covered half the corridor.

Both Tim and Saint fired at the blackness. Saint discharged both barrels, but it seemed to have no effect on the blackness ahead.

"Mark says to stop wasting your time and to bring him the board," Bobby said.

Tim shrugged, picked it off the floor and dusted it off. He walked over to where the little soldier was emanating waves of power and held it out to him. The action figure acknowledged him only by turning his head to study the board.

Bobby continued to act as medium. "Mark says that the most important thing is to stop the demon from placing the white king in the center of the modern board. I can't really understand all the words he's using, but it seems that that would open a portal of some kind. One way to confuse her, is to set up the pieces on your board. It doesn't matter where you put them, as long as they're in a square and not directly on top of a line. He says that this won't stop her, but it will make her much less powerful, and maybe slow her down enough to..." The boy sat down hard and put his hands over his ears. "Too many voices! They need to stop." He began to sob loudly, rocking back and forth on the floor.

Saint ran over to him, while Tim, responding to energetic gestures from the Soldier of Valor, cleared the chess set from its board and began to place the pieces carefully in the squares of the *Ashtāpada*. As he worked, he listened to Saint telling his son that everything was going to be all right, and to Bobby saying things like "That's impossible, my mom is dead." It sounded like there were two separate conversations going on at once, but it was hard to tell over the boy's loud sobs.

He glanced at the corridor as well. On two separate occasions, the darkness pushed forward, and on two separate occasions it broke against the light like a wave against the shore. It seemed like the action figure had things well under control.

As soon as Tim finished setting the pieces down, the doll did something unexpected. He stood to one side just as the darkness began to re-form. Tim barely had time to dive to one side as it exploded into the room.

He cursed and turned to see if he could save Saint and the boy, but realized that the darkness hadn't simply destroyed the room. It seemed to be enmeshed in the waves of light that Mark was sending out, struggling, stretching in what looked to be agony and slowly being herded.

He watched the darkness shrink, solidify and finally coalesce into a solid shape which dropped neatly onto a square of the *Ashtāpada*. The black queen had finally come home.

Bobby let out one last sob and opened his eyes. "Oh, God, that was terrible, I'm so glad the voices are gone." Then he jumped, but relaxed and looked vacant for a second. "Mark says we're safe. The black queen can't move effectively on the *Ashtāpada*; the old oaths hold her back. The black queen can only be truly unchained on the modern board—that one over there. The original Spanish board linked to the promises made by Fernán Valdemar de Jaén, the ones sealed with his own blood."

"What does that even mean?" Saint asked.

Bobby's shoulders drooped. "He says it doesn't matter. He says that all we need to know is that we'll be safe if we stay here for a couple of days until the Sha'Daa blows over."

"What."

"It doesn't matter, don't you see?" Bobby exploded at them. "He's wrong. None of us will ever be safe when a demon queen can come and promise to bring back my mother. How can anyone resist that?" He approached the action figure. "And you, did you hear all that? Was she telling me the truth?"

He stopped and listened.

"What do I care about the cost to the world? If her word is good, then it's good!"

Before Tim could react, Bobby rushed across the room, picked up the black queen and, pausing only long enough to kick the Soldier of Valor toy into the wall beside the *Ashtāpada,* he placed her triumphantly on one of the central squares of the board, the modern board.

At that moment, everything seemed to happen at once. The remaining black pieces on the board evaporated into smaller versions of the darkness that had been attacking them, leaving no trace of their presence on the *Ashtāpada.*

The figure of a slight blond woman, no more than thirty years old at the most, appeared in the center of the room, looking around in confusion.

"Mommy!" Bobby said and ran towards her.

Tim was only peripherally aware of these things. His attention was focused on the chess piece that the boy had deposited. It was growing bigger, but also growing darker. Gone was the insubstantial shadow that was only strong enough to destroy a mansion, and in its place, was something black and shiny as a cavern pool. It grew, sinews visibly stretching as it took shape.

"First things first," the former black queen said in a voice like the rustle of ancient paper. "The promised price." She took two longs strides and stood in front of the immobile form of Saint. The anger had left him, and he was petrified with fear. The useless rifle fell from nerveless fingers.

Before Tim could react, the Queen drove two long black arms, tendrils of darkness, into Saint's chest. Despite the volume of his friend's scream, Tim could still hear the soft sound of satisfaction that the demon emitted as the life was sucked out of her victim. Saint collapsed into a pile of dust on the floor.

"Allow the boy and the woman to live," it roared with a voice like daggers across Tim's soul. "Deal with the toy."

Bobby looked away from his father as he died, but by the way he clung to his mother, it was clear to Tim that he felt he'd also gotten a good bargain. Just how much had the boy suffered, what fantasies of being a child again lived on inside his head? Enough to give his Dad—the man who'd raised him lovingly for ten years—to a demon in exchange?

The smaller black shadows immediately converged on the *Ashtāpada,* but the Soldier of Valor wasn't there. Tim caught sight of the action figure huddled beneath a chair, invisible from above. It was hunched over, holding something in its arms.

The white king, the key to the portal, in the confusion, it must have managed to grab it.

The doll saw him looking and nodded. Then it nodded toward the open window, and Tim understood. Every second's head start that the action figure got would mean one more second that the forces battling the demon attack would have to defend themselves. Without reinforcements from a portal, the Black Queen was much less formidable. It was up to him to provide the diversion.

With a yell, Tim shot behind the shadowy figure in the center of the room, making a beeline towards the *Ashtāpada*. He picked up a number of pieces at random and dashed towards the open door of the room, on the opposite side of the chamber from the window.

One of the smaller black shadows hit him before he made it through the threshold. He fell back on his butt, risked a quick glance behind him and saw the Soldier of Valor climbing out the broken window.

"I'm much too old for this," he muttered, but pulled himself off the floor and headed for one of the side walls, passing his hand across the shelves and pushing books and priceless curios onto the floor into the path of the pursuing black shadows. Then he headed back towards the door.

Another minor demon buffeted him, then a third. Tim cocked his arm back and threw all the white pieces into the hall one after another. The demon queen screamed.

He ignored her and tossed the final piece, the white queen, after the rest. He hoped the size was similar enough that the shadows would be confused enough to try to find the king in the hall…and to give the action figure time to disappear into the woods.

The great crowned head turn Tim's way. He looked into two eyes ablaze with darkness and felt his sanity crumbling—an actual physical sense of the world of logic and thought disappearing. Drool rolled down his chin, and something warm ran down his leg.

The only satisfaction he felt as his soul was leeched away was that the smaller black shadows had flitted desperately into the long-darkened corridor. His ruse seemed to have worked.

But the balm of that knowledge was short-lived. Pain like needles tearing into every nerve of his body racked him in waves that came and came and never seemed to recede.

It was almost a relief when the blade of pure night, thinner than the sharpest razor, approached from below and bit into his neck at a steep angle.

The last thing he saw before awareness faded was Bobby, leading his dazed-looking mother away from the carnage. Then there was nothing.

The Price Of A Toy

AS HE FELT LIFE BEGIN TO SLIP FROM HIS body, and his vision started to turn red, William Thomas Carrolton suddenly took notice of a tall stranger standing just a few feet above him. The colony was not all that large and this figure definitely was not one of the mob that had brought him to this end.

"Looks like you're in quite a bind there, lad," the stranger said with a hint of humor, "definitely at the end of your rope."

Anger flooded William but the ever-tightening rope prevented him from speaking. The tall man was dressed in dark undertaker's clothes, and surprisingly, an ebony great coat with capes, more than an oddity on this sweltering hot day. Atop his head the stranger sported a sable French tricorn hat that cast a long shadow over his clean-shaven face.

"I see that we don't have much time, good sir," the stranger said, "so I shall speak with alacrity. My name is Benedict, the trader, and I am here to offer you a proposition. No, no, no, this is not jape to mock your current circumstance. It just so happens that I am in need of your noose. You see, the rope used to hang an innocent man possesses unusual properties, ones that I will need to conclude another transaction. If you agree to give me your noose, I have an item that I promise will be of great value to you. What say you good sir?"

A minute or less away from unconsciousness and death, William could not believe what he was hearing his last moments before embracing eternity and this madman Benedict was toying with him.

"Quickly, Sir William," Benedict said, "have we a deal?"

Wishing he could laugh aloud at the absurdity of it all, William, his sight growing dark, moved his lips in an approximation of the word, yes. Then everything went black.

Sometime later, perhaps minutes, perhaps seconds, William found himself sitting on the ground a mere foot from the crevasse into which he had previously dangled. Sea water splashed up through it and William knew that the tide was coming back in. His hands and feet were unbound. He put his fingers on his neck and immediately regretted the action as the tortured flesh sang with pain. Looking up he saw Benedict standing over him, tucking away the hangman's rope into an inner pocket of his great coat.

"Ah yes," Benedict said, "to conclude our transaction. Here."

Benedict reached into the very same pocket that had swallowed up the long rope and suddenly pulled out what William quickly recognized as a finely carved wood, horn, and seashell composite bou-mar-rang, a deadly weapon he'd seen used by some of the large island's aboriginal population. This device looked highly unusual to William as he'd only seen versions of this object carved from single pieces of curved Mulga tree branches, and not complex decorative constructs like this. The swirls and shapes carved into it were crude but pleasing to the eye.

"Take it quick, lad," Benedict said, "I know this will be hard to believe, but if you wish it hard enough while holding this clever weapon, you will appear invisible to those who wish you harm. You'd best be moving on before your judge, jury, and executioners return."

"Where can I go?" William regretted asking as the words were a lightning bolt of pain in his harshly abused throat.

"Inland," Benedict said, "the natives will respect this weapon of yours as a noble talisman…assuming that you show them the same respect, something your brethren have been lacking in since they arrived on this ancient continent. And on that note, good day, sir."

Benedict flashed a smile that exposed a wide mouth full of perfect white teeth marred only by a dark gap that once housed a left upper tooth, and just as quickly and magically as he had appeared, Benedict the trader simply vanished.

William heard shouts from the main settlement and quickly stood up. A pounding headache was filling his skull but instinct took over as he turned away from the encroaching ocean and walked inland, away from the settlement, and toward his destiny.

Gwen's Gamble

R.J. Ladon

"Toys are merely ideas brought to life."

–Melissa Crawley

G WEN OPENED HER HAND TO REVEAL A rolled-up strip of paper tied with a red bow, a golden cross with the word courage, red slippers and a heart. She looked at me and said, "It's what Dad wanted."

"If you'd rather keep them, I would understand. He would understand." I closed her hand around the small tokens.

"No, Mom. We made these together; he carved, and I decorated. We wanted to do this every year." Gwen placed the slippers on the pedestal of Dorothy and Toto.

"Someone might take them." I reached for the tiny wooden shoes.

"Mom. Stop. Please, I need to complete my promise to Dad."

I let the slippers stay on the pedestal and followed my daughter to the Scarecrow statue. Gwen placed the diploma on the pedestal. Lion received his badge of courage. And Tinman was given his heart.

"For Dad." Gwen's voice cracked, and tears streamed down her face.

My tears joined Gwen's. The world seemed gloomy and broken since my husband Marshal died, one month ago. Even Oz Park, with its whimsical statues, didn't have the charm it once held. But I made a promise to Gwen to visit the park she and her father enjoyed.

I tapped the outside of my pocket, feeling the hard outline of the old pocket knife Marshal loved. He treasured the knife because his father passed it to him. I couldn't think of a time or place he didn't have the old knife in his pocket. For me, the blade was a memento, a way of keeping Marshal close to me.

For years he whittled and carved bits of wood, leftovers from his cabinet or shelving projects. When visiting random parks, he would stash the small tokens near trees or on benches. He wanted to leave wonder and beauty wherever he went.

Often Marshal would cut himself while creating his works of art. He'd smile and say, "No job is complete until there is blood on it." His comment always made Gwen laugh. Under their paint and decoration, a drop of blood stained many of the tiny statues.

After a long day of reminiscing about what Dad used to do and say, and hours of laughter and tears, Gwen's solemn mood lifted. *We should have made the trip to the park weeks ago.* We crossed the street, making our way back to the apartment.

"Whirligigs, can we go?" Gwen pulled my hand toward the eclectic toy shop that sat opposite Oz Park.

I rolled my eyes. "That place gives me the creeps."

"Seriously, Mom?" Gwen pulled my hand even harder. "They have the neatest toys. Dad used to take me there after we spent time at the park. Besides, Willy and Dad were friends. I'd like to see him today too. Please?"

"Oh, all right." I smiled at my thirteen-year-old daughter. She looked so much like her father, with her dark hair and eyes. She loved all the crazy things he loved too, like shrunken heads and dinosaur droppings.

Gwen climbed the stairs and opened the wooden door. A gentle tinkle of bells announced our arrival. Cabinets and shelving held a strange array of toys. Some old and refurbished, some new, and some were cheap knockoffs of high-end toys. Smells of cotton candy and popcorn filled the store.

"I'm going to the book section," Gwen called to me as she scampered to the back corner. She enjoyed books, but what she loved more was watching the conveyor belt move boxes of toys from the warehouse in the back to the storefront. Sometimes she would catch a glimpse of a new item that she *had* to have.

Gwen told me that children worked in the warehouse helping Willy because she saw small hands pushing a box once. I let her know that there were laws preventing children from working until they were sixteen. Someone was probably playing a trick on her, just one more reason why I didn't like Whirligigs.

Bright colored shelving lined the walls. Bean-bag chairs filled with pampered kids actively playing with toys, giggling and begging their wealthy parents to buy whatever was in their hands.

I didn't dare step far into the store. It always felt strange to me, like the building itself was alive and judging. Sometimes it seemed as if the eyes of the dolls and stuffed animals watched me. I tried to avoid eye contact with the toys near me.

I turned away from the porcelain babies and noticed a basket filled with blocks, connected with colorful ribbons. Jacob's ladder. As a small child, I loved the sound of the blocks striking the others. I picked up a series of plain wood blocks connected with blue ribbons on one side and red on the other.

I flipped them over, mesmerized by the illusion of blocks cascading down, yet never moving. I flipped the top block again. *Click-clack, click-clack.*

"Excellent choice, madam," said a gentle masculine voice with an Aussie accent.

Startled, I sucked in air. I had lied to Gwen; it wasn't just the store that gave me the creeps–the owner Willy did. His personality and mood changed with every customer, sometimes he was accommodating, and other times he was rude. His shock of bright red hair and pale skin reminded me of a clown, a sick and demented clown; one that would eat babies or juggle kittens. *I hate clowns.* And there was something wrong with his eyes, I couldn't look at them for more than a second.

"If madam wishes, I can hold your selection at the counter until you're done shopping." Willy bowed slightly holding out his hand, averting his eyes, as if he read my mind.

I dropped the Jacobs ladder into his palm, silently wishing for him to go away. *I don't think I want that toy now.*

He flashed his over-white smile. *Was that a diamond on the right side?* Willy slinked away, toward Gwen perusing the books. *Willy, there couldn't be a more perfect name for that man. He certainly gave me the willies.* But Gwen adored Willy, claiming that the sight of him brought back memories of Dad.

"Elizabeth? Vos miremini. I'm surprised to see you here," said a familiar voice.

I turned to see Seth, a co-worker from the University. He taught Latin and Archeology, specializing in Persian culture. "I could say the same thing. You don't even have children."

"One does not need children to buy toys, specialis nugas." Seth pushed his glasses up the bridge of his nose, giving me his best haughty-professor stare. A smile cracked his face, and he chuckled deep and low; a contagious laugh. "Especially not today, right? That is why you're here, isn't it? Dies irae dies Ahriman."

I worked with Seth for years. He often spoke in riddles, using Latin, and fancy professor language, assuming everyone knew exactly what he was talking about. I was a secretary for the incoming freshman class, and half the time, I had no clue. Never the less, I pretended to know exactly what he meant, so I nodded. "Today is a great day to buy a toy from Whirligigs. Did you know they sell Jacob's ladders here?" I pointed to the basket. "I haven't had one since I was little." I held my hand out to indicate my size as a child.

"Indeed?" Seth raised an eyebrow. "It is the Sha'Daa and Ahriman is coming. Perhaps he would like one, scala Iacob." He reached into the basket.

"Excuse me, sir," Willy said, appearing out of nowhere. "But what you are giving Ahriman tonight is everything he could possibly need. The Jacob's ladder is not for you." The store proprietor held out his hand.

Seth looked into his bag of purchased items, some of which appeared to be costumes, masks, and decorations, then to the Jacob's ladder in his hand. He gave the wooden toy to Willy, nodding. "Yes, of course, you're right. He cannot ask more of me. Non quaeritur quid amplius a me." Seth became introspective, staring off into space.

I ignored Willy and continued my conversation with Seth. "Are you having a costume party or play tonight?" I pointed at the bags in Seth's hands, over-flowing with strange and wondrous things.

"No, no it is bigger than a party, more like a pageant, a festival. Convivium." Seth continued to wistfully gaze at nothing. "I'd like it very much if you came to witness my gift, my offering to Ahriman." Fear contorted his features for a moment, and then he met my gaze. "Ahriman has expressed his desire to meet my friends. Sacrifice pro sua redempcione persolueret. I'd be delighted if you came, if I can count you as one."

I instantly felt horrible for Seth. He had few friends from the University. "I'll be there. When and where?" A nagging voice in the back of my mind asked, *did he just say sacrifice?* But there was no way; Seth was a sweetheart.

"Southern side of Lincoln Park just before sunset. North Ave. and Clark."

"Tonight? By the Children's Fountain?"

"Yes, Ahriman will love it there. There is so much history. Tot funera, multo igitur mortem."

"How do you know this Ahriman?" I wanted to help Seth, but I felt uneasy about this Ahriman person. I scolded myself. *I don't even know who he is. How can I be afraid? You're probably just upset being in this store.*

"A colleague introduced us, while we were excavating a Neolithic temple near Palmyra, in Syria. We excavated a ziggurat and found Acheulean tools, dating the earliest part of the site, some 130,000 years old, maybe more. Can you imagine?" Seth paused shaking his head. "Anyway, Ahriman was unable to stay long due to the turbulent nature of the region, but never-the-less, we hit it off, and I invited him to Chicago for the Sha'Daa, the longest day of the year. I know he will love it here. Fructus maturus legendo."

"Sha'Daa? Is that similar to Midsummer's Night? You know, Shakespeare?" I loved The Bard's plays, though Marshal insisted I didn't fully understand the tragedy Shakespeare was trying to express.

Seth thought for a moment. "Yes, a parallel can be drawn. It is very much like Shakespeare's tale and a door opening for fairy folk to enter the land of humans. Casus belli." Seth chuckled softly, his eyes sparkling. "Yes, Ahriman will like you, and your innocence."

I nodded, *fairies don't sound bad.* "Gwen and I will be there for you Seth." I loved the theater and hoped he and Ahriman were up to putting on a fantastic show.

"You mean you'll be there for Ahriman." Seth corrected me.

"Yes, I suppose we will be there for him too. I'm excited to see the performance tonight and to meet your mysterious friend."

"Most excellent." Seth saluted me. "Ad finem!" He shouted as he reached the door and left the toy store.

"Ad finem." I parroted back.

"Do you know what 'ad finem' means? Or Sha'Daa?"

I turned and saw Willy staring at me with his unnatural eyes. "Well, no. Not really. I think it's Latin."

Willy tsk-tsked and shook his head while walking away. He approached Gwen while she sat on the floor with her nose in a book. He bent over and whispered to her. He gave her something, which prompted Gwen to jump up and throw her arms around him. I shuddered involuntarily; *my baby is hugging an evil clown.* Willy ruffled Gwen's hair, smiling sweetly at her.

Gwen ran to me. "Guess what Willy gave me?" She held up the Jacob's ladder for me to see. "He said you changed your mind and didn't want to buy it. But he said it was important that I have it tonight."

I looked at Willy, narrowing my eyes. *How did he know I decided not to buy the toy?* A shiver ran up my spine. "Come on, Gwen let's go."

✠ ✠ ✠

Gwen and I entered the southwestern side of Lincoln Park at eight o'clock, one half hour till sunset. Despite the time, the sun hid behind the Chicago skyline.

The storks that made up the base of the Children's Fountain appeared different than I remembered. The cherubs on the upper tiers looked darker. *Were they moving?* I shook my head, *must be my imagination.*

A tall, thin man stood on the steps that led up to the pool under the fountain. He wore a black trench coat and hat. He bowed to an elderly man, then approached him and said, "Good evening Edward. I have something I would like to give you."

I didn't hear what the old man said, but he seemed excited.

"Please, sir, call me Johnny, and you're welcome." The tall man tipped his hat as the old man shuffled away.

Johnny pulled a long black cane out of his coat and leaned into it, shaking. As we passed him I heard giggling, excited and chaotic giggles, accompanied by mumbling, as if he were arguing with himself. I pulled Gwen closer to me and away from the crazy man. Suddenly, Johnny pointed his cane at me. "I'll be talking to you, later." His cane dropped to the ground, and the giggling continued.

I looked toward Johnny, to see if he followed us or posed any kind of threat, but he seemed to have forgotten about us. He talked to a young couple with a stroller. The couple did not appear afraid of him. Chicago brought out the weird in everyone, especially in the summer months.

We followed a bike path toward the center of Lincoln Park. My daughter pulled me off the trail, toward a cement building that had 'Couch' embossed in the roof. An interesting but short black iron fence surrounded the small structure, keeping people out. "Couch? For sitting? If this is some kind of art, I don't understand."

Gwen leaned on the fence. "Dad told me it's a mausoleum. Couch is the surname. This is the last part of the cemetery that used to be here. All the other grave markers and mausoleums were removed when they transformed the cemetery into a park. Ten thousand bodies were disinterred, some predated the civil war, and some were even Native American. There must have been mounds here with all kinds of interesting artifacts." Gwen's eyes twinkled.

I stared at her. She sounded so much like Marshal that I could imagine him standing in her place, explaining with the same conviction, spouting off the same facts and figures, looking just as excited. "When did you grow up? Seems like yesterday you were a baby."

"Mom, I'm almost fourteen. I'm not a baby." Gwen placed her hands on her hips, suddenly looking much older than her years.

"But, Oz Park? Whirligigs? Those things are for little kids."

Gwen shrugged. "Dad always said growing older is mandatory, growing up is optional. He was the oldest kid I knew."

She was right; Marshal was professional, intelligent, and a big child. His toy collection of superheroes, N gauge trains, video games, and comics rivaled Willy's store. It wasn't surprising that Willy and his toys reminded Gwen of her father.

Gwen pulled the Jacob's ladder out of her purse, and let it fall. *Click-clack click-clack.* "Willy said the sound is like a baby's rattle."

"It doesn't sound anything like a rattle."

"No, that's not what he meant. A long time ago, a rattle was created to scare off monsters or demons, to keep babies safe. But, those were ignorant times, long before science." Gwen continued to turn the top block of the Jacob's ladder. *Click-clack.* "I wonder what he meant. He wanted me to bring it to the Sha'Daa your co-worker talked about."

I saw something strange in the light of twilight. It seemed to pulse with the sound of the blocks striking one another. "Look over there."

"Where?" Gwen stopped turning the toy and stared in the direction I pointed.

"There by the tree."

"I don't see anything."

"Try turning the blocks again," I suggested.

Gwen turned the toy, the sound revealed what at first it looked like a dog. With each strike of block on block more detail appeared. The hindquarters were not dog-like. They curved too much. It looked more like a crouching man on hands and feet, with knees close to the armpits, in a frog position.

Gwen twisted her wrist flipping the cascading blocks quicker than before. The click-clack sound reverberated in my ears. Voices and laughter from others in the park were muffled like I was underwater.

The figure pulsed with light and clarity, expressing more detail with the speed of Gwen's wrist, *click-clack*. It was no man. Thick sword-like spikes stuck out of its back at odd angles. Its slick green-grey skin looked wet and oozing.

A man in a three-piece suit walked on the path next to the tree, oblivious to the beast. The creature, remaining on all fours, crept up behind the man. *How could he not see or sense the monster?* The creature's arms struck out toward the man, enveloping him, twisting and ripping him in half. The actions were so quick the man didn't react. The monster placed each half in the tree as if saving the meat for later or perhaps, some kind of macabre decoration.

Blood streamed from the corpse. My stomach flipped, threatening me with a reshowing of dinner. The man's mouth opened and closed as if he were trying to shout. His limbs jerked. Bitter bile assaulted my palette. I swallowed hard. A scream caught in my throat.

Gwen nudged my arm, putting her finger to her lips. She pointed to the top of the Couch mausoleum at another creature while her other hand continued to turn the Jacob's ladder.

The creature's face contorted in a snarl. Short black spikes covered its head with punk-like hair. Dark, unblinking, glassy eyes stared through us scanning the area, nostrils flaring. The beast seemed to know we were there. Perhaps my perfume gave us away. Gwen and I cringed as the monster's arms flung out in our direction. I leaned back to avoid contact and stumbled, pulling my daughter down with me.

The toy fell silent.

Gwen rolled past me, wooden blocks clutched in her hand.

The beast stared at me with lethal intent. The pulsing of the creature lessened, and it slowly became transparent. I watched it climb off the mausoleum picking its way over the fence, before it disappeared completely. I scrambled backward. The strap of my purse tangled my arms, impeding my progress. Blades of grass bent and twisted under its invisible feet. I couldn't move fast enough. Heat from its breath and spittle struck my cheek and lips.

"Mom!"

The crushed grass turned away from me, edging toward Gwen. The creature grunted, as if jumping. Gwen flipped the blocks and side stepped. The beast landed, throwing its arms wide trying to locate her. It shrieked with anger then looked back to me.

Gwen stood at my side, hiding us with the sound of cascading blocks. "Move–it could come back!" she hissed. I scrambled to my feet, stumbling as Gwen guided me away.

The monster turned away from us, something caught its attention. The beast jumped, disappearing from view. We heard a woman's scream. Assuming the worst, Gwen and I moved away from the growling and commotion.

Gwen continued to turn the toy, revealing hordes of monsters all around us. They stalked people, attacking and killing with ease. Screams of pain and fear came from the children's fountain. Gun fire resounded off the buildings. *Someone was fighting back.*

Lights from the skyscrapers and park lamps flickered and went dark. The thick smell of ozone and smoke enveloped us. Soon night would be at its darkest. I shuddered, feeling alone, naked, and paranoid as the world fell apart around us. I held Gwen close, knowing the toy hid us. I felt guilty not helping others, cowering behind our shield.

We carefully picked our way away from the noise, stench, and darkness, toward an area lit up with overhead arena lights. As we approached we heard the hum of a generator. Aluminum bleachers were slick with blood and bodies of children and their parents. The beasts must have come from here.

"What the fuck?" Gwen stared at the carnage around her, at a loss for words. The click-clack of the Jacob's ladder stuttered for a second. The light and pulsing of the monsters returned. The parent in me wanted to yell at her for swearing, but I was too terrified to say anything.

Movement in the baseball outfield caught my attention. Men in light blue scrubs stood around a casualty of the chaos. The people seemed to pulse like the beasts. I looked closer, staring at the person they were working on. *That looks like Seth.* We moved to the chain link backstop.

As if he heard my thoughts, Seth's head twisted to look in my direction. His thick sandy brown hair framed his face. A subtle jerking convulsed his head and shoulders. He smiled, but his eyes belied the pain he felt. Cords of what looked like wet rope were thrown on his chest. Seth grabbed at it, rubbing it over his face, chest, and arms. He licked his lips and then arched his back as if reaching orgasm. The men moved away, except one. Seth's naked body was flayed open, exposing his intestines.

"Malum hoc sacrificio daemonum evocare!" Seth shouted. He cleared his throat. "Entrails..." his voice shuddered.

"Entrails exposed,
Thick blood flows,
Centuries of hardship,
Evil grows,
Sacrifice freely given,
I release thee,
Ahriman!
Ahriman...
Ahriman..."

The remaining man standing at Seth's side raised a heavy sledge hammer, swinging it, letting it strike the back of Seth's skull.

Seth never looked away from my eyes, his smile permanently affixed to his face, even as the light of life was extinguished. The men in scrubs moved away from Seth, stripping fabric and masks off their bodies. They shimmered, and turned into beasts.

"Oh, my God! What the hell is going on?"

"Depends on your god, but Hell is an excellent description–it's the Sha'Daa."

"That's what Seth said." I spun on my heel to look at the speaker. The tall, thin man from the fountain looked at me from under his fedora. His black hair stuck out like porcupine quills between coat collar and hat rim. The man's eyes held me like thick pools of tar. "You're Johnny, right?"

The man looked over my head and all around as if expecting to find eavesdroppers. He grinned, moved his head closer to us, and spoke out the side of his mouth. "I'm also known as The Salesman." Johnny pressed his finger to his lips, a twinkle in his eye.

Suddenly he straightened to his full height and patted down his long coat. He opened the front and checked the interior pockets on one side then the other. The man nodded sharply then turned his attention to me. "You have something I want, and I have something you need. Two somethings to be exact." Johnny giggled, rising up onto his toes and then back down, like a child unable to contain their excitement.

"You want something? At a time like this? Is this some kind of sick joke?"

"Does this look like a joke to you?" The strange man swept his arm slowly like he was presenting a prize on a game show. "Does that blood or smoke smell like a joke? How about the screams of the dying or the moans of anguished, do they sound funny to your ears?" He lifted himself up on tiptoes, giggled, and dropped hard to the soles of his feet. "Well, this is no joke, Elizabeth, this is the Sha'Daa."

"How do you know my name?"

He shrugged. "Your husband's knife, I want it." Johnny held out his hand, his eyes narrowed, biting into my soul.

I mentally felt the weight of the knife in my pocket. I kept it with me since the day he died. It was his favorite, even after he sharpened it past the hardened steel and it was unable to hold an edge. I fished the knife from my pocket, holding it in my palm. The Walnut casing was worn, and the brass ends loose. "Why would you want this? It's old and dull."

"It doesn't matter." Johnny flashed a smile. His white shark-like grin was marred by a single gold tooth. "That is not where the value of the knife lies." He held out his hand.

I closed my hand around the knife, clutching it to my chest. "What do you mean?"

"There is love, honor, respect, and blood on that blade. All of which are powerful in these times." He extended his hand further.

My thoughts turned inward. Blood. In my mind, I heard Marshal say, "The job isn't complete until there's blood on it." Sometimes I wondered if he cut himself purposely to mark his work. Perhaps, the blood gave the carving some kind of power. Or he was simply marking his territory.

The strange man nodded as if agreeing with my thoughts.

Johnny was right of course. I still had Marshal's memory and his daughter. I pulled Gwen close. I didn't need the knife, but I felt like I had to have it.

"Willy must like you if he parted with a Jacob's ladder," Johnny said to Gwen.

"He gave it to me. He told me it is like a baby's rattle." Gwen eyed the thin man with distrust.

"Indeed? He *gave* you the toy and *told* you what it does. For certain you *are* special." Johnny's smile dripped with sweetness.

He patted Gwen on the head as if she were a puppy, and then turned sharply to me. "The toy exposes the demons that surround you and allows you to hide within the waves of its sound. But there are other demons, archdemons. They will see you. You need to defend your daughter and yourself. I have a weapon you need."

"Weapon? Do I look like I can use a weapon? I'd end up hurting myself. I can't even open a pickle jar." I looked down at my skinny body and straw-like arms.

"It is amazing what someone can do when their life is at stake." Johnny walked around us, circling, looking me over. "No, you're right, but strength isn't the only thing you are missing. First Minerva's Needle and then a weapon." He handed me a sewing needle the size of a pencil, sharp on one end and an eye on the other. "It must puncture your flesh for it to work."

I recoiled, stepping away from Johnny. "How can that needle help us if it kills me?"

"Yes, you definitely need Minerva's wisdom. Put your hair in a bun and skewer the hair. Flesh, after all, comes in all shapes." Johnny giggled then quickly covered his mouth, as if embarrassed by the outburst.

Gwen took the needle. "Mom, play with the ladder." She gave me the toy. The air around us shimmered as the toy was silent for a moment.

I turned the top block, *click-clack.*

"Mom, Minerva is the Roman Goddess of Wisdom, War, and Weaving. The strange events of the past few minutes make me think this needle will help you, and me." Gwen pulled my hair back, sweeping it off my face and twisting it around her fingers into a bun.

"Now I understand Willy's desire to keep you around, keep you safe." Johnny's eyes sparkled with mirth as he spoke to Gwen.

Gwen stuck her tongue out at Johnny then stabbed my hair with the needle.

I felt light headed as a wave of consciousness overpowered me. A gentle voice rang in my head, *let go, I can protect your daughter.*

Gwen took the toy back, deftly without losing a single sound.

I shook my head trying to clear my thoughts. Gwen needed me. She couldn't turn that toy all night. If the chaos of Ahriman's demons only lasted one night. We needed others to help, take turns playing with the toy if we were to remain hidden. We also needed a weapon for protection against the monsters that could see through the sound. The solution was obvious. I placed my husband's dull, worthless knife into Johnny's hand.

You can't handle a weapon, but I can. Let go, trust me, the voice in my head told me.

I didn't like the idea of relinquishing control to the voice, to Minerva. I reached up to remove the needle. But I was also afraid of what would happen if she didn't take over. My hand stopped then dropped to my side.

"Mom? Are you okay?" Gwen looked at me with worried eyes.

"Of course, darling, your mother is fine. She's resting," I said. The voice was mine, but it wasn't me. Minerva spoke through my mouth. I turned away from Gwen and addressed The Salesman. "Johnny, we have a deal, do we not?"

Johnny opened his trench coat and from within pulled out a dagger in a matching curved metal sheath. "This ancient blade was created and blessed by Amesha Spenta, who serves Ahura Mazda; the Bringer of Light and Ahriman's brother. This weapon, in the right hands, can defeat Ahriman and any of his demons."

I accepted the dagger, pulling blade from sheath; its gentle curve was breathtaking. The metal had waves of depth and color that ran the entire length, Damascus. Small jewels wrapped around the grip. The head of a golden ram was carved into the pommel. Its curved horns echoed the curvature of the blade and sheath. I felt power and strength radiate from the hilt and enter my body. "Thank you." I looked up, but Johnny was gone.

The rolling crash of thunder drew my attention back to Seth's corpse. A crack appeared as if lightning ripped a hole in the air. Massive hands gripped the edges, forcing the void larger. A cloven hoof the size of Seth's body stepped through. Surely this was the Archdemon Johnny spoke of. *A fight worthy of a goddess.* The tingle of excitement and adrenaline surged through my muscles.

I kissed Gwen on the forehead. "Your mother and I will be right back. Keep that toy moving. Stay hidden."

I saw my daughter look at the needle, slightly above my head, and back to my eyes. Her stare was steel hard. "Keep her safe, Minerva."

Indeed, Gwen is an excellent specimen. I smiled reassuringly at her then ran onto the outfield, tossing and catching the blade. *It's nice to have a weapon in my hand again.* I cut my left palm allowing my blood to anoint the steel. "No job is complete until there is blood on it!" I raised my weapon and attacked.

Toys Are Made In Heaven

"**P**LEASE," THE CUSTOMER BEGGED FRANTIcally, "you must have one left. I just know it."

Willy frowned and shook his head at the teenage couple sporting bright-blue punk haircuts. "No, I'm afraid we are all out of Kappa Kick Russian Roulette Hippo guns. However, I do have a Face Bank and Shave The Baby Doll."

"Deal," the teenagers spouted in unison.

"Wow, I've never seen the store this packed before."

Willy looked up to see Johnny at the counter, smiling wildly and holding a small gunny sack.

"Don't tell me," Willy said, "you want to make a trade. What are your interests?"

"Something very special," Johnny said.

"Well," Willy replied, "I suppose you know exactly what you want, and I just happen to have it, right?"

"Bingo," Johnny said, "I have my heart set on an authentic, mint-condition nineteen-sixty-three Big Loo red and gold robot from Marx."

"One of the few gems from my personal collection," Willy said in shock, "what in the world could you have that would even make me consider giving my little robot up?"

Slowly, Johnny reached into his sack and pulled it out.

"No," Willy said as his eyes grew wide, "it's a replica, right?"

Johnny shook his head and slid it closer to Willy.

"I think we have a deal?" Johnny asked.

Willy nodded his head and slowly picked up the mint condition nineteen-seventy-eight, Luke Skywalker Action Figure, still in its original packaging.

"May the force be with you," Johnny shouted over his shoulder, as he exited the shop.

Overhead, the speakers began playing a muzak version of Aerosmith's *Toys in the Attic.*

The antique phone booth rang and Willy rushed into it and picked up the receiver.

"Hello, this is Kvasir your interface," Kvasir said.

"I know who it is," Willy snapped, "what do you want?"

"The Midnight Laborers have requested three barrels of grape juice and two bottles of whole grain alcohol."

"What for?" Willy asked.

"To celebrate the festival of Euphoriant Expectation," Kvasir said, "during their fourth work-shift break."

"Aha," Willy shouted, "I've got them. Of their current thirty-three festivals, this Euphoriant Expectation is totally new. I have an eidetic memory and recall no such event."

"Yes, well," Kvasir replied, "they said if that was your reply, to tell you that this festival occurs but once every hundred years as a celebration of the second birth of the Goddess of Succulent Surprises…and, uh, to also supply them with one hundred pounds of crushed ice—"

"Bah," Willy snapped. "If it will keep their productivity up, they can have it. I'll have the supplies on the conveyor belt ASAP. And tell them no more shirking, dammit!"

CHAPTER FIVE

Off-Key

Larry Atchley Jr. and A.E. Atchley

"I like boxes because of the secrets they hide."

–Kate Williams

THE FRECKLED ACOUSTIC CEILING OF THE Music Box was tinged with ringed ginger-colored blotches. Benny reasoned that there were baby alien corpses leaking pus from the loft above. The pestering chiding from his grandmother for him to get off the floor interrupted Benny's state of shopping-educed ennui. Since lying on a shop floor was "inappropriate," Benny meandered through rows of frou-frou noise boxes to the counter where the shop owner, Morty was standing in a mess of packing peanuts, whistling an old familiar tune as he was peeling bubble wrap away from yet another breakable girly object "that the rambunctious should avoid."

Morty Winters was Chicago's authority regarding everything "music box." That may have been a bit unusual for a bachelor; presently turning forty-two years old, but with his sixteen-going-on-seventeen-year obsession with music boxes, he pretty much knew all there was to know about them. His full beard and bushy sideburns, along with a top hat he wore gave the Old Town shop owner a Beau Brummel-esque appearance that gave the illusion, at least to Benny, that he was a much older man.

The little boy's eyes widened with the creeping anticipation of discovery as Morty pulled away the last layer of bubble wrap. Morty scoured the cast metal box with his eyes, and fingered the hinge because it squeaked a little. Not expecting much, Benny mumbled, "What's in that one, Mister?" Morty held the painted box open so that Benny could see a little pirate seated inside. Taken a little aback, Benny exclaimed, "Wow!! That one's actually kinda cool!" Spotting the ratchet handle, he asked, "What does that one sound like?"

"Let's see, shall we?" suggested Morty, who already knew the tune. He wound the ratchet, and *What Shall We Do With A Drunken Sailor* began to play as a tall, thin, weathered-looking man wearing a black trench coat and a wide-brimmed hat entered the store. Morty set the music box safely behind the shop counter as he turned away from the boy, and greeted the other oddly-dressed man. "Sir, what can I help you with today?" Morty asked.

As Morty's attention was now focused on the man, and the pirate box was out of reach, Benny spread his arms like wings, and made airplane sounds as he ran to the opposite side of the store. Torn from his customer, Morty's eyes widened, as his gaze fixed on the boy in terror. "Don't run in the store!!" shouted Morty as Benny's wheels slowly came to a stop. Morty beckoned to Benny's grandmother to keep an eye on the boy, as he tried to turn his attention back to the man in the coat and hat. His eyes constantly darted back and forth between the man and Benny.

"Bull in a China shop," the darkly clad man chortled, as his eyes honed in on a key that was dangling from a silver chain around the shop keeper's neck. "Looks like I'm in the right place at the right time," the man said after an awkward giggle. Looking at Morty's chest, the customer finally stated, "I need a key, and you need something to keep that boy from wrecking your store."

Morty held out his right hand, and offered, "I'm Morty Winters." And then after a pause and another strange laugh from the man, the customer responded, "I'm called Johnny the Salesman. I make deals people can't turn down."

"The sign says NO SOLICITORS," Morty pointed out to Johnny, as he gestured toward the front door, noticeably perturbed.

"I'm not asking you to spend any of your hard-earned money, Mr. Winters," said the stranger. "Salesman's my name, but trading's my game. I'm kind of old fashioned. I barter for what I want." Then after a pause Johnny continued, "I've got something you could use, and you've got something I want."

"Look, man," Morty reasoned. "I've got bills to pay. I don't need things; I sell my items for money."

Getting to his point, Johnny reached into his inside coat pocket, causing Morty to flinch, and pulled out a portable video game device. Morty visibly relaxed, realizing Johnny hadn't gone for a weapon as Johnny offered, "You need something to keep that kid occupied, and I need a key." Once again, Johnny set his eyes on Morty's necklace.

Though he desperately wanted the video game, Morty hesitated, and clasped his key in his hand. The music box enthusiast had kept it on him for years, hoping to one day find its box. "What do you want with an old music box key?" he asked Johnny, as Benny nearly brought down a small display when he turned an imaginary corner, extending his invisible pistol at the ready.

"Somebody's going to need it tonight in order to do something that will benefit you and the rest of the world greatly," replied Johnny. Not having time to wait for the salesman to make sense, Morty took the chain off of his neck, and held it out to Johnny in one hand while he reached for the video game with the other.

"Okay," Morty sighed, as he zeroed in on Benny, and lunged toward him, holding the video game out like a relay baton. With Benny pacified, Morty let out a huge sigh of relief, as he looked back toward the spot from which Johnny had suddenly vanished.

⊕ ⊕ ⊕

When she tired of preparing for British Lit. lectures at De Paul University, Edith would sometimes walk to Oz Park for a little jaunt her pedometer could record. Today, Edith's sister Lorina was with her. She'd flown in from London for a visit. The sisters cut through the park to a little Italian café Edith had raved about. Lorina thought it amusing to look at the statues of Dorothy and Toto, the Tin Man, the Cowardly Lion, and the Scarecrow. They reminded her of the excitement, joy, and terror the book had evoked when she read it as a young girl. Back then she actually believed that there was magic, both good and evil. Sometimes she wished she could still believe there was something more to this mundane world…

After an early dinner, the sisters combed the shops that were nestled between the alleyways that branched off of North Lincoln Avenue. The heat of the summer day had finally started to relent with the coming of evening. With it being the longest day of the year, the sun still hung well above the horizon. Lorina knew it would be nice to be back in London next week where it was cooler, even if it meant the usual rainy weather. Spotting a shop that caught her interest, Lorina said, "Whirligigs! What a fun name for a store."

"Oh, that place is great. It's one of Chicago's hidden treasures." Edith replied. "They have all kinds of neat and things. You'll see stuff you never imagined existed."

"I'd like to look for a present to bring back home for Alicia."

"That's a good idea. I'm sure we can find something she would like from her favorite aunt too," said Edith, smiling.

Taking turns spinning the revolving door they entered into a wonderland. A sign on the wall proclaimed: TOYS FOR ALL AGES. A young woman wearing a shirt with the store name printed on it greeted them with a smile.

"Welcome to Whirligigs! Feel free to pick up and play with anything in the store. Let us know if you are looking for anything in particular. And be sure to have fun!"

Walking down the main aisle, Lorina noticed that this wasn't like any toy store she had ever been to before. It was like an antique mall and modern store all jumbled into one. There were toys and dolls that she remembered playing with as a little girl, and many that she had never seen or heard about that looked very old, possibly antique even. Scattered throughout were also the usual toys that were popular with kids today.

"Toys for all ages, indeed," Lorina said. "You were right about this place. And I could swear it's bigger on the inside."

They looked around, awestruck at the variety that surrounded them. Children were everywhere, playing with toys, running, laughing, and smiling. *What she would have given to have been in a store like this when she was a little girl,* Lorina mused. She was overwhelmed by the huge variety of toys. She didn't know what her daughter would like best.

"Does Alicia still collect music boxes?" Edith asked.

"She still has a few, yes. That's a good idea. Surely, they will have some here somewhere, what with everything else they carry."

Lorina stopped a young man who was wearing a Whirligigs cap, and a shirt donning the phrase: I AM THE WALRUS. His badge introduced him as Stephen.

Suddenly aware of loud hammering being done by a seemingly out-of-place carpenter, Lorina raised her voice and inquired, "Excuse me, do you know if you have any music boxes?"

"Yes ma'am. I'll show you where they are." Stephen said as they followed him.

"Hey Fish!" said a girl in a Whirligigs t-shirt, touching Stephen on the shoulder. "Have you seen Willy recently?"

Stephen shook his head, and she dashed off to another part of the store.

The two sisters exchanged puzzled expressions.

"Inside joke. Somehow, I got the nickname Fishman. It's a long story," Stephen responded to appease the ladies' questioning faces. "I guess it's better than Tweedle-Dum," he said motioning to another coworker. "Is it your first time in Whirligigs?"

"Yes, it is," Lorina answered. But my sister has been here before. This place is phenomenal!"

"Thanks. It's a lot of fun working here. I like your accent. Are you from England?"

"London."

"That's cool," he said as he led them to an escalator that would take them down to a lower floor.

There was a sign suspended from the ceiling at the end of the escalator which had two arrows: one pointing toward BOARD GAMES on the left, and another indicating that the MUSIC department was in the opposite direction. As the escalator ride ended, they were confronted by a larger than life chess board. Following Stephen's lead, they wove their way between towering game pieces until they were past the checkered part of floor.

Stephen turned his head and commanded, "White Knight to King's Rook three!"

The floor vibrated as the marble stead moved forward and to the right. As Edith braced herself, Lorina exclaimed, "What happened?"

"It's something Willy rigged up," Stephen replied.

"Who is Willy?" Lorina asked.

"He owns Whirligigs," the young man answered.

As they reached the music department, Stephen dramatically bowed to the sisters before turning to leave, explaining, "This is Cat's department, she'll guide you from here."

Greeting the ladies with a broad grin, a girl with almond eyes and pink and purple hair quizzed, "What can I help you two find today?"

"Where are your music boxes, please?" Lorina inquired.

"Right this way," Cat said, leading them through the department. "We have a lot to choose from. I'm sure you'll find something you like. May I ask who you are shopping for?"

"My daughter," said Lorina, "she collects music boxes."

Cat led them to a series of shelves that displayed dozens of music boxes. "Is there a particular style that you are looking for?"

"Well..." pondered Lorina, "She already has plenty of carousels, dancers and the usual sort. Maybe something different this time would be good."

"We do have these singing bird boxes." Cat suggested, as she flashed a grin full of bright white teeth.

"I think she has some like that as well, but thank you. Maybe we'll just look around at these others for a while."

"Just let me know if you need help with anything. I'll be around."

Cat disappeared behind a counter-height glass display case, and opened a cabinet in the wall, taking out a fresh roll of cash register paper. When she did, Lorina spied a bisque music box that had a white rabbit sprouting from the center of a green cabbage.

"Could you show me that one in the cabinet?" Lorina asked, pointing to the strange but beautiful music box.

"The one with the rabbit?"

"Yes. That one please."

"I can show it to you but it's not for sale. We don't have the key to make the music play. The estate Willy bought it from didn't know what happened to it. But apparently there's something really special about it because Willy bought it anyway."

She set it gently upon the glass display case in front of Lorina and Edith. Lorina traced her fingertips along the scalloped edges of the delicate cabbage leaves. She could see every detail, including raised veins that made the cabbage appear almost life-like.

"The rabbit even has realistic whiskers on his face and eyelashes above his cute little doe eyes!" Edith exclaimed, as she pulled out her reading glasses.

"I'm really interested in this one," declared Lorina. "Would it be possible for me to speak to the owner?"

Cat slinked around the counter. "I can try to find Willy, if you don't mind waiting here a minute."

Lorina turned to her sister, and asked, "Is that okay? I'd really like to see if I could get this for Alicia. I could swear it seems familiar, but I know Alicia doesn't have one like it."

"Sure," replied Edith. "I don't mind waiting a little while. I think it's very unique. I think Alicia would love it, if we could just find the key…"

"I'll be back as quick as I can. Hopefully with Willy," Cat said, as she sauntered away.

A few minutes later Cat returned with a tall pale man who looked to be in his mid-thirties, and had bright red hair that looked like it had defied all the efforts of brush and comb. The disheveled look of his hair was offset by his clean shaven, but freckled face, and he smiled a broad grin that showed bright white teeth. A tiny diamond in his right lateral incisor sparkled under the store lights.

"Hello ladies, I'm Willy Carroll. Welcome to my store, Whirligigs." He said with an accent that sounded like he was from Australia or New Zealand. "Cat tells me that you are interested in this piece."

"Yes," Lorina said, touching the realistic fur on the rabbit's head. A spark jumped from the music box to her fingertip.

"Ouch! It shocked me," Lorina exclaimed as she felt a strange tingling that spread throughout her body.

"Sorry about that," Willy said. "It's this carpet. Happens to me all the time."

Willy noticed the spark that shocked her was green instead of blue, as it should have been.

"It's okay, it just startled me is all," Lorina said, trying to shake off the odd feeling.

"I think this piece was meant for you," Willy suggested. "Tell you what. If you ladies will excuse me for a moment, I may be able to find out where a key like that could be."

The sisters waited while Willy made off.

On his phone, Willy tapped a thumbnail photo of Johnny The Salesman, who promptly answered the call. Trying not to be overheard, Willy half-whispered with a sense of urgency in his voice, "Johnny, I've got a green one. It's a music box with a rabbit in a cabbage."

"Alice caught the rabbit. Good. I've got the key. We have our opportunity for check mate," the salesman squealed.

"Johnny, you've got to hurry. The little green men are gonna be here any minute," Willy remarked.

"Show me the lady," Johnny responded. Willy sent a picture of Lorina to Johnny. "Tell her to look for me at the airport. I'll make the exchange, and hopefully we can enjoy another 10,000 years of peace before the bastards try again."

✛ ✛ ✛

At 2 A.M. at Chicago O'Hare Airport, Edith gave her sister a tight squeeze. "Love you, Ina." She watched as Lorina walked through the automatic sliding glass doors at the entrance to Terminal 5 with her little suitcase, purse, and the carefully packaged music box.

Sliding into a seat at her gate to await her flight, Lorina glanced up at a television screen that was showing a live news report about something happening in Tokyo. There was a green glow coming from the flat screen TV, through which Lorina could see people running in panic as an unidentifiable threat gave birth to chaos. Lorina couldn't hear the television, so she was very confused about the broadcast. Cupping her earpiece, the reporter paused before she passed along close-captioned news of a second "inexplicable event" that was quickly painting the faces of people in Beijing with expressions of terror.

Glued to the information scrolling across the television screen, Lorina hadn't noticed when a man in a black trench coat and a wide-brimmed hat landed upon the seat next to her, his knees much higher than the seat. Lorina caught a glimpse of the lanky, dark character when she turned to reach for her cell phone, and froze, her eyes darting up to the man's shaded face.

Johnny offered his right hand and spoke. "Hi there, Ms. Lorina. I'm Johnny, the Salesman, Willy told you about me."

Lorina furrowed her brow as her blind gaze traveled through the man who had spoken to her. "Excuse me?"

"Willy from Whirligigs," offered Johnny with a giggle. "The place where you got that music box," he continued as his eyes moved to the box in front of Lorina's feet. He laughed as she looked down toward the floor, then back up at him with a confused expression.

"Lady, you bought a music box today for your daughter?" he verified.

A little embarrassed, Lorina shook her head as if she'd just come out of a dark tunnel. "Oh! The man with the—"

"Key," interrupted Johnny.

"Forgive me, but there's something awful on the news…" Lorina explained as she looked at the TV screen and back at Johnny, slack-jawed.

"That's why I'm here," explained Johnny, his patience wearing a little thin. Though she was still feeling dumbfounded, the muscles in Lorina's face visibly relaxed. Johnny reached behind the front panel of his trench coat, causing Lorina to scoot back in her seat abruptly. She watched in wonder as he pulled Morty's key, still on the chain, from his pocket. "Put this in your front pocket," Johnny told her, as an airline employee announced that passengers could begin to board the plane that was destined for London. "You'll know when to give it a try, Johnny said to her.

Lorina looked at Johnny as if to ask, *Are you coming?*

Johnny gave a nod toward the bridge door. "When we're in our seats, we'll talk some more."

After spotting her seat on the plane, Lorina carefully stored her belongings in an overhead compartment. She did a double-take as she noticed Johnny was heading for the window seat next to her. She attempted to make herself compact as Johnny shuffled past her to his seat. There was an extremely awkward silence between them until the airplane began to taxi away from Gate M21.

The jet took off; when it reached cruising altitude, Johnny turned his head toward Lorina and began, "The stuff on the news… It's real, it's dangerous, and it's about to be happening all over the world." At this, Lorina's eyes and mouth opened wide. She turned toward Johnny, and with one swipe of her arm, she removed Johnny's hat and glared intensely into the salesman's dark eyes, her mind reeling. Her head felt like it was splitting as feelings of confusion, anger, and fear took over her ability to rationalize. The plane started dipping and swerving like the wind was about to tear off the wings. Flight passengers became alarmed and cried out.

"Let me show you something," Johnny said to her. "Close your eyes." As soon as her lids dropped, Lorina saw Alicia, surrounded in blinding green light, silently shouting, 'Mum!!! Muu-uuum!!" Clearly, Alicia was terrified. Before Lorina could open her flooding eyes, the pilot's voice came through speakers in the ceiling, announcing that they'd have to make an emergency landing.

Lorina's eyes shot open, and she spun toward Johnny. Past his tall, thin frame and pale face she could see out the window a sickly green glow coming from a jagged patch of darkness that looked like part of the night sky had been torn open. The wind howled and moaned and churned like a maelstrom as it batted the plane around.

"Try the key!!" Johnny urged her.

"N- now??" she asked as her trembling fingers fumbled with her seat belt buckle.

"NOW!"

Lorina got her seatbelt buckle to release, and then, working to gain balance, she shimmied past the passenger on her right. With a tremor, she reached up to the overhead compartment, and felt around for the latch before her body had even cleared the man that had been bumping into her right shoulder for the past few minutes. Just as Lorina stumbled into the aisle, from where she could more easily get the compartment door open, a flight attendant yelled at her from a jump seat in a strained saccharine voice, "Take your seat, Madam!! The pilot has turned on the FASTEN SEATBELTS lights!"

In response to Lorina's lack of compliance, the flight attendant worked to get her cumbersome torso down the aisle toward her. The woman stood on her toes, and reached her arms up across Lorina's to the open compartment. Lorina managed to pull the package containing the music box out of the overhead space, and immediately toss it to Johnny.

The flight attendant looked at her disdainfully.

"You must sit down and fasten your seatbelt. It's the rules and it's for your safety, madam. Now please sit!"

"Sorry," Lorina said to the flight attendant. "I'm just trying to save the world."

"Well you'll just have to save it while sitting in your seat, with your seatbelt fastened," the red-faced stewardess proclaimed.

Lorina sat and clicked the seatbelt halves together. With a satisfied nod, the flight attendant hustled back to her jump seat.

Johnny opened the thick cardboard box and removed the bubble wrap from around the carefully packaged music box. He went to hand it to Lorina, then drew his hands back.

"Wait," the Salesman said.

The plane continued to buck even harder through the turbulence. The green glow was getting more intense. Inside the plane, people were starting to scream and cry.

"Johnny, the music box, please! So, I can stop this."

"Hee-hee," Johnny giggled. "First, the Salesman has to make a sale. Got to maintain 'the balance' you see. I gave you the key. Now I need something from you." Johnny flashed his biggest smile yet, exposing his glaring bright white teeth. The airplane cabin lights glinted off his one gold tooth. Lorina swore it sparkled for an instant.

"I don't have very much cash on me, only a few American dollars. You can have all of it."

Johnny kept on smiling with a maniacal look on his face, and said, "The Salesman doesn't take cash, credit, or personal checks. Those earrings you're wearing look mighty fine though. I know someone who sure could use them. Mmmm hmmmm."

"My daughter gave them to me," Lorina said, reaching up to caress them with her fingers. "No, they have too much sentimental value for me to give them to you."

The plane dropped about thirty feet in altitude abruptly and pitched to the left as if some unseen force were trying to snatch it out of the air. The passengers screamed even louder than before, and Lorina let out a startled cry. The storm clouds now had a gangrenous look to them, and spilling out from the rent in the sky unidentifiable forms writhed.

"Ma'am, If you ever want to see your daughter again, you'll let me have them!"

"Okay!" Lorina exclaimed as she snatched them from her earlobes and placed them in Johnny's, long, pale, outstretched palm.

"A sale!" Johnny whooped as he slid them into an interior pocket of his long black overcoat. Then he handed her the music box.

Lorina turned it around so that she could insert the key that she'd retrieved from her pants pocket. The long chain dangled down and shook as her hand trembled, trying to get the key in the hole. She fumbled with it while trying to hang onto the music box with one arm as the plane continued to be violently swatted around the sky. She managed to push the key in, and she turned it. The music box radiated a phosphorescent green aura. Over the cacophony she could just barely make out the song, "Come Into the Garden, Maud" playing.

Then, the turbulence disappeared. The terrible sounds ceased. The passengers had stopped screaming and crying. The awful looking rip in the sky and the sickly green color outside were gone, as if they had never been. Johnny the Salesman had also disappeared from the seat next to her.

✦ ✦ ✦

Back together in London, Lorina and her daughter, Alicia did their best to put the still fresh past behind them, and carry on with life, though it wasn't the easiest thing to do. Strange events and disasters were still occurring around the world according to Internet reports. Lorina did her best to keep Alicia's attention on other things. Before she'd filed away memories of the recent events in her mind, and headed to bed, Lorina looked to Alicia and said, "we'll mark this day with a white stone."

Toy On The Run

WILLIAM THOMAS CARROLTON HAD NOT slept in three days. His former colleagues from Botany Bay were still on his trail and seeking him out in their unfair and unjust manhunt on the largely unexplored continent of Australia. The seemingly supernatural character, who called itself Benedict the Trader, had told William that the composite native Wo-mur-rang he now gripped had the power to make him invisible to his pursuers. Unfortunately, no instructions beyond wanting it to happen were ever given.

Standing at the edge of a wide and possibly deep river, an exhausted and starving William focused harder on the ceremonial weapon in his hands than he ever had before. Suddenly, two colonists, soldiers named Andrews and Caruthers who'd arrived with the third wave of supplies from England, appeared on the bluff behind him and raised their rifles. William's heart skipped two beats and then the soldiers rotated their weapons in a complete circle.

"I thought you said you saw him," Caruthers said

"I know I did," Andrews replied, "damn his soul. Let us follow the river as far as we can."

Moments later they'd walked out of sight. William let out a slow deep breath, before walking into the river and swimming toward the far side with the last of his failing strength.

He finally crawled up the opposing shore, and lay on his side panting. Dark naked feet appeared just a few feet away. He looked up into the eyes of two Eora men; the aboriginal warriors slowly raised their spears.

William shoved the composite wo-mur-rang forward. Both warriors gasped when they saw the markings on it, and rushed forward to help William to his feet, half-carrying him inland away from his former British colony and towards a completely new life.

CHAPTER SIX

Sketches From The Apocalypse

Lou Antonelli

"By the way, is there anything sadder than toys on a grave?"

–Fannie Flagg

I DON'T KNOW WHY I WENT TO THE OFFICE yesterday. Force of habit, I suppose.

My late wife would joke—half in jest and half seriously—that she was a "Newspaper Widow" and used that line from *Citizen Kane*:

"I wish I had a rival made of flesh and blood."

Newspapers *do* have a way of sucking up all your time, and the smaller the paper, the more time consuming, because you do it all.

When you're running a small Southern county seat weekly, deadlines are your enemy and time a valuable commodity.

The Sha'Daa was the second time I ran out of time—well, we all did now, didn't we?

The first time was when my wife was diagnosed with breast cancer, I never left her side all the months she was undergoing treatment

My retired predecessor came out of retirement during that time so I could help take care of her.

It didn't matter. She died in my arms.

After she died, I couldn't think of anything else but go back to work. What else was there to do?

Now that the world was dying around me, I did the same exact thing. I went to work.

The sky was streaked with red that morning. The last thing I did before I closed the door of my house was look back towards the living room fireplace and its mantel.

It held a display of childhood toys my wife and I had put together years earlier. It was a cute collection.

One of my most prized items was a vintage Sketch-O-Matic, still in its original box, propped upright beneath the mirror. Just as I closed the door, I thought I heard a rustling sound.

"Just my imagination," I thought.

Once the Sha'Daa had started, people quickly began to disappear from the streets. Screams, cries and gunshots echoed throughout the small city, but there was little to be seen.

A poet in New Orleans, Andrei Codrescu, once did a poem about the end of the world, from the viewpoint of an old man sitting on a park bench. By the end, you realize the old man had simply died.

But it was the end of the world for him.

I guess death and the apocalypse is a personal thing for everyone.

I put the key in the office door and noticed the electricity was on. I was impressed—strange what you think of in a time like that—that the electricity remained on despite everything. But the power plant was only 15 miles away, and it had its own coal supply from an adjacent lignite mine.

No one else was at the office, of course.

"The Captain always goes down with his ship," I thought.

I considered briefly putting out one last edition of the newspaper.

"WORLD ENDS!!!"

That would be wood.

Excuse me, that's jargon. "Wood" is what we used to call exceptionally large type. Back in the days when type was cast in lead, the largest standard size was 144 points. Anything larger than that would have to be custom-carved for making the plate...from wood.

I started in the business when type was cast in lead. I went through the photo-typesetting era, and on through desktop publishing.

With the internet, I thought that print would be ending soon.

Not the whole damn world.

But a printing press is too large and complex a piece of machinery for one man to operate. I sat down behind my desk and waited for...what?

The doorbell tinkled. I opened my middle desk draw a little and put my finger on the trigger of the sawed-off shotgun inside

It's an old used car salesman's trick that works with a wooden desk. Pull the trigger and the shotgun blasts through the front of the desk. I installed the gun the day before after the Sha'Daa started.

A tall man in a long black trench coat stepped inside. He touched the brim of his fedora but didn't remove it.

"Peace, Mister Redstone," he said as he stepped inside.

He turned to face me and tugged at his lapels. His face was in shadows but looked drawn.

He smiled, showing a gleaming gold tooth. "May I speak to you for a moment?"

I kept my finger on the trigger. "I don't know you, and I know just about everyone in this town."

"As well you should, as the local newspaper editor," said the stranger. "But I'm not from here."

"Where are you from, then?"

He made a gesture of futility. "Does it matter?"

I cocked an eye at him. "At this point, I suppose not. What do you want?"

He gestured to a chair. "May I sit down?"

"No. Speak your peace on your feet."

He smiled enigmatically and came across the room, tugging a chair with him as he approached the front of my desk.

He squared the chair, and then sat down.

"You have nothing to fear from me," he said. "You could pull that trigger if you want."

"OK, then, are you here for me? To haul my ass away? What's next for me, then? Do I get to be the copy boy for Joe Goebbels?"

"No, I'm here to see you *don't* get that assignment."

"How?"

"You can survive, if you are willing to give up something you value. And I have what you need the most," he said with a slight nod.

"I already lost the thing I value the most, May fourteen of last year."

"No, you didn't lose the *love* of your wife," said the man. "She still loves you."

I leaned forward and hissed. "Who are you?"

"A friend, as in '*A friend in need is a friend, indeed*'." The man steepled his fingers. "By profession, a tradesman, as salesman, if you wish."

"So, I sell you my soul...for what?"

The Salesman smiled again, the gold tooth glowing. "No, I'm on your side. You're one of the people who can stop this. I want your help. They..." he cocked an ear towards the sounds outside..."*need* your help."

I listened. The late afternoon shadows were lengthening and screams and cries were growing louder.

The Salesman looked across the desk at me. "In a world going insane, you're an oasis of normalcy. You're mundane, grounded in the real world. You've written millions of words and read millions of stories over a half a century about the real world."

"That's why I'm not losing my mind, why I haven't been attacked by any demons?" I asked. "Because I'm so well grounded in this world?"

He nodded. "Exactly. You are the definition of prosaic. You neither rejoice... nor fear. But you will not go through this unscathed. I have something that will help you."

He reached in a pocket of his trench coat and pulled out a small white disk. He dropped it on the desk. It made a sweet "ting", and he pushed it towards me.

I looked at it, and he nodded. I picked it up and looked it over.

"This is a 1916D Mercury dime," I said. "It looks like it's in brilliant uncirculated condition."

"It is, and it is," said the Salesman. "The last dime you need to complete the collection you started when you were in the third grade."

I laid it in the palm of my hand. "What do you want for this?"

"Something of great value to you."

I already told you..." He raised a hand.

"Love cannot be bought or sold," he said. "But a memory..." He trailed off and looked at the photo in a frame on my desk."

I grabbed the picture frame. "Here, if this is what you want, then." I handed it to him. "It's only a photograph. I have many, many more, and she will always live in my heart."

"Excellent." He slid the photo inside his coat and stood up. "That wasn't so hard, was it?"

He turned to walk away. "That dime is not truly what you want; it is what you will need. Before the battle with evil is done."

I stood up behind my desk. "I suppose it would be too much to ask what I'm supposed to do with it?"

"You will know when the time comes, and you face your challenge," he said. He put his hand on the door knob.

I held up a hand. "Hey, I do have simple question?"

"Yes?"

"Over the years, in my line of work, I've learned the only place you get a gold tooth is in prison, What prison were you in?"

He smiled, showing that tooth again. "I have been in prisons of unfathomable depths in regions you could never imagine."

He looked at me a bit sympathetically. "Always the journalist, always asking questions." He turned the door knob. "Keep on as usual. Like Edward R. Murrow said, 'Good night, and good luck.'"

I'm not sure I even saw him open the door and leave. But he was gone.

I was startled to see it was almost dark outside. I looked at the clock on the wall. It was almost 6 p.m. Somehow our seemingly brief encounter had taken nine hours.

"Isn't that a saying, '*time has run out?*'" I thought. "I guess time has broken down entirely."

I closed my briefcase and snapped the latches shut. "Time to go home… one last time."

✠ ✠ ✠

My home was only a mile from the office—this is a small town—and I kept my eyes to myself for that short distance. Still, there was an orange glow in the sky, and in the distance, you could see fires—and hear screams.

As I walked into the living room, I heard a quiet squeaking sound. I thought for second it sounded like a mouse. I moved towards the fireplace, where it seemed louder.

"There's a mouse in the grate," I thought as I leaned down.

As I cocked an ear, I realized the sound was coming from above me. I stood up and listened. It sounded like it was coming from the mantel.

It was decorated with mementoes and children's toys from both our youths. Her favorite Barbie doll was there and a Suzy Homemaker kitchen oven. I had a stuffed toy dog and a GI Joe.

We set up the display in the house when we moved in. It became poignant over the years, as we never had any children. I guess in a way there was always a lingering sadness in the house, and there on that mantel.

Which is why the Sha'Daa came after me there.

I cocked an ear again and realized the squeaking sound was coming from my Sketch-O-Matic box.

I was given it as a Christmas gift when I was in the third grade. You know the classic Sketch-O-Matic. A rectangle the size of a lunch box, with a bright red plastic border and a dull metallic screen that shone through a glass screen like a television set. In each lower corner there was a plastic knob, like the tuning knobs on a television set, and you turned then to make a stylus inside peel away the aluminum dust from the inside of the screen.

With skill, you could manipulate that stylus inside along the X-Y axis to make pictures, or even words.

I had preserved it lovingly for all those years, and it was still its original box. I picked it up. It still had the sales label on it: "Whirligigs, Chicago, Il. $7.99."

I opened the box and realized the squeaking sound I heard were the knobs. They were turning on their own—and writing a message.

I pulled the Sketch-O-Matic from the box. The knobs turned faster now, and spelled out:

I'M COMING FOR YOU.

I flipped it over and shook it horizontally to erase the message, then turned it right side up again.

The screen was blank…for a moment. Then the knobs began to spin furiously, and another message quickly formed, like by a computer controlled engraving machine.

NO STOPPING ME.

I flipped it over and shook it again, then laid it down on a table and grabbed the knobs myself. It let me spell out my message.

WHO?

Underneath, a message quickly formed.

THE HELLNEWSHOUND.

Damn, years earlier, when I was just a novice, I was out drinking one night with some newspaper friends in the East Village. We were all very plastered in a goofy giggling sort of way. As we staggered from street light to street light, we noticed an emaciated stray dog was following us.

One friend asked, "I wonder what the dog wants?"

Another said, "He's obviously looking for a handout."

I pointed and said. "He must be a newshound. He knows we're all journalists!"

We all laughed. Then I waved at the dog. "Scram, mutt! We don't have any food!"

The dog whimpered and looked behind itself.

I took a few steps forward and lunged at the dog. It yelped and ran into the street, where a taxi smashed it.

We all stared in silence. Then someone said, "Well, he's a hellhound now."

Parts of the crushed dog were still twitching in the street. I turned around and ran to the end of the block, and threw up violently.

It was the worst thing I ever did in my life.

I stared at the Sketch-O-Matic, then grabbed the knobs again and spelled out:

SORRY.

There was no room left on the screen, so I flipped it over and shook it.

When I turned it right side up, a new message spelled itself out.

TOO LATE.

I shoved the Sketch-O-Matic aside. "So, this is the way it's going to be, eh?" I thought.

I pulled a slim display case from the mantel. It held the folder with my dime collection. I pulled it out. "Well, if I'm going to die, I'll at least have completed the collection."

I unfolded the holder to the first page where there was one empty spot. I took the 1916D dime from my pocket and snapped it in its place.

I looked at the pages. "Well, that's finished."

I heard a scratching at the front door. "So probably am I," I said to myself.

I heard that squealing sound again, and looked down to the Sketch-O-Matic to see the knobs turning again.

This time the message spelled out slowly...and it was in a feminine cursive style.

I read the message as it formed word by word, as the scratching grew louder at the front door.

You...

can...

do...

this...

I gasped as I read the last word:

Babe.

"Babe" That's what my wife always called me.

The Sketch-O-Matic was bridging worlds now, and she managed to get a message off to me.

The door was starting to splinter. I went into the bedroom and took the shotgun from the gun safe.

It was a "Street Sweeper"—a giant, single-action, revolver-chambered, 12 Gauge shotgun. They had been illegal for years, but it had been handed down to me by my father. It was loaded. Since we never had any children, we had never taken some of the precautions other people might have.

I walked into the living room as the door broke apart and the demon dog leaped inside. It was a smoldering, sulphur-dripping version of the dog whose death I caused that drunken night. It resonated with evil. I knew instinctively it was a demon that took the form so it could come after me—and it did.

It turned to face me and leaped at me across the living room; I leveled the Street Sweeper and blasted away. I was on the far side of a table the demon had to hurdle, and the blast struck the dime collection folder, which I had set down upright on the table.

The blast tore through the dime collection and sent dimes and fragments of dimes into the demon, which screeched in pain and fell on the table. The table collapsed and the demon fell dead onto the floor.

I looked down. "Mercury Dimes—silver dimes," I thought.

The Salesman *had* been my friend. He traded me for the dime, which made me bring out my collection, which provided the ammunition that killed the demon.

I reloaded the empty chamber, and then went back to the bedroom, where in the same closet that held the gun safe there was an old glass water cooler bottle.

Filled with silver dimes, quarters and half dollars. It was a trove started my father and also handed down to me.

I rolled the bottle on its edges into the living room, and sat down on the couch, with the Street Sweeper across my lap, and waited out the night.

#

As the sun rose and the day brightened, I could feel the darkness at the edges of the world receding.

I was tired, very tired, but I also knew I had survived.

Then I heard the very slightest squeaking sound. I jumped up and ran over to where the Sketch-O-Matic lay smashed on the floor. The glass screen was badly cracked, but a message was still spelling out, in cursive.

PROUD

Then, beneath it, slowly spelled out:

C U LTR

I picked the Sketch-O-Matic up, but the shards of the screen fell to the floor.

I stepped outside onto the porch. I still saw smoke in the sky, but I also heard fire sirens.

We were surviving. The Sha'Daa was close to being over. The worlds would soon be parted again.

I was alive to help with the rebuilding. I could be useful. I scratched my chin and looked towards downtown.

"I wonder how many of the old crew are still with us?" I thought, "I wonder how long it will take to get the next edition printed?"

I suddenly realized I would have to digitally manipulate a headline to be big enough for the occasion, assuming the Earth survived these last few hours of this mother of all apocalypses.

SHA'DAA

OVER!!!

Yep, that's wood.

The Toy That Got Away

"I'M SORRY, MISTER G," WILLY SAID. "YES, IT'S true he worked for me back in the nineteen-sixties, but I have not seen him since the eighties."

"Yes," the elderly hunched man nodded and replied with a strong Italian accent, "I understand. I'm just so lonely since old Figaro passed away. I miss my son. He came to America and his letters stopped arriving in Toscana last year. Well, I'd best be on my way."

The overhead speakers began playing a muzak version of Duran Duran's *Bedroom Toys*.

Willy watched the ancient wood carver hobble out the front.

"Shame you couldn't help him out," Johnny said.

Willy turned to his left to see Johnny grinning and leaning on the front counter.

"Yes," Willy replied. "Pino left a long time ago and never left a forwarding address."

"Guess he found some other city or state to sink his roots in," Johnny said.

"So how are things out in the real world?" Willy asked.

"Almost a third of the way into The Sha'Daa," Johnny replied, "and we're still holding firm."

Willy's eyes opened wide. He hadn't realized so much time had passed. The nonstop flow of customers had really made time fly.

"You..." Willy started, "you really think humanity has a chance?"

Johnny grinned knowingly. "At this stage of things, I'd say a whole string of miracles couldn't guarantee this blue-white ball's survival. Still, I'm contracted for the long haul; meaning I won't give up until the fat lady sings. Now, what do you think of this?"

Johnny laid it out on the counter.

"The original Monopoly game," Johnny said with gusto, "owned by Charles Darrow himself, in all its nineteen-thirty-three, hand drawn, oil cloth glory."

"You amaze me, Salesman," Willy said.

"Now," Johnny replied, "in exchange, I want your nineteen sixty-three, first edition of Maurice Sendak's, *Where The Wild Things Are*."

Willy's jaw slowly dropped, "I don't think I've ever hated anyone as much as I hate you right now."

"And put it in one of those rare, red silk book boxes you've been hoarding since forever," Johnny chuckled evilly. "Helps with the presentation, don't you know?"

From overhead came the muzak version of Randy Newman's *You've Got A Friend In Me*.

Willy growled, then walked toward his office and personal safe. Before he reached it the antique telephone rang, and Willy quickly ran into the booth.

"Hello, this is Kvasir the Interface."

"Yeah, yeah, yeah," Willy said. "What is it? I'm busy."

"Sorry, sir," Kvasir said. "The Midnight Laborers have a very important question, that if not answered immediately, may very well cause a long delay in at least three separate production lines."

"What," Willy shouted, "three whole lines? For Aditi's sake spill it."

"The laborers need to know," Kvasir said, "Why are we here? Do we serve a greater design beyond the pleasure we get from our daily labors—however mundane or heroic they may be? Is the meaning of life internal to our own limited toy-making existence—to be found inherently in this workshop's many practical activities. Or is it external—to be found in a realm somehow beyond our factory, but to which life leads? Is it a vast shopping center with a three-dimensional cinema, or an all you can eat buffet run by grad school dropouts?"

"Dammit, Kvasir," Willy said, "you gave them a link to Wikipedia, didn't you!?"

"Well," Kvasir said, "I might have accidentally let a few of the younglings peruse the ether for a few days..."

"Tell them," Willy snarled, "I gave them free will, and it is for them to decide. Also, if they don't get back to work right this minute, not only are they all fired, but they'll receive neither a severance package nor a recommendation." Willy slammed down the receiver and headed toward his office.

The muzak version of The Monkees' *All of Your Toys* started up.

Samuel Meant Well and The Little Black Cloud of the Apocalypse

Shebat Legion and Joe Bonadonna

"What is man? Ally of God or simply his toy? His triumph or his fall?"

–Elie Wiesel

SAM PULLED A STOCKING CAP LOW OVER his bald head. Although it was summer, it felt like a cold winter's day. A bitter wind blew through Chicago with all the force of an angry tempest. Sam donned his mittens and then wrapped his favorite, most beloved, very green scarf around his neck. He left his apartment building on Dickens Avenue and headed to Oz Park.

A single, amorphous black cloud hung in the ghostly, gray, overcast sky.

A group of boys tossed a Frisbee back and forth between them. As Sam passed the statues of L. Frank Baum's memorable Oz characters, one of the boys missed catching the Frisbee, which had been thrown too high above his head. The icy wind caught it and sent it flying until it landed near Sam's feet. With well-meaning intent, he picked up the Frisbee and threw it back to the boys. Sam watched as the disk went flying into one of the nearby trees, getting caught among the bony branches.

Sam quickened his pace through the park and shouted, "I'm sorry, boys! I was just trying to help. It was an accident. I meant well."

And that was his nickname: "Meant Well." Throughout his life, every time Sam tried to do something good, tried to help somebody, Fate would turn against him and disaster would strike. For instance: a birthday barbecue for a cousin resulted in him burning down the porch. Then there was the time Sam attempted to fix a sister's leaky faucet, only to break a pipe, flooding the kitchen. There was also the time when he was stringing lights on the Christmas tree for an elderly aunt. When Sam plugged the lights into the socket, he blew a fuse, shorting out every circuit in her house. Startled by the fireworks display of sparks, his aunt clutched her chest, collapsed and later died.

Insecurities, self-doubt and an inferiority complex had plagued Sam since childhood. Everything he touched ended up broken. Everything he tried to do wound up creating havoc. That was his life. That was *him*. And why his family kept on trusting him with tasks was a complete mystery to Sam. He had considered refusing to offer his services for future good deeds, but this was his *family*, after all.

And besides, what would a super hero do?

◈ ◈ ◈

Sam reached the gate at the other end of Oz Park and paused to catch his breath. There was a strange odor in the air…a mixture of sulfur and ammonia. *"Hell must smell like that."*

Sam whirled around but no speaker was in sight. An unexpected rumble of thunder sounded in the distance like the laugh of a beanstalk-dwelling giant. Sam stared at the dismal sky, where a solitary black cloud floated above his head. Crossing Webster Avenue, Sam reached the sidewalk where a line of trees, a row of frame houses and several brownstone apartment buildings towered over him. He turned his head and glanced over his shoulder.

The little black cloud was still there.

Sam stared at the cloud and the cloud stared back.

"Wha…" Sam started to say when a tentacle extruded from the rumbling cumulonimbus. He froze as it inspected him, its concentration halting him in mid-gape. Another tendril reached out, yanked at his cap and insinuated itself into a handy ear canal, eventually retreating and coiling back up into itself before releasing Sam, who howled and clutched at his ear.

"Fanny Flaps!" he swore, his big thumbs tugging at his stocking cap.

Sam raised a fist and the cloud laughed at him. He began to run, and the black cloud moved across the sky, keeping pace with him. He dodged left, it dodged left. When he zigzagged to the right, the cloud zigzagged to the right. The cloud hovered in the sky, directly above him and shot out another tendril, grabbing Sam's scarf firmly in its clutches. Sam cried out, "Let me go, you creepy douche-biscuit!" He grabbed at his scarf but the oily tentacle held on tight, shaking him violently and lifting him from the sidewalk. He began to gag, tearing at his scarf, hooking his overly-large thumbs beneath it and wriggling until it loosened. "Ha!" He shouted in triumph, and the cloud sent a fireball into a fire-hydrant, causing it to explode. Drops of watery sparks exploded, causing Sam's skin to blister. "Ouch, you evil cloud! Get off, then."

The cloud snatched Sam's scarf and it disappeared inside of its amorphous, billowing blackness. He stumbled away but the cloud persisted in its torment, rolling out wafts of flickering, hot vapor and searing Sam's backside with a series of burning jabs. Sam swatted at his rear, howling, tears streaming. "Why?" He screamed as he ran, "What the hell?"

In the distance, he saw a flickering light.

Sam ran. "Help!" He gasped and almost ran into the large display window of a store whose sign read, "Whirligigs"…a toy store that had not been there yesterday.

Reaching for the door handle, Sam stopped suddenly, spooking like a skittish gelding. A man wearing an overcoat and a fedora on his head stepped out of the shadows.

"So. That black cloud there. That happen often?" asked the man.

Sam wheezed. "What?"

"That one." The man pointed.

Sam looked at the cloud and the cloud sneered at him. "It's just," he began to say, his bottom lip moistly quivering and his jowls a-wobble. "It's been that sort of day."

"Looks like you have a problem."

"I usually do."

The man's mouth turned up with a quirk of a smile, revealing a shiny gold tooth. "Might be something you could do about that."

The cloud growled.

"You mean, about the cloud?"

"What do you think?"

Sam fingered his collar. "Well, I'm not stupid. I mean, I am. I know I am, but I know evil when I see it. It stole my scarf!"

"A pity," the man told him.

Sam looked at the brightly lit display window offering a veritable cornucopia of toys, and then back to the man. "Look you, I'm going inside. That cloud is trying to kill me!"

"It does stuff like that."

The cloud growled again.

"I'm going in," Sam repeated. "You should, too."

"We go way back, that cloud and me," the man replied. "By the way, my name is Johnny."

"Um…my name is Sam." The cloud moved away slightly and then froze into a holding pattern. "Okay. Nice to meet you. Now let's go inside."

"How 'bout we talk a bit? I got things to say."

Sam edged flat against the entrance of the toy shop, his hand clutching the door handle. "And what would that be?"

Johnny hesitated before answering. "There are things—"

"Things?"

"Yes. And with them, great power."

"Power? What kind of power."

Johnny shrugged and grinned mysteriously. "Wanna be a super hero?"

"Why— yes! All my life!"

"Fight the good fight?"

"I'm not much of a fighter," Sam admitted, fidgeting.

"Well now, you could be. Just takes the right kind of elbow grease. A little bippity-boppity-boo."

"How do I get super powers? If say, I was interested, like?"

Johnny waved a hand toward the door of the toy shop. "Seek and you shall find."

"In there?"

"Could be."

"Powers?"

Johnny nodded and winked. "You fight, you get powers."

The cloud maintained its holding pattern.

Sam stared thoughtfully at the cloud. "It attacked me, it really did."

"I know." Johnny shook his head sadly. "That ain't right."

"So, what kind of powers are you talking about?" asked Sam.

"Could be an assortment."

"Like, more than one?"

"Could be!"

"Do I get to keep the powers? Say that I fought it, like?"

"Let's see what happens first."

"What if I lose?"

Johnny shook his finger in disapproval. "Wrong attitude, Sammy. It's all about the fight. The ol' college try. The 'not what you can do for yourself, but what can you do for the world' sort of thing."

"Nothing ventured and all that?"

"You got it, kid."

"Right. Okay. Well, this has certainly been a strange day, rather."

"Gonna get even stranger, count on it." Johnny's gold tooth glittered as the sun briefly appeared in the sky. "And anyway, can't have clouds just attacking people whenever they feel like it."

"Ain't right," Sam grumbled. "And I want my green scarf back. It's my favorite."

"See? So maybe we can make a deal, you and me."

"Power," Sam reminded Johnny.

Johnny beamed. "What I'm sayin'!"

"Super powers?" asked Sam.

"Go inside and see what you can find, then come talk to me."

Sam looked at the cloud again and then at Johnny. "Do I even have a chance? You know, with it being evil and all? I don't want to die."

"Well, we all die, but I don't think you will. Not today. Then again, what do I know?" Johnny shrugged. "Things happen."

"That's not very, um, what's it called. Brave talking? Courage thing?"

"So it's inspiration and encouragement you'll be wanting then? I can do that."

"Maybe you should."

"I will!"

There was complete silence.

Johnny cocked his head to one side and studied Sam. "Oh, you mean now? Okay, Sam. You can do this thing. You sure can. Yep."

"That's the worst pep talk I ever heard."

"Yeah, but I meant it."

"Let me think about it." Sam pushed down on the door handle. "I will. Really."

"Please do."

Casting another look at the waiting cloud, Sam pushed open the door and walked into the shop, which was so much larger on the inside than its exterior had led him to believe. There was the loud sound of whirring machinery as a conveyor belt, delivering a constant stream of toys, chugged along in a tantalizing fashion. Sam could see the shadowy movements of small men who shuffled back and forth, loading the conveyor belt.

"Blimey! *Elves?*" He stared with his mouth open and then began to search the store.

There were all sorts of toys. Each one tugged at his heart and mind with a feeling of nostalgia and a sense of *déjà vu*. Stuffed animals and wooden dolls greeted him. Metal and plastic soldiers of all eras saluted him. Puppets, toy rifles and pistols, dollhouses and battlefield playsets beckoned to him. Model cars, sailing ships, airplanes, spaceships and famous monsters called to him. There were wind-up toys, battery-operated toys and remote-controlled toys. There was also a huge assortment of board games, video games and computer games.

One particular toy caught Sam's attention, a doll. He stared at it. It stared back and slowly blinked. Sam blinked back and somehow ended up with the doll in his hand. He poked it with a finger. It blinked again. "Wow! It's all a motion thing and stuff."

"Mama," said the doll.

Sam exclaimed, "It talks, too!"

And for that brief moment in time, Sam forgot about the little black cloud and he forgot about the man named Johnny. He hugged the doll, which snuggled into his arms with great affection. He stroked its cheek and the doll's head turned slightly. Its lips parted and it bit him on the pad of his oversized thumb.

"Ow!" He tried to remove the doll, but it refused to let go.

"Howdy do? Can I help you?"

Sam looked up as the proprietor appeared from the shadows at the back of the store. The man gave a slight bow. "Willy Carroll, at your service." A small diamond in one tooth presented itself when he smiled.

"The doll bit me."

"Special doll, that." Willy winked.

Sam tried to shake the doll loose again. "It won't let go of my thumb!"

"You it likes, I think. It wants for you to buy it." Willy spoke with an odd accent. He gave a little laugh. "If you buy, it will let go. Take it home. It will give you much happiness."

"It will?"

"For certain."

"Well, then." Sam's brow furrowed. "Wait now. This can't be right."

"Excuse you?"

"Super powers," said Sam.

"Come again?"

"There was a man named Johnny. He said I could have super powers. I'm looking for super powers."

"Ah."

"You got those?"

"You take the doll?"

Sam nodded. "Yeah. I mean, sure. But the powers? Will this doll give me superpowers?"

"Maybe yes. Maybe no." Willy coughed politely. "Super powers, super powers. . . ." He scratched his nose thoughtfully and then snapped his nimble fingers. "I got just the thing for *you*." He scampered to a shelf, reached up and took down a Pez dispenser. Willy demonstrated it for Sam, using one slender thumb to pull back on the, plastic head of the goblin. There appeared, in the goblin's mouth, a small, rectangular, pink sugar tablet. "Powers," he said. "You take?"

Sam looked at it eagerly. "What kind of powers?"

Willy let the goblin head close with a click, and the sugar tablet disappeared into the dispenser. "Depends. Could be anything."

"I'll take it!" Sam crowed with joy. "Do you take Visa?"

"I do!" Willy said from where he now stood beside an ornate cash register and credit card scanner.

"Ring 'em up and that takes care of two things." Sam reached into his wallet, pulled out his credit card and handed it to Willy, who slid it through the scanner.

Once the purchase was made, the doll, having been complacent for the duration, released Sam's thumb, gave a whirring sound and said, "Mama."

"Oh, I never asked how much," said Sam.

"Not to worry, mate — not too little, not too much."

"Hum," Sam hummed. "Do you know anything about this cloud thing? It attacked me. It stole my scarf."

"Bad cloud."

Sam handed the doll to Willy. "Yes. It's evil. And I really want to get my scarf back."

Willy carefully wrapped the doll in tissue and placed it in a decorative bag. The Pez dispenser he placed on the counter in front of Sam. "You hold onto this," he said, returning Sam's Visa card to him.

Sam reached over, taking the bag in one hand and the Pez in another. "How many of those, um, things — those pill things — are there?"

"You mean the candy tablets?"

"Yeah, the candy tablets."

"Twelve."

"Do you have any refills?"

"No. Special order, those are."

"Gotcha. Huh. So twelve whatever. But are they strong?"

"Could be."

"You don't know?"

Willy shrugged. "Could be very strong."

"Huh." Sam's overly large thumb fondled the goblin head and he pushed at it. The head bobbed back and its tongue presented a tablet. "Huh." He turned toward the window. The little black cloud was not visible from his vantage point. "It could still be there. The cloud."

Willy nodded. "Right."

"Evil just shouldn't be floating around like that."

"It's crazy," Willy agreed.

"I'm thinking about fighting it."

"With super powers?"

"Super powers, yes." Sam nodded. "Because it isn't right."

Willy gave a noncommittal grunt.

"And it took my favorite scarf," said Sam.

"Rude," Willy murmured.

"Quite!" Sam squared his shoulders and clutched the bag until it crinkled.

From within the bag came a muffled voice. "Mama."

"Hush," Willy whispered.

Sam looked out of the window again. "I don't see it. But I know it's still out there."

Willy walked over to the door and opened it. "Pleasure doing business with you."

"Oh. Erm. Right-o. I'll just be on my way, then."

Willy nodded.

"To fight evil."

Willy nodded again.

"Off I go." Sam cleared his throat, walked through the doorway, stopped and looked behind him. The door had shut, Willy Carroll was gone, and a sign now hung from the doorknob: CLOSED.

⊕ ⊕ ⊕

Outside, the first thing Sam noticed was that Webster Avenue was deserted; not a soul on the street. It was quiet, as well. Too quiet. There were parked cars, along with discarded sleds, ice skates, snowboards, and even a bicycle lying forgotten on the sidewalk. But the street was vacant of people, as if the whole neighborhood had been evacuated.

The second thing Sam noticed was that the little black cloud was still hovering in the sky, watching him.

"Interesting, isn't it?" said Johnny, appearing suddenly out of nowhere and carrying a large, old-fashioned megaphone in one hand.

"What *is* that thing, exactly? That cloud?"

"Sha'Daa. A piece of it, anyway. "

"Okay. So what's that supposed to mean?"

"It means what it means. Sha'Daa," said Johnny. "Things go boom."

"That doesn't sound good."

"Think of it as a portal, Sam. A portal that leads to Hell." Johnny squinted up at the little black cloud. "It's like an event horizon that opens up and allows Chaos from Hell to come through."

"That cloud?"

"It noticed you, Sam. It wants you. Through you it intends to wreak havoc and, well…Chaos. That's what it does."

Sam swallowed the lump in his throat. "It wants *me?* And just what am I supposed to do about that?"

"You can fight it, Sam."

Sam hesitated a moment, thinking things through. "So you were saying, earlier."

"You always wanted to be a superhero, didn't you?"

"Yeah. Ever since I was a kid."

"Well, now here's your chance."

"But what exactly do I *do?*"

"You have your weapon?"

Sam held up the Pez dispenser and flipped its goblin head. "This, right?"

"That. Yes, candy. Candy's good."

"What do I have to do to become a superhero?"

Johnny pointed to the street. "Just step off the curb when you're ready. And eat a piece of candy. That's all."

"Wait! You said something about a deal. I get to keep a power or two, right?"

"Sure. Deal," Johnny said easily, holding out a hand for Sam to shake, which he did, although with some uncertainty.

"What about a costume? Do I get a costume?"

"Costumes will be provided by the wardrobe department."

"And that's it? That's all?"

"That's all. Are you game? Do you want to give it a try?"

"What about the doll?"

"The doll?"

"I bought a doll because it bit me and would not let go until I bought it."

Johnny shook his head. "Dolls these days."

"I'm asking, does the doll do anything?"

"You just said it bit you."

"Will it maybe bite the Sha'Daa?"

Johnny appeared to consider this, adjusting his fedora. "It might. You just never know what a doll is going to do." He snapped the brim of his hat. "So, you in?"

Glancing at the cloud, Sam noticed it pulsing…expanding and contracting as if it was breathing. "I — I guess so."

"That's great!" Johnny grinned and punched Sam lightly on the shoulder. "Okay. The first rule is…there are no rules. Anything goes."

"Anything?"

"Anything and everything. It's a free-for-all, Sam."

"But what if I get tired?"

"Then you just step out of the arena — step back onto the sidewalk. Got it?"

"Yeah. I guess."

"There you are. Now off you go. And good luck to you!"

Sam studied the street where a shimmering portal appeared. "I walk through that?"

"You do," said Johnny.

"And then?"

"Eat some candy"

Sam set his gift bag down but then, unsure of what he should do, he picked it up again. Then he put it down, only to pick it up again. "I have a feeling I may need to use both hands, what do you think?"

"Good idea," Johnny replied.

"Okay," said Sam, placing the bag at Johnny's feet. "Keep an eye on it for me."

"Mama," said the doll.

"Sure thing," Johnny said, as Sam turned away. Then he laughed. "Looks like you have some company, Sam."

"What?" Sam asked without bothering to stop.

"Look."

This time, Sam stopped, turned and stared.

The doll wriggled its way out of the bag and crawled toward Sam. It scampered on its hands and knees until it reached his side.

"Mama," said the doll.

"Well, that's unnerving," said Sam.

"It's like a valley of dolls, except without the valley."

"So, you gonna help me?" Sam asked the doll.

"Mama," the doll replied.

"Guess you have yourself a sidekick," said Johnny.

"Like a real superhero." Sam nodded, "makes sense."

Johnny held the megaphone to his lips. "You guys ready?"

Sam stared into the whirling portal. "I guess so."

"Then go for it. Badda-bing, badda-boom."

"You aren't coming?"

"I'll be right where I need to be, Sammy."

"What?"

"Never mind, never mind. Fight the good fight."

"Right." Sam eyed the portal with suspicion. "That portal. You were talking about portals. Does it lead to Hell, because I don't want to go to Hell?"

"No, no," said Johnny, "just a stadium."

"But…"

The doll sank its sharp little teeth into Sam's ankle with such ferocity that Sam hopped around on one leg, lost his balance and tripped into the portal, yelping. He landed on a street with colors as bright and vibrant as a Technicolor cartoon.

"Hey!" Sam exclaimed, still shaking his leg.

The doll let go of Sam's ankle and said, "Mama."

Sam watched in amazement as the Yellow Brick Road materialized from a vibrant echo of Oz Park and the statues of Dorothy and Toto came walking toward him.

"You're not in Chicago anymore," Dorothy said to him. She gave him a meaningful look, then turned and headed down the road. Toto barked, nipped at Sam's ankle and followed closely on her heels. They vanished without a sound.

From somewhere behind Sam, Johnny shouted, "Eat your candy!"

Sam whirled around in shock, reached into his pocket and pulled out the Pez dispenser. He fumbled with it and dropped it. The dispenser landed on the asphalt street and broke with a loud crack, sending pills spilling into the gutter.

The cloud snickered.

Sam dropped to his knees, scrambling for the candy, shoved them into his jacket pocket and dislodged his mitten. The little black cloud shot out a billowing limb, snatched the mitten and struck Sam across the face, not once, not twice, but three times.

"Mama," said the doll.

"Yeah, I know what that means," Sam grumbled. "I've just been challenged to a duel by an evil black cloud."

Johnny shouted through his megaphone, "Are you ready to rumble?"

"Wait!" Sam cried.

Far off in the distance, an unseen audience cheered and jeered, whistled, hooted and applauded.

The black cloud closed in, flashes of lightning bursting all around it. Colors swirled and thunder grumbled and roared.

"Wait!" Sam screamed as he ran, his legs taking him in huge strides to where he trembled behind a mailbox.

"Fight!" Johnny yelled from wherever he was. "Eat some candy!"

"Mama!" said the doll.

Sam shoved his hand into his pocket, grabbed his first Pez tablet and chewed it rapidly. He began to grow and, looking down, saw that he was turning green. Holding his hands out in front of him, he watched his fingers curl, shorten and sprout claws. He stomped his tail in confusion — and then realized that he *had* a tail.

"A tail?" he shrieked.

"Mama," said the doll.

"I'm Godzilla?"

The invisible audience cheered.

"But Godzilla isn't a superhero!" Sam bleated.

"That's a matter of opinion," Johnny told him.

Sam opened his mouth to complain, but sprayed the air with his fiery breath instead.

"Hot damn!" Johnny shouted.

When Sam's radiation breath had almost reached it, the little black cloud scattered into fragments to avoid being incinerated…and then threw a refrigerator at Sam. His attempt to flee was all for naught as the open fridge slammed into him and knocked him backward. The fridge fell over with a thud and the door swung shut on Sam, trapping him inside.

Johnny yelled, "Eat more candy!"

The crowd screamed. *"Candy! Candy! Candy!"*

In a panic, Sam chewed a second tablet and punched his way out of the refrigerator. He rose to his feet and stood there, his burly hands on his hips…a hero's stance. A lumberjack.

A shower of trees rained down on him — palm trees, pine trees, fir trees — and Sam felt a tickle in his throat. He coughed, and from out of his mouth flew scores of iron nails that drilled into the trees, splintering and shattering them into kindling. He spat again and another three-score and ten nails burst from his mouth, destroying the rest of the trees, but also puncturing automobile tires, cracking windshields and shattering windows.

A tentacle extended from the center of the cloud, bitch-slapped and punched Sam in the stomach. Down he went, falling against a lamp pole, first bending it and then breaking it in two. Sam's power failed and his costume disappeared.

"Seriously? You made me a lumberjack?" he shouted.

Boos and catcalls echoed in the air.

A disembodied voice cried out, *"And the crowd goes wild!"*

"*What* crowd?" Sam asked, popping a third Pez candy tablet into his mouth.

"Mama," said the doll.

"And once again our intrepid hero is up and ready to rock and roll!" Johnny announced.

Sam was now dressed as a cowboy, holding a lariat in his hands. "What the hell?"

The cloud transformed itself into a longhorn steer.

Sam twirled the lariat over his head and somehow managed to lasso the steer on his first try. "There — gotcha!"

Back and forth, up and down the street he pulled and tugged as the cloud pulled back and struggled to break free. Sam sweated and panted, his muscles aching as he used all of his strength to reel in the nasty, little black cloud. Then the steer opened its mouth and stuck out its tongue — a forked tongue holding a huge pair of scissors, which it used to cut the lariat in half. Thrown off balance when the rope was severed, Sam tumbled backward, landed hard and rolled over and over until he crashed into a garbage truck, which exploded and tossed rotten and foul-smelling garbage all over the street.

"Kayo!" Johnny shouted through his megaphone.

Sam laid there, momentarily unable to move as his cowboy costume vanished, another of his super powers spent.

"This is not what I expected!" Sam cursed and struggled to his feet. "You said I would be a superhero!"

"It's all a matter of interpretation," Johnny said.

The unseen audience chanted, *"Sammy! Sammy! Sammy!"*

Sam popped another piece of candy into his mouth and looked down at himself, holding his arms out for inspection. He now wore a yellow sweater, red-plaid knickers, Argyle socks, and black and white shoes. In one hand, he held a golf club — a driver, — and in the other hand he held a bucket filled with golf balls.

"Are you kidding me?" he shouted at the sky.

The little black cloud closed in, shooting off sparks and flames.

Sam set the bucket down, removed a few golf balls and lined them up on the street. "I've never even golfed before!"

"Mama," said the doll.

Swinging the golf club, Sam aimed for the first ball, but missed. He took another whack at the ball and smacked it hard, but it missed the cloud. Swiping at the second ball, he missed that one, too. On his next try, the ball scored a direct hit and punched through the cloud, but caused no damage. Sam swung furiously at the golf balls, hitting them one by one into the air. A number of golf balls broke windows, put huge dents into parked cars and shattered all the street lights…but many more flew straight toward the enemy cloud.

Then, from the center of the cloud emerged nine tentacles holding baseball gloves — catchers' mitts. The cloud expertly caught each golf ball and threw them back at Sam in a barrage that knocked him to his knees.

"What a day! What a battle! What a show!" said Johnny.

The audience again chanted, *"Candy! Candy! Candy!"*

Not quite as fast as a speeding bullet, Sam lurched to his feet, popped a fifth Pez candy tablet into his mouth and was soon dressed as a gunslinger, in denim and black leather. He reached for his weapons and discovered that the guns he toted were a pair of water pistols.

"What kind of game is this?" he squawked.

"Mama," said the doll.

Shaking his head in despair, Sam started squirting at the cloud, hoping to freeze it. Ice formed around the cloud, trapping it like an insect encased in amber. But just as Sam gave a yodel of triumph, the cloud transformed itself into a ball of fire and melted the ice. Sam desperately shot water at the cloud, which then covered itself with a half-dozen umbrellas. As the water rained down upon the umbrellas and splashed in all directions, an electrical transformer got soaked and then shorted out, exploding in a huge shower of sparks, smoke and flames. The umbrellas beat Sam and knocked him to the ground.

"He's down, folks!" said Johnny.

The crowd roared, *"Meant well! Meant well! Meant well!"*

"Mama!"

Bottom lip quivering, Sam tossed another piece of Pez candy into his mouth and climbed shakily to his feet. This time he was dressed as a knight in shining armor, complete with a huge broadsword in one gauntleted hand.

"No, he's up again!" shouted Johnny.

A tentacle wrapped in chainmail slithered from the cloud, bearing a battle axe.

"Mama Mia!" cried Sam.

Slam! Crash! Scrape! Squeal! The sound of metal banging against metal was sharp and ear-shattering. Sam lunged. The cloud parried. Sam thrust with his sword. The tentacle battered it aside with its battle axe. Like two opponents from the days of old when knights were bold, Sam and the cloud whacked and hacked and smacked away at each other. *Crash! Clang! Bang! Boom!* Sword against axe, Sam against the little black cloud, the battle raged on. But Sam was tiring quickly, his arm growing numb and limp.

"I don't know how much more of this pounding Sam can take, ladies and gentlemen," Johnny informed the invisible audience.

Crack! Snap!

The battle axe came down with all the force of Thor's Hammer and shattered Sam's sword. The force of the blow caused the cover of one sewer to shoot upward and fly into the chimney of a house, knocking it over and causing it to crash down upon the roof of the house next door. Sam's suit of armor popped out of existence.

"Darn it, damn it, blast it! I can't beat this thing!" he wailed.

"Keep trying, Sam," Johnny urged him. "Don't give up!"

"Mama," said the doll.

Tired and aching all over, but still with a little bit of the fire left in his belly, Sam ate another candy tablet — and this time he turned into a policeman. The cloud sent out nine smaller clouds with big, red clown shoes sticking out from their bottoms. The tiny clouds morphed into creepy, demonic killer clowns, jesters, harlequins and mimes.

"He has a gun! He has a gun!" the crowd roared.

Sam looked down and saw a .45 automatic in a holster hanging from his belt.

The clowns were armed with seltzer bottles, balloons and pies. They began squirting him with seltzer water, hitting him with pies, bopping him on the head with their balloons, and touching him with hand-buzzers that sent electrical shocks throughout his body. Outnumbered and burning with pain, Sam drew his weapon and started shooting.

Bullets flew in rapid succession. Clowns and jesters, harlequins and mimes exploded into mists of circus colors. Slugs tore into buildings, causing them to shake, rattle and crumble. Windows broke as bullets ricocheted every which way, causing as much damage as a bombardment of blockbuster bombs dropped from the belly of a B-52.

"Ouch! That's gotta hurt," Johnny commented.

"Candy! Candy! Candy!"

"Shut it!" Sam yelled at the unseen audience. He struggled for another tablet, counting with his fingers: five. He had five left. With a trembling hand, he popped another Pez tablet into his mouth and shouted, "I'm not afraid of you!"

But Sam *was* afraid.

The lie caused his nose to grow longer and longer.

"My God — I'm Pinocchio!" he cried.

The crowd cheered and laughed joyously.

"What kind of bloody superhero is this?" Sam screeched.

Sliding forward and, for the first time, descending lower toward the battered and shattered street, the cloud floated toward Sam with one tentacle slithered forward like a cobra dancing to a snake charmer's tune.

Sam faced the cloud fearfully, when suddenly his long nose started itching and twitching. He felt a sneeze building... and he sneezed with all the force of a hurricane. Windows exploded. A 3-story brownstone blew apart. Two trucks tipped over. Sleds and snowboards and the bicycle were sent flying into the air.

But the little black cloud remained untouched, undamaged, and still very much a threat.

Running low on his super powers, Sam swayed on his feet and staggered backward. He shook his head, leaned against a crushed and broken car, and caught a glimpse of himself in the cracked side view mirror. His nose had returned to its normal size.

The invisible audience booed and hissed.

Sam shook his head again and rubbed his eyes, crying, "Oh, what the hell! I'm tired and I ache all over."

"Come on, Sam!" cried Johnny. "Eat more candy!"

The doll wailed, "Mama!"

Reluctantly, and with a heavy sigh, Sam once again reached into his pocket for another tablet of candy and flipped it into his mouth.

"Orange!" he yelled as if it was his battle cry — and abruptly found himself dressed as a NASCAR driver. "*Nascar?* What the heck kind of super power is that? What kind of trick is this, now?"

Laughter from the unseen audience set his temper to boiling.

And suddenly he was sitting behind the steering wheel of a 1963 Aston Martin DB5. Sam yelled to Johnny, "I want to be a super *hero*, not a *spy*. This wasn't part of the deal! *None* of this was part of the deal!"

"Mama," said the doll.

Sam cursed. "James Bond is *not* a superhero!"

"Say's you," said Johnny.

"Mama," the doll muttered again.

The engine of Sam's Aston Martin hummed and purred as the little black cloud dropped nine automobiles onto the street — all 1969 Dodge Chargers, like the "General Lee" from the old *Dukes of Hazzard* TV show.

The Dodge Chargers sped toward Sam. He stomped on the pedal and his vehicle darted forward, straight at his nine opponents. He cranked the steering wheel to the left, slammed into the side of a parked Cadillac and bounced off of it just as the first three Chargers crashed into him. The Aston Martin spun around and rammed one of the Chargers, pushing it into another. The first Dodge spun out of control, sideswiped an old station wagon, then knocked down and rolled over a Honda motorcycle. The second car skidded to one side, did a quick U-turn and maneuvered around Sam. As the first Dodge rejoined the others, they spun their tires, burned rubber and formed a circle around the 007 automobile, their front ends pointed directly at it.

Sam flipped a switch on the dashboard that brought the Aston Martin's front-end machine guns into play. Slamming pedal to the metal, he cranked hard on the steering wheel, turning it as far as it would go to the right, which sent his car into a mind-blurring spin. As he whirled around in a circle, the machine guns blasted away, their bullets ripping into the front ends and into the engines of the Dodge Chargers. The cars exploded into a million flaming pieces, raining fiery bits of metal all over the arena.

The invisible spectators cheered.

"He's almost out of ammo, folks!" yelled Johnny. "But it looks like he's gonna make it!"

And then Sam felt it happening again…his power was fading.

A hush fell over the crowd as Sam's NASCAR uniform vanished and his Aston Martin disappeared, followed by all nine Dodge Chargers.

But the little black cloud was still there, hovering in the sky.

"*Sam! Sam! Sam! Sam!*" roared the crowd.

"Lemme think about this!" Sam yelled, fingering his Pez candy.

"Come on, Sam," said Johnny. "You're winning."

Sam looked around, searching for the sidewalk hidden beneath the rubble. Then slowly and with great determination, he walked away from the street and headed toward the curb with the doll crawling along beside him.

"I'm not winning. The fight is rigged," he muttered. "Fixed like a neutered fox! And I did *not* even get my favorite scarf back!"

Before Sam stepped onto the sidewalk and through the shimmering portal, the statues of the Scarecrow, Tin Man and Cowardly Lion emerged from Oz Park and approached him.

"What the hell do you guys want?" he demanded.

"Listen, Sam," said the Tin Man. "You have the heart of a true hero. Don't give up."

The Cowardly Lion told him, "You have the courage of a superhero, too."

"And you have the brains to know when discretion is the better part of valor, my friend," said the Scarecrow.

"You know, you people are all nuttier than an attic full of squirrels," said Sam, taking his anger out on them. "Go back over that stupid rainbow and leave me alone. I quit!" And with that, Sam stepped through the portal to where Johnny stood waiting for him.

Having followed Sam back through the portal, the little black cloud hovered in the sky, waiting and watching...

"Why did you give up, Sam?" asked Johnny.

Sam took a moment to catch his breath. Looking around at his neighborhood: it had remained untouched and affected by the events that happened in that bizarre arena. "You wanna know why I gave up? I'll tell you why I gave up," he said. "Enough is enough. I'm *done!*"

"So, what's the deal?"

"There is no deal!" Sam yelled. "The fight was rigged. You cheated me."

"You should have read the fine print, Sam."

"*Fine print?* What fine print?"

Johnny laughed softly. "You wanted super powers, you got super powers."

"But I wanted to be a super *hero*, not some spy or cowboy or dorky golfer!"

"You gotta understand. This fight could have ended badly for you. It was all a test."

"What the hell do you mean, it was a *test?*"

"A test of your abilities, Sam. Don't you want to be a superhero?"

"Yes — that's all I ever wanted to be, even if just once," said Sam. "And you know why I always wanted to be a superhero?"

"No. Enlighten me," said Johnny.

"Because nothing I do ever does any good at all. I mess up everything. I'm just a guy who screws up all the time. I mean, I meant well, but things just never worked out right for me. They never do."

"You just have to keep trying, Sam."

Sam shook his head. "But superheroes don't walk away from a battle. They don't quit. They don't give up. They have their moments, sure. But in the end, they always come back to finish the job."

"And you can finish it, too, Sam."

"Maybe I don't want to!"

There was a silence.

"So, did I pass the test, then?" Sam spat.

Johnny pushed his fedora back from his forehead. "What do you think?"

"I think I'm just a gorker who means well, but never seems to get it right."

Johnny nodded. "Okay. If that's what you want to think, so be it. But the question now is — what you gonna do next? You think that little black cloud has forgotten about you?"

Sam glanced at the cloud, saw it pulsing and throbbing with cosmic energy. "I don't really give a cat's ass whether it has or not."

"Well then," said Johnny. "I guess all's hell that's meant well."

Sam glared at Johnny. "Even if I knew what you meant, it wouldn't matter. It just doesn't matter anymore. Some people are heroes, and hats off to them, bloody right. But me?" He shrugged. "I just don't have it in me. I've been fooling myself, and that cloud knows it. And if it gets me in the end, well, shit happens."

"Apathy. Man's great excuse for everything."

"Maybe. And maybe that little black cloud up there has had its fun. If not," Sam shook his pocket and the three remaining tablets rattled, "at least I've got a shot at getting away or —"

"Or what, Sam?"

"Or maybe I'll just join it. If you can't beat 'em, join 'em, and all that junk and stuff."

The little black cloud blazed with a bright orange light for one brief moment, and then turned pitch black again.

Johnny stepped back, an incredulous look on his face.

The doll stood and gestured with its little doll hands. "But you *are* a hero, Sam."

Sam looked at the doll. "Y-you…you can really talk?"

"Of course I can talk!" said the doll. "Look. Real heroes don't need super powers. Ordinary people can be heroes. It happens every day. A hero fights for what is right, for what he believes in. A hero thinks nothing about his own needs or his own desires…he fights to defend those who can't defend themselves. Cowboys, lumberjacks, golfers — anyone can be a superhero when the chips are down. You did well, Sam. You proved yourself worthy. Remember what the Scarecrow told you, and live to fight another day."

Sam put one hand into his coat pocket, felt the three remaining Pez tablets, and addressed the cloud. "And what do *you* to say about all this?"

A long, sinuous tentacle responded, holding Sam's favorite green scarf. The tentacle ever so tenderly wrapped the scarf around Sam's neck, patted him on the back and curled itself around his free hand.

"Hey! I got my scarf back!" Sam smiled at the cloud. "Thank you!"

Johnny frowned. "I can't believe you just thanked the Sha'Daa."

"If there's one thing you can say about me, it's that I always express my gratitude."

Both Johnny and the doll remained speechless.

"It doesn't matter whether or not I passed your test. I made my decision," said Sam. "I went nine rounds with that little black cloud and guess what? I'm still here to brag about it, Johnny. You want me to continue with the fight. The doll said I did well — and them three misfits from that *oh so* wonderful Land of Oz told me that I *am* a hero. They have confidence in me. And now...I got no more self-doubts, no more insecurity and I'm bursting with a confidence I ain't never had before. My life has always been chaotic, and everything I've ever done has gone bollocks up. But I know one thing now: this is who I *am*. I can't change my nature. I've tried, and like everything else I've ever tried, it's all gone horribly wrong. At least now I know what I have to do. I know what I *can* do. I know what I *wanna* do."

"Wait," said Johnny.

Sam took one of the Pez candy tablets from his pocket and offered it. "Here. Have fun. And good luck to you, mate."

Johnny stared at Sam for a long moment and then popped the candy into his mouth. He nodded to the doll. "Well, it looks like it's just you and me, kid."

"Mama," said the doll.

Sam stuck his hand back into his coat pocket, fiddled with the two remaining Pez tablets, then turned and slowly walked away, hand in tentacle with the little black cloud. He started whistling a merry tune and the cloud joined in, in perfect harmony.

Making Toys

FOR THIRTY YEARS WILLIAM THOMAS CARROLTON traveled across much of the Australian continent, always wary of anyone not of native origin, welcomed by every clan after displaying his ceremonial composite aboriginal weapon, and given food, drink, and a place to sleep. Over those decades, he learned many languages, slowly coming to realize that the wo-mur-ang was granting him the ability to memorize the languages of all the native peoples he spent any time with: the Alyawarre, the Anmatjera, the Arrernte, the Gurindji, the Kunibidji, the Luritja, the Murrinh-Patha, the Pitjant-jatjara, the Tiwi, the Warlpiri, and the Yolngu.

After all this time in the Northern Territory, having learned many secrets and forms of ritual and practical aboriginal magic, William decided he wanted to know and experience more. He made the decision to meet and learn from all the peoples of Queensland, South Australia, Tasmania, Victoria, and Western Australia.

A shaman among the Gurindji told William that the Dieri were powerful practitioners, not only of the Dream-Time, but also of the practice of imbuing nature's objects with the spirits of the living, through the creation of talismans, sculptures, and even children's toys. Thus, William began his long walk to South Australia.

Pox in Blocks

Beth W. Patterson

*"The more things that you READ, the more
things you will KNOW.
The more that you LEARN, the more places
you'll GO"*
–Dr. Seuss

"**M**OMMY, WHY DID YOU MAKE THAT LADY CRY?"
The boy's enormous brown eyes were wide with confusion.
Standing in a sunbeam cast by the dining room stained-glass
window, he looked like a paint spatter, even in his immaculate clothes.

The smug woman, looking like a spun-sugar decoration in her retro fifties
polka-dot dress and flip hairdo, crouched to face her son, perfectly balanced on
her stilettos. "Sweetheart, there are some things you wouldn't understand. I had
to explain a very grown-up thing to her," she replied in a delicate voice, like a
wasp lighting on a cherry pie. "It's not my fault that she didn't want to hear it."
She tenderly tousled his downy sable hair before whipping a plastic comb out
of her pocket and returning every strand to its rightful position across his scalp.

"I'll take that for you, Petra," her husband rumbled, his usual booming voice
now a muffled thundercloud. He knew that she would not want a dirtied comb
on the kitchen island, but he also knew he'd been banished from the kitchen.
He reached out as far as he dared, tucked the comb into the brim of his fedora,
and beat a hasty retreat into the dining room.

Petra Shelley was all about order and control. Once the guests had cleared
from the Midsummer brunch in her expansive house, she had set about making
certain that nothing had soiled the freshly-painted, yellow walls. She now
returned to her task of reloading the dishwasher, since her oaf of a husband
never got it right. But her child was not going to drop the issue.

"You shouldn't have made her cry, Mommy. She was nice to me. She was the only grownup at the party who played with me, and there were no other kids around. She showed me how to make a house with my Legos."

His father chose that time to snort. "That's not what they're called, Winston. Remember our trip to Chicago? The man Willy at Whirligigs Toys had a funny accent when you picked out your…"

"It doesn't matter, Horace!" Petra, rising up onto her toes until she could glare up her husband's nostrils, was not up for a change of subject. "He also gave you a pop from what he called a 'chully bun,' and we all know that's just a cooler. Anything to make a sale! He certainly charmed you two, but he didn't fool me." Petra stared down at the boy, happy to have a height advantage over someone. "Look, Winston, you know how you're better at drawing in school, but some of your friends are better at math? That's fine when you're a child. But honey, when you're a grownup, sometimes other grownups don't know their place. Their ambitions exceed reality, and you're actually doing them a favor if you step on them. *Ow.*"

"What happened, dear?" Horace dared to ask.

"I stepped on one of Winston's Legos," she fumed. One of them got into my shoe somehow. Winston, I told you not to play with those in the dining room!"

"But I wasn't playing with them in the dining room," the boy protested. As usual, Winston couldn't win. "The lady and I went to the playroom after you made her cry," he tried to explain. "Before she left, we made a circle of Legos, and she made a little design in the middle. Then she whispered some funny words. They sounded like 'ta-daaaa,' like what that magician said at his show last week. They made me laugh.

"Why were you so mean? You made fun of her, Mommy, and you tried to get the man she was holding hands with to laugh at her too! And then you took her aside and whispered something in her ear." Winston knew that he should hold his tongue, but he had just been denied his only potential playmate all summer. The familiar tethered sensation wound around his heart, which began to flutter erratically like a trapped bird. He tried to find his special make-believe land in his mind, a place where everyone liked him and wanted to play.

Horace Shelley stroked his beard and peered over the rim of his glasses at his wife. "What exactly did you tell Willow anyway?"

Petra arched one dark eyebrow. "I told her that she wasn't going to be good enough for Jacob. He has such high standards, and I know he's going to dump her any day. It was best if she heard it from me first, so it wouldn't be such a shock."

"Pet, that's really none of your business. Are you still bitter that Jacob quit your firm?"

"Don't be silly. Everyone knows ...*ow.*" Another offending plastic block had lodged itself between the overbearing woman's toes. She took off her stiletto and shook out the brightly colored piece of shrapnel, glaring at her husband. "Are you actually defending Willow? She's just a dumb blonde."

"She brought gourmet cupcakes." Horace patted his ample gut in satisfaction. "Green frosted pistachio cupcakes with bacon on top. It sounds weird, but the sweet and salty combination was to *die* for. I ate six. She's got quite a creative recipe."

"She probably just bought them from Byerlys. And I couldn't eat them. I'm allergic to eggs, and I haven't eaten pork products since I read *Charlotte's Web.*"

"Sometimes I think your empathy is a bit misplaced, my dear," grumbled Horace.

"Empathy? That book helped me to realize how dirty pigs are," she sniffed.

"You really ought to try respecting other people's comfort zones," he ventured.

Petra was not about to be criticized. "So, I upset one guest at our little summer gathering," she shrugged. "I didn't even know her, and I'll probably never see her again. It's not like it's the end of the world."

The kitchen smoke detector chose that moment to chirp. Horace threw up his hands before Petra could utter anything that matched her glare. "I'll change the battery, dear," he assured her.

"Mommy, will you play a game with me?" Winston had tried to amuse himself for several hours after the brunch, but the passage of time was an eternity for a young child.

Mrs. Shelley looked up from her crossword puzzle, resplendent in the regal living room recliner. "I'm busy, sweetheart. Why don't you go play with your set of Legos?"

"I've already played with them. And all of my dinosaurs, too. Maybe we can take a drive to Lake Superior?"

It was Mr. Shelley's turn to be stern. "It's too dangerous to go there as of late. There have been some mysterious fires—spontaneous combustions around some of the trees—and a few people have gone missing there in the past twenty-four hours. Plus, do you remember what happened last time we went there?"

The little boy hung his head. "Another kid. . ." he struggled to find the right word, "*urinated* into the lake." He knew his father would take a belt to his backside if he said a bad word like "peed." The thought of company his age—and lack thereof—made his small chest go tight with yearning. "Why can't I play with other kids?" he pleaded. "It's summertime, and I only get to see them at school."

Petra rolled her eyes. "Do I have to tell you this every time?" she sighed. "We've tried having other kids over. Bjorn always wipes his nose on his sleeve. Erik's mom is a convenience store clerk, and I don't want that family to be a bad influence. Sarah laughs too much. Anders only talks about cars, and not only that, he showed you how to strike a match."

"And don't forget about Agneta," boomed Horace. "She still uses very bad grammar. She can't even get her pluperfect subjunctive right."

"We're all only seven years old, Mommy," pleaded Winston.

"I don't care," his mother shot back. "I can't have a perfect child if he's around all these little losers. Soon you'll have a little brother . . ." she patted her swollen belly, "and then you won't be so lonely."

"But I'm lonely *now*. I wish I could be friends with someone in my story-books. Daddy, will you read to me?"

His father sighed. "Okay, fine. What story do you want to hear?"

"Doves in Gloves."

"I am so sick of that book, I could cry," Mr. Shelley muttered under his breath. "Son, that's not real poetry, you know. *I'm* the one who writes poetry around here!" He puffed out his chest. "Don't forget that I'm a teacher."

"You're a substitute gym coach," corrected his wife. "We'd be much better off if you'd only get a real job. Your writing is garbage, and it doesn't pay a single bill. If I didn't have my own law firm, we wouldn't have this nice house."

Horace held his tongue. He personally didn't care how big the house was, and didn't know much about his wife's pocketbook. But the more she was working at the law firm, the more she was commuting to the Twin Cities, which meant less time he had to deal with her in their little cookie-cutter suburban neighborhood.

In the span of their argument, Winston had gone to his room and returned with his book, pouting. "Read," he demanded. "You're always talking about Lord Byron, but he's boring for kids. I like Dr. Zeus much better. There are pictures."

The ringing of the doorbell was such a welcome subject changer. "Saved by the bell," Horace crowed. He threw open the door, but his grin froze on his face at the sight of the lanky man with dark eyes like two ancient gunshot wounds. The visitor's wide-brimmed hat put his own prized fedora to shame. This man wasn't even breaking a sweat in the long, leather trench coat, which was a relief, because Horace didn't want to have to invite him in for a cold beverage. The newcomer was even taller than Horace, who was certain that his pint-sized wife, with her Napoleonic complex, would hate him right away if she came to the door.

"I just might have a solution to the tedium you feel about your child's favorite book," said the stranger in a low, silky tone. "May I offer you a book exchange? I've got one by the same author, and it's loved by children everywhere."

"How did you know...? Oh, you must have read my venting on my litera-ture blog! Out of the thousands of people who probably follow it, finally someone decided to take action. Hmmm…*The Goat in the Coat?* How much are you asking?"

"Who're you talking to, Daddy?" Winston had inserted himself in the doorway and was staring intensely at the newcomer.

The tall, dark stranger gave the child his undivided attention, as if he were the most important person in the world. "Why, hello there young man. My name's Johnny."

Winston gawked. "Hey, you're really cool, mister. You have a gold front tooth like some bad guy in a story!"

"I'm not a bad guy, young man," Johnny said, crouching to meet the boy at eye level. "I am a trader, of sorts. Would you like to make a trade and try a different book? It's by the same author, and it contains some important lessons."

"Like what?"

"There's a big event coming, and some frightening things will happen. You might have some visitors. But they won't hurt you as long as your mommy shows them some respect."

"Do I have to give up *Doves in Gloves* for this book you have?"

"Not necessarily. Whatever you want to trade."

"I've read enough of *Hanson Hears a How* that I think I've got it memorized. Hold on, mister, I'll go get it. I think I want to hear this new story!" The little boy pelted to his room.

"So, you're a trader?" chuckled Mr. Shelley to Johnny. "Can I trade my irascible wife and thirty pounds for a decent writing career and a little peace and quiet? Haw, haw, haw!"

The patter of footsteps returned. "Take good care of *Hanson Hears a How*," Winston instructed, holding out his beloved battered copy.

Johnny slid the shiny new copy of *The Goat in the Coat* into the boy's small hands. The salesman's eyes crinkled at the corners as he watched Winston savor the glossy cover before flipping it open to delight in the uncracked spine, stiff new pages, and strange new illustrations of imaginary beasts.

"Now, you'll have to pay careful attention to the words," Johnny told the child. "I was telling you about a scary event that is coming soon. Everything might be very different after that, and you'll have to make a very important decision. Are you ready? I get the feeling that you don't get a chance to make many decisions, but believe me, this is all on you, kiddo. Enjoy your new book."

With a hastily mumbled, "Thanks," Winston was off to his room with his new treasure.

"Who's there?" demanded Mrs. Shelley, heralded by her rapidly approaching stomps.

"He's some sort of salesman named Johnny," Horace called backward over his shoulder. "He wanted to swap some books with Winston."

"I would like to be able to monitor what my child reads, thank you very much. Oh!" She stopped ten paces short of her husband.

"What's wrong, dear?" asked Horace with as much feigned concern as he could muster. "Did you get another Lego in your shoe?"

"No, the baby just kicked," she said with a frown. "He seems more agitated than normal."

The smoke alarm beeped.

Petra scowled at her husband, then frowned into the kitchen. "I thought you changed the battery!"

Horace adjusted his glasses and squinted in the same direction. "I did," he insisted.

When they both turned to face the doorway again, Johnny was gone.

"This is bullshit," snapped Petra and tossed the book aside onto the living room couch.

"Mommy, you said a bad word," protested Winston. He scurried over to his new treasure and cradled the book in his arms, trying to comfort the tome over his mother's rash dismissal. The smoke alarm in the living room chirped a warning.

Petra ignored her son's outburst. "What kind of junk are kids reading these days anyway?" she demanded to her husband. "That goat looks really creepy. He's like a cross between Satan and some kind of pervert flasher. Was the author Satanic?"

Horace stroked his beard, pleased to impart his knowledge. "Actually, he disavowed organized religion. And he had an interesting life. He even drew political cartoons at one point."

"Just the first page is sickening. *Don't read too quickly. This book is hazardous.*"

"It's to make it interesting and set the tone," Horace pointed out. He may have found the rhyming patterns of Dr. Zeus to be petty, but he wasn't about to let his wife criticize literature so irresponsibly.

"This author doesn't even use real words. Like 'sprox' and 'olenoDady' and 'Sha'Daa.' What does it all mean, anyway? It sounds like an incantation:

Summer solstice, florus, faunus,
The great Sha'Daa is now upon us!
You're the key to its prevention
Join us in the next dimension!"

"I think it would be cool to go to another dimension," piped up Winston. "Then I wouldn't have to be perfect all the time. Nobody would be telling me what to do and then tell me I was doing it wrong."

"Winston, how dare you," hissed Petra. "Go to your room this instant if you can't show some respect for your father and me."

The boy wiggled off of the sofa like a fugitive tadpole and skittered toward the playroom before his mother could see his face and call him a crybaby.

"*Ow*," Petra shrieked. "There are now Legos in my *bra!*"

Horace moved his bulk to shake several out of his own sweaty undershirt. "Where are they coming from?"

"How am I supposed to know?" she snarled. "They were supposed to be in the playroom. I don't even recall having bought that many."

"Mommy! Daddy! Look what my Legos are doing," came a shrill voice from the playroom.

"This had better be good," growled Horace as he stormed into the playroom, his wife on his heels. And he froze in incredulity.

Where the circle had been was now a floor-to-ceiling structure comprised of the tiny plastic blocks.

Winston was elated. "Look, Daddy," he squeaked. "The Legos have formed a spiral staircase!"

Mr. Shelley could not let a mistake go by, inexplicable phenomenon or not. "That's not a spiral staircase, son," he corrected the boy. "That's a model of a DNA helix."

"What's that?"

"It's a genetic code for all that your body is made of," he defined, no longer caring whether or not his son even understood. "It's in every one of your cells."

"Maybe it's for one of my new storybook creatures?" Winston breathed. "Wouldn't it be cool if *The Goat in the Coat* could be here right now? Or maybe one of the other monsters. 'And what would you do if you met a Sha'Doo?'"

The foundation of the house gave a violent shake. Pictures on the walls rattled, and something shattered in the dining room.

Horace's face darkened. "What have you done, boy?" he roared. "Are you trying to invoke one of those characters?"

The helix began to turn just then, rotating faster until it was a blur, then became a column of green light.

When the light faded, there was a charred hole in the ceiling, through which father and son could see some alien night sky. Streaks of fire shot across the stars, and incomprehensible singing was coming from somewhere, as if nobody had ever made someone cry or stopped Christmas from coming.

Where the helix had been stood a dark, shadowy figure. The creature was black as night but could have almost passed for comical, with its absurdly long eyelashes and prodigious birdlike beak. Thick tufts of downy feathers ringed its throat and wrists. It had long, gangly limbs, a potbelly, and oversized fuzzy feet. Only its glowing red eyes gave any hint that Mrs. Shelley had just made a terrible mistake.

It recited in a rhythmic, singsong voice:

"I don't wish to make your day darker or eerier,
Nobody can make you feel small or inferior
Without your consent, though that word's an annoyer
"Consent' is ambiguous. Ask any lawyer.
Now why do you treat people's dreams like manure?
Could it be that you're secretly most insecure?
If others are happy, then what's it to you?
Have you met a Sha'doo? How do you do?"

It extended a hand to shake, which was more like a large, ungainly mitten with an opposable thumb and pinky. There was nothing comical, however, about the several rows of razor-sharp teeth that it bared as it suddenly smiled.

"Say your prayers and hug your pillow,
I'm the one you knew as Willow.
We'll vamoose for one small price
We demand a sacrifice!"

Petra had had enough. "No wonder you're not good enough for Jacob. You're not even human!"

Winston, on the other hand, was quivering with excitement. Another figure had joined the Sha'Doo: he recognized it as the Goat in the Coat, only it was made realer than flesh and blood. Every pen stroke of his book's illustration was now a fur pattern, the striped coat looked so soft and comforting, and it was tall enough to hug Winston, perhaps even cherish and protect him. The horned figure smiled directly at the child, blinking its long eyelashes. Beckoning to him, it said,

"Blameless child, must you abide
With such oppression, rage, and pride?
Leave this world and come with us
And we will stop this awful fuss."

The shadowy figure produced a platter out of thin air. "Ooo, she's brought more of those green cupcakes and bacon!" was all Horace could say.

The hole in the ceiling began to widen, the edges simply melting away like burning paper. The boy could see the dimension that could be his new home if he so chose: a pink candy-striped volcano that erupted green lava, trees with colorfully banded trunks and fluffy pom-poms for foliage, and a bright yellow terrain that constantly rose and fell like a waterbed begging to be jumped on. Its inhabitants smiled and beckoned to Winston, making his little heart go tight with longing to be one of them. They were smiling long-lashed humanoid beings, some with floppy ears or long snouts. Some looked like birds with stars on their bellies. Half of them didn't even open their eyes, but they all seemed to know where they were going and what they were seeing.

The Sha'Doo formerly known as Willow presented the confections to Petra.

"Will you eat them in a void?
Eat them or the world's destroyed."

Petra Shelley's face darkened. "I don't eat eggs or pork products. You'll make me throw up and ruin my dress!" she snapped.

The dusky creature sighed and rolled its burning eyes before uttering,
"Oh what an ugly tone of voice,
It seems that you have made your choice."

The thick mittens darted out and latched onto each side of the ill-tempered matriarch's face. Mrs. Shelley's screams were muffled by the enormous beak forcing itself into her mouth. When the Sha'Doo released her, she fell to the floor in a slump, blood spurting from her open jaw. She could not even articulate what had just happened.

The Sha'Doo made quite a show of slowly devouring Petra's tongue in front of her. The blood was barely visible against the black beak, but the juicy smacking sound was unmistakable. "Now is your tongue dumb?" it asked through a gory mouthful.

From the rent in the dimensions, an endless cataract of Legos poured into the room, a chute of red, yellow, blue, and white. Winston was borne up on a platform of the blocks under the rising tide of plastic pieces, but Mr. and Mrs. Shelley were not so lucky. They began to scream in agony until the tiny toys filled their open mouths. The crushing weight of the tiny plastic blocks was nothing compared to the infinite number of sharp corners digging into their soft, yielding flesh. The Legos worked as a single organism, assembling itself into formations of its own accord: cages, strange creatures, and abstract designs. It was a sight that would have made a medieval torturer weep with envy.

The next thing everyone felt was heat, an uncomfortable temperature at first radiating from the ceiling, quickly escalating to dangerous levels. Smoke began to bank down, descending until the playroom was plunged into pitch-blackness. Nobody could see a way out, but the groaning sound of the walls beginning to bow threw the three humans into a coughing, gasping panic. Glass windows exploded in the hallway. The draconian parents tried to aimlessly swim their way through the Legos, managing to get their heads above the plastic level even as the sharp corners made every stroke excruciating. Horace screamed, "Light! We need some light over here!"

And with the word there was soft illumination, but it wasn't any more comforting. Flames began to lick the edges of the ceiling, giving Horace only time to exclaim, "My, my, my..." His fedora burst into flame at that moment, and he bawled in devastation. He'd loved that hat, perhaps more than anything—except for sweets and listening to himself talk.

The ensuing flashover ended all of Horace's woes. The particles of the smoke and the vaporized chemicals from the Legos and other toys combusted in one enormous conflagration. Complete darkness became inferno in an instant. The fire itself was an angry creature, unpredictably devouring furniture and sucking all the oxygen in the atmosphere for itself. It blinked its long-lashed eyes and flashed an incendiary grin at the surviving boy. Legos began to melt, encasing husband and wife in partial sarcophagi of primary colors.

The Goat in the Coat gripped the boy in its arms. He covered the youngster's mouth and nose with his striped wrap, protecting the child from breathing the acrid smoke as Winston shrieked at the grisly demise of his parents. They had isolated him, they had mocked him in every waking moment, but they were still his mom and Dad. And yet—a tingling wave coursed through his little body—he was free at last.

As the black smoke enveloped him, he fell under its spell. He saw wondrous things flash past his closed eyes: exotic rock formations, fantastic inventions, exotic pets that surpassed imagination. There were faraway lands to explore, animals that did funny things, and outrageous parades. He was still letting these images swirl in his mind when the umbrage stopped and the Goat in the Coat slowly released him.

The house had been reduced to a smoldering heap of wood and brick. All that was still standing in the wreckage and carnage was the little boy, transformed by the event. His hair was now an uncontrollable mop of bright blue, his clothing now a red body stocking with a white circle on his belly that read *Beast One.*

Something stirred under the pile of detritus. There was a sucking, chewing sound, like something trying to tear its way out of wet sackcloth. The top layer of Legos fell away to reveal a dead human. She was barely recognizable as a woman under all the molten plastic, but she somehow looked familiar in the charred remains of her polka-dot dress. Had he known her from somewhere?

Something began to writhe within the dead woman's body cavity. There was an unholy popping sound, startling amid the hissing embers. In a spray of blood and lymph, the woman's swollen belly split down the middle like a seed pod. A defiant red mitten reached through the grisly fissure, another protruded to hoist up the rest of its bulk, and then a miniature version of himself now stood in a pool of afterbirth. Fully clothed like Athena springing from Zeus' head, the body stocking read *Beast Two.* The baby did not cry with his first breath, only blinked his enormous eyes at the dimension that awaited them.

Beast One took his baby brother by the hand. The premature sibling followed on legs oddly stable for one so small. The older brother told his new companion,

"Willow was just too annoyed
Now we will join her in the void."

A series of graduated discs floated down to meet them like slow flying saucers. Beast One and Beast Two found they could easily ascend them like stairs and walk straight through the hole where their new friends were waiting, welcoming them home.

The hole in the sky began to shrink after them like the puckering of a wound healing. Tighter and tighter it went until like the belly of a starfish, it was whole again.

Only a single page torn from a book fluttered across the smoldering remains of the once perfect house. It read:

"Should we tell you about it? What tales to bestow?

Well . . .where would you go if your mother said no?

Think up and think down and think burn and think die

Oh, such nightmares await you if only you try!"

INTERLUDE 8

To Toy Or Not To Toy

WILLY PICKED UP THE ANTIQUE PHONE receiver. "What?"

"Hello, this is Kvasir the Interface."

"Now what do you want?" Willy spat.

"A public quorum has been raised that is causing havoc amidst the Midnight Laborers," Kvasir said, "and fearing this could cause production delays, I have contacted you in hopes you could make a decision on their behalf."

"A decision?" Willy asked. "Isn't this a quorum? Why can't they vote on whatever for themselves?"

"They have," Kvasir said. "It is a fifty-fifty split, something that has not occurred in over a century. Now, if you could make a choice, I'm sure they'd accept your judgment...."

"What's the issue?" Willy asked.

"Whether or not to have you replace their bathtubs with personal indoor swimming pools, therefore tripling the size of their domiciles to make way for said swimming pools...heated ones...with adjoining Jacuzzis..."

⊕ ⊕ ⊕

Willy left the phone booth and returned to the box full of antique books, blocks, bowls, and game pieces that sat on the counter in front of an expectant customer.

The overhead speakers began playing a muzak version of Carrie Underwood's *Little Toy Guns*.

"These are the last of them?" a wizened, old man asked, leaning on a steel hospital cane with his right hand. "You're sure of that, Mister Carroll?"

"Absolutely, Philip," Willy replied. "You should have no problem recreating the heart of Polistarchia with these objects."

"Yes," Philip coughed, "I've an eighth great deed to accomplish. The Sha'Daa don't you know? It must be stopped. Won't be easy without Lucy, of course."

"Once again," Willy said, "my condolences on the loss of your sister."

"Yes, well," Philip started, as he hobbled toward the front with his box under his left arm, "over one hundred and twenty years of age, you can't say Lucy didn't have a full life. Good day, sir!"

"I wouldn't bet against that old man," Johnny laughed. "Pip is strong as a brick, though I worry about his hip."

Willy turned to find Johnny practically dancing from foot to foot.

"Oh me. Oh my," Johnny spouted almost maniacally, "at least he's gotta try."

"Right," Willy said, realizing Johnny was having one of his rare but famous spells, where he appeared to be on the verge of going completely insane. "You okay, Johnny?"

"Okay, Okay," Johnny laughed. "Oh what a day. Gotta trade, trade, trade, Willy my boy."

Johnny slammed something onto the counter.

"Wait," Willy said, "that's not…"

"Absolutely right," Johnny shouted, "an Alpha Black Lotus trading card for Magic The Gathering." He cackled.

"And in return?" Willy asked.

"That legendary prototype set of Happy Meal Toys that was never copied, mass produced, or sold," Johnny demanded. "All ten of the Replicant and Blade Runner figurines from the first classic movie and its bizarre sequel, and yes, this includes the Roy Batty version with the nail in his hand and the Mister Tyrell toy with imploding eyes." The cackle sounded again.

"Well," Willy replied as he reached down under the counter, "nobody could ever claim you weren't a modern renaissance collector, Johnny."

The muzak version of Joni Mitchell's *Shiny Toys* filled the store.

When Vulcans Cry

William Joseph Roberts

"Anybody can jump a motorcycle. The trouble begins when you try to land it."

–Evel Knievel

BRAXTON CRUISED ALONG THE EMPTY COUN-
try road. The early morning air was warm and smelled like summer
dew. Thin wisps of moonlit fog hung lazily in the air. The open
exhaust of Valerie, his twenty-year old Vulcan 800 reverberated among the trees
along the roadway. Ragged strings of his gray corduroy cut; what was once a
jacket, now a roughly-cut sleeveless vest, fluttered in the breeze. Braxton found
his Zen. The rhythmic pounding hum of the bike chanted a mantra to his soul.
The wind felt as if it wanted to lift him away. The numb bliss of nothingness beckoned to him. In that brief moment his soul transcended time, space, and deer.

"Shit! DEER!" Instinct possessed Braxton in that moment. He squeezed the
clutch, stood on the rear brake lever and leaned the bike hard to the right as he
turned the front wheel to the left. The bike skidded with a belched cacophony of
rubber against pavement. The doe leapt away into the darkness just as Braxton
braced himself for the impact. He downshifted then released the clutch with a
slight roll of the throttle to right the bike and brought it to a stop.

"WOO! Shit! That was close." Braxton shifted the bike into neutral and
removed his helmet. "Dammit man, that'll wake you up for sure." He rubbed his
face vigorously and shook off the tension. "Nearly back to the house and I almost
get splattered by a deer. Damn. You did good, Val," Braxton lovingly stroked
the bike's fuel tank. "That's my dirty girl. You'll never let me down, will you?"

Beyond the idle of the motorcycle, Braxton heard a yip from the darkness to his right. Then another followed by two or three, then a dozen or more. "Oh, what the hell now," he turned the handlebars to the right and shined his headlight on a pack of coyotes. "Hell no, go on now GIT!" He rolled the throttle to the full extent. Valerie roared to life. Flames leapt from the downturned exhaust pipes onto the pavement in a blinding pyrotechnic display. The coyote pack exploded into motion and melded back into the darkness.

Blop blop blop ...

"Are you fucking serious?" Braxton hit the starter button over and over, but the engine refused to turn over. *Maybe I just flooded her.* "At least the sun is coming up," he muttered as he stared at the reddening sky. He pushed the bike to the side of the road then leaned back on the seat and propped his feet on the handlebars.

"He must rise early, the one who wants to have another's wealth or life. Seldom does a lying wolf get a ham or a sleeping man victory," warned an unseen voice. A chill ran down Braxton's spine at the sound of a tight-lipped giggle that subsided with a deep nasally breath. He leapt to his feet.

"Well this just turned into a B-rate horror flick. Who's there? Show yourself."

"Should you sleep your day away, then mayhaps you sleep your life away as well? If that be the case my friend, I will wait for the crows to pick your bones to conduct my business." A chorus of caws and flapping wings filled the air. The odd voice blurted out a maniacal giggle, then suppressed it. "Be leery and tend to yourself before all others guardian," warned the strange voice.

Braxton focused his gaze in the direction of the voice. Perched on the upper branch of a nearby oak he spotted a tall, slender figure silhouetted against the morning sky. The dark apparition was oddly dressed for this time of year. He wore a full suit, long coat and a wide brimmed hat all in black. The figure grinned. One golden tooth shone bright in the shark like smile of his sunken face.

"I am Johnny, Johnny the salesman." He pulled a pocket watch from his vest, glanced at the time then returned the watch. "I trade, I barter, I wheel and deal. This for that, thing for thing, but all of importance and tied to the wheel."

Johnny leapt from the branch as the sky erupted with life. Hundreds of crows took to the air and began to circle as he floated the last few feet to the ground.

"What the fuck? How..."

"How is not important now that the Sha'Daa has begun."

"Bullshit, you just floated to the ground man. How is that not something important?"

"We all have our gifts," Johnny grinned.

"Well yours are a tad bit on the weird side, wouldn't you say?"

"Perhaps, perhaps not," Johnny produced a scroll from his jacket and briefly examined it as he walked toward Braxton. He then bent at the waist and stared at the underside of the bike. "A guardian bell for a true guardian," he sang.

"Gremlin bell, man, not guardian bell. It knocks those pesky gremlins off the bike every time it rings."

"This bell is much more special than that. It has an ancient power to protect that few can comprehend. Another is in need of it before the night is over and I offer a trade."

"How about hell no man, I'm not about to trade you my bell."

"All things have a price my friend; the greater the need, the higher the price." Johnny flung open his long coat like a flasher in a nunnery. An assortment of strange objects dangled on the inside of his coat. "Name your price my friend."

Braxton scratched at his scruffy face in thought. "Tell ya what, buddy. You show me a wallet that never goes empty then we might have a trade."

Johnny smiled wide, then reached into a pocket and produced an ordinary looking wallet on a chain. He tossed it to Braxton.

Braxton checked the wallet and pulled out five, twenty dollar bills. "Well hell man, if you're just giving it away I'll not argue." He tucked the bills into his pocket and tossed the wallet back to Johnny.

"You may wish to look again," he said, as he returned the wallet to Braxton.

"Okay, sure, I'll play your game." Braxton opened the wallet and removed five more twenty dollar bills. "What the hell man. Are you serious or shitting me?"

"Open it one last time," Johnny chortled.

Bewildered, Braxton dug inside the wallet once more, then froze. He stared at Johnny for a silent moment. "You aren't shitting me. You got a deal," he said, with excited reluctance.

"A deal is a deal, a trade has been made," Johnny chortled with a snort. He waved his right hand and rolled his wrist. Out of thin air, Braxton's bell dangled between Johnny's thumb and forefinger. With another quick flourish of his hand, Johnny dissolved and soaked into the surface of the paved country road.

⊕ ⊕ ⊕

Bells chimed as Braxton opened the door of the Phantom Horse pub. The scent of fresh-baked biscuits and bacon filled the air. A group of twenty some-things mingled around the pool tables and juke box in the side room. A few sang along with a classic rock tune. Two individuals danced apart from the rest of the group. A young man in what could qualify as rags and a graceful young woman. She was petite and covered head to toe in sweat-streaked body paint.

Braxton pulled his attention away from the dancers. "Oy, James," he shouted toward the kitchen as he leaned against the bar. "I'll take my regular with a stout."

A middle-aged man with a massive pot belly and baker's apron, appeared from the kitchen door. "Brax, you ugly son of a bitch. Biscuits are almost done. Let me get back to the kitchen and I'll send Suzi out with your order. Good to see you again." James smiled, then disappeared through the kitchen door. Braxton took a seat in a nearby booth and stretched out on the bench.

The door bells rang again and a familiar figure in black entered. Johnny flashed his toothy grin as he approached Braxton. "I must apologize for my outburst earlier," Johnny said, as he slid into the booth across the table from Braxton. "My work has taken its toll on me as of late.

A waitress appeared with Braxton's order. "Here you go, hun. Can I get you anything else?

"No, that'll be it Suzi. Thank you."

The rumble of motorcycles rattled the windows of the pub. Braxton sat up to look out the large front windows and saw a dozen bikes roll into the parking lot. As the bikers turned and backed into the parking spots, Braxton caught sight of their colors, a grinning skull over a Confederate flag. "Damned Confederate Reaver assholes," he mumbled to Johnny. "Just don't look at them and they might not cause us any trouble."

"James! Beers and house specials pronto," the lead biker shouted as he entered the pub. "Well, would you look at what we got here. Ain't you just a pretty little thing, darlin." The lead biker sucked on his teeth in a lusty smile as he admired the young woman in body paint.

Johnny turned in the booth and glanced at the biker for moment. His head tilted at a slightly odd angle. He scanned his scroll then stared at the biker.

"You got a problem, Preacher? There ain't no souls around here to be saving."

"Get him, Hound," a massive biker urged as he sauntered up to the young girl near the juke box.

"A cross of silver, a cross of blood, the one to possess, a compulsion will come," Johnny fitfully chortled. "A deal to be made, a cross to trade," Johnny stood and moved toward the biker. A gaunt finger pointed to an iron cross pinned to Hound's leather vest.

Hound looked down at the pin on his chest then back to Johnny. "Hey buddy, you can fuck off. My great grandfather pried that from the corpse of a Nazi General he'd killed."

"Johnny, sit back down," Braxton urged as he shoveled down his breakfast.

"Listen to my counsel and you will fare well. It will help you much to heed my words. Pain of one to profit another, the Valkyries frown upon such things.

The Sha'Daa will prove a man's worth, be he fodder for the crows?" Johnny flashed a grin at Hound.

"What the fuck? Did ya hear that Moose?"

"Is he speakin' in tongues or something," the massive biker at the juke-box replied.

Hound shoved Johnny. As if a choreographed move, Moose shoved the girl toward a rat-faced biker and pinned Johnny's arms behind his back. Hound gut punched Johnny over and over again.

The room burst into motion. The group of hippies scattered and ran for the side door, followed by six of the road worn bikers.

"Shit!" Braxton leapt from the booth and shoulder-charged into Hound. The pair collapsed to the ground. In one swift move, Braxton kneed Hound in the groin and head-butted the biker into a dazed stupor.

"Let go of me," the young girl screamed. Braxton jumped to his feet and sprinted toward the girl. He leapt into the air with his arm outstretched and hooked Rat Face around the neck. Braxton perched himself on the man's back and locked the choke hold in place.

Another biker, whose name patch read, Bubba, picked up a chair and swung it at the Salesman. Johnny melded backwards through the man called Moose and rematerialized behind the massive biker. The chair hit Moose across the jaw and he collapsed to the floor. Bubba pulled a spiked trench knife from his boot and lunged at Johnny. Johnny caught the man's wrist and snapped the joint backwards with a sick crack of bones. Bubba screamed and dropped to his knees.

"Be leery of yourself, Braxton. These men be enforcers. They answer to the one who be the true master of none. The Piper plays and the sheep obey," Johnny sang.

"You gonna die, Preacher Man!" Hound pulled a revolver from his waist-band as he sat up, and aimed it at Johnny.

Johnny opened his longcoat wide. Inky black tendrils of oily smoke expanded from the depths of his coat like a living vine. The tendrils sprouted new offshoots that pursued and engulfed each of the bikers.

Braxton gaped as the group of bikers fell unconscious then walked back to his table and sat down. Unnerved, he took a quiet sip of his now warm stout and grimaced.

"Are they dead?"

"Only the one," Johnny restrained a giggle with a giddy smile. "He was taken by the hand of his associate, not by I, nor you."

The young, painted woman appeared from behind Johnny. Visibly shaken, she stepped cautiously around the salesman and approached Braxton. "You came to the aid of a stranger when you didn't have to. I invite you to our circle tonight and offer you a gift of the heart."

"No worries. It's all good, Miss." Braxton sipped at his beer.

"My name is, Laura. The memories that this gift represents are precious and dear to me," she continued. "It was a gift from a dear friend who helped me when no others would. I was stranded in Chicago and met Willy in Oz Park a few days after being abandoned. He offered me a safe place and a job if I wanted it. So, for six months I worked at his toy store, Whirligigs. When it was time to move on, he gave me this to remember our time together." She slid a thin metal armlet off of her paint-streaked arm and lightly tossed it into the air above her palm. It exploded and formed a torus of thin metal strips. "I now pass it and all the warm kindness that it embodies to you." She collapsed it back into an armlet and gently slid the ring onto Braxton's forearm.

Laura leaned forward over Braxton and placed her forehead to his for a brief moment. "Bless you brother."

"The name is, Braxton. Thank you."

"Bless you, Brother Braxton." Laura smiled. "We will be celebrating the summer solstice at Four Quarters Farm this evening. Please join us to call in the ancestors." A horn honked from the parking lot. She turned and ran out the door.

The sound of metal on metal drew Braxton's attention. "What the hell now?" he growled. Braxton ran out the door, to find Valerie lying on top of a line of fallen bikes. The door bells chimed as Johnny exited the pub.

"What the hell Val, you decide to take a nap all of a sudden or some shit?" Braxton turned to Johnny. "Ya see what you caused? I want my bell back."

"A deal is a deal, a trade has been made," Johnny replied in a plain tone.

"Then what's the cost? You can have the wallet back."

"The bell is intended for use by another."

"If I've learned anything, it's that everything has a price tag. I thought it was a good deal at the time. A chance to change my life a little. You see how my luck has gone to shit? I need my bell back. I should have never traded it in the first place. There has to be something worth trading," Braxton begged.

Johnny pulled out the scroll and glanced over it, then he looked back toward the building.

"Oh, what the hell? I can't ride without my bell and you're worried about a pin?"

"You have nothing else that interests me, though I do need that cross." Johnny looked back to the building. "He must willingly offer it. I cannot merely take it."

Braxton stood his bike back up and set the kickstand. "Oh, fucking hell, man." He stomped off inside the pub and quickly returned. He handed Johnny the iron cross with a forceful clasp of the Salesman's hand. "Possession is nine tenths of the law. Now, how about my bell?"

"You are the persistent interesting sort aren't you my friend? That has sweetened the pot to be sure." Johnny forced a deep breath to restrain another fit of laughter.

"I tell you what," Braxton started. He stared at the ground in contemplation for a few moments, then looked back to Johnny. "I don't have anything worth an ounce of what you traded me to start with. But any real man's word is as good as gold, and I live by my word. If I say I'll do something, then by fucking God I'll do it, come hell or high water. I don't know what kind of business you're really in, but I've learned to not ask too many questions in my line of work. I do what needs done and that's that. A contract is a contract, an oath an oath."

Johnny stared at Braxton with a curious grin. "We are somewhat similar in that manner, Mister Hicks."

Braxton unsheathed his belt knife and sliced his palm then held out his hand to shake. "I give you my word stranger. If you call, I'll answer. I can find nearly anything if I dig deep enough. If I can't, then I know folks that can. Day or night, my services are yours." Braxton gave Johnny the thousand-yard stare. "Karma is a bitch, and right now she's dry humping the hell out of me. With this shit-ass luck, I can't ride another mile without my bell."

Johnny doubled over into another spasmodic fit of laughter. He fought to hold it back. His jaw clenched and his cheeks puffed as he regained control of himself. Johnny marked the scroll, then tucked both scroll and cross into his coat.

"I have another matter that I must attend to immediately, or all will be for naught. This is an absolute rarity that has never before happened, but the Sha'Daa is fully upon us. Your offer is both enticing and absurd, but nonetheless may be critical to our success. Payment in full for services to be rendered in the near, present and future time as I see fit on your promise of blood oath. The aforementioned payment; the bell, will be available for my use in the minutes prior to its intended utilization and returned afterwards in the event that the Sha'Daa has been overcome."

Braxton stared at Johnny in dismayed confusion. His bloody hand hung slack by his side. "Sha'Daa? What the hell is that? You keep saying it like I'm supposed to know what it means."

"Tonight, the veil between worlds will be at its weakest. Portals will begin to open and many lives lost. Tonight is the Sha'Daa. Armageddon. By midnight tonight, it will literally be Hell on earth," Johnny quirked. "I have need of your services while I…" Johnny forced a deep breath, "while I attend to a personal matter." Johnny held out his right hand to shake. The bell dangled from his left.

"Ooookay. You are certified bat shit crazy aren't you? But after seeing what you can do, there's got to be some kinda truth to it. I've worked for the government and seen all kinds of weird shit. This can't be any worse." Braxton enthusiastically grasped Johnny's hand and shook. "Son of a…" he leapt away from Johnny. Smoke lingered around the cauterized wound.

"A contract is a contract and you agreed by blood." Johnny tossed the bell to Braxton. "The armlet that you now wear, placed there by a maiden's hand. Another has need of it and you of another, a trade for a trade, a tit for tat." The salesman chortled then produced a small leather pouch from his long coat.

"Sure, boss man," Braxton slid the armlet off and tossed it at Johnny. It spun and expanded to form a whirling torus as it soared through the air. Johnny caught and examined the torus with childlike wonderment.

"Yes yes, this will do nicely. So, we have a deal?"

"Sure, man," Braxton said in a firm, but unsure tone.

"A sale! A trade! A deal is done!" Johnny collapsed the torus, then slid it out of sight within the sleeve of his coat. Johnny opened the small, leather pouch and poured six dark jack-like objects into his hand. Braxton watched as Johnny sniffed at the objects. He prodded each of them with tip of his tongue. "Yes, this is exactly what you need my friend," he gleefully sang. He returned the jacks to the pouch and tossed it to Braxton.

"You must seek out the maiden that gave you this treasure. In her possession is an enameled bronze censer that once hung in the temple of Athena. Your first assignment is to retrieve the censer."

"Censer? What the hell is that?"

"It is a decorated bronze pot that hangs from a chain."

"Ok, gotcha, but how do I get it to you?"

"I won't be far, you need only call….hee hee… Out…tsss ha….my name." Johnny took a deep breath, then doubled over in a fit of laughter. He straightened to his full height with a conniving grin and glowered at Braxton. "To the south and to the west they journeyed during the night. The Piper called and the children followed." Johnny chortled and vanished as a shadow fades in the morning light.

"Oh, what the hell? The devil did come down to Georgia and I just sold him my soul."

⊕ ⊕ ⊕

Braxton spotted the sign for the Four Quarters Farm. He turned off the main road onto hard-packed clay. He eased the throttle and crept along the rough dirt road. The road meandered through the thick Georgia forest. A few hundred yards from the highway, the road opened up to a small clearing. At the far end of the clearing, stood what looked like an old church.

Why do I get a bad feeling about this? Random church in the middle of nothing. Naw, can't be anything wrong with that set up. Just your average every day snake handlers or something way out in the woods. Oh sweet, bikes…

Four highly polished motorcycles came into view as Braxton neared the building.

A little heavy on the chrome and polish but…wait, those look like…

"You son of a bitch! My brother is dead because of you and that preacher friend of yours!"

Braxton spotted Hound on the small side porch that jutted out from the far side of the building.

"Aw hell, fucking Reavers." Braxton squeezed the front brake handle and rolled the throttle hard as he turned the bike on the spot then released the brake. He exploded from a massive cloud of dust and raced down the dirt road as fast as he could.

"Shit, shit, shit. There's the pavement, Val! Bite hard and let's get out of here," Braxton shouted, as he skidded in a hard lean on the blacktop. He could hear the heavy rumble of a large v-twin close behind him.

"You're a dead man," Hound shouted and slid into formation to Braxton's right. Another large, fully-dressed bike rolled up along his left.

Braxton downshifted and throttled hard. His eight hundred cubic centimeters were no match for the two large bore motorcycles. Hound pulled a pistol from his waist band and pointed it at Braxton.

"Pull it over and I'll make it quick." Hound chuckled, as he nodded to the other biker.

Braxton looked to his left, just as the other biker swung a long-weighted whip at him. The opposite end of the whip was attached to the bike's right-hand grip. Braxton snatched the end of the whip out of the air with his left hand and grabbed his handlebar grip. He cut the throttle, and sparks flew from his foot peg as he leaned hard right, throttled and swung in behind and to the right of Hound. The other biker and bike were unceremoniously yanked off balance.

"Fuck you, asshole," Braxton shouted, as he straightened the bike and released the whip. He tapped the brake, leaned left and rolled the throttle hard. The two large motorcycles collided with a sheet metal crunch. The second bike flipped and threw the biker ahead of the pack. He landed flat on his back on the pavement. Braxton glanced to his right. He watched as Hound became the soft gooey center of a Harley crunch. The mangled mess tumbled and sparked on the roadway as it skidded past two parked police cars.

"Fucking hell, can my day get any worse?" He dropped a gear and rolled full throttle.

⊕ ⊕ ⊕

"It won't be too much longer before the sun fully sets. Are you sure that you want to go wandering over there in the dark after what happened with the Reavers?"

"No choice in the matter, Doll," Braxton replied as he stretched. "I got a job to do. Though I do appreciate you letting me lay low till dark. I know it's been awhile since I came around. It's just lucky for me that your place is just over the ridge from Four Quarters Farm." He smiled with a cheesy wide-mouthed grin.

"Those guys are egotistical psychopaths," Amy said. "Why don't you stay here and wait till daybreak? I'm sure we can find something to keep ourselves busy."

Damn fine sight, Braxton thought to himself. Amy was a cute little redhead with big doe eyes and braided pigtails. "As tempting as that is, I can't. I have to find the girl and the package before midnight," Braxton replied. He stretched again and shifted on the couch.

"Why? Is she going to turn into a pumpkin?" she snickered.

"No. Nothing like that. Or at least I don't think so. Trust me. If what Johnny said has an ounce of truth to it, we're all screwed if I can't pull this off."

"What if the Reavers catch you snooping around?"

"Don't know. Hell, I'm just winging it. Just gotta hope that my luck gets better before the night is over."

Amy sat on the edge of the couch and hugged Braxton close. "Don't do anything stupid. This evening has been the best I've had since Dad died. I haven't had much time for anything but running the farm. It isn't much, but it's all that I have left of him. But it can get lonely after a while."

"No worries. I don't plan on getting myself killed…" Braxton sat up with a jerk at the sound of something outside.

"That sounded like it came from my Dad's shop. Think it could be a thief?" she asked.

"Probably just a critter; you stay here and I'll go check it out. Time for me to get off this couch, anyways." He kissed her temple then stood.

"Wait," Amy ran into the bedroom and returned with a shotgun in one hand and a box of ammo in the other. "Here, it's my Dad's old gun. It's already loaded."

"Alright. If it'll make you feel better." He took the shotgun from her and admired the carved walnut stock. "Nice looking piece. Don't worry. I'll take good care of it." Braxton put a handful of shells into his vest pocket and headed for the shop.

A loud *pop, pop, groan* came from the rusted hinges of the shop door. Braxton reached in and fumbled for a light switch. With a loud *click*, the hum of electrical current flowed through the overhead shop lights with a warm orange glow.

"Come out with your paws up and no one gets hurt." He looked around in the dim light. A thick layer of dust covered old car parts, tools and assorted other mechanical bits. *She wasn't lying. It doesn't look like anyone has been in here for years. I don't see anything. Time to get my lazy ass to work.* He turned to leave and felt an odd vibration against his side. His lower vest pocket began to heat up. "What the hell?"

Braxton started to reach into his pocket when something launched him into a set of shelves. The shotgun flew from his hand as the shelving and all of its contents toppled over him. Braxton blinked to clear away the fog of unconsciousness.

"That's going to hurt in the morning." He blinked again. An oily, black figure emerged from the shadows on the other side of the shop. It took on the shape of a man. It was as if it absorbed all of the light around it.

"Holy fucking hell! I did sell my soul to the devil and now he's come to collect!" Braxton searched around him for anything that could become a weapon. His hand grasped something long, cold, and, metallic. "My debt hasn't been paid yet, Salesman," he shouted. Spittle flew from his mouth. He charged the figure and swung with all of his might. The camshaft connected with the side of the thing's head. The creature clutched both of Braxton's wrists; its mouth agape with what looked like a scream, but there was no sound. A high-pitched siren shrieked inside of Braxton's head.

"Get out of my head," Braxton screamed, then slammed his forehead into the thing's face. He tore his wrists away from the creature and swung again. Bits of inky-black ooze splashed to the floor with each strike of the camshaft. Over and over again he struck, until it fell to the floor. He straddled the thing and struck until what might have once been a head, rolled away from the body of the thing. "AHHHHHHHHH!" His lungs gasped for air as he paced. He glared at the black mass.

What in the hell is that thing? Did I really sell my soul?

"I didn't send that creature to collect your soul, Braxton."

Braxton spun around to see Johnny leaned against the doorframe of the shop. "What in the hell was that thing?"

"That is merely one of millions of creatures that are about to engulf the Earth. That is what we are trying to stop. Time is ticking away and the gates have begun to open."

"Feeling a bit better, I take it," Braxton asked.

"Yes, indeed."

Braxton took a deep breath. "I can't say that I've ever seen anything stranger or worse, but it is what it is. I made a deal, and I keep my word."

"Retrieve the censer, while I deliver the bell as we contracted," Johnny rolled his wrist and the bell once again dangled between his thumb and forefinger.

"Will do, Boss Man, I'm on it."

Johnny faded away as if a shadow himself. Braxton dropped the camshaft and picked up the shotgun. **BOOM! BOOM!** Two rounds ripped through the thing. Braxton turned and walked out of the door. Three steps outside of the shop and twilight ignited into the blinding surface of the sun.

"Drop the gun and put your hands above your head!" A metallic, male voice shouted. "Hey, isn't that the guy that wrecked those bikers earlier," another voice insisted inadvertently over the loudspeaker.

"I think you're right, Grady," the first voice said, amidst the sound of shuffled papers. "That sure as hell looks like him. What's the name on there?"

"Braxton Hicks," the second voice replied.

"Braxton Hicks, you are under arrest."

"What in the world is going on out here?" Amy shouted, as she ran out onto the porch.

"Back inside!" Braxton sprinted for the porch and pulled Amy inside with him.

"What the hell happened out there?"

"It's hard to explain. Just trust me. You don't want to go out there." The front windows of the small farmhouse exploded with white light. "These guys need to go away. Too many people are counting on me now."

"Braxton Hicks; drop the gun and let the girl go," the voice echoed over the loudspeaker.

"Run out the back through the field to the county road and just go," Amy pleaded.

He stared into her glistening eyes. "I can't Doll; a job is a job. I'm sorry that you got wrapped up in all of this." Amy nuzzled into the hollow of his chest as he pulled her close. The faint smell of her vanilla perfume mingled with sweat tingled in his nose. He kissed her slowly on the forehead then turned her face upward. He leaned down and kissed her tenderly on the lips.

"I'm sorry," he whispered, then took a step back and struck her in the head with the butt of the shotgun. "It'll hurt in the morning, but at least you'll be alive." He pumped the shotgun, reloaded and opened the front door of the small farmhouse.

"Lay down your…"

BOOM!

The shotgun slug plunged through the cruiser door and the deputy that hid behind it. Blood splattered the interior of the cruiser.

"Oh, my God! Grady," the Sheriff screamed.

Another slug demolished the cruiser's roof lights.

The sheriff dove into the car and pulled the deputy in. "Grady! Talk to me! Grady!" The police cruiser plowed through the yard, leapt the roadside ditch and sped away down the dark country road.

"It can't get much worse at this point." Braxton sighed, as he reloaded then set off at a jog. He turned the corner of the house and skidded to a stop. Tiny red eyes glared at him from a moon-lit, gator-like face of another beast. It grunted and sniffed at the air.

"Well hell, you're just big and ugly, aren't you?"

A thunderous growl rumbled from the thing's throat as it charged. It barreled into Braxton's motorcycle and became entangled. It roared and pounced on the downed machine. Claws and teeth alike ripped through leather and steel.

"Valerie! No!" Braxton ran toward the creature. The creature crouched on the bike, like a wolf defending a kill. It roared again. Braxton heaved, as the stench of week-old, sun-baked fish engulfed him.

"Die, you son of a bitch." Point blank he leveled the shotgun at the thing's face and fired.

It fell on top of the bike with a solid thud.

He fired until it clicked empty. A loud, ear-piercing squeal came from beneath the creature, as air escaped a tire. Braxton sniffed at the heavy scent of gasoline.

"Shit, see what you made me do!" Braxton smashed the butt of the gun into the thing. "I'll do what I can later Val. I've got more important things to tend to at the moment." He sprinted off into the moonlit night.

⊕ ⊕ ⊕

From his hillside perch Braxton could see the full length of the valley. Groups of people mingled about the numerous bonfires below. Some danced, some sang, while others laughed or made love.

"Damn, that looks like a good time," Braxton mumbled.

Other shit to do, time for that later.

At the far end of the valley, dozens of torches illuminated the entrance to a cave. Two men in what looked like loincloths guarded the entrance. A man in black robes with a large curved ram's horn exited the cavern.

A horn reverberated through the valley below. All activity came to a halt. Individuals hugged one another, some laughed, others cried. A portion of the gathering made their way to the cave entrance. Braxton waited and watched. The celebration continued below as the chosen group entered the cave.

A flash of light caught his attention. Braxton's eyes locked onto a single dancer. Laura danced around a large bonfire, in all of her painted nude glory. The intricate body paint that covered her petite frame enhanced her well-defined curves. Like a master martial artist, she spun and twirled around the fire as she swung a pair of firepots in wide arcs. Her cat-like grace, entangled within the swirl of flame, mesmerized Braxton. He shook his head and rubbed his face.

"Time enough to daydream after this is over with." He set off for the valley below at a quick but quiet pace.

"Laura. Pssst. Hey, Laura." She turned with a start. She scanned the darkness for the voice. Braxton took a step into the firelight from behind one of the many tents.

"Brother Braxton!" She ran over and gave him a tight hug. "Oh, no, your vest. I've gotten paint all over it. Let me fix it. Hold this." She handed off the fire pots to Braxton and sprinted over to a stack of bags near the fire.

"Well shit, that was easy. Now, where the hell is Johnny?"

"Right where I am supposed to be," Johnny replied from the shadows, as he edged into the light.

"How the hell do you do that? One day you'll have to teach me that trick." Braxton held out the firepots in Johnny's direction. "As promised, Boss Man."

"Thank you," he replied and tucked the censer into his coat.

"What's next boss?"

"A delivery," Johnny grinned. "You already possess the key to close off the gate deep within that cavern. You'll know what to do when you get there," Johnny reassured, as he melded back into the shadows.

Laura returned with a wet towel and began to wipe down Braxton's cut.

"No, wait. It's all good; you just gave me an idea," he exclaimed, as he took the leather pouch from his vest and put it into his pants pocket. He removed his vest and shirt and laid them to the ground with the shotgun. "I need you," he said, as he pulled Laura close and kissed her deeply. Braxton double-clutched her butt cheeks and lifted her to him. She wrapped her legs around his waist as he kissed and bit her neck.

"Ohhhhh, God," she leaned back and moaned as she began to grind herself into him.

Braxton lowered her back to the ground with a gentle kiss.

"Wait, what?" she asked, confused.

"Keep that thought for later and get yourself out of here. There's a house on the other side of that hill," he pointed behind him with his thumb. "Go there, and wait for me. You'll see what's left of my bike out back. There's a girl there named Amy. She may still be unconscious. Stay there with her till I get back. No time to explain, just do it."

"Okay," she whimpered, before Braxton picked up the shotgun and sprinted through the darkness for the cavern.

Dark silence greeted Braxton at the cave entrance.

Well, that's not suspicious at all. No guards, no priest, no nothing. This seems too easy.

"Now or never I guess," he mumbled to himself, as he stepped toward the opening. Braxton followed the line of torches that flickered in the damp corridors of the old mine. Broken, rusted and otherwise discarded equipment littered the floor of the mine.

I've gotta be halfway to China by now.

The torches branched away from the main tunnel and sloped upward toward a narrow passage. The rhythm of a low, guttural chant echoed from the confined space. Careful of his step, Braxton made the short climb up the slimy slope to a small landing. The passage turned sharply then opened into a large chamber.

He tiptoed to the edge of the opening. Torches mounted high on the rough-cut walls dimly lit the large chamber. At the far end of the room, two large, stone doors stood in drastic contrast to the darker surrounding stone. Their surfaces polished smooth. A small, balding man in black robes knelt before the doors. His head tilted back and arms outstretched, he chanted.

A hum resonated within the chamber in rhythm to the chant. Dust fell from the edges of the doors as they shuddered.

Braxton gasped. "That can't be a good sign." An odd reflection from the floor caught his attention. He crouched low and crept slowly into the chamber. Braxton groped about in the dim darkness.

What the hell?

A wet sticky mass blocked his path. He felt along its length and locked fingers with an unknown hand.

Did this bastard kill all of those kids that came in here earlier?

The man's chant grew louder, more forceful. The hum of the doors grew louder in time with the priest. Braxton felt the heat and vibration in his pocket again.

What the hell?

He reached into his pocket and pulled out the leather pouch of jacks. It droned along with the sound that resonated from the doors. The heavy grinding of stone-on-stone, drew his attention.

The chant grew louder, its rhythm faster. Dark forms writhed and slithered from the opening as it widened.

"Oh, fuck me. This is gonna hurt for sure." Braxton took aim with the shotgun and stepped forward and fired. Black ooze splattered from one of the man like forms. The head of another exploded. The next slug severed a thick tentacle that extended from the opening and left a crater in the face of a door. He fired until the shotgun was empty.

"Your blood will complete the opening. Bring him to me," the priest shouted.

"Oh shit." Braxton fumbled in his vest pocket for more ammo.

A pair of the shadow creatures charged at Braxton. He took the shotgun by the barrel and wielded it like a club. The first shadow creature to reach Braxton somersaulted from the impact of the gun stock.

Braxton dropped the gun and pouch as he clutched his head. His brain erupted in pain from the second shadow creature's unheard scream.

"Shut the hell up," he shouted as he drew his belt knife and heaved it at the shadow creature. The blade of the knife disappeared into the thing's head.

Sudden waves of warm pain washed over Braxton. He shook his head and cleared the fog. The scaled snout of a gator thing pressed down on his left shoulder. He collapsed to his knees under the weight of the thing as it bit deep into his flesh. It shook him like a rag doll and flung him to the ground.

Braxton could feel the sticky cold of the mine floor seep into him. A soothing silence engulfed him, held him close in this cold womb of the earth.

A distant reverberating hum broke into the dark silence.

"Will someone please shut that off," he muttered, as he rolled over onto his back and opened his eyes.

"Dammit man, not a dream." Braxton forced himself upright. He fumbled for the small leather pouch and poured the jacks into his hand. The smell of burnt flesh filled the air. The odd little objects glowed red hot and scorched his palm. Instinct screamed at him.

Throw them!

He slung the jacks toward the doorway as the gator thing approached. The scattered red specks formed a grid-like pattern as they soared through the air. They doubled and tripled in size. Their points elongated and connected to one another. Sparks flew from the white-hot points as they welded themselves together, forming what looked like a large, iron, castle gate that collected and impaled priest and beast alike. It slammed into the stone doors. Tentacles and other appendages projected from between the dark, iron slats like a festive Thanks-Hallo-Mas display.

"Don't let the door hit you in the ass on the way out," Braxton said, with a chuckle and a wince of pain. "Ungh," he poked at his left shoulder. Blood seeped from the deep puncture wounds of the gator thing's teeth.

Braxton slumped to the cold sticky ground. He smacked his dry lips together. "You owe me a beer Salesm…"

Toys With Roots

THE NINETEENTH CENTURY WAS ENDING, AND the twentieth century beginning, when a two hundred and thirty-two-year old, William Thomas Carrolton (who now went by the moniker, Willy Carroll) decided it was time to leave Australia. He had outlived his own infamy, and the sons, daughters, and grandchildren of those who'd once sought to kill him.

For over two hundred years, he had traveled every square inch of this grand continent, learning all the languages, culture, secrets, and powers of the oppressed, first peoples of this once mystical land.

Immortality was the most notable and well-guarded of Willy's powers. A boon and a curse, which had required a great sacrifice by Willy, a secret he would never share with anyone, even those few women he would eventually fall in love with, outlive, and grieve over.

Willy traveled the world for many decades, finding that he had skills as a salesman, trader, and expert in antiquities, and toys.

A couple of decades before the start of World War Two, Willy opened up the first Whirligigs' toy store, at Leipziger Platz, less than a block from the renown Wertheim Department Store. His shop was a grand success. Life was good.

CHAPTER TEN

A Warm Cuppa

Terry Maggert

"Each cup of tea represents an imaginary voyage."

–Catherine Douzel

ASH BEGAN FALLING ON THE CITY AS BRETT stared upward in disgust. He was, as usual, in a state of mild irritation, forced to do something other than crossfit with the hottie who'd taken his class over a week earlier. Serah was a free spirit in range of his charms, if he wasn't forced to miss class in order to shop for fucking toys.

Rain mixed with the ash, making a bizarre gray sludge that spattered against his coat. Swearing richly, he slunk under the tattered awning, looking at his phone to verify that he was at the right place on the edge of Oz Park.

He was. *Whirligigs.* The sign was hand painted, glossy, and clung to the heavy glass and wood door like a limpet, its edges worn from the touch of many hands. A warm, buttery light spilled out of the interior, casting shadows that hinted at treasures unseen.

Was it even worth it? He was only here because he needed a gift for his current girlfriend's brat, a repulsive little troll with blonde curls and a face like a clenched fist. She was surly, needy, and dumb, but she slept like the dead so Brett could have her mother in any room of the house she'd won in a divorce three years earlier. After three solid days of mind-bending depravity, she'd gone cold as a stone after he mentioned that things might be even better if the kid went to bed earlier.

It was a rookie mistake and he'd known it as the words tumbled out of his mouth. The effect was instantaneous. She'd closed up shop, but allowed him to come around, plying her with gifts in between nights out with his boys. He'd found himself drawn to her, and the inexorable tug of sexual memory brought him here, to this dripping awning amid a night in which the city had gone stark raving mad. If Serah hadn't been magic in bed, he would have cut her loose weeks ago, especially if he'd know that closing the deal on a Thursday night meant wandering around in the rain among fires, car accidents, and sirens. It sounded like the end of the world, but Brett was inured to the worst of the chaos. He'd spent the day sleeping off a legendary hangover, adrift on the wonders of painkillers and a nip or three of bourbon upon rising from his sweaty couch.

Earlier, he'd been steadied by a drink at the corner bar, listlessly scrolling through his phone while looking for gifts that might keep a kid quiet. Quiet long enough for him to have a sail-away bang with her mother—or more, given the memory of Serah's tits bouncing in the lamplight of her bedroom. He knew nothing of kids, and planned on keeping it that way. But for Serah, he'd dip his toes in the pool of whatever it was children needed to let the adults play without fear of being disturbed.

He hadn't noticed the guy next to him at first, but the stranger slid his stool closer, smiling under the wan light of the dingy bar. His face was obscured by the light, a mass of shadow that gave him an air of friendly conspiracy. Brett held up a cautious hand, his natural city sense keeping him slightly back from anything that could be construed as interest.

"Johnny. I'm in sales, but I have a background in keys, you might say, and you look like a man with an access problem." He stuck out a confident hand, smiling broadly.

"Access?" Brett asked, curiosity piqued by the term. It might have been the booze, too, but he wasn't used to people being quicker than he was.

"Access. Opportunity. Ingress. So many terms for the thing you need, but it all comes down to solving a simple problem." Johnny cracked an ice cube on his molars. It sounded like a gunshot, fading behind his smile.

Brett warmed to the guy like a drunk to the bottle, wanting the quickest path to Serah's lockbox. A single mother with dark hair and milky skin, she was one of those undiscovered gems he specialized in, and he was determined to get back into her bed at any cost.

They spoke for a moment until Brett balked at the way their dynamic was shifting. Johnny had a way with words, like he knew what Brett needed but wasn't in any hurry to get to the point. After watching him drain three Manhattans in short order, Brett stood to walk. He wasn't anyone's bitch, and he wasn't going to start now.

"Brett, you seem to think that Serah is the same woman she was when you first met." It was simple, flat, and factual in the way that brooked no argument.

Brett fell back onto his stool as his resolve faded, replaced by the seeds of interest. "She isn't. But"—

"I presume that you care about her in ways other than what she can do for you?" Johnny interrupted, a knowing smile creasing his face. A gold tooth winked cheerfully from the shadows of his smile.

He nodded, slowly, letting the companionable moment wash over Brett, who returned the nod in a mirrored gesture that every salesman looked for. Syncopation. Understanding.

Accord. It was what Brett needed, even if he didn't know it yet.

"Okay, maybe I do." The words tasted like mud, alien and earthy. Far from the slick game that he'd used to bag Serah in the first place. Inside him, something began to warm, like a feeling. It sat unused, a potential emotion rather than the kinetic use of his charms.

"In that case, let me help you. You want help, don't you, Brett?" Again, the nod.

Again, the return by Brett, as if in a fugue state.

"I don't pay for women," Brett protested, though he had, and when it suited him. He felt the hollowness of his lie, a husk that vanished as the words left his mouth. Johnny looked away, letting Brett stew in his own untruth.

Pockets lined the heavy garment, their shapes as varied as the bulges within. Johnny plucked a key from one of the smaller pockets, placing it carefully on the bar with a brass *click*. He nodded toward the key with meaning, indicating Brett should pick it up.

"This is?" Brett asked, his eyes never leaving the worn metal. The key looked old, and heavy.

"It's what you need, Brett. You *think* you have a problem, but you don't. We *all* have a problem, and the most fortunate set of circumstances has brought you to Serah, and then, to me. It's my job to see that you get what you *need*, not just what you want," Johnny said, deep in his pitch.

"But?"

"Ah, a realist, and a man who understands that doors do not open without keys." Johnny fussed with his napkin as if embarrassed. "There is, of course, a minor fee." He smiled into his drink, an honest rogue doing an honest service. There was weary nobility to the gesture, verging into self-deprecation.

Brett reached for his wallet, but Johnny put a hand on his arm, shaking his head once. "Not money. A thing."

"Thing?"

"Yes, something with an accrued history. Tell me, Brett—what was your first car?" Johnny asked.

Without hesitation Brett answered. "Mustang. An '88. White with a five speed."

"And tell me, did you name your car?" The question was rapid fire, on the heels of Brett's answer.

"Dusty," he said with a smile. Brett's eyes stared into the middle distance, their focus somewhere far from the dim light of the bar.

"I thought so." Johnny favored him with a smile that verged into warmth. "Which car is worth more, Dusty, or what you drive now?"

Brett smiled again, and this time, he eyed Johnny with clarity. "Dusty, of course."

"Then you'll understand why I say that, there is money, and there is value."

Wordlessly, Brett reached into his wallet and withdrew a small, crinkled ribbon. It had been purple at one time, and a small metal cross dangled from it, bent and dull. He held it toward Johnny, who lifted a brow of inquiry. "From my aunt's funeral. I was late, and the flowers I'd sent were—they were cheap. Nearly dead. This was the only good part of my shitty gesture." He slid the ribbon and cross to Johnny, who made them vanish into his coat. "Why do you need them?"

Johnny turned to Brett, regarding him in silence. "Do you regret being late that day?"

"I do." His voice was heavy with an old shame, the kind that only youth can truly create. He'd been nineteen the day of the funeral.

"What if I told you that for Serah, you could be exactly on time?"

The Deal

So, Brett now stood, hand on the burnished knob of the door to a shop that could solve his problem, which seemed all the more urgent given his pleasant buzz. Even in the strange air of a night that seemed unraveling around him, he knew a good thing when he saw it. Brett was a closer. He fished the key from his pocket, turned the lock, and pulled the door open with a surge of confidence, stepping out of the night into the stillness of a store lost in time.

Brett stopped after one long step.

It wasn't a store; it was a repository of his own memory made real. Toys of stunning detail and materials rested on heavy wood shelves, shining with care under the muted lights that hung from long, scarred beams.

"Welcome. I know a man with a problem when I see him, and your problem is of the very worst kind." He was young, or not, and might have been Australian, though he trilled his words with the singsong ease of a carnival barker at the height of his powers. An unctuous smile crinkled his freckles into a starry pattern under startling red hair. He was nearly Brett's height of six feet and an inch, but slender, and posed like a bird watching a worm.

"Problem?" Brett asked, feeling a repeat of his earlier conversation coming on. Brett hated being trite, but he sensed a chasm opening underneath him as instincts began to fire in the presence of this unknown operator.

"Indeed. Willy Carroll has an uncanny ability to discern the most knotty issues, and like any master craftsman, he can untangle the knot in a mutually beneficial manner." He smiled. It was oily with use.

"You're Willy, I take it?" Brett got his sea legs back, feeling his competitive nature surging. "What is my, umm, problem? If it's so bad, that is." His lips twisted in a mulish sneer. The real Brett was emerging, like a ship from a rogue wave. Johnny had pushed him to this moment, but Brett would finish the sale. He always did.

"I am, and you do." Willy pointed skyward with flair, moving around the counter to stand before Brett. "You've the look of a man who knows how to take charge. I like that." He grinned, rocking on his heels with practiced ease. "Your problem is of the heart, and you're here to find a gift suitable for a young lady. *Very* young, if I make my mark?"

"How'd you"—Brett cut himself off, thinking of how he'd bagged Serah the first time. It was sales. Anticipating needs, and closing the deal. He knew he was a good-looking guy, maybe rough from the booze, but still at a reasonable hunting weight from the crossfit. Brett knew how to pry the legs of single mothers apart, and he even scored with a few solid 9's he met at the gym, when he was bright-eyed for a week or two at a stretch. Underneath his simmering want and drive, he sensed that Willy was a seasoned vet of *something*, even if he wasn't entirely sure what the hustle was. Not yet. He could learn a few things from this guy, but for now, he let Willy take the lead. His only answer was a conspiratorial nod.

That was all Willy needed. He went to a shelf that groaned with toys of all shapes and origins. There was a brass horn of some incomprehensible design, and a model truck made of burnished tin. Behind these hefty items was a box, inlaid with no less than three kinds of wood and gleaming with polish. A chased silver hasp kept the lid closed to prying eyes, hiding the toy within. There was nothing else of distinction on the box, which had a soft, feminine quality to the lightly burled woods.

"That's the one," Brett felt himself say.

"Ah, decisive and discerning. Two qualities I do love in my clients. Perhaps you'll take a look before we conclude the sale? I do like to know that my people are, ah—properly instructed in the care and use of their new acquisitions." Willy lifted a brow, one hand on the lid. When Brett nodded, he proceeded to open the case with a flourish.

A scent of velvet and age wafted upward as the light struck a tea set. It was plain white, small, and designed for a child, being sturdily thrown on some forgotten potter's wheel. Four cups faced inward like piglets around the sowbelly teapot, all free of chips and cracking. It was old—even Brett could see that—but the condition was flawless. Saucers lay flat in their own side compartment. A yellowed envelope poked upward from the divot under a cup, its edges curled with age, and Willy plucked the paper from its place with a delicate twitch of his long fingers.

"What's it say?" Brett leaned forward, careful not to disturb the items in their cradle. His curiosity burned now, a runaway conflagration that eroded his will with each passing second. He *needed* this—whatever it was.

"A most unusual find, even more me. This is a letter from the previous owner, one Ruby Detweiler, late of Des Moines, Iowa. I came across the set while"—he stopped, a look of embarrassment crossing his features. "But of course, you'll want the bare details so that you can deliver this gift to a deserving child, of course. Pardon me, I do ramble. The only question it might seem, is the price, but you've already found a key to my establishment." He gave Brett a measured look, then nodded slightly to himself before moving behind the counter without looking back.

Compelled to follow, Brett felt himself pull his wallet out, unbidden and the sheer sign of a rank amateur. Disgusted, he put the wallet back and folded his arms. "How much?" His voice grated with need.

"Two days ago, this item would have been sixty dollars, but tonight? The situation has changed." Willy's eyes flickered out into the night, where muted chaos reigned. In the shop, there was only the deal, and silence.

"I asked you how much. I won't ask again," Brett lied.

Drumming his fingers, Willy pushed the case across the counter to Brett. "I'll take all the cash you have in your right front pocket, and not a penny less. I'll also ask that you let the gift do its work. So many items are, ah, interrupted before they can fulfill their purpose. Much like you, Brett." The cryptic comment fell in the space between them, failing to reach its mark.

Brett narrowed his eyes, thinking that the guy was a poor echo of Johnny. Without looking away, he pulled out a wad of cash and receipts from last night's debauchery. Counting quickly, he arranged the bills to see three twenties and a lone, heroic single, crumpled and stained with what appeared to be taco sauce. "Sixty-one," he sneered. The flare of victory crept up his spine to bolster his confidence. He liked winning. He hated losing, and this idiot handed him the keys to Serah's treasure for a single dollar, if he believed the original price.

He didn't. Something began to unfold within Brett's awareness, a gentle insistence that he listen to the sirens. When he did, he began to wonder if Serah was really his goal, or was it something else entirely. Altruism was an ill-fitting show for Brett, but he let the emotion roam free in his mind for a long moment, concluding that there was only one way to understand the path he'd found himself well along on a night filled with distant violence.

Brett ceased his woolgathering. "Take your cash and let me go."

"A deal, as they say, is a deal." Willy collected the money, which vanished in his hand with the speed of a rumor. "I trust you'll sip in good health."

"I won't be drinking from the damned thing," Brett spat, sure of his plans for the night.

Willy merely grinned. "I wouldn't be so sure. You know how winsome children can be. Oh! A thought, Friend. When you leave? Turn right. I sense some—difficulties to the left."

Brett snatched up the gift, but it was a petulant gesture. He was at the door before he turned, a question bubbling upward in the swamp of his mind. "The lady, Judy?"

"Ruby, you mean?"

An airy wave with his free hand, Brett asked, "You said *late* of Des Moines. What'd she die of?"

"Oh, that." Willy busied himself with the counter, wiping smudges away with a dark cloth. "You might say she died of consumption."

Tea Time

Like a fucking charm. A charm for fucking.

Inside, Brett roared with laughter, but he schooled his face into a warm gaze, looking down at Serah's enormous gray eyes and the beaded sweat on her milky skin. Jesus, she was beautiful, almost glowing if you believed in that kind of shit. He had a hard time focusing in the soft cloud of her perfume, her breath, all of her.

The brat was silent, sleeping or playing with the tea set in her room, a disastrous place of pink and glitter and all the things that Brett hated. She'd taken the box without a sound, dropping to the carpeted floor and setting up a tea party as if she'd been waiting for the toy her whole life. With a feigned smile, Bret had steered Serah to her room, a firm grip on her elbow as he made his wishes known.

Firm, not rough. Smiling all the while, then flashing a heated look of need to her that told her she was *the one.*

Like. A. Charm. She'd thrown gates open to him, working his body like the levers of a device made for pleasure. She didn't even want to chitchat, muttering that she'd missed him and other meaningless things—at least to Brett. Serah looked like some kind of hero, her eyes shining with thanks. All Brett could think about was the flawless expanse of her body, and how she gave over to him in totality. She was a work of art, and he was inspired to give pleasure for once, making her all the more wild in the hour of their need.

Around them Chicago came apart at the seams, but it didn't matter. Serah was an art instructor who was off during the summer, so unless they ran out of water and food, there was no reason for Brett to open the front door. Ever. They were well into their third hour of enthusiastic sport when a timorous knock came at the door just as Brett was rolling her over for yet another go at that perfect ass.

"Hold on, honey." Serah withdrew, mind and body, sliding from the steaming sheets to slip on a robe and open the door. Brett bit a curse off at his tongue, then smiled into the pillow with a lecherous glare he could feel all the way to his toes. The murmured conversation was somewhere between cooing and babytalk, meaning that the brat needed something.

Brett smiled again as the mattress depressed with Serah's weight. He smelled her and rolled over, forcing a welcoming look on his face, no matter what she was going to say. Brett didn't make the same mistakes twice, especially not with something like her on the line. Their sex had pushed his caring back into the recesses of whatever soul he still had, despite the lingering sense of something else clouding around them.

"Welcome back. She okay?" He mouthed the words, keeping his tone light. He was learning.

"Our presence has been requested at a tea party." Serah spoke into his neck, charging his skin like a lightning strike. Her lightest touch was a command, digging into his head with ease and leaving him leaning, off balance, and awash with need. Outside, a distant siren wailed and went silent with a truncated squawk. Whatever was going on out there couldn't be better than what was going on in here, even if it meant playing house with a kid and her idiotic imagination.

He took a moment to get the pitch right. "Love to see her use the set. I bought it, after all." His subtle reminder worked as Serah slid up his body with untold promise.

"I can't tell you what this'll mean to her. She's frail. I love her, but so many things frighten her." The hint of a tear danced in her voice, and Brett realized he felt bad for the kid. He'd never been lonely, given his ability to talk shit under any circumstances. A class clown by nature, he'd realized his true calling was chasing women, and every decision after that was designed to further his favorite hobby.

In a rare moment of gallantry, he rose to the occasion. Standing from the bed, he held out a hand. "Join me for the party, won't you?" Affecting a little bow, he saw Serah's face light up like a carnival midway and knew he'd made the right call. Twenty minutes in the kid's room and another day here, maybe two. After a few minutes of restoring order to their appearance, they were ready to leave the bedroom. Brett worked hard to keep his smile neutral, even as he admired Serah as she slid into mommy clothes that covered her treasures with cruel efficiency.

Who knew? He might find this setup to his liking. Looking at Serah's body as she dressed, he knew that there were worse things than dying in her arms every night, and when they went into the kid's room, his smile was almost genuine. That faded after they lowered themselves to the floor in a room lit only by the twilight pouring in from the single window. A tiny, battered radio played soft music that sounded like a funeral dirge, and there were clothes scattered across the room with the fury of a child who could not find the perfect thing to wear.

Brett sat on the pink carpet trying not to look bewildered. The smell of something dead hung over the child's table, filling the room with hints of something old and rotten, but Serah paid it no mind, so neither did Brett.

"Sorry, gotta clean in here. She keeps snacks in her day bed," Serah whispered, a mild blush rising in her pale cheeks. Brett waved her off with a smile, taking one hand for a brief kiss and then letting go. Best not to overplay his hand around the kid, who fussed and busied herself with setting up the table, moving tiny plastic placemats in a series of spasmodic gestures that made Brett want to scream. She'd put on a little apron over a dress that had seen better days, and Brett took his first good look at her. She was plain but cute, he guessed, knowing less than nothing about children.

"What's your name, Sweetie?" He knew they'd been introduced, but thought it was a good icebreaker given the weird atmosphere. Serah's answering grin told him he'd scored, despite looking like a forgetful asshole.

The girl didn't look up from her work, putting saucers on each placemat. "Junie." Saying nothing else, she let a tiny frown pull his lips to the side. "That's better." Cups went down with surprising speed, earning raised eyebrows and a clumsy thumbs-up from Brett. Junie was a strange little thing, but she moved with utter certainty. It was like watching an adult at work, though her wild curls made the image veer into absurdity.

"It's a beautiful party, honey," Serah said. Her voice was fat with pride, and she dropped a kiss on Junie's head as she passed by to the toy kitchen along a wall.

"Thanks, momma. I'm trying." She reached into the toy fridge, pulling the teapot out with surprising delicacy. It sloshed as if full, a liquid noise that sounded oddly thick.

"What are we having, Junie?" Brett asked. He hoped she hadn't left milk in there to sour. That would explain the smell, at least.

"Magic tea," she stated, matter-of-factly as she began to pour.

Brett recoiled. A dark, viscous liquid slid out of the pot into Serah's cup. In the low light, it looked nearly black.

"Honey, where did you get the tea?" Serah asked, mild alarm in each word. She was keeping calm, but Junie looked up sharply, a strange look on her broad face.

"I told you, it's magic. I asked the pot to fill up and it did. I drank some, and then it came back. I didn't even have to use my wand, momma." She finished filling Serah's cup to the rim. The fluid lay inert. "It's special. You can only get it when the shu—shah," she struggled with alien syllables, looking to Serah for help.

"Okayyyy." Serah said, raising her cup for what Brett hoped was a mock gesture. Junie moved to his cup but he put his hand over it, watching her mother instead. Serah brought the cup close to her mouth, winced at the scent, and twitched as if stung. A thin tendril of oily liquid shot out to land on her bee stung lips, winding into her mouth with a speed that rendered it into a flicker. She shivered, then slowly put the cup to her lips and drank. A whisper escaped from her, then again in a sibilant his. *Sha'Daa.*

Brett sensed the air in the room change, turning to see Junie standing far too close for his comfort. She watched her mother with a furtive smile, joy suffusing her face. It was a grotesque parody of childish joy. With smooth motions, she tied her apron again, looping the bow with flair.

"Manners are so rare these days," Junie said in the accent of wide open plains. There was a flat formality in her words, like she spoke through the words of a person from the days of plowshares and dirt roads.

"I couldn't agree more, child. Look at Brett here, so full of avarice and lust. It's shameful that I let him into our home. You'll forgive me, of course?" Serah tsked in Brett's general direction as he felt vertigo take hold. Something was hideously wrong, and he began to lift himself from the carpet as raw terror bloomed in his gut. "So transparent, now." She twitched her robe down to cover a creamy expanse of thigh. "We won't be doing *that* kind of thing anymore."

The teapot rattled, impatient to serve. "Where are my manners?" Junie lifted the pot and began to pour for herself, and then her mother. With a grateful smile, Serah tipped the cup upward without hesitation. Gummy fluid gathered at the corners of her mouth as Brett watched her skin drain of color. In seconds, she was pale as a corpse.

So was Junie. He'd missed it in the low light, but the kid looked dead, or near to it. Something crashed hard against the house, unleashing an unearthly wail that made Brett's guts go to water.

They leapt on him, nimble as grasshoppers, their grips like iron. Serah straddled his chest, her own barely moving as she forced his arms out like Christ. With muffled snaps, his tendons gave as he fought against her in complete silence. He didn't scream until Junie wrenched his ankles into shards of bone, pulling his shoes off with a smooth motion to expose his feet to the warm air. Tiny fingers separated his toes, cracking each with a vicious twist. The pain was a searing invasion of his mind, already crowded with raging fear and disbelief.

He looked past Serah's blank face to see Junie lower her mouth to his foot. "Junie, kid, for fuck's sake don't"—

She looked up from her work in confusion. "Junie? You mean Ruby."

"Ruby? No, I—whatever. Please, Christ, please, listen, I'll drink the tea, let me have a cuppa with you or whatever, right?" He was bargaining hard, his voice cracked with fear and shame. He was fucked and he knew it, right down to the howls outside the window. Something was coming in to the party.

Serah spoke, her breath meaty and warm. It hinted at things kept away from the sun. Old things not meant for his sight, or anyone else.

A growl from the window after it shattered inward, the words in a tongue from before men plowed rows or mastered the beasts. It vibrated in Brett's chest, loosing his bowels and ripping into his psyche with the power of a hot knife. Serah answered in kind, smiling at the blackness that flowed through the frame. There were tentacles, or limbs with scales but no bones. A hook gleamed at the end of the closest limb, moist with something vile.

The voice coughed again. The thing that had been Junie put chubby hands on hips, turning form her perch on his legs. "I don't think so. It's my room and my toy and my party. I get to say so." Her head dipped to his feet as she splayed his toes again, now throbbing with pain. Tiny teeth crunched clean through his first two toes, earning the night a howl of raw pain from Brett that died as he coughed himself into a spasm. "Mine," Junie mumbled around her feast, noises of cracking bone echoing in the room as she chewed.

"Agreed. Tea is only for those with manners, Brett." Serah leaned down to caress his cheek with a tongue that seemed far too long for a human. Where her saliva trailed, his skin rose to greet her with the expectation of her touch. He whimpered as she looked at him, blushing and shy. "Brett! Now? Surely you can't—but you would, wouldn't you?" She bounced lightly on his groin breaking free into an open-mouthed laugh that revealed a new row of teeth. They were round, and made for grinding.

"Refill, Momma?" Junie asked in her new voice. It was silken with manners, and old. Very old.

"Of course, sweetheart. I'll need something to wash this down." Serah tore at Brett's clothes as the unseen beast laughed from its window perch, a ragged gasp booming deep from the center of a beaklike mouth. It held on to the window frame with too many arms to count, their wet rasping leaving trails across the cheery pink walls. Above, the ceiling began to warp inward as things pushed from places unseen, their laughter a wet chorus of miserable hope.

Brett tried to scream as her teeth bit slowly down, jaw snapping in an inhuman motion. Serah's voice was a wet mumble as she laughed, chewing methodically.

Outside, the last siren wound to a halt. Rain lashed at the open window as the last party guest flowed forward to eat, stopping only to rend at Brett's hip, the beak coming down on his thigh—

The key struck against its mouth with a flare of golden light, unleashing the seed of a promise made, and a body unwillingly offered. It seared into the beast, sending its own tentacles of flowing light to dive in and out of the gelatinous body like avenging angels. Wrapping tighter, the promise of Brett's sole good act whipped around the demon to lift it, shrieking with hate, toward the growing vortex that began scouring the child's room with a fervor unmatched in this plane or any other. Serah lurched toward the creature, her hands flaming into ash as she contacted the glowing metal. Her screams were the sound of a dying storm rolling across a prairie in the heat of August.

Then Junie threw herself at the old one, her tiny hands elongating to monstrous proportions. They fell on the key, and for a black moment, her eyes went round with triumph as she pried the object of pain away from the creature who would open the door between worlds and grant her endless nights of wicked delights.

Brett's knee split Junie's mouth with a savagery he hadn't known possible, spraying fluids that no longer resembled anything ever found in a human. Junie collapsed into the wriggling mass of the ancient beast, its snapping beak reflexively biting through her body to send a spume of gore into the collapsing void that ripped the ceiling in every direction. The key snapped back into place, burrowing further into the suppurating mass. Light began to break through on the creature as it voice rose to a titanic howl of denial and frustration.

It was the Sha'Daa no longer. The gate closed with a subsonic tearing as Brett rolled to his side, dislodging the thing that had been Serah. Outside, sirens wailed again.

Inside, Brett's heart gave the first honest beat of his life, and then, the last.

Boys And Their Toys

"**L**ISTEN, MISTER PARKER," WILLY TOLD the angry, blonde middle-aged man with thick framed glasses who stood on the other side of the counter, "I told you. The Red Ryder BB gun you sold to me ten years ago is no longer here. We re-sold it. Fair and square."

"My son turns nine this year," Mister Parker said, with a slight whine in his voice, "I can't explain it, but I just have to give it to him this Christmas… it's…a coming of age thing. Passing of the torch, as it were…"

"Well I just can't help you with that," Willy said.

"Do you have records of who you sold it to?" Mister Parker asked.

"No," Willy replied. "We didn't upgrade to computers until a couple of years ago. A fire in the store room destroyed all of our earlier paper receipts. Though, if memory serves, I think it might have been some pale, balding, red haired guy, with yellow eyes no less, and wearing a ratty old imitation coon skin hat who bought it. That's all I can remember."

Parker's face quickly turned red and for a moment. Willy thought that steam might burst out of the customer's nostrils.

"Farkus," Mister Parker yelled at the top of his lungs, before turning around and pushing his way through the small crowd and out the door.

The muzak version of The Beach Boys' *The Man With All the Toys* stared playing from the overhead speakers.

"So, what did you just double-dog-dare that poor fella to do?" Johnny asked.

Willy spun to his right to see a smiling Johnny leaning on the counter. The earlier spell of madness seemed to have passed.

"Huh," Willy said, "Oh that. Nothing. He's probably just going where all the little piggies go. So, what do you have in your bag of tricks?"

"This," Johnny placed a polished, dark, narrow, two-foot tall box on the counter, grabbed both sides, and lifted what was quickly revealed to be an outer shell to reveal a strange, polished-bronze sculpture of two birds amidst leafy foliage in and around a small bowl of water.

Johnny dramatically splayed both of his hands. "None other than Hero of Alexandria's very first pneumatic chirping bird automaton." He reached inside the remaining half-shell of the wood base to flip a lever. Water started pouring down from the upper bowl to a holding pot below, and beautiful whistling sounds began emitting from the birds' beaks.

"Well," Johnny asked, "what do you say?"

"I don't suppose you've got documented provenance on this acquisition?" Willy asked sarcastically.

"I find your lack of faith, disturbing. Oh, that's right," Johnny smirked. "Time travel wasn't one of the powers you sold your, ummmm, most important aspect for way back when, huh? Guess you'll just have to take my word on this, Toyman."

"And in trade you want…" Willy started.

"I want," Johnny replied, "that one-of-a-kind, gold and platinum Korbanth Lightsaber, decorated with rubies, diamonds, and sapphires…you know the one. It is hiding in the very rear of that large safe of yours."

"A treasure from antiquity, for the most desired treasure of modern pop culture," Willy said. "I'd be lying if I told anyone I had foreseen this."

A couple of minutes later, Johnny snatched the light-saber from Willy's hand, turned around and shouted over his shoulder, "take care, Willy. And by the way, you can't keep avoiding the Sha'Daa, any more than you can stop the sun from setting."

The muzak version of Elvis's *Teddy Bear* echoed throughout the store.

Willy frowned for a moment, and then dashed to the phone booth as it began ringing.

"What?" Johnny shouted.

"Hello, this is Kvasir the Interface," Kvasir said.

"Well, what a surprise," Willy said. "What is it, now?"

"The Midnight Laborers have come to a profound decision," Kvasir said, "something they feel speaks to the heart of their noble purpose and ancient pride."

"And what is that?" Willy asked.

"They want you to stop referring to them," Kvasir said, "as the Midnight Laborers."

"And call them what, instead?" Willy asked cautiously.

"They wish to be called…the Wyrd Honorable Order of Professional Exceptional Engineers," Kvasir said.

"Whoopee?"

"I take that as an approval, sir?" Kvasir asked.

"Tell them to shelve this conversation. We can pick it up at the end of the Sha'Daa," Willy said.

"The Sha'Daa," Kvasir gasped.

"Oh," Willy said, "did I forget to mention what was happening in the real world? Oh my, how thoughtless of me. Yes, probably best to hold off on forwarding this particular news. And to answer your unasked question, yes, the Midnight Laborers wonderful pocket universe will cease to exist if Whirligigs does not survive this most frightening of events."

The Poppet

R.J. Ladon

"Living toys are something novel, but it soon wears off somehow."

–Philip Larkin

SETH WALKED AWAY FROM WHIRLIGIGS, AN enormous smile on his face and a bag filled with brightly colored Carnival and Marti Gras costumes in his hand.

"What a woman, so stupid and gullible, but so beautiful too," Seth talked to no one in particular as he strolled to his apartment on a quiet sidewalk. "Can you believe she thinks we're putting on a play tonight? Elizabeth always falls for anything, once I say it in Latin."

"She had no choice," said an incorporeal voice, emanating directly behind him. "Truth spoken in Latin coupled with your amulet will make a follower out of anyone." The voice chuckled. "How else could the Ancients convert the Pagans?"

Seth knew the voice was Sauru, an archdemon and devoted follower of Ahriman. He chuckled at the irony. *Priests and missionaries used the amulet to convert natives to the Christian faith, while I use it to bring the faithful to the other side.* He fingered the gold relic hanging around his neck. Ahriman gave it to Seth during a brief encounter at an archeological dig in Syria.

Sauru had been following Seth closely for the past couple days, helping and instructing him in preparation for the Sha'Daa. The demon's voice had grown in strength as the event drew closer.

"Surely the sacrifice of one so pure and innocent would help our master enter this world." Sauru continued. "Her blood mingling with yours would entwine her soul to you. She would be your mate, yours to command on the other side. For eternity."

He let his mind wander. *The things I will do to that woman once she is mine.* He smiled. They turned down an alley filled with box trucks, garbage, and slumbering homeless.

Seth's smile faltered. Tonight he would die on this plane to be reborn on the next. His flesh and blood, freely given, will be the final step that allows Ahriman to enter this world. He shuddered not knowing exactly what to expect, beyond the pain.

"Alleviate your fears young one. Soon this life will be over. Only then will you receive all that you deserve. Ahriman entrusted his plans to you, entitling you to your fondest dreams." The demon paused. "You will be the highest ranking human I know, a prince among men." Sauru's voice soothed Seth.

Five minutes of pain for an eternity filled with riches, women, and power. Seth shook with anticipation.

Together they turned a corner out of the alley, into a section of the Chicago Loop, an area frequented by tourists looking for a deal. People filled the sidewalks, gawking at window displays, and eating from the street carts. Seth lamented how many people he would touch crossing the street.

"Not all are human," Sauru told him. "Look there's an imp, one we agreed to meet today." Sauru's bond with Seth was complete and allowed the demon to know all his thoughts.

"Where?"

"With the man wearing khaki shorts and a Green Bay tee-shirt." Sauru chuckled, rich and pleasing. "Football, what a pathetic human sport, I miss the gladiatorial games."

"There are at least twenty people who fit that description. Can I use your eyes?" Seth disliked the feeling of being possessed by Sauru, but it was the fastest way to understand what the demon saw.

"That is why I am here," the demon said.

Bone chilling cold, followed by oppressive heat, encased Seth's body. He blinked a couple times, getting used to the strange visual elements demon sight provided. Streaks of bright light zipped past; these were souls departing a human host. Blobs of transparent color hovered above the street, others bobbed among the humans on the sidewalk, while others hung off buildings and trees. The shapeless-ones appeared in every tincture and pigmentation imaginable, like the streaks of color oil releases when it floats on water.

More and more of the incorporeal appeared as the Sha'Daa approached. Some of the shapeless-ones were demons, some were neutral, and far fewer could be described as angelic.

Seth spotted a blue-violet blob hovering over a man in Green Bay attire. *That must be the imp Sauru spotted.* Seth was never certain what each blob was as they all looked the same to his untrained eyes.

"That's the one," the demon's voice vibrated inside Seth's head.

"The man gets a costume?"

"Yes." Sauru's voice shook Seth with intensity.

"Please release me, so I can walk." Seth preferred to move of his own accord, instead of having the demon drive him like a marionette.

"Of course, young one."

Seth's body returned to its normal temperature, and his eyes only detected the colors of the rainbow. *How boring.*

"Soon, my child, you will have demon sight of your own."

Seth shimmied his way through the crowds. The bald man looked at him, frowned, and looked away. "I have something for you," Seth said.

"Quickly, my wife and children are in that store. It would be best if they didn't see us talking." The man shifted his feet, tilting his shoulders as if adjusting the weight of the imp on his back.

Seth positioned himself next to the man, appearing like he was window shopping. He stuffed a costume into one of the bags the man was standing over. "Will your family join us tonight?"

"Oh, yes. The more sacrifices, the better." The man spoke out the side of his mouth.

Seth nodded then moved down the street. Once away from the congestion of the tourists, he picked up the pace, almost running to his apartment. *Others would be arriving soon. Too much to do and so little time.*

☦ ☦ ☦

Eleven men and women came to Seth's apartment to retrieve a costume. Adding the man on the street and himself, thirteen imps and demons would be released tonight. But Seth had to wait to be the last sacrifice. His offering would be pivotal to the opening of the portal and bringing Ahriman into the world. His reward would be the greatest. *A prince among men.*

Fully nude and covered with oils and perfumes, Seth paced back and forth in his sparsely furnished apartment.

"Patience, young one," Sauru encouraged. "The Sha'Daa is nigh."

"How do I make it to Lincoln Park naked? Someone will notice, the cops will pick me up, and I will fail."

"This was foreseen. That is why you have a costume."

"But the fabric would touch my skin and remove the magic." His skin glistened under the harsh fluorescent light. Herb and ash encrusted symbols covered his body.

"The costume is for me," the demon proclaimed.

"What? But you really aren't here. What I see and hear is just pressure on the veil between our worlds. We communicate through our bond because Ahriman commands it."

"With the Sha'Daa so close, the veil weakens, and my power and presence grows. I can wear that costume and hide you."

Seth stared at the voice. The red and black shimmer of Sauru's colorful blob reminded him of a ghost, or what television depicted as a poltergeist. He knew from experience a real spirit looked like a streak of light. Over the past few days, the demon's physical appearance had become more apparent to his human eyes. *Perhaps Sauru could wear the outfit.*

"Quickly young one, gather your wits and fetch the costume. And your amulet, you will need it–for a trade." The demon chuckled, the shimmer brightened.

Seth entered his bedroom where the costume was laid out. The obnoxious colors and patterns of the Brazilian Carnival one-piece clashed with his flannel bedspread. The mask was decorated in an equally hideous style. *How the heck are we going to be inconspicuous in that monstrosity?*

The amulet, a gold cross with a ruby in the center, sat on the dresser. Seth collected everything, carefully holding it at arm's length so nothing would mar the oil or magic. It took four hours to cast the spells and six people to anoint his flesh. He did not have the time to redo the magic and symbols. He dropped the costume and amulet on the kitchen table.

"Excellent. Now hold the shoulders of the costume at the proper height of a man."

Seth did as he was instructed.

"Let go I have it."

The costume hovered above the floor, but it was still ugly.

"Now the mask, hold it at the proper height for the clothing. Good."

Seth stepped back to get a better look. The costume and mask floated in space with the slight shimmer of Sauru's red-black blob behind it. *No one would believe that is a person.*

"It'll work," Sauru assured. "Walk behind it and go to the mirror hanging over your couch. You will see a glamour spell, an old witch's trick. All the costumes have one."

Seth stepped into the shapeless-one's blob. He could see with demon eyes again. The outfit drifted in front of him, close but never touching. His movements choreographed the clothing, forcing the arms and legs to swing with the motion of his steps. *Okay, I have to admit that is kind of cool.*

"Of course it is," Sauru snapped. "You must have faith."

The mirror displayed Seth standing behind the floating costume. His heart fell.

"Look again, this time let your eyes become unfocused. Remember you are using demon sight."

Seth relaxed his eyes to a point where his apartment and the mirror went out of focus. Within the reflection was a massive man wearing gray sweats and a blue baseball cap. *An easily forgettable visage.*

"That's why these costumes are perfect."

"Okay, let's go. I want to get this over with." Seth wanted to go before his courage diminished.

"We need to bring the amulet." Sauru's voice vibrated inside Seth's skull.

"Right." Seth stepped out of the demon's shapeless body, picked up the amulet from the kitchen table, and returned. "Wait a minute; I've never been able to break free from your possession before. What is different now?"

"You stepped into my body. I allowed you to possess me. In doing so, your movements are projected to the clothing I'm wearing. And the glamour will talk when you talk. Simple and elegant, don't you think?"

"Fascinating." Seth walked around the floating costume. The visage of the fat man flashed in and out of his sight, like a hologram. But it always returned to the unsightly outfit.

"Our time approaches. Come young one."

Seth stepped into Sauru and mentally noted there was no heat or cold when *he* possessed the demon. He walked toward the door, and the costume copied his movements.

The puppet collided with the entrance-way before Seth realized his mistake; the costume had to operate the doorknob, not his physical form. It took a few mental adjustments until Seth was able to control the outfit, like playing a third-person video game.

They walked out of the apartment building and down the street. Everyone moved aside to avoid touching the glamour of the disgusting overweight man. Seth began to relax; his body and its magic covering would arrive at Lincoln Park unscathed.

The Children's Fountain on the southwestern edge of Lincoln Park pulsed with shapeless-ones. The colorful blobs floated in the water and interacted with the bronze statues. The blobs moved toward people, hovering, getting close, and then retreating back to the metal cherubs and storks, like Native Americans playing counting coup.

A tall, thin man stood on the steps that led up to the pool under the fountain. He wore a black trench coat and wide-brimmed hat. The man appeared to be a street performer, but he had no crowd or tip can. The shapeless-ones skirted around him, either out of respect or fear.

"There's Johnny. We need to trade with him," Sauru said.

"Johnny?" Seth gripped the gold and ruby cross tightly in his fist.

Johnny bounced on the balls of his feet giggling and talking to himself. He leaned on a cane and scanned the crowd. His dark eyes snapped on the glamour. Johnny didn't acknowledge the costume; instead, he stared through the image of the humongous man to Seth. "You have a trade for me, Seth? A trade?"

"How do you know my name?"

Johnny snickered. "I know many things. I know you have an amulet to trade. I know your *friend* Sauru." The man tipped his hat. "We have done business before."

"Good to see you, Salesman." Sauru's voice rumbled in Seth's head.

Johnny nodded as if he heard what the demon said.

"You know the amulet and what it can do? It is quite valuable. What am I to get in trade?"

"Does it matter what you get or what you leave? Soon you will be done with this plane. If you so desire take your amulet with you–I will collect it later when it has no value." Johnny giggled and spun his cane. "You'll be happy with what I give you. It has only one purpose." He flashed a small blade three-inches long with a skinning hook at the tip. "And none that come after you will be interested in its *features*. For Sauru, I have something to complete the ritual." The Salesman's hands disappeared into his pockets, and the blade was gone.

Seth knew Johnny was right. He had no more need of the amulet. It was almost worthless unless you spoke Latin or Greek. He nodded to himself, it was time. He dumped the cross into Johnny's out stretched hand.

Seth wondered what the people around him saw. Did the glamour of the ginormous man drop something out of his armpit? He laughed at the thought.

Johnny bit the cross then deposited the amulet into an inner coat pocket. "A deal is done, a trade made." From another pocket, The Salesman pulled out a huge bag, dropped the small knife into it, and gave it to the glamour.

The obese man grabbed the bag, and they walked away from Johnny.

They passed the Couch mausoleum. Seth grinned, the souls that were feeling unrest after being disinterred would be added fodder for the army of the damned that was about to break upon the Earth. And *he* was the catalyst; the last in a procession of thirteen. He was the one who found and converted most of the willing sacrifices. Seth smirked. Without him, there would be no Sha'Daa. He should ask for more.

"Feeling greedy Seth?" Sauru's voice echoed in his mind.

"Perhaps."

"The Sha'Daa will happen with or without you. Your sacrifice is for my benefit and Ahriman's. You would be wise not to anger an archdemon."

Seth stopped.

Sauru continued, "The blade Johnny gave you allows your sacrifice to be less painful. That was your concern, was it not? I felt pity for you. So, I asked Johnny's help. I could withhold it so that you feel every stab and slice."

"I possessed you; you have to do what I say." Seth's frustration broke to the surface. "You will do my bidding, or I won't sacrifice myself for you or anyone."

"Do I?" Sauru's voice rose. "You said yourself I am not really here. I am on the other side of the veil. All I have to do is move away and step deeper into my realm, and I will no longer be your *pet*." The demon purred with contentment. "And then I'll return to possess you and force you to do anything I want."

Seth stiffened. He didn't have a choice; he never did. One way or another he was going to die. "Sauru, you have to understand. I was just trying to get the best price for what I offer."

"I'm the only buyer. Don't make me steal the product." Sauru's voice turned into a snarl.

A scream echoed across the park, startling Seth.

"Ah, music to my ears. The Sha'Daa begins." Sauru's voice softened.

Park lamps and skyscraper lights went out. A gentle beckoning glow from the sports area called to Seth like a moth to a flame. The main baseball diamond had a generator.

Fast moving shapes bounded along the bike path.

"I'll make good on my agreement," Seth said. He plodded toward the light. "Will you and Ahriman follow through on your half of the bargain?"

"If you follow through on the self-sacrifice you promised us, we will give you everything you deserve." Sauru chuckled.

More screams and shouts flowed around them. People ran from gray monsters covered with spiky black hair. The beasts moved like dogs chasing rabbits.

"What are those…things?"

"Spiked Fiends. The first of many demons. Look, young one, we are almost there."

Grotesquely displayed men, women, and children were sprawled across the aluminum bleachers, facing the baseball diamond. Seth stared with morbid fascination. Blood and death were beautiful to demon eyes.

A group of men in blue scrubs worked like industrious ants in the outfield. They helped, guiding a willing sacrifice to the bloodied earth for the others to dissect and disembowel. Then the body was meticulously displayed on the bleachers.

"Those first sacrifices allowed some of our forces to come through the veil, to get an early start as it were. The more that are sacrificed, the more demons can enter. But sacrifices that are freely given can release the most powerful."

"So you do need me."

"Need? No. one or two hundred forced sacrifices will work just as well. One freely given is simply faster."

A naked woman sauntered toward the men working in the outfield. She chanted and sang, sweeping her arms above her head. Symbols and glyphs marked her oil covered body.

"Behold, your brethren, giving herself freely."

"Janet…" Seth's voice choked. This woman was braver than him. She deserved more riches in the next plane than he did.

The men watched the woman approach, the tools of their trade dripped with blood. Janet stood among them, spinning in a circle, she touched each man, and then gracefully lowered herself to the blood and flesh covered ground. The men got to work, looking more like vultures than the doctors their blue scrubs implied. Janet never made a sound.

Seth saw with the help of Sauru's demon eyes that these men were not human; they were demons hiding behind the glamor charged costumes he bought hours ago at Whirligigs.

Elizabeth. Seth remembered seeing her for the last time at the toy store.

"If you want her to join you on the next plane, you will need virgin ground. To ensure her blood mingles with yours, and only yours."

A dull crack reverberated.

"The veil weakens further. Come, young one, you're next." Urgency sounded in Sauru's voice.

"The Sha'Daa is here, isn't it? Nothing can stop it, can it? My death can either be meaningless, or it can amount to something, like helping you. And who would blame me if I gained something from the apocalypse?"

Sauru didn't respond right away. "Are you trying to justify your actions?"

"I'd feel a lot better if you told me I'm doing the right thing; that there is no other option." Seth's voice cracked.

"You know I can't lie. But I can't see the future either. You must be satisfied with your choice."

Seth stepped from the glamour exposing his nakedness. He didn't feel confident like Janet appeared. He felt exposed and terrified. The loss of the demon sight made him feel sick. He scanned the ground quickly looking for a clean patch of earth before the sights and smells of butchery forced him to faint.

"I'm ready." Seth looked to the ginormous male glamour and watched it change into a smaller man wearing scrubs, matching the others. "How did you do that?"

"We are at the physical location where the veil is the thinnest. All the other sacrifices have made sure of that. I can do so much more even as an incorporeal form. With your offering, the veil will inevitably fail. Then Ahriman and I will be able to enter completely, with hordes following." Tears formed in the glamor's eyes. "I owe you so much."

"Please give me Johnny's knife."

"Of course, young one. Do you promise to say your spell?"

"With my last breath."

The glamour reached into the bag and pulled out the knife placing it in Seth's waiting hand.

Sauru motioned for the other men in scrubs to surround Seth. They spoke in unison, in a guttural language. They swayed and bounced, dipping to their vocal harmony.

It's time.

Seth lifted his head to look down his prone body. His hands shook. Before he could back out, he pressed the knife against his flesh above his pubic hair and shoved the blade through his taunt skin and muscles. He caught his breath. The pain was there, he recognized it, but it dissipated, transforming into euphoria. Quickly he pulled the blade up his belly to his sternum. The sharp pain of agony was replaced with an intoxication so intense his body shook with excitement and release. He gasped again, but this time it was with pleasure.

The knife fell from his hand. He didn't care. One of the men picked it up and continued to carve. Each cut drove pain followed by exhilaration coursing through his body.

Click-clack Seth turned his head toward the sound. Elizabeth stared back from the other side of the backstop. The young girl next to her played with a Jacob's ladder.

Intestine was thrown on his chest. His fingers massaged and caressed the rope-like structures. *Who knew torture could be so stimulating?* Seth arched his back, completing his arousal.

All the men moved away except for Sauru. "All right young one, it is time for your spell."

Seth blinked a couple times but continued to stare at Elizabeth. "Malum hoc sacrificio daemonum evocare!" he shouted.

"In English, young one, you traded the amulet remember?"

Seth cleared his throat. "Entrails…" his voice shuddered.

> "Entrails exposed,
> Thick blood flows,
> Centuries of hardship,
> Evil grows,
> Sacrifice freely given,
> I release thee,
> Ahriman!
> Ahriman…
> Ahriman…"

Sauru pulled a heavy sledge hammer from the bag, swinging it, and letting it strike the back of Seth's skull.

The impact of the hammer tossed Seth's soul into the air. He looked down at what remained of his body, his friend Sauru, and Elizabeth.

His feelings became diluted. Seth no longer cared if he was a prince among men. Money and power in the demon realm held no sway. Hunger to touch and own Elizabeth's body and soul dissipated. Johnny was right; once he was dead, his earthly desires and physical possessions had no value.

Nothing mattered.

Without the influence of his primitive body or the insubstantial promises of Sauru and Ahriman, his soul was free, at peace.

The spirit drifted away from the madness of humans and demons. It followed the course other flashes of light–other souls–were taking.

Toys In The Attic

NEAR EVENING ON NOVEMBER 9, 1938 IN Berlin, Germany, Willy was wondering why business was so slow. The reason soon became clear as a horrendous wave of violence occurred all across Germany proper: Kristallnacht, also referred to as the Night of Broken Glass.

The sounds of people screaming and glass shattering had Willy running to the front display window of Whirligigs to see SA paramilitary forces and German civilians attacking the storefronts of several nearby businesses, dragging the owners out into the streets to be beaten and spat upon.

Without notice, four men and two women, Willy recognized as owners of a laundry service and a haberdashery burst into the front parlor of the store and slammed the door behind them.

"Mister Carroll," a young man yelled, "can you hide us? I beg you. I fear hatred has driven them mad."

Willy knew the man, Samuel Felix Cyfer, his business neighbor for over six years. The two of them shared breakfast and lunch at least twice monthly. Willy took one step forward, then stopped, his mind working furiously. Even with all his weird learning he considered himself an agnostic, and liked both atheists and theists like Samuel and his friends and families equally. Prejudice like this, which he had witnessed long ago in Australia, was certainly wrong, and nothing that he ever approved of, but the anger of the authorities for helping these innocent people might cause him much trouble, if not worse. He was an immortal and had gone to great lengths to keep this aspect of his life a secret from the public at large.

Biting his lower lip, Willy also found himself questioning his own thinking. How could he be thinking so cold-bloodedly at this moment? A recollection of an arcane ceremony he underwent over two centuries ago flickered through his mind…something about a sacrifice meaningless at the time, with the reward being powers, and even immortality, though he wasn't indestructible and could be killed, if he wasn't careful

"Mister Carroll," Samuel pleaded, "please."

Some long-forgotten corner of Willy's consciousness screamed for him to help these victims. Yet Willy's sense of empathy did not well up within him.

The front door flew open and eight SA Brown Shirts rushed in, eyeing Samuel and his colleagues with vicious eyes and snarling lips.

"I know you're Aryan, Carroll, just relax and let us do our business" the leader of the SA shouted. Willy recognized him as a boy who had shopped here with his parents much of his life. Karl Metzger.

"Don't be stupid and try to protect these animals," Karl continued. "You six, show me your identification papers. Immediately!"

All six, letting out sighs of defeat, slowly reached into pockets, jackets, and purses and reluctantly offered up the demanded forms. They were quickly dragged out into the streets, helpless at the hands of the raging mobs.

For two days Jewish homes, hospitals, and schools were ransacked. Nazis destroyed buildings using sledgehammers. They burned 1000 synagogues and 7000 thousand Jewish businesses were destroyed or damaged. Hundreds died and 30,000 Jewish men were arrested and sent to concentration camps.

Decades later Willy would pick up a copy of the book, *The Sociopath Next Door* by Martha Stout on a whim while in a small bookshop in New York City. It took him just five hours to read from cover to cover though he spent several days considering all that it had to say about the human condition.

He'd owned multiple dogs since leaving Australia, loved them, and grieved their passing. The same was also true of all his half dozen successful marriages (none which ever ended in divorce), as he managed to conceal his immortality from his wives, and wallowed in genuine bereavement after their passing. So surely he was not a sociopath?

But beyond these facts, Willy came to realize that these feelings only sprang between himself and those few people, animals, and beings that he had a strong personal relationship with. Humanity as a whole, however, though he felt no desire to see anyone suffer harm, he also did not care if disaster fell on them either.

He knew that this somehow stemmed from some ritual he underwent long ago in Australia, but every time he found himself close to remembering, all thoughts of this matter would slip away like water through the fingers of an open palm, and might only return late at night, moments before sleep struck.

Thinking back on his time in Germany from the front parlor of his Greenwich Village toy store in the 1970s, Willy remembered running his small business throughout the length of world war II, watching his Jewish business colleagues disappear from every aspect of finance and sales across Berlin. While that tiny part of his consciousness seemed to demand he address the horrors that surrounded him, no reciprocating emotions surfaced. Eventually the constant bombing of Berlin by the allies, and the unrelenting approach of Russians, eager for revenge upon anyone who wore the label, German, convinced Willy to relocate to London under cover of his own eldritch abilities.

Tommy Talker

Robby Hilliard

"People used to play with toys. Now the toys play with them."

–Idries Shah

"**I** CAN'T BELIEVE I'VE NEVER NOTICED THAT SHOP before," Maureen said. Across the street from her and her son Sean, right next to Oz Park in Chicago, was a shop called, 'Whirligigs'. Sweat trickled down her back, the day already hot even though it was not yet noon, the sweat tickling, like a spider crawling down her spine. Maureen shivered in spite of the heat.

"Shall we give it a try? Even if I can't sell anything, we might find you a birthday present, okay?"

Sean looked up at her and nodded. He held up one of her ceramic samples.

It was a candy cane with an elf holding it at the top, arms and legs wrapped around the stem. It was designed to sit on a mantle, the elf part, and allow a stocking to be hung from the hook of the candy cane. Several times a year, she and Sean would go into the city to show her pottery crafts and art work to independent shop owners. Although Maureen produced some high-end art pieces, what paid her bills were simple things that sold a lot. And right now, that was this candy cane stocking hook.

"Let's go," she said and took Sean by the hand.

Sean was small for his age, seven, and rarely spoke. Often, Maureen worried that he wasn't being socialized enough. She hoped that seeing her interact with potential clients might help.

The shadows along the front of the building were dark and the recessed doorway a darker patch of shadow. As the two of them stepped up onto the sidewalk, a large figure loomed, separating itself from the shadows of the store front.

"Hello there," a deep, male voice said. "Have I got a deal for you fine looking folks."

Maureen stopped abruptly, unconsciously pulling Sean to be behind her. With her other hand she shielded her eyes from the bright solstice sun.

"Excuse me," she said. She slowly sidestepped towards the building face and the shade so that she could see better, guiding Sean as she went. The man was tall, wore a long coat and hat that seemed out of place in the mid-summer heat. The hat that cast a dark shadow over the man's face. He held out a piece of wood. It was an old-fashioned back scratcher.

"For just a small donation of any kind, I have this very fine back scratcher. It's guaranteed to get the job done, if you know what I mean." He smiled as he spoke. Light shone off of a gold tooth.

"I don't think we're interested in trading anything today," Maureen said. She felt Sean tug on her hand. When she looked down, he was holding up the candy cane stocking holder.

"Looks like someone is ready to make a trade," the man said. He extended the back scratcher to Sean.

"Stop!" Maureen's voice was sharp and stern, her free hand interposed between Sean and the man.

The man froze in position and Maureen felt Sean jump slightly.

"I'm sorry," Maureen said. "It's just that I don't usually allow my son to interact with strangers."

The man drew back slightly, his arms relaxed. "Of course. I didn't mean to startle anyone."

Maureen took the candy cane ornament from Sean and exchanged it for the back scratcher.

"My name's Johnny, by the way," the man said. "And it's a pleasure doing business with you."

Maureen smiled but didn't introduce herself or Sean. "Thank you, Johnny. And you have a good day."

Johnny reached up and touched the brim of his hat. "Solstice today. You know that?" he said as he turned away. "Gonna' be a hot couple of days."

Maureen moved to put the piece of wood in her sample bag and noticed there were the words on one side. 'Beware! The Sha'Daa is here!' Maureen flipped the implement over and looked for some kind of lodge or religious symbol, but found nothing, she asked, "What is 'shadaa'?"

Johnny didn't answer her.

"Excuse me," she began, looking up.

Johnny was nowhere to be seen.

Maureen gave a start and looked around.

"Damn," she said. "That was weird." For the second time that morning, she shivered.

The two of them entered Whirligigs.

✛ ✛ ✛

"What do you think happened to its face," Sean asked. His voice was so soft Maureen almost missed it. She stopped looking around the store. She'd seen enough to know that Whirligigs was probably not in the market for Christmas decorations. Maybe some of her higher end sculptures, so that was promising, but not candy canes.

The store was packed from floor to ceiling in some places with odd things, both vintage and new. They were crammed into glass display cases, sat on furniture, and randomly filled shelves. Maureen couldn't quite tell if the store's interior was 'artfully arranged', or just chaotically thrown together.

"What are you looking at, honey," she asked.

Sean pointed at something in a glass display case and Maureen could tell by the look on his face that he'd found something he really wanted. She knelt down next to the display case. It was a doll that looked like a ventriloquist doll from the '50's or so. Its eyes were large and its mouth was a permanent smile, the lips prominently colored in what must have been a bright red years ago. One side of its face drooped, much like when someone has had a stroke. Either way, it looked like it might be expensive. Maureen would have to be gentle with how she appraised it in case she couldn't afford it.

"It looks old. It might not in such good shape."

"But what do you think happened to its face," Sean said, again.

"Well, let's see," Maureen said. "It looks like it melted or something. Maybe left in the sun, or sat too close to a furnace or someth—".

"It was a fire," a male voice, much older than Sean, said.

Maureen stood abruptly and looked about. The kiln glazed samples of her work clinked alarmingly in the bag she carried.

Standing at the far end of the glass counter case was a tall, gangly man, dressed in clownish colors, with a head of shocking red hair.

"A horrendous fire," the man continued. His eyes opened wide as the word 'horrendous' rolled off his tongue. His hands splayed like someone signing 'sunrise' or 'boom'.

"Some say it was started by a stranger passing through town, but others say," his smile broadened and his voice lowered in a conspiratorial manner, "it was the mother of the children who started it. A terrible tragedy. Four children burned to death." He shook himself and clenched his hands into fists as he said, "Gruesome."

"Excuse me," Maureen said, her voice rising. She leaned towards the man, raised her eyebrows, and gestured with a nod of her head towards Sean. "I think that may be inappropr—".

"Stranger still," the man leaned forward, hunched as if to share a secret, "the mother claimed it was the doll itself that started the fire." His eyebrows rose and fell two or three times and his smile, as big as it was, grew bigger. "Sodder family fire, West Virginia, 1945. Surely you've heard of it?" The man's head turned slightly, his mouth open as if ready to laugh. He looked like someone who has just told a joke, waiting for the audience to get it. One of his teeth sparkled. "No?"

Maureen's mouth hung open for a second before she closed it. She glared at the man.

The man drew back abruptly as if he had been lightly smacked on the nose. "Huh. Well. Okay." He suddenly found something on the front of his jacket that needed brushing and whisked at it with one hand. "It's very collectable you know. Preserved by one of the surviving siblings. Said she wanted to 'break the circle' or some such." He made a dismissive, shooing away motion with his hands. "Curse or something."

Maureen's mouth opened again, and closed. It was obvious to her that this person lacked some kind of awareness of social cues. Without breaking eye contact with him, she reached out and put a firm hand on Sean's shoulder. "Come on Sean, we'll find a birthday present for you somewhere else."

Shock displayed on the man's face, his smile now gone. He moved quickly, inserting himself in front of Maureen. One hand went up in a, "stop, wait" motion while the other reached into a waistcoat pocket and whipped out a business card.

"Willy Carroll," the man said, his gigantic smile once again on display. "Proprietor. Seller of curiosities and..." As he spoke, his other hand began to make a sweeping gesture indicating the store's interior and contents, but then stopped, his smile diminishing some as he appeared to search for the correct word. "...and oddities." The large smile returned. "I'm the owner. At your service." He didn't quite bow but the attitude of his posture suggested that he had just done so. "Forgive me for any assumptions I've made. I thought you were perhaps a...collector." Again, the eyebrows rose and fell as if to indicate he was speaking in code. He looked back and forth between Maureen and Sean. "It seems I've overwhelmed you. Please. Allow me to start over." He took a small step to one side, stood up straight, and said, "Welcome to Whirligigs. How may I help you?"

Maureen waited a second to see if Willy was through speaking.

"If," she began, she made a limp handed sweeping gesture mocking the one Willy had begun earlier, "by 'oddities' you mean, 'used and not too expensive', then maybe you have something we might want."

Willy laughed out loud, his head flung back and his hands clasped in front of his chest. "Touché, madame. Touché!"

"How about this doll," Sean asked. His voice was much louder than before.

Maureen looked at Sean, her eyes opening wide. This was the first time she could recall he had voluntarily spoken with a sales person. He usually just smiled and tried to hide behind her.

"Ah, yes," Willy said. "The doll." Willy stepped to the far side of the glass case, took the doll out, and sat it on top of the counter. A large key like handle stuck out of the doll's back, like on an old-fashioned windup toy.

"This is the famous, 'Talking Tommy'. A toy that appeared in the 1940's long before that 'Chatty Kate' or whatever it was. This doll was modeled on the original Thomas Edison talking doll of the late eighteen-hundreds. Of course, I've never been able to get this one to work." He looked at Maureen and said, "Hence the reduced price." He finished with an exaggerated wink.

"Can you take it out of the case," Sean said.

"No, Sean," Maureen said, "I don't think that's a good ide—."

"Of course I can," Willy said. He opened the display case, took the doll out, and sat it on top of the glass counter. "You are supposed to be able to wind the key to make it work." Abruptly, he grabbed the doll again, turned it around, and gave the key a few turns. He turned the doll back around and let it sit.

A mechanical grinding sound like metal teeth sliding across each other could be heard.

"Sadly," he said, "it has 'never worked for me." He stood and stared at the doll, his hands on his hips. "See," he said. He looked at Sean, and the Maureen. "Nothing."

"Well," Maureen said. She looked at Sean. "Would you still want it? Even if it doesn't talk?"

"Of course," Sean said. "I wanted it before I even knew it was supposed to talk. And besides," he reached for the doll. "Maybe we can fix it."

Willy laughed and looked at Maureen. It was a big laugh like you might expect from a stage actor. "Well then, it sounds as if this young man might be just the sort of person who could appreciate a fine collectable."

Maureen sighed and looked at Willy with a stern expression. "Fine. I'll take it. But at the 'reduced price' you mentioned."

"Of course," Willy said, his face making an expression of faux seriousness to match Maureen's. "How does thirty dollars sound?"

"Hello," a tinny voice said, "My name is Tommy. What's yours?"

Maureen and Willy both turned to look at Sean and the doll.

The doll's head was turning slightly from side to side, a soft metallic clicking emanating from its neck. The eyes were also moving slightly giving the impression that the doll was actually looking around as it spoke.

"Oh my," Willy said. Both hands were on the sides of his face, his eyes opened wide. "It actually works!"

"Can you draw a circle," the doll asked.

"I can," Sean said, his head nodding.

Maureen produced cash from a pocket so fast it seemed as if she'd performed some slight-of-hand feat. "Thirty dollars sounds perfect." She held the cash out to the Willy.

Willy scowled at Maureen for a few seconds before snatching the cash from her hand.

Maureen finished drying the last of the dishes from lunch. She could hear Sean playing with his new toy, talking away in the living room. The house was old and small, a catalog order home from the 1930s. Two bedrooms, bathroom, kitchen and living room. The property itself wasn't so rural as to be considered out in the country, but farms could be seen just a mile or so down the road. It was quiet and simple. And it was the best she could do after Sean's father had left them. Maureen like to think of it as 'wholesome'.

She could hear Sean talking to the doll in the living room. It made her smile.

She dried her hands and hung the dish towel on the oven handle. She moved towards the living room door and stopped, just inside the kitchen, to listen. She couldn't remember when Sean had talked so much and the thought made her smile.

She stepped into the living room. "Sean, I'm going out to the pottery shed to…"

Sean stopped talking. The doll stopped talking. The dolls head snapped to one side, towards her. The droopy side of its face made it look evil.

A trick of the light, Maureen thought.

It seemed as if she had just walked into a room where two people were talking and she had interrupted the conversation. Something about it made her stomach tighten with anxiety.

"You know, Sean, maybe you should set the doll aside for a while and play outside, huh? What do you think?"

Maureen approached Sean, knelt down and reached for the doll. "Why don't you let me put the doll away for a little while."

Sean jerked the doll away and his face twisted in anger. "No!"

The change in Sean's demeanor was so abrupt, Maureen flinched.

"Sean," she said, her voice tinged with anger. She pointed at Sean for emphasis. "You know you aren't allowed to talk to me like that."

Sean hung his head. "I'm sorry momma." When he looked up, his eyes were brimming with tears. "I'm just having fun."

Maureen felt a pang of guilt. "Alright, Sean. You continue playing with your new...friend until dinner. Okay?"

Sean nodded his head, affirmative.

"I'll be out in the pottery shed." She stood up and made her way back to the kitchen. She picked up her sample bag and headed for the back door. As she stepped out into the back yard, she could hear Sean talking again in the living room. And the doll as well.

⊕   ⊕   ⊕

The shed was small, but it was enough for Maureen to have an old kiln, work benches, and shelves for drying her ceramics. She placed the sample bag on a work bench and removed the ceramics. She came across the back scratcher and thought perhaps it would be useful for shaping clay at some point. She put it on the work bench that ran along one end of the shed and went to inspect her kiln.

Even though the kiln had been cooling since the day before and should be ready to open, it still radiated a tremendous amount of heat. Donning oven mitts, she grabbed a pair of tongs, opened the kiln door, and began unstacking the ornaments. Next, she would apply colors in the glazing process and load them back into the kiln. She carefully unstacked the now hardened decorations and began lining them up on the work table that occupied the center of the shed.

Once the pieces were all lined up, she got out her brushes and paints, and allowed herself to relax and mindlessly apply the colors. Red, green, white. Red, green, white. It was a slow, repetitive process, but Maureen found it to be almost therapeutic.

A bead of sweat dripping from her nose roused her from her work, and she looked up. the shed was darker. Outside the windows, the sky was a burnt orange.

"Damn. Dinner's going to be late tonight!" Maureen took off her work apron, turned out the shed lights, and headed for the kitchen.

⊕   ⊕   ⊕

When Maureen entered the back door, she turned on the kitchen light.

Several bags of salt were on the kitchen floor, the cabinet doors open. She kept a great deal of it on hand, buying it whenever it was on sale for future salt glazing projects.

"Dammit Sean," she called. "What have you been up to?"

She walked towards the living room. Ahead of her she could hear what sounded like someone talking in long sentences, but the voice was not Sean's.

Before she got to the living room doorway, the voice stopped. It had been a tinny voice.

The fine hairs on the back of Maureen's neck felt as if they were standing on end. Her pulse beginning to quicken for no reason that made sense to her, she stepped through the doorway of the living room.

"Young man," she said, her voice full of the sternness that mothers often have to use with their children, "what have I told you about getting into my salt..." Her speech slowed and faded in volume as she took in the mess of the living room.

Sean, a bag of salt in his hands, pouring thin lines in the shape of a circle, one inside of the other. The outer circle, about six feet across was finished and he was now attempting to pour another circle inside of it.

"What in the hell are you doing," Maureen yelled. She rushed forward, hands outthrust. "Give that to me!" She grabbed the bag of salt from Sean. "What is going on here?"

Sean seemed to jump when Maureen grabbed the bag of salt out of his hands. He looked around at the circles as if disoriented for a second and then he looked up at his mother.

"I'm drawing circles."

"Well, I can see that," Maureen said. She held the bag against her hip, her other hand going to her forehead. "Why are you using salt of all things? Why can't you just draw on things with chalk or crayons like other kids?" She looked around in frustration. "And why in the hell are you drawing circles in the first place? And for heaven's sake, why on my floor?"

Sean pointed at the doll. "Tommy asked me to."

Maureen looked at the doll. It was positioned in an easy chair as if watching Sean. "What do you mean it 'told you to'? It's a toy. It just says things that are prerecorded on little metal plates. That's it."

Maureen looked at the amount of salt on the floor and wondered if the vacuum cleaner could would be able to handle all of it. She realized she'd probably be finding salt crystals for weeks.

"You go to your room, young man, and don't come out until I call you for dinner. Do you hear me?"

"Yes ma'am," Sean said. He moved to pick up the doll.

"Oh no," Maureen said. She took a big step towards the chair. "No, you don't." She snatched the doll up by one arm. The doll's head spun to one side and the mouth again made the chittering sound from earlier.

Maureen half dropped, half threw the doll down on the floor. Salt spilled out of the bag on her hip.

Sean rushed towards the fallen doll, arms outstretched. Maureen caught him with her free hand.

"No," she yelled. "He's going in the closet."

She kicked the doll so it was out of Sean's reach.

As Sean struggled in her grasp, she couldn't help but stare at the toy as if it were alive.

The doll's head thrashed from side to side, turning in rapid, jerking motions.

After just a few seconds, the thrashing motion began to stop, slowly winding down. Maureen set the bag of salt down. She then picked the doll up by the back of its shirt, holding it at arm's length for what reason she wasn't sure.

"This thing is to be put away until you have shown me you know how to behave."

"But mommy," Tommy cried, "he's my friend!"

Maureen felt a pang of guilt at the sound of her son's voice, but the tightness in her gut reminded her to be firm.

"Dammit, Sean. It's just a toy. It'll be there whenever I decide to let you play with it again."

Maureen jerked the hall closet door open. She shoved the doll onto the top shelf beside some hats and slammed the door shut. When she turned around, Sean stood in the middle of the living room, quietly beginning to cry.

"It stays there until I say so. Understood?"

"I said, 'understood.'" Maureen said. "Do you hear me, Sean?"

Sean nodded his head.

"Good. Now go to your room. I'll call you when dinner is ready."

Sean walked slowly to his room, dragging his feet across the lines of salt.

Maureen just stood there until she heard his bedroom door close. She looked at the circle and almost circle of salt, the lines now blurred and broken in places by their feet dragging through them and stepping on them.

"At least we have wooden floors," she said to herself.

Φ Φ Φ

Dinner had been a sullen affair. Sean had gone back to his usual self, no talking unless spoken to. And then it had been only mumbles and single word responses. After dinner, Maureen had watched television in the living room and Sean had sat on the floor making a show of being very dissatisfied with his old toys, every once in a while stealing an angry glance at his mother which she pretended not to notice. She was still quite upset with him, but she was determined not to behave as if anything unusual was going on. As much as she loved hearing him talk so much earlier in the day, discipline was important. She had to follow through with what she had said she would do.

Eventually she put Sean to bed. After a while, she checked in on him to see that he was sound asleep. Maureen wasn't quite ready for sleep herself, she still felt wound up after so much yelling earlier in the evening, but she thought perhaps going through the motions of preparing for bed would help.

She went to her bedroom, changed into pajamas, and headed to the bathroom to brush her teeth. It was when she was trying to put toothpaste on her toothbrush that she realized she was trembling.

She sat down on the side of the tub and held her toothbrush up in front of her face.

Yes, she was trembling, no doubt about it.

But why, she wondered. Was she upset with herself for having to discipline Sean? No, that was something that all mothers had to do from time to time. Was she that angry at him? Not really. She was sure that someday it would be a funny story to tell and embarrass Sean in front of his friends. Was it the doll?

When she asked herself that, she felt her stomach tighten more and realized it had been tight all day. Something about the doll was having an effect on her, causing her stress.

But it was so wonderful that Sean was so talkative today. She loved hearing his voice! Was she jealous of the doll? She pondered that for a moment. Toothpaste dripped onto her knee.

She quickly stood up and faced the sink, her trembling having subsided somewhat now that she was dealing with the issue. She brushed her teeth and watched herself in the mirror. Thinking back to Sean talking throughout the day and how weird she was for imagining that she was hearing real conversation, a realization came to her.

Sean was obsessed. He was too fixated on the toy.

This was something she had never experienced with Sean. The stress of it must be influencing how she perceived reality, she thought.

"Damn," she said thought, her mouth still full of toothpaste. She bent over and rinsed, spitting into the sink.

If Sean was too fixated, too consumed by the toy, she would have to find a way to wean him off of it. But so soon? After only one day? She'd take it slow and see how he reacted to less time with the toy. Surely, that way, he would simply grow out of it. Wouldn't he?

Maureen took a deep breath and looked at herself in the mirror. She imagined she could see her whole body trembling ever so slightly. She opened the mirror vanity to put away the toothpaste and toothbrush, and her hand brushed against a bottle.

Sleeping pills.

She hadn't had need to use those in a long time. The prescription was out of date, to be sure, but that didn't bother her as long as they worked. She'd probably need two of them to get to sleep tonight.

Better not, she thought.

That's when she heard the talking.

Maureen turned off the bathroom light before opening the door. She stepped out into the space between her bedroom door and Sean's bedroom door.

The talking was a little louder. She crept closer to Sean's door and put her ear up against it. It was obvious that Sean was talking. The other voice, the tinny voice was talking to. But it didn't sound like the little canned phrases she'd expect to hear from a toy. It sounded like complete, complex sentences!

Maureen gently put her hand on the doorknob and slowly turned it. The door opened without a sound and she could see that the room was still dark. And through the crack she could clearly hear what was being said.

"You know I love you, don't you, Sean," the tinny voice said.

"Yes," Sean replied. "And I love you to, Tommy."

"Good, good," the doll said. "And that is why it is so important for you to follow my instructions. You must do just as I've told you."

"I will," Sean said.

Maureen felt as if her blood was frozen. Her entire body began to shake.

Maureen's mind reeled. The doll was talking, really talking.

She shoved the bedroom door open and flicked on the bedroom light. There, in the middle of the bed, the doll sat as if staring into Sean's eyes.

Sean stared back.

When Sean turned to look at Maureen, she could have sworn the doll's head turned as well. The side of its face that drooped gave it a sinister look, as if it were an expression of anger. Not so much as a thought-out action but more because of a mother's instinct, Maureen launched herself across the room, lunging at the doll. She all but tackled it, one hand shoving Sean away from it.

The doll made that horrendous chittering noise and Maureen, now fully on the bed, flopped away from the doll and kicked at it, shoving it with her feet to get it away from her.

The doll flew across the end of the bed and slammed into the wall.

She rounded on Sean, rising to her knees on the bed, her hands-on Sean's arms.

"What were you doing," she yelled. "What were you saying to that thing? Who told you that you could play with it? I didn't!"

Sean's face was white with terror.

Maureen realized that she was shaking him. Violently. Her fear and terror being translated into the too strong grip on his tiny arms.

"Oh, Sean," she said as she released her grip. "I'm sorry. I'm so sorry." She gently put her arms around him, hugging him, trying to refrain from hugging him too tightly. Her body shuddered and she sobbed as realization of what she had been doing swept over her. Tears streamed down her face. She held him out from her. "Are you all right, Sean? Did I hurt you?"

Sean shook his head, his eyes still wide. He tried to say, 'no', but no sound came out. Only his mouth moved.

"I am so sorry," Maureen said, again. "You frightened me." She sat on the bed, her legs folded beneath her, and wiped at Sean's face as if there were tears there. "I thought I heard you talking to that thing. You know, like real talking. I'm so sorry. I don't know what's wrong with me."

"It's…it's okay, mom," Sean finally managed to say.

Maureen hugged Sean, rocking gently back and forth.

After a while, long enough for Maureen to calm herself somewhat, she drew back away from Sean.

"Now listen," she said. "It was wrong of you to take the doll out of the closet. Do you understand?"

Sean nodded.

"But I think I've over reacted and punished both of us enough for one night, so I'm just going to put it away. We'll both get some sleep and tomorrow will be a brand new day, okay?"

Sean nodded. Maureen could see that he was still in shock at being treated so harshly.

"Why don't you sleep in my room tonight. I think that would be best."

"Yes," Sean said, his head nodding.

"Alright." Maureen stood up and ushered Sean out of his room and into hers. She tucked him into her bed. "I'll be back in just a minute."

Maureen stepped lightly back into Sean's room and moved around his bed to the far side where she had kicked the doll. She felt her pulse rate increasing and could hear her heart beating in her chest.

The doll lay there on the floor. Maureen felt as if she had been expecting something else. It was clear to her now that something was not right with this doll.

She bent down and picked it up by the back of its shirt. Holding at arm's length for no reason that she could explain to herself, she moved into the hallway, through the kitchen, and out to the pottery shed. She turned on a light and looked around the pottery shed. She had never had any issues with people breaking into her property, so there were no boxes or pantries with locks on them. But still, she felt as if she needed to put the doll in something. Some space that she could close off.

At the back of the shed there were old crates she used for shipping. She found one with a loose lid and shoved the doll inside, replacing the top. She stared at the crate for a few seconds, and then looked around. She found a bag of powdered clay, fifty pounds worth, and hauled that up onto the top of the crate.

As she made her way back into the house, back through the kitchen, she could feel her hands trembling worse than before.

⊕ ⊕ ⊕

The next day began as if nothing had happened. Maureen had left Sean sleeping in her bed while she got up and fixed breakfast. Even though they were not religious, Sundays were days for not doing too much in the way of work. Still feeling not quite herself, she thought maybe pancakes and eggs with a nice glass of orange juice for Sean and a stout cup of tea for her would be a good way to start things off.

Sean eventually got out of bed and, oddly enough, was rather more talkative than usual. But most surprisingly, and to Maureen's great relief, he didn't ask about the doll.

Maureen made no mention of it either.

Around noon, Maureen was half sitting, half reclining on the couch reading a book when Sean came in. He had made a cup of tea and was trying his best to make it across the living room without spilling it.

Maureen sat up quickly, her hands reaching out to take the cup as soon as she could. "Why, thank you Sean. How sweet of you."

Sean smiled. Fixing tea was one of the things she had taught him how to do using an electric kettle. The teabags were kept on the counter, so no need to climb up on anything other than the little steps kept just for that purpose.

"You looked so relaxed, I thought I'd make it for you," he said.

"My," Maureen said, "that's a rather grown up thing for you to consider." She looked at him for a moment. "Thank you very much."

"Do you mind if I turn on the TV," Sean asked.

"I think that would be fine."

Sean took the remote and sat on the floor. He flipped through a few channels until he found something he that interested him.

Maureen sipped her tea. Too much honey, she thought. But damned if she was going to spoil a moment like this with that kind of comment. It occurred to her that her hands were no longer trembling. Life was good.

⊕ ⊕ ⊕

It was dark outside when she woke up. Her head was swimming and her vision was blurring like she needed to wipe sleep from her eyes, much like after having a deep sleep. On the floor in front of her was her tea cup and saucer as if they'd been dropped. There was a dull pounding sensation in her head.

This was a sensation she had felt before, but where— sleeping pills.

Oh my god, she thought. *I've been drugged.*

It took several long seconds for the obviousness of her next thought to formulate itself in her mind.

I've been drugged by my son.

She must have left the sleeping pills out in the bathroom. But why would Sean do something like this?

A chill settled over her.

The doll, she thought. The doll put him up to this.

Even as she thought it, she thought she must be crazy for thinking it. But just as unsure as she was at that moment about her sanity, there was one thing of which she was certain. She had to find Sean.

Maureen lurched up off the couch. Her legs felt as if they were still asleep and rather than walking in the direction she was trying to go, she staggered severely to one side. She would have fallen if she hadn't caught herself on the shelving there, pictures and ceramics crashing to floor as she did so.

"Thon," she called out. Her speech was slurred, her tongue thick. "Thon!"

Maureen managed to stay upright and make it to the kitchen door. What she saw there made no sense.

Several cabinets were left open and in the middle of the floor was the partial bag of salt. She looked back up at the open cabinets were there had been more bags of salt.

They were gone.

A movement of light caught her eye as she stood there in the darkness. Through the kitchen window she saw a bluish glow. It seemed to flicker, grow brighter, and then weaker. It was coming from the pottery shed.

Maureen stumbled, her hands moving from one door frame to the next, attempting to catch herself before she fell down. She managed to get the back-door open and then fell down the two shallow steps down to the back yard. She started crawling even as she was trying to stand, struggling to make her way to the pottery shed.

Now that she was outside it was obvious what was illuminating the interior of the shed. She'd worked with fire enough to recognize it when she saw its light.

Maureen managed to make it to the door of the pottery shed. She tried in vain to open the door, her hands not wanting to obey her brain, and on her third attempt she managed to catch the handle and press down on the latch. When she opened the door, a wave of heat hit. The sound of flames licking the air was a palpable, fluctuating drum beat thrumming against her chest. Maureen flung herself through the doorway, stumbled, and fell on her face.

When she managed to look up, what she saw made no sense. Sean was standing with his back to her, a wall of blue flame dancing in the middle of the floor., his hair flickering in the thermal updraft. Her work table had been turned on its side and shoved against the wall. The floor was covered in ceramics.

And the voices.

"Sean," she screamed.

Sean's voice was stronger than she had ever heard it before. But what he was saying made no sense to her.

"Shadashadashadasha."

"Sean," Maureen yelled again. "Get back!"

And then she heard the tinny voice of the doll. To Maureen, it sounded like Sean was trying to repeat what the doll was saying.

Maureen pushed herself to her feet, one hand grasping the edge of her work bench for support.

"Come to me my chosen one," the tinny voice said. "The Sha'Daa is upon us. It is time for you to commit yourself."

Maureen now could see that the doll sat at the center of the blue flames. Al around it, blue flames danced. It was then that she realized the flames formed a circle around the doll. She could see two concentric circles outlined in what could only be salt. There appeared to be squiggles, letters perhaps of some foreign alphabet in the space between the two circles.

Sean stepped towards the blue flames and he spoke, "I welcome you to this world. I am your willing host."

"Sean," Maureen screamed. Her hand scrabbled around the top of the work bench closing on anything she could grasp. She launched herself forward, reaching out for Sean but her drugged body was slow to respond. Her body hit the floor with a sickening sound of crunching, her arms outstretched. The heat of the blue flames licked intensely at the flesh of her hands. Sean was still out of reach.

"Yes," the tinny voice said. "You are my host. And through you I will find others. The Sha'Daa is finally here!"

"No, Sean, no," Maureen sobbed. She stretched out her hands, trying to reach Sean, but to no avail. She realized at some point that she was holding the back scratcher the stranger had given them. It caught fire and blue flames flared. She dropped it, pain searing through her now blistering hands.

A memory jumped into her thoughts. Something the salesman had said about the doll and fire and the children lost before. What was it? As insane as it was in this moment when her son needed her, part of her mind felt that it was something important that had been said. And then she remembered. Something about a surviving sibling and the 'circle must be broken'.

Circle. Broken.

The words stuck in her brain. She began to claw at the dirt floor and the lines of salt that formed the outer most circle.

"Stop her," the doll screamed. "Stop her Sean! She wants to destroy me!"

Sean paused and looked around, dazed. He took a hesitant step towards his mother.

"Yes, Sean, yes," the doll said. "You must stop her!"

Maureen kept clawing towards the outer circle, her hands gouging the dirt floor to no avail. The blue flames seemed to grow in intensity, reaching for her. She felt their heat as if it were lashing out at her. Maureen managed to pull herself closer to the flames, the heat searing her face. Part of her brain was conscious of hair burning. She shoved her hands through the flaming ring of salt. Blue flames danced across her arms.

The doll screamed. Sean screamed.

Maureen stretched.

The inner circle was beyond her grasp. She collapsed, sobbing.

And then she remembered what the strange man outside the shop had said when he gave them the scratcher. "It'll do the job."

The back scratcher.

Maureen reached to her side and grabbed the thin piece of wood, even as it burned. In one quick stroke, she thrust her arm into the blue flames and scratched through the salt that made the circle—

And her world erupted in blue flame. The flames rushed out of the circle, intense heat crashing over her.

Sean stumbled and fell, one of his hands landing on top of one of Maureen's.

The familiar touch of her son gave her a surge of energy. She grasped Sean's tiny hand in hers, and stumbled to her feet. Maureen lifted him off the dirt floor and wrapped her arms around Sean as she stumbled towards the door to the shed.

Maureen fell through the shed door, rolling on the yard outside.

Sean kicked and screamed. "No! No! No!"

His body bucked and convulsed, his head slamming into Maureen's chin, stunning her. Finally, Sean broke free.

He got up ran back towards the shed.

"Sean," Maureen screamed. She flailed out with one hand and caught him by an ankle.

Sean ripped his foot from her grasp and ran back into the blue inferno.

"Tommy," he cried. "Tommy!"

Maureen, her body wracked in pain, her hands blistered with burns, her head still spinning from drugs, struggled to roll and crawl to the shed entrance. She pulled herself up by the door frame. She saw Sean reach the doll still in the middle of the floor. There was a loud rending noise. Maureen glance dup just in time to see the roof come crashing down on her.

When Maureen came to, there was a man talking to her. His face was a blurred blob.

"It's okay," he was saying. "Just take deep breaths, okay? Can you do that for me?"

Maureen felt cool air blowing inside the mask on her face. She took a huge gulp of air.

"Easy now," the man said. "Take it easy. You've got extensive lung damage, okay? You just try to take normal breaths for me and we'll get you all taken care of."

"My son," Maureen tried to say. "Where is my son?"

"Don't try to talk, ma'am. You may hurt yourself. Just try to breath norm—"

Maureen grabbed the man's hand in hers, blisters bursting as she did so. She pulled him closer to her. His face became clearer and she could see surprise there.

"Is he all right," Maureen gasped.

"Okay," the man said as he used the ambulance gurney to push himself back up. "We'll get someone over here to give us an update. Okay? But you take it easy. You're in no condition to move."

Maureen wasn't sure but she thought she might have lost consciousness once or twice. It was impossible to know. The flashing lights, people running past her, the sound of water rushing and gushing. Then there was a person blob standing next to her. Next to him was a smaller blob.

"Ma'am," the larger blob said. "Here's your son. He's just fine. A little worse for wear, but he's just fine."

"Sean," Maureen asked. She reached out to her son and tried to pull him closer. "Sean, is that you?"

The smaller blob jerked back.

"Sean," Maureen said.

The small blob moved closer, but still avoided Maureen's touch. Even before her eyes were able to focus on the small face, she knew something was wrong.

One side of his face was drooped, like someone who had had a stroke. Or like a doll that had been set too close to a fire.

Boy Toy

"**L**ISTEN," WILLY SAID EXASPERATED, "I KNOW I don't look that old, but I can assure you I've seen every kind of toy that was ever made and I have never ever seen a toy car with matching tollbooth that was designed for a nine-year old child to play with."

The elderly white-haired man on the other side of the counter slouched in defeat, "it really wasn't for me," he said, "but my family and grandchildren. You know for years I've laughed at all the fools who built their own personal bomb shelters. But you've been watching the news. It's Armageddon out there. The world is on the verge of total collapse. If we could cross over, we'd be safe from this madness spreading around the globe. I just know it."

"I don't know what to say," Willy started.

"No no," the elderly man said, "not your fault son."

He turned from the counter and slowly walked towards the front door.

"Just an old man's quirky memories surfacing," he mumbled, shuffling away, "childhood dreams and what not. Probably that Alzheimers surfacing…"

"Yeah," Willy shouted to the retreating figure, "see you on the flip side, Milo!"

The Four Season's song, *Rag Doll*, began playing in the store's muzak system.

"Well," Johnny said, "he's not the only one with memory issues about his early years, eh Willy?"

Johnny was suddenly standing on the other side of the counter and smiling his startling smile. Willy emptied a small aluminum thermos cup and burped.

"Dexedrine and Jamaican Blue Mountain," Willy said, "care for a cup?"

Johnny waved off the offer, "thank you, no. I'm here with my wares," whereupon Johnny placed a large oversized black briefcase on the counter and slowly began to open it.

"The suspense is killing me," Willy said with a smirk.

"Ta daaaaaa," Johnny said as the case popped the rest of the way open.

Willy's eyes sparkled as he leaned forward, "sweet."

"A mint nineteen forties Superman Action figure," Johnny started, "a rare double star Pikachu Illustrator card, a Bye Focals Matchbox Car, and a nineteen sixty-nine Hot Wheels Rear Loader Beach Bomb van, and all yours for the low low price of…."

"Spill," Willy said.

"That old toy you keep in that display case," Johnny pointed to a far wall.

Willy turned to follow the salesman's finger though he knew with certainty what the object was. Framed in a shadow box made of Australian Blackwood with an unbreakable palladium-based metallic glass front was the composite boomerang that Johnny had given to him after being freed of a noose over two hundred years ago.

"Not for sale, Johnny," Willy snapped.

"Yes," Johnny smiled, "but this is a trade, Willy boy."

"No," Willy said, "there anything else you want here?"

Johnny pursed his lips, "well, push come to shove…I suppose I'd be satisfied with your Russell and Case platinum pacifier…yeah, that should do it."

"Deal," Willy said.

The phone booth began ringing incessantly and biting his lower lip Willy rushed to it.

"Hello," Willy shouted into the wall-imbedded mic.

"Hello, this is Kvaris the interface," Kvaris said in his lazy sounding drawl.

"What do you want, Kvaris?" Willy asked, "and make it snappy."

"Well, sir," Kvaris said, "the Midnight Laborers are getting fed up with the lack of variety at all three of the company stores."

"What do you mean the lack of variety?" Willy asked.

"Well, there's only five varieties of ice cream," Kvaris said, "chocolate, vanilla, strawberry, butter pecan, and maple walnut. Then there's cookies. They only sell chocolate chip, oatmeal, and Hydrox. As for soft drinks and soda pop, there's just the six-type variety of company product, aka, Whirligigs Cola, Whirligigs Ginger Ale, Whirligigs Orange Soda, Whirligigs Cream…"

"Enough," Willy yelled, "they've always loved this junk food. Why the sudden complaint?"

"Well, sir," Kvaris said in a self-conscious voice, "when the younglings had access to the internet they managed to download quite a few, um, commercials, and the Midnight Laborers are now aware of the rather large variety of soda, cookies, ice cream, and many other products in the real world. There's even speculation among the population that you've been short-changing them with the quality of food. They want a vastly improved menu, sir."

"Why those ungrateful little…," Willy started.

"And considering the rather intimidating number of orders you've been placing this past day," Kvaris said, "it would, in my humble opinion, be a reasonable compromise to start shipments of food brands other than Whirligigs generic…if you know what I mean."

"Okay," Willy said, "tell them if we can get through another day and a half of orders they have my word that they will have order access to any and all food depositories on the planet."

"Very good sir," Kvaris, "may the angels of summer bless your every endeavor."

The muzak version of *Barbie Girl* by Aqua began playing from the overhead speakers.

Saint John's Day

Richard Groller

"The more fascinated we become with the toys of this world, the more we forget that there's another world to come."

–Aiden Wilson Tozer

I AM TELLING THIS TALE OF ST. JOHN'S DAY because my friends and I were once grognards and folklorists, but that is forever changed. They say the difference between the men and the boys is the price of their toys. I guess we were still boys at heart. Old men and their toys—ours were butt blister games—Napoleonic miniatures, strategic board games, card games of every sort, but mostly old school wargames, the types you could lose yourself in for months on end. Play by mail. Or even these days with the internet, play on line. We were confirmed bachelors, former and retired military, competitive to a fault and set in our ways. Life was good.

As a group, we also came together as folklorists, who loved the stories of the Brothers Grimm, Hans Christian Anderson's fairy tales, the Arthurian and Grail Legends, Charlemagne and his Paladins, stories of Teutonic Knights and Norse mythology and Prose Edda and all things Viking. Including mead. Especially mead!

My name is Stephen Driscoll. I am the American of the gaming group, an ex-pat New Yorker and retired Army officer working as a logistician for US Army Europe in Wiesbaden. Together with Dietrich Andersson, Dieter Hornburg, Erwin Fassl, and Björn Thorsson we formed the Solstice and Equinox Gaming Club. As folklorists, we honored the traditions and history of the solstice and equinox celebrations of yore. That became our calendar for gaming. Four times a year we travel to each other's homes to gather, take a long holiday, make merry, eat well, drink better than well, discuss our many researches, and game. Into the wee hours. Sleep. Then game some more.

Dietrich Andersson was also a logistician, late of the Norwegian Navy. We met while on a NATO Exercise. Our mutual love for gaming led to a long-term friendship that lasted decades and led to the expanding circle of gaming friends. Dietrich's sister Rosewitha married a German mining engineer named Gerhardt Weiss, and with their two children, Liesl and Jochen had settled in the far North in Longyearbyen on the island of Spitsbergen on the Svalbard archipelago. Last year, Rosewitha convinced Dietrich to take a job working at the Norwegian mining company where her husband worked. Our next gaming session was to be in Svalbard—for me a new and fascinating location, so close to the Arctic Circle. Land of the Midnight Sun and the Polar Night. A desolate place where you can ski during summer from the south to the north of Spitsbergen with almost no land not covered by snow.

Desolate, yet not without romance and charm, Svalbard is home to polar bears, caribou, reindeer, walrus, Arctic fox, orcas and puffins. It is covered with glaciers, mountains and fjords, but only one road outside of settlements to a mining town. To get where you are going, it is generally by boat (in summer), aircraft or snowmobile. Longyearbyen is a settlement of roughly 2000 souls, and the only incorporated town on the archipelago. It is the seat of government, a demilitarized zone, and economic free zone. It does have some amenities, to include primary and secondary school and university, a hospital, sports and culture centers, and several museums. To support tourism, there are buses to get around town and to its several hotels. Food is expensive, but alcohol is cheap, and Svalbard Airport Longyear serves as the main gateway to the archipelago. But the veneer of civilization is but a veneer—if you venture beyond the settlements, you carry a rifle in case the wildlife, especially if any of the thousands of polar bears, get too curious.

A small fraction of the mining activity remains at Longyearbyen. Dietrich works there in port logistics while Gerhardt, an engineer, commutes weekly by bus to Sveagruva, a dormitory town co-located with the coal mine.

So, it is for us a sad coincidence, that in this potential gamer paradise, where you can lose yourself to the desolation and solitude, the Sha'Daa falls upon our holiday.

⊕ ⊕ ⊕

The first murmurings of trouble began on St. John's Eve. St. John's Day, the traditional Midsummer celebration of the solstice with revelry and bonfires that will draw the entire city, was still to come. The members of the Solstice and Equinox Gaming Club began to arrive in Longyearbyen. First to arrive were Erwin Fassl from Graz, Austria, and Björn Thorsson from Oslo, Norway. Their flights were close, so Dietrich met them at the airport and using the company van and drove them to his well-appointed rustic cabin to settle in. Next to arrive was Dieter Hornburg from Munich. That pickup did not go as expected.

Dieter Hornburg was a scholar and the true historian of the group. He had been rumored to have dabbled in the occult. In truth, he was a student of the paranormal sciences and had a morbid fascination with the Nazi Occult Bureau and the history of "Germanic Applied Research," the Allgemeine and Waffen SS esoteric philosophy concerning parapsychology, runes, Germanic mysticism, extraterrestrial beings, the Thule legends, ancestor worship, and a host of other dubious beliefs and practices. He was "aware" of the coming of the Sha'Daa, and welcomed it. He had a plan. He would create Valhalla on his little corner of Earth, and we would forever be his brothers in arms. What we in the gaming group viewed as a fun pastime, he obsessed over as a means to a very dark end.

Svalbard would be the perfect out of the way place to thrive and survive the apocalypse. Easy to control or so he thought, since he had obtained an orb of summoning that was once housed in Castle Wewelsburg, in the Library of the Schutzstaffel. A tool of the cosmic forces of the Sha'Daa.

The orb was made of a luminous green crystal, and contained an ancient occult symbol— twelve jagged arms branching off a black circle, composed of three circles and twelve rays—The Black Sun. And he knew how to use it to "immanentize the eschaton"—to use the occult vernacular.

But unbeknownst to Dieter there was another orb in play.

⊕ ⊕ ⊕

Dietrich ordered *it* from the catalog of Willy Carroll's toy shop "Whirli-gigs" in Chicago. The global economy was amazing. Excellent internet access via undersea cable and satellite. Payment by PayPal. Delivery by DHL. Very pricey gift for his 6-year old niece Liesl, but he was her only blood uncle and she was worth it. Besides, what else did he have to spend his money on besides his games. A magical musical Christmas snow globe, hand-made, artisanal, one of a kind, created personally by one of St. Nick's elves at the North Pole and guaranteed to enthrall with sight and sound. It would play and visualize every Christmas song known to man. He planned to give it to her for the Yule celebration—but *it* wouldn't wait. I guess the Yuletide spirit reigns year-round here in people's sensibilities.

There had always been a friendly rivalry between Dieter and Dietrich as gamers. When Dietrich picked him up, Dieter seemed warm, yet distracted. It was as though he was already deep in thought into a game, but the game had not yet begun. Then Dieter surprised him with an announcement, "Please take me to the Radisson Hotel. I have some things to do this visit and will need some alone time. We will game, but I have some business I must attend to first."

"Business, here in Longyearbyen?" Dietrich asked, astounded. "Why didn't you tell me ahead of time? I could perhaps have been of assistance since I now live here."

"No," Dieter replied. "It would be too much of an imposition and an inconvenience, especially when you have our other compatriots in the group to attend to while they stay with you. It is best this way."

Dietrich was hurt at the thought, and didn't buy it, but what could he say? So being polite, he let it go. It was later that evening when the nightmare began in earnest.

⊕ ⊕ ⊕

I was the last to arrive later that evening. After Dietrich dropped off Dieter at the hotel, he stopped by the DHL office to pick up a package, then went to the house to check on Björn and Erwin, and inform them that Dieter would not be available to game that evening. When he returned to start the vehicle, it was dead. The battery died for no apparent reason. Dietrich called the shuttle service for the airport, and then informed me that it was too late to get the vehicle back into working order tonight and that he had made arrangements for someone to pick me up.

"Johnny" was providing limousine services at Longyear Airport that night. He was a most peculiar man. A fellow American I thought, but somehow "off." Tall and slender with jet black hair and eyes, an angular face and a wide smile with gleaming white teeth punctuated by a shiny gold left lateral incisor. The man in black apparel seemed out of place here—I mean, did a limo driver near the Arctic Circle really need to wear a black undertaker's suit, black shoes, a long black trench coat, and sport a black fedora hat? Maybe he was a Goth? Johnny confided obliquely that his former helper, the *Krampus*, had gone rogue and would have to be dealt with to deter him from permanently giving Svalbard a lump of coal and the switch. Then he let out a cackle that raised the hair on my skin.

I thought he was nuts. He had a Santa Claus suit on the seat beside him—the full Monty, with red and white fur, a broad belt and black leather boots. I am portly and sport a white beard, so I was mildly amused, since I had done the role before for friends. Then he said the suit was for me and that I would be needing it if I intended to win the game. I was tempted to get out and walk, but it was cold, dark and starting to snow, so I thought better of it.

"What game?" I asked.

He smiled, ignored the question and said. "I'll trade you for it."

"What could I possibly have to trade for that?" I replied.

Without missing a beat, he replied. "You seem the type of gamer that might have a set of poker dice in his pocket."

"What are you, psychic?" I exclaimed. I had an old set of poker dice in a thin plastic sleeve I carried with me everywhere for the last twenty years, that often came in handy in bars when the hour was late and the company needed to be livened up. "I dunno, I've had these babies a long time. They are pretty lucky. I'd hate to give them up."

Johnny replied, "How about if I sweeten the deal. Your buddy Dietrich has a gift for his niece that is missing a key. I happen to have the very key she needs. Shall I throw it in?"

I thought to myself, how the hell would this guy know that? But then, with Dietrich moving to this new locale and it being a small community, who knows? Maybe everybody knows everybody's business!

"Sure, anything to make Dietrich's niece happy," was my reply. I figured I would find out which game I needed the suit for soon enough.

$$\phi \quad \phi \quad \phi$$

After Dietrich went home, he started to feel ill. Luckily his sister and his niece and nephew were already there, visiting with their "uncles" and already playing board games that were "gateway drugs" to more complicated and intricate strategy games that they would be exposed to as soon as they were of age.

He decided to lie down and take a quick cat nap while he had the time and left his cronies to her tender care. He immediately began having a nightmare—vivid images that he recognized as Nordic folkloric archetypes. The images flooded into his somnambulant mind and told him of terrors to come. In his mind, he knew he must try to stop them. He was mesmerized—his body rigid, it felt like his spirit was trying to leave his body. He tried to will himself awake, but couldn't. The archetypal figures were so real, and as the images became clearer, he realized it was a premonition of things to come. *Wilde Jagd*—The Wild Hunt.

Folklorists across the European continent have many versions of the myth of spectral huntsmen passing in wild pursuit. The hunters may be the dead, elves, fairies, or gods. The leader of the hunt can be a legendary or historical figure like Odin, Charlemagne or Satan, or a nameless lost soul. It was believed that witnessing the Wild Hunt presaged great catastrophe such as war, plague, famine or more personally, the imminent death of the witness. Common folk who are awake during an encounter with the Wild Hunt might be abducted by the fae or dragged to the underworld. A sleeping mortal's spirit could be pulled from its body to join the hunt.

In the vision, someone was summoning the participants of the hunt to do their bidding—that someone was Dieter! Suddenly a word crystallized in his thoughts—*Sha'Daa*. What is the *Sha'Daa*? I would say perhaps an incarnation of Ragnorak, but it will take the form of an assault by archetypes of the North upon the citizens of Longyearbyen, archetypes chosen by Dieter to fulfill his dark predilections!

When Johnny and I arrived at Dietrich's house, I was tired and disoriented. The sun is visible for a full 24 hours a day on the summer solstice here. It was night my body told me, but yet not night. And I wasn't the only one disoriented.

As we pulled up outside, Dietrich arose from his bed, sleepwalking. Not quite free of the vision, he exited the front door of his house and lumbered towards the vehicle. Johnny stood before him, and Dietrich shouted "Loki, what mischief are you up to here?"

Johnny, nonplussed, replied "Special Delivery!" winked, hopped back into the limousine and drove off. Dietrich's knees buckled as a wave of dizziness overtook him as he returned to full wakefulness. I bent down to help him up, and Dietrich asked in a moment of clarity, "Did he give you anything?"

I said, "Why yes—a key."

Once he had regained his legs under him, we grabbed my things and went inside. I asked Dietrich why he called Johnny "Loki." He did not know. He just said it felt right to call him that—a subliminal affirmation of a fact that he knew, but he did not know why he knew it.

By now everyone was awake. I greeted my fellow grognards and Dietrich's extended family, and wondered to myself if we were about to find ourselves a part of some family drama.

I handed Dietrich the key. He said, "What is this to?"

I replied, "I don't know. It is something that your niece needs."

Dietrich's face went white. I followed him as he quietly went to the back bedroom with the package that he had picked up from DHL and closed the door. He slit the wrapping tape and opened the flaps on the small cardboard box. The whole package was about a cubic foot. Inside was a schneekugel—a snow globe, but it was no ordinary snow globe. It was encased in a rather compact and solidly built bell jar with a wooden base. The bell jar acted as a schusterkugel, a liquid filled container used to focus light since medieval times. Within the wooden base was the music box. It had 3 keyholes in it, and a place for 3 keys, but there were only 2 keys present—one copper, one silver. The key I handed Dietrich was gold.

A "Whirligigs" business card was also in the box. Calligraphed on the back of the card were the words: *For the Christmas song to start, a wish must come from the purest heart.* Knowing that Liesl was close by, he quickly closed it back up and hid it in a closet. Then he sent his sister and her children home saying he would call for them later.

Dietrich addressed the group: "I have something to tell you that will be difficult to believe." His tone was solemn and measured—not at all like his normal jovial self. "All our lives will depend upon you believing what I tell you. There is a game that is played once every 10,000 years, and it is called Sha'Daa. It is a game of life and death for the entire human race. I have had a revelation about it—a vision. In it, I saw Dieter. Unfortunately, we are on opposite sides in this game. I believe he is too involved with the wrong side to be swayed. We must convince Dieter that the "sporting" thing to do is to play the game out as we always done. Otherwise, every life on Spitsbergen will be at risk of a fate too terrible to imagine."

I was incredulous. I thought to myself that Dietrich must be having some sort of stress reaction adjusting to the change in daylight since he moved North—a bad case of seasonal affective disorder. I did not want to upset him, so I just nodded and kept my doubts to myself, too tired to argue. "Whatever you say Dietrich," was my reply, "Just show me to where I am bunking tonight!"

⊕ ⊕ ⊕

Dieter arrived at the house about an hour after he received the call from Dietrich that the gaming group had a proposition for him with respect to the Sha'Daa. He was pleasantly surprised that any of them had knowledge of the event. Being friends for years, he was willing to give them the benefit of the doubt and hear them out.

Dietrich eyed him warily as he let him in. The rest of us exchanged greetings and hugs of welcome. Then we waited for Dieter to speak. I (and I believed the others too) expected that Dieter would repudiate the claims of Dietrich. He didn't. He confirmed them and explained that he was *glad* that the Sha'Daa had been revealed to the group, since we were all part of his plan all along. His original intent was to keep it a surprise, and just present *the new world* to them as a fait accompli.

Dieter believed that mankind was too weak to survive the event alone, and that positioning himself with the dark forces was our "best option" for survival. Fore knowledge through his occult studies of the Nazis led him to a plan to be the channel for the energies for this small corner of the world as the door opened to "the other side." He would control the dark forces here, channel them, and control the outcome, so his friends might survive, to the detriment of everyone else. To him it was a fair exchange—a rational choice—he would lead and we would follow, so that we could remain together while the world devolved into chaos and terror.

The choice of the location came about from the happy coincidence of Dietrich moving to Spitsbergen—the place where the Svalbard Global Seed Vault resides. The Seed Vault is a highly secure seed bank cut inside a sandstone mountain. It was created to preserve a wide variety of plant seeds as duplicate copies of seeds held in gene banks worldwide, as insurance against the loss of seeds in other gene banks during large-scale regional or global crises. After the Sha'Daa events are over, the world will need to be stabilized. Control of the seed store would insure a power base that would be priceless as the coming apocalypse unfolded.

Dietrich in his vision had perceived Dieter's grand strategy and also was given a glimpse of a counter-strategy to undo it. Dieter would evoke the Wild Hunt and include the specific spirits he needed to control the populace in perpetuity. The spirits would be those of long dead Vikings and mythical creatures they believed in. They would conquer like the Vikings of old—kill the men who are willing to fight and enslave the rest, along with the women and children, and take the spoils to be the start of their new kingdom in the North. He would call forth the legendary Viking Leader Ragnar Lothbrok and his sons and to slaughter the men and enforce the new order; *Fossegrim* to control the women to his will; the *Krampus* to control the children; *dökkálfar* or dark elves to control Seed Bank.

Dietrich then challenged Dieter, "This is nothing if not the chance for the highest stakes *Krieg Spiel* we will ever play. Will you agree to a competition? We will come with you as you make your moves. If we can dispel what you summon we win. If we cannot, you win. If you win, we will willingly be your companions in the new world order of the Sha'Daa. If we win, you will allow the folks of Spitsbergen to live in peace and will not make any attempts to assist the dark forces of the Sha'Daa. Are the terms amenable?"

Dieter acquiesced to the gaming group. "I agree to your terms. You seem to think you understand my motivations, but just so you know what you are up against, and to dispel any doubts among you that this game is in fact real, let me show you something. Please step outside." We filed outside, and Dieter pulled a glowing green orb from within his coat. He held it aloft and the green light that shone from it was mirrored in the sky. Dieter was bathed in a green aura, and transfigured into something larger than life, an avatar of great power. The sky darkened and a green aurora borealis formed in the sky. The waves cascaded and formed the symbol in the sky from within the orb—a Black Sun! The power suddenly went out to the archipelago and with it, communications to the outside world. Spitsbergen was more alone than it has been in a long time. "I will take my leave now. If you still want to play, meet me in town in two hours by the St. John's Day bonfire and the competition will commence. Or not. Either way, the Sha'Daa will occur."

⊕ ⊕ ⊕

Once inside, the group was visibly shaken. They checked the radios—the wireless crackled, the satcom links were silent. Dietrich silently mused—two orbs, one of light, one of darkness. In terms of magickal folklore invoking and evoking—one prays and one summons. For a hymn is a sung prayer.

Dietrich announced, "The game is afoot—we are now all players for good or ill."

Dietrich turned to me and bade me to put on the Santa suit, while he went into the closet to wrap presents for Liesl and Jochen. We then walked over as a group to his sister's house.

"Yule is coming early this year!" he announced when we arrived. "We will hereby celebrate the Winter Solstice on the Summer Solstice!"

I did my best St. Nick belly laugh and handed Jochen the first gift. "Your uncle tells me you will be 13 this year, so this should be an appropriate gift for a young man so close to the North. Pole." The gift was a .22 long rifle. Dietrich chimed in, "It was my father's gun—good for hunting small game, and since you are already a good fisherman, I figure this would be a good family heirloom to pass down that will help you learn new skills." Jochen hugged his uncle with an ear to ear grin and went off to show the others his new prize.

My next belly laugh was for Liesl. I handed her the box with the toy from Whirligigs. "Your uncle's gift has a strange history. It was built by my elves here at the North Pole, yet he found it overseas—all the way in America." Liesl, very wise for her 6 years, said, "But America isn't that far away if you fly there!" I belly laughed again and said, "Very true, even if these had to come by reindeer!" She opened the box and saw the encased snow globe. Within the globe was a traditional alpine village with a Christkindlmarkt. She shook it, and the snow swirled around the village.

"Very pretty," she said. "What else does it do?"

Dietrich knelt down and said, "It is also a music box. What is your favorite Christmas song? Think really hard about it."

Liesl says, that's easy—Its "Kling, Glöckchen, Kling!"

The globe darkened momentarily, then began to brighten and swirl, and the sound of "Kling, Glöckchen, Kling" began to chime, and the globe showed an image which was magnified by the bell jar to show little golden bells ringing. It was magical. How did it know what to play? Was it voice activated?

Dietrich was pleased that it performed as advertised, and we all sang along:

> Kling, Glöckchen, klingelingeling, kling, Glöckchen, kling
> Kling, Glöckchen, klingelingeling, kling, Glöckchen, kling
> Laßt mich ein, ihr Kinder,
> ist so kalt der Winter,
> öffnet mir die Türen,
> lasst mich nicht erfrieren!
> Kling, Glöckchen, klingelingeling, kling, Glöckchen, kling!

Dietrich then told Liesl that we were going to play a game with Uncle Dieter and that she needed to be really attentive and do exactly what he told her to do if we wanted to win. And the game involved her wonderful new toy! Liesl gave Dietrich a big hug, and a smile and couldn't wait to get started.

⊕　⊕　⊕

The bonfire for the Midsummer celebration lit up the beach not far from the town center. Though there was no power in town, that did not stop the town folks from coming out and enjoying the celebration. Folks danced to guitars and flutes and drums. All were sure the power outage would pass soon and things would go back to normal—probably a strong solar flare. But the odd aurora and the strange shape in the sky was pretty out of the ordinary.

The Solstice and Equinox Gaming Club, along with Dietrich's sister and children, all turned out for the celebration, including Dieter. For his first summoning, Dieter began with a mild display of power, a being of folklore, the *Fossegrim*. The *Fossegrim* was a nøkk—a male water spirit who played enchanted songs on the violin, not unlike the siren song of a mermaid. The enthralled women would, according to legend, either be lead to death by drowning or fall in love with them and do their bidding. Dieter's plan was the latter.

He removed the green orb from his coat, which flared as he spoke a few words in Old Norse, and suddenly, a very handsome naked man emerged from the shoreline, wearing only a sly smile, but carrying an ancient violin. He walked towards the crowd around the bonfire and began to fiddle—an uproarious sight that caught the attention of all within earshot and made the women dance and sway in unison. The folks pointed and laughed at the mad man who played so enchantingly, and even Rosewitha began to dance. But then as he started to walk down the beach away from the bonfire, the women all began to follow him, including Rosewitha. The men who escorted the women protested, but the women did not respond. They danced on, ignoring the entreaties of their boyfriends and spouses. It was as if the women could not hear them. If there was any doubt about Dieter's power to summon and control, it was now gone. Liesl asked "Where is Mommy going?"

Dietrich turned to Liesl and said, "The game has begun. We must get your mother to turn around. Use the magical music box to concentrate on the specific verse of the Christmas song "Stille Nacht" we talked about. Will you do that?"

Liesl, shook the globe, then turned the copper key one turn and concentrated on the words:

Silent Night
Holy Night
All is calm
All is bright
Round yon virgin
Mother and child
Holy infant so tender and mild
Sleep in heavenly peace
Sleep in heavenly peace.

The globe clouded, and when the image inside emerged, it was that of the Holy manger containing the sleeping Christ child, with snow quietly falling, serene and silent. The music from the violin suddenly could not be heard. As hard as he fiddled, no sound emerged. The women swooned into a deep sleep, oblivious to any sounds around them. The nøkk enraged, threw the violin into the sea, ran breakneck to the shoreline, and dove in head first in frustration. He disappeared into the breakers and was not seen again. The women began to waken, quite refreshed, after the *Fossegrim* returned to the sea. Rosewitha gave her daughter a hug of approval, but you could tell by the look in her eyes, that she was worried, and recognized there were powers at work here beyond the grasp of humankind.

Dieter was not amused. "Well played, my friends, but let's see how you handle this." This time, the target was the children. He summoned the *Krampus*, the cloven hooved, long tongued, horned god avatar that in some traditions, accompanies St. Nicholas to give lumps of coal and whippings with a birch switch to the "bad" children. He was black as night, and carried a sack on his back, to carry away the evil children to Hell. The bonfire suddenly flared and black smoke billowed from it. He appeared menacingly from a cloud of smoke. He wore chains that he rattled to chilling effect. The children attending the festival were instantly full of dread and clutched their parents. The *Krampus* pulled the sack from his back, brandishing it, and saying in a come-hither voice from the grave, "Who will be the first to come with me?"

Liesl saw the effect on the other children, and immediately said, "I am not afraid of him—I know I am good—I already have my Christmas present!" Dietrich nodded and she once again shook the snow globe. This time she turned the silver key a single turn, and concentrated on this verse from O Komm, O Komm, Emmanuel that she had discussed with Uncle Dietrich:

> Draw nigh, O Jesse's Rod, draw nigh,
> To free us from the enemy;
> From Hell's infernal pit to save,
> And give us victory o'er the grave.
> Rejoice! rejoice! Emmanuel
> Shall be born, for thee, O Israel!

The image that formed this time was like a picture out of the Book of Revelations. Angelic choirs on a field of clouds, welcoming new souls to heaven, while looking down into the faces of despair, as lost souls in the fiery pit of Hell stared longingly heavenward.

The *Krampus* held the bag in his left hand, and with his right reached for a frightened boy who was there but separated from his parents. The bag suddenly took on a life of its own. A fiery light shone inside it—like the deep embers within a fireplace or perhaps the embers of Hell itself—and the bag wrested itself from his hand and engulfed the *Krampus*. Then it righted itself and flew into the center of the bonfire, which exploded, sending burning embers into the sky, some scattering into the crowd. At this, the citizens of Longyearbyen began to realize that the world around them was no longer following natural laws. Families with children decided the festival was no longer safe, began to head home. Several men came to us to ask what was happening, since they saw that we seemed to be calm in the face of these events. As a group we said, "Go home—you will not be safe otherwise—this is not your fight." They did not listen. Undaunted, it was obvious that whatever was happening, they would not shy away from a fight. Some went to their cars and armed themselves with rifles.

Dieter was clearly disturbed, "I have underestimated you—it will not happen again. You will now see the full fury of the *Wilde Jagd*!" He strode to the beach and turned to face the sea. Again, he intoned in Old Norse. This time the orb's light was diffused, almost cloudy and a dense green fog arose from the sea. From out of the fog, there appeared three Viking long ships, manned by spectral Vikings in full battle gear!

He then turned his back to the sea, and pointed at the mountain side over a mile distant, and intoned again. A stream of green fire arced from the orb and bathed a point on the side of the mountain. The mountain side melted where the green fire splashed, and suddenly an opening appeared from where it caved. From within that cave emerged a swarm of creatures, dark elves out of fantasy, but *real* and bent on a purpose, to take and hold the Seed Bank.

The spectral Vikings jumped into the surf and began to stride ashore, battle axes at the ready. They were a horrific sight. The armor and weapons were substantial, while the spirits that motivated them were more ethereal. One of the men with a high-power rifle he carried in case of bear attacks levied it at a Viking ghost and fired. The round punched through the armor but passed through the spirit with no visible effect. The Viking laughed, responded with a francisca. The throwing ax was solid and embedded in the poor soul's head. At first blood, the Viking host let out a blood curdling battle cry and surged forward.

Dietrich told Liesl to concentrate on the Christmas song for the Vikings first. She shook the globe, twisted the gold key, and concentrated on the Christmas song "O Du Fröhliche", specifically the verse:

> O you joyful, O you blessed,
> Grace-bringing Christmas time!
> Heavenly armies rejoicing to honor you:
> Rejoice, rejoice, O Christendom!

The snow globe formed an image of St. Michael leading the heavenly host and projected it into the sky. The image became real and a legion of angels appeared, not unlike Valkyries, and swept in on the thin strand between the Vikings with their backs to the sea, and the citizens of Longyearbyen. The angels pressed forward, and every Viking touched exploded in a ball of green light, dissolving into atoms. Archangels with spears stabbed at the long ships, and they were engulfed in green fire.

Dieter was furious and shrieked, "This cannot be!" and strode towards Liesl. Björn and Erwin rushed to stand between him and the child. Dietrich told Liesl to not be afraid, and implored her to quickly wish for the last Christmas song we discussed, and then he also turned to face Dietrich.

Dieter once again emanated power, this time like an angry avatar. He stretched out his hand and flicked his wrist, and Erwin went flying twenty feet away. He did the same to Björn.

Liesl, shook the globe, turned both the copper and the silver key, and thought of the song "Es Ist Ein Ros Entsprungen." The verse she concentrated on was:

> The floweret, so small
> That smells so sweet to us
> With its clear light
> Dispels the darkness.
> True man and true God!

He helps us from all trouble,
Saves us from sin and death.

The globe became murky, and then there emerged a bright piercing white light. Above the mountain the sky opened like a cloud moving to reveal the sun, and an intense bright light shined down on the dark elves. The light dispelled the darkness that was within the elves, like a searing fire, and they simply dematerialized.

Dieter growled, "You have won fair and square. Unfortunately, the Sha'Daa is really not a game. It is life and death. And I cannot abide such defeat!" He stretched his arm out toward Dietrich, made a fist, and arced it violently upward. Dietrich was lifted off the ground and hurled high into the air.

I grabbed the globe from the now screaming child, turned all 3 keys and with an American carol from Longfellow in mind invoked this verse from "I Heard the Bells on Christmas Day:"

Then pealed the bells more loud and deep:
"God is not dead, nor doth He sleep;
The Wrong shall fail,
The Right prevail,
With peace on earth, good-will to men."

No image formed. The bell jar shattered with a sound like a giant bell, and the wooden base exploded, sending glass shards and wood splinters across my body, and knocking me backwards. The green orb imploded, turning Dieter to dust and sucking him into the void—a miniature black hole, which blazed for a moment, them winked out of existence. The snow globe remained, unbroken, at my feet. But Dietrich's crumpled body was lifeless on the shoreline.

⊕ ⊕ ⊕

Some folklorists maintain that Santa Claus and Odin are two sides of the same coin, that a procession through the sky led by eight reindeer at Midwinter and the ghostly Wild Hunt are corollaries to the duality of nature. Life and Death. Good and Evil. Light and Darkness.

So, I conclude my St. John's Day tale with the observation that it is true that all things pass into mystery. For the gaming group is now gone, and the folklore and stories that were once the stuff of myth are in fact, all too real, but in time, will once again become legend. And the bitter truth has not set us free.

Throw Your Toys Out

THE MAIN BODY WAS SOLID PLATINUM WITH a solid-gold stock and fore end, and was a perfect replica of a Remington M11 shotgun at five inches in length. A tiny, ruby jewel served as the site-bead atop the barrel (a part that the original never had).

It was February of 1992 in Greenwich Village and Whirligigs was having a slow year. So, when the diminutive man walked into the nearly empty store, Willy greeted him with a large smile.

"The floor is yours, good sir," Willy said. "Please take your time viewing our wares and just give us a shout if you have any questions."

The young man spotted the rifle ornament almost immediately in the glass-fronted display case that also formed the main counter for the cash register. The potential customer had long, dirty-blonde hair and wore a flannel shirt and ripped blue jeans. His pale blue eyes fastened on the item.

Willy noticed that all five of his employees had gathered feet behind him, whispering frantically with surprised looks.

"Excuse me, sir," Willy said. He turned to confront his employees. "Break time isn't for another hour, folks,"

"Don't you know who that is?" Debbie, a gaunt, brunette New York University freshman whispered fiercely, "his band was on Saturday Night Live last month. He's the lead singer/songwriter!"

"What band?" Willy asked.

"Nirvana, dude," Chris, a slacker in his late twenties spit out, "this guy's the savior of the current music scene."

"Hey," the budding rock star yelled out plaintively, "I like this."

"Back to work, people," Willy said before returning to the cash register.

The young man pointed to the shotgun ornament in the display case.

"Tell me about that," he said, "I'm getting some freaky vibes off of it."

Willy reached into the display, grabbed the pendant, and placed it before the customer. The long black leather lanyard showed it was meant to be worn as pendant.

"That's not paint," Willy said slyly, "but pure solid platinum and gold, with a small ruby chip at the end of the barrel. I received this from a craftsman/ sculptor in Shropshire, England, shortly before he died: a man purported to be the tail end of a lineage that stretches directly from Richard Munslow, the last of the sin-eaters."

The young man picked up the item. His pupils dilated.

"What's a sin-eater?" he asked.

"Oh," Willy said, "it's an old legend. A sin-eater was a person who consumed a ritual meal in order to magically take on the sins of a person or household. The food was believed to absorb the sins of a recently deceased person, thus absolving the soul of the person. Therefore sin-eaters were believed to carry the sins of all folks whose sins they had eaten."

"Weird, dude," the young man said.

"Quite," Willy smiled, "the craftsman told me he couldn't believe his ancestor, or any human being, could hold all those sins in his heart and mind without going crazy, and on some odd bit of inspiration, created this little talisman in a short fit of near madness while chanting various Latin incantations that sprang from memories of his Catholic childhood in Ireland. He actually believed he had crafted something that could absorb sins…a battery for evil, as it were."

"I'll take it," the young man said.

"It's a five-figure deal, sir," Willy said, "and I'm not talking the low end."

The young man laid a huge roll of bills on the counter.

"Take what you need," he said.

Months later, on Debbie's prompting, Willy watched Nirvana at the Video Music Awards. At one point, near the end of the song 'Lithium,' the group seemed to lose control of their senses, and the lead singer began stumbling around, toppling speakers, and even leaping upon the drums and cymbals. To the crowd and the audience around the world, it no doubt looked like the rock star was acting out, but to Willy's keen eyes he could see that the lead singer was frantically looking for something he had misplaced, albeit for a short amount of time, the shotgun amulet.

It then came as no great surprise to Willy when on April fifth, nineteen ninety-four it was announced that Kurt Cobain, lead singer/songwriter of Nirvana, had committed suicide by shotgun.

Later that same day, Willy found himself listening to a live rendition of 'Smells Like Teen Spirit' over the radio, and for a few minutes the mild cloud of indifference that had suffused Willy's soul for over two hundred years seemed to dissipate. And in that short stretch of spiritual awakening, Willy's sense of empathy overwhelmed him, and he saw with a crystalline clarity, the doom that had overtaken Cobain.

For two years the shotgun talisman had absorbed the demons that wished to ravage Kurt's soul. But it could never be removed for any length of time, such was the curse's strength, for the wild lifestyle that Cobain and his band and his wife lived, it was too easy for the talisman to eventually be misplaced, lost, or stolen. When it was gone, the demons quickly found their home in Cobain himself.

Suicide was the rock star's only escape.

The song finished, and the clarity that had briefly imbued Willy was replaced with that spiritual fugue that had inundated his thoughts for centuries…still, off and on throughout his following years, Willy would find himself occasionally hearing Nirvana's most popular songs, and in those moments a pain would take his chest, and inexplicable tears filled his eyes.

Mr. Hopps

Cecilia Star Kachina, Magda Jones, and William Joseph
Roberts

"Toys are children's words and play is their language."

–Garry L. Landret

MY GRITTY EYES OPENED AT THE SOUND of heavy footsteps on the creaky wooden floors downstairs. *Papa is home!* I ripped the covers off and hit the cold floor at a run. I ran downstairs and leapt into his arms. As he put me down, he smiled from ear to ear and reached into his bag. *Yay! This meant he got me something good from his recent adventure. My Papa gets me something every time, sometimes sweets or a token.* Papa pulled out something of the size of a stuffed bear and held it behind his back.

"Papa! Why must you hide it from me?" I asked.

He chuckled as I chased it around him several times until I finally caught it.

"Oh! I love it!" I shouted.

I squeezed it tight, and then hugged Papa again. He brought back the best gift so far. It was a stuffed frog with round gold spectacles, a wide smile and a black bow tie. He showed me a small wooden frog that he had found for Momma in a place called Oz Park.

"Mr. Hopps," I said.

His name just popped into my head and had a nice sound to it. I ran upstairs to go play with my new friend. I replaced the baby doll at my play table with Mr. Hopps. He looked like he would enjoy a good tea party.

"Want some tea Mr. Hopps?" I asked as I held up a tea cup with nothing in it.

"No child I do not want your tea."

"Who was that?" I asked.

The voice was soft and kind of soothing, but it startled me at the same time.

"Was that you Mr. Hopps?" I carefully asked the stuffed frog.

"Yes dear. I can talk, but only to you," he replied.

"But your mouth doesn't move? How do you do it?"

"I am special," he explained, "and I can only talk to special people. You are one of those people."

"Oh...okay cool," I said.

I turned and went back downstairs. I felt kind of confused and guilty at the same time. I wondered where Papa had gotten this unusual frog. I found him in the kitchen talking to Momma. He turned toward me as I walked in.

"Papa, where did you get Mr. Hopps?" I asked as I sat down slowly at the kitchen table.

"Well while I was on this last adventure I went into this store that had a peculiar name," Papa said as his face went blank, "Whirligigs was the name of the store. It had old timey toys, brand new toys, stuffed toys, dress up costumes, and many other things, but they all seemed too similar. On a shelf in the back of the store, I saw Mr. Hopps. This frog seemed to call out to me. It was the only one of its kind so I got it immediately. Then as I was walking out of the store, this odd man dressed in all black came up to me."

Papa's face suddenly grew serious as he continued, "and he kept laughing like a nut. I'm pretty sure he was an escapee from the mental hospital in that area. He told me his name was Johnny. He tried to trade the frog that I had gotten for you, but I just knew this was the thing to bring back to you."

Papa rubbed his lower chin for a moment, "and I have to say this Johnny fellow had gold and riches like I'd never seen before. Now he had to have stolen them. No one carries valuables like that on the street in their jacket.

All of the things were great but would never have forgiven myself if I had traded this frog for something so pure...and probably stolen."

Papa bit his lower lip then said, "and then he said the strangest thing when I left him behind. It was almost a whisper, but, it seemed to echo..."

"What was that, Papa?" I asked.

"He said," Papa spoke, "*just remember, fire cleanses all evils, and closes all doors....* So strange." Then Papa's expression returned to normal.

"Okay, thank you Papa," I had this odd feeling that I should not tell them that Mr. Hopps could talk. I got up and kissed his cheek and went back upstairs.

"Okay Mr. Hopps, we are going to play outside," I said.

I grabbed him and went to the field behind my house.

"How old are you child?" Mr. Hopps asked while I sat him down on the ground beside the dirt patch that I play in.

"Eight," I blankly stated, while moving my finger in the dirt writing my full name. ANNA MARIE LORSO, I wrote in the dirt.

"Ah, Anna. That is your name," Mr. Hopps said as if I had just answered his next question.

"I go by Anna Marie actually," I stated matter of factly. There was a silence that lingered for a few moments as I gently ran my fingers through the soft dirt.

"I stand corrected," he soothed, "I do not wish to offend."

"It's alright Mr. Hopps, you didn't know," I said.

I loved my new friend. *Papa always knows what to get me to keep me happy.*

"Hey Anna Marie, do you see that kitten over there by the shed?" Mr. Hopps said.

I turned and looked towards the shed.

"Oh, you mean Ginger? That's the neighbor's kitten. Why do you ask?" I asked.

I watched as Ginger chased a field mouse, played with it and pinned it the ground.

"Do you see what it is doing to that mouse? It is torturing it. I want you to hurt the kitten like it hurts the mouse," Mr. Hopps said.

His voice was so soft in my head and I felt angry at Ginger for being so mean. As I walked towards the kitten, he killed the mouse with one swipe of his claws.

"Kill it dear child," spurred Mr. Hopps.

I swept down and grabbed Ginger by his tail. The startled kitten screeched a horrible sound of pain. It was getting on my nerves with its racket. I reached around the other side of the kitten's head and in a single movement, snapped its head towards me. The kitten's neck broke with a single snap. Its body went limp and was now silent, never to make its racket again.

"Good job Anna Marie, you avenged the death of the mouse," Mr. Hopps said.

His voice sounded very pleased with me. I tossed the kitten's dead body into the brush beside the shed and made it look like it fell out of the old oak tree. I went back to the soft dirt and started drawing a picture of the mouse with a large piece of Swiss cheese. *That would make the poor mouse feel better.*

"Hey, are there any big events happening soon in town?" Mr. Hopps sounded hopeful.

"Yes! Ms. Magdu and Mr. Lazar are getting married!" I shouted, "There will be a big celebration and the entire town will be there. Everyone will be bringing food and gifts for them. I can't wait for the day I marry the love of my life."

I gazed at the bright sky, day dreaming of the big white dress, the flowers, and the people dancing and laughing at my wedding. Mr. Hopps was silent for a few moments.

"When will this be?" He purred.

"Tomorrow," I answered, "They picked tomorrow because it is the day they fell in love. They spent the entire night staring at the stars during last year's Midsummer festival. The next morning, they knew they were meant for each other. The church doesn't have any outside lights. And since it is one of the longest days of the year, we get more time to celebrate. I get to wear my green and blue dress and my black shoes with the heels."

I twirled around like I was on the dance floor at the wedding.

"Is your mother going to cook for the delightful event?" Mr. Hopps asked.

He sounded very interested in the event. Maybe I should take him with me.

"Yes, she will be cooking her famous Mexican chicken casserole," I said, "it has chicken, rice, black beans and tomatoes. Everyone loves it."

My mouth was watering just thinking about it.

"Mmmm that sounds good," Mr. Hopps replied, "but I bet we could make it even better. Are there some plants they use for cooking near here?"

I thought for a moment.

"I don't know about for cooking," I said, "but the woman next door has a garden. She is not really a nice lady though. She got mad the last time I went over there to see how much her plants had grown. Momma told me to stay away from her. All the kids at school say that she's a witch. No one dares to trick or treat her house. She might toss us in the oven or cook us in her witch's cauldron."

"Well do you want to help your Mother's food taste even better than it does now?" Mr. Hopps asked.

He sounded quite excited when he asked this question.

"We could make it a surprise."

"Oh yes!" I said, "She would love that so much."

I was now excited and picked the stuffed frog up.

"Okay, go to the neighbor lady's yard and I am going to help you get what you need to put in it," Mr. Hopps said.

I ran down the road and opened the neighbor's backyard gate. I crouched down so that she would not be able to see me from her window, and crawled to her garden of weird plants. All of them had wooden sticks stabbed into the ground with names tags in front of each row. I read them out loud to Mr. Hopps, "Basil, Borage, Chervil, Dill, Fennel, Hemlock, Tarragon Oleander."

"Did you say Hemlock and Oleander dear child?" He inquired.

He seemed very intrigued.

"Yes, I did," I said, "do you want me to get those?"

I reached for the plant that was labeled with the name Hemlock. Then the one labeled Oleander

"Yes, those will make your Mother's food taste extra special," Mr. Hopps said.

I quickly stuffed handfuls of each plant into my pockets and took off at a run back to my house. I opened the door and went quietly into the kitchen to see if Momma was in there. Nope. She must be napping. She had five pans of the tasteful meal sitting on the counter. None of them have been baked yet. Perfect.

"Okay, Anna Marie," Mr. Hopps said, "all you have to do is crunch it in your hands and rip the plants into tiny shreds."

I started doing what he had told me to do and an odd smell came from the crushed plants. After I was done with that part, I mixed it into the casseroles. Searching through Momma's cookbook, I found the recipe and turned the oven on to the temperature it listed. When it was hot, I put all five pans into the large oven, two on top and three on bottom, to bake. I even remembered to set the timer to remind me when to take them back out. Sometimes, Momma forgets. I went up to my room to play with my toys until the timer went off.

Momma woke up with the buzz of the timer and saw how much of a help I was. She was worried at first, but was pleased that I had done it all just as the recipe called for. She took the hot heavy pans out. She and Papa were so proud that I had helped with casseroles; they gave me ice cream as a treat for helping without being asked to.

✛ ✛ ✛

The next day Momma came to wake me up and helped me put on my blue and green dress and black shoes with the heels. While Momma was fixing my hair, I wondered if I could take my new friend to the wedding.

"Momma, can I bring Mr. Hopps with me today," I pleaded.

I gave her my sweetest smile and made my eyes big. She always falls for that look.

"Yes, you can," Mama said, "but you have to be good today, okay?"

She looked me in the eyes, waiting for me to answer.

"Oh! Yes Momma," I said, "I will be very good."

I hugged her neck and jumped down from her lap. When we were finished dressing, Papa put the casserole dishes and our gift for the bride and groom in my red wagon. He pulled the wagon while we all, including Mr. Hopps, walked hand in hand down to the Catholic Church.

When we arrived at the church, Momma arranged our food on one of the tables. Papa and I found a seat. We were lucky. The building was so full that some people had to stand. The couple was so beautiful, the flowers smelled sweet, and the music was grand. After the ceremony, people gathered under the pavilion by the church to dance, eat, and talk. Kids played while a few of the older men took slabs of meat off of the large trailer mounted grills. Folks gave speeches about the newlyweds until the father of the bride joked that he would starve to death before we got to eat. The priest smirked and blessed the tables of casseroles, steamy crockpots, crusty breads, and sundry salads. After prayer, we all got in line. Momma had planned it just right because everyone got a helping of her dish. I got the last spoonful. Mr. Hopps had told me to not eat until everyone else had eaten.

Once the meal had been eaten, it was time to dance. The newly-wed couple started the first dance and many people joined them, including Momma and Papa. People swung close to tell Momma how good her chicken dish tasted. I watched everyone dance while I finished eating my food.

Towards the end of the dance, the bride and groom slowed down. Pain was written all over their faces. They clutched at their stomachs and dropped to the floor. Then almost like dominos, people started dropping to the ground, holding their stomachs. I looked for Mamma and Papa and noticed that the Bride was now spitting up blood.

"Finish your food dear child," Mr. Hopps crooned, but I could not. I was worried about my parents.

"Eat it now!" he barked.

His normally smooth voice was now harsh and frightening. I shoveled the food into my mouth and swallowed painfully. When I looked back up from my plate, more than half the town was on the floor. Most were not moving and many were lying in pools of their own blood.

Fear gripped me as I spotted Momma and Papa on the far side of the dance floor. I started shaking and crying. I ran to them to make them get up, but they were not moving. I tried to get other people up but none of them would respond. Now all of them were on the ground bleeding and motionless.

"What is going on, Mr. Hopps?" I cried as a great pain stabbed my belly.

I coughed and blood poured out of my mouth.

"Dear Anna Marie, that hemlock and oleander was not to make the food taste better," Mr. Hopps said, "It was to make everyone in the town bleed on the inside until you died. You, Anna Marie Lorso, have killed everyone in town. You have even sacrificed yourself. Now see, I told you to do so, but I am only a helpless demon trapped in this stuffed frog. It was my job to provide sacrifices to open the portal under this church. Can't you feel the eldritch energies flowing upward from below, Anna Marie?"

I didn't really understand half of what Mr. Hopps was saying, but yeah, on top of the pain in my stomach, I was feeling a strange warming tickling all over my skin.

"This is The Sha'Daa, Anna Marie," Mr. Hopps said, "it happens once every ten thousand years during the Summer Solstice. All the hell dimensions in existence are granted the opportunity to open a doorway to your world, and with your help today my job was made real easy you stupid, murderous little brat," he cackled, "and that horrible and plotting Johnny the Salesman tried to save you all, but I prevented it. Once your precious Papa picked me up, controlling him was a piece of cake."

My heart was breaking and I just wanted to go home. This was supposed to be a happy day. I had ruined it for everyone. What have I done? And then it popped in my head. What had Papa said? Johnny said something to him...*fire cleanses all evils, and closes all doors...*

"You are not my friend any more Mr. Hopps," I said and ran to one of the large still burning grills near the pavilion. Papa always warned me to stay away from them, but I had a mission. I needed to make things right. *To make amends,* as Mama always said.

"What are you doing?" Mr. Hopps shouted in a panicked voice, "it is over. You're a horrible evil little girl who has killed everyone she loves. Accept your fate and just die."

"Bad Frog!" I shouted and tossed the Mr. Hopps into a flaming grill and closed the lid.

Mr. Hopps voice changed into something high pitched and nasty as he screamed in agony while the fire quickly ate his body, "damn you Anna Marie!"

"Ow," I yelled as tears streamed down my face. I had burned my hand badly on the hot grill cover, but I didn't care. It was *the price I had to pay,* another one of those sayings mama always told me.

I made my way back to Momma and Papa. As the pain got worse, I cried harder. I lay on the cold concrete wishing this was just a bad dream, but I was smarter than that. I had been fooled by evil.

Then I suddenly noticed...the tingling, the tickling I had felt earlier, it was going away...I couldn't feel it anymore...the Hell thing Mr. Hopps had said I'd opened...the door was closing...

Now it was my time to be with Momma, Papa, and the rest of the town. I felt the sickly-sweet blood pour out of my mouth. My eyes dimmed. The pain faded. I couldn't move my lips but I managed to say one last thing in my head, praying I was heard, *I'm so sorry mama and papa, I thought, please forgive me. It...it is my turn now. Wait for me...*

INTERLUDE 14

Baby Doll

THE MUZAK VERSION OF EMINEM'S *Like Toy Soldiers* played from the overhead speakers.

"No, Ms. Derkins," Willy said sadly. "I'm afraid we have not had any stuffed tigers in stock for many years."

"Please," the pretty and polite middle-age woman replied, "call me Suzie. Oh, I'm sorry to be such a pest, but, well, this was a really special toy, belonged to a childhood friend of mine who is in dire straits. A friend who lived in Los Angeles over a decade ago swore they saw this stuffed tiger when Whirligigs was situated there…I guess it was silly of me to think you'd still have it on your new shelves here."

"Hmmm…," Willy scratched at his head, lost in thought, "you know, I do think I remember that item."

"You do?" Suzie asked hopefully.

"Yes," Willy replied, "If memory serves…which it often doesn't, an elderly man purchased it…a foreigner, British I believe…went by the name of Christopher Milne. This was back around February 1962. He didn't look all that well though, I believe he said he was only seventy-five years old. Seemed he was looking for a long-lost stuffed bear his father had given him as a child. Said he felt a strong connection to this stuffed tiger. Paid in cash I'm afraid. Did not leave any forwarding address. I believe he might have hailed from Devon, by his accent, not at all like my Aussie drawl. Ha."

"Oh, I hoped to track it down today," Suzie sighed, "but with all that I see on the television, I don't even know if the world will exist this time tomorrow. Goodbye, Mr. Willy."

Willy pursed his lips as he watched Suzie walk way.

"A lot of heartbreak in this store, Toyman," Johnny said, "can't say it bodes well for the longevity of this establishment, which, by the way, looks pretty serene considering what is occurring all over Chicago."

"Everyone…and everything, knows Whirligigs is neutral territory," Willy shot back.

"Keep telling yourself that," Johnny said with steel in his voice, "though I don't think you'll truly be able to convince yourself of it…not completely. Here."

Johnny reached into his trench coat's seemingly bottomless inner pocket and pulled out a large item with great solemnity before placing it on the counter.

"An authentic game board for the Royal Game of Ur, complete with full black and white sets of markers and tetrahedral dice. Mint condition and all set for gameplay on all twenty squares. It was created in twenty-six seventy-five BC."

"You just never cease to amaze me, Salesman," Willy said. "So what's the asking?"

"Rumor has it," Johnny said, "you've got a mint condition 1932 original Mickey Mouse poster, safe and sound, in a titanium poster tube and long hidden in your mattress. I want it."

"Is nothing sacred?" Willy asked.

"Not on this day," Johnny replied.

A minute later, the trade was made, and Johnny exited out the front doors. The phone booth rang; Willy sprinted inside and snatched up the receiver.

"What?" Willy asked.

"Hello, this is Kvaris the Interface," Kvaris said.

"I know who you are, imbecilic imp," Willy said, "and if you ever leave that quantum nook between realities that you reside in, I swear I'll wrap my hands around your annoying throat and..."

"Mister Carroll," Kvaris cut in, "the Midnight Laborers have been unusually productive during this last internal quarter shift and wish to notify you that they want to sell off their surplus to third-party-buyers at a discount, to supplement their current income."

"What?" Willy said, not quite believing his ears, "are they nuts? If they have a surplus, it was created from my supply chain and using my equipment. How the hell is that logical?"

"They said they would be willing," Kvaris replied, "to provide you with a five percent royalty on every item sold."

"Five percent," Willy said, "sure, I'll take that...as well as an outgoing fifty percent tariff on every one of these surplus sales that rides the main conveyor belt...the only route they'll ever have for transporting product out of their comfy little lair."

"That hardly seems fair, sir," Kvaris said.

"Consider it a lesson in big time economics," Willy smirked and hung up.

The muzak version of Julie Andrews' *Let's Go Fly A Kite* began playing from the store's speaker.

Last Flight of the Weirdos

Arthur Sánchez

"A toy has no gender and no idea of whether a girl or boy is playing with it."

–Letty Cottin Pogrebin

"**H**EY, WHO'S THAT AND WHAT'S HE DOING with T?" Malcolm demanded, letting his bad mood get the better of him. They'd been waiting outside of *Whirligigs* for almost an hour and was starting to think that T had stood them up. Now, he saw the petite blonde 15-year-old girl standing on the street corner conversing with some guy in a hat and trench coat.

Beijing, Malcolm's wingman, stepped up to see what he was looking at. Beijing was a foot shorter than Malcolm with thick glasses and a smart mouth. Ordinarily that'd get you killed in the tenth grade but he also had a world class smile. He could charm the crankiest Assistant Principal just by flashing it and he was using it now.

"Don't know who the guy is," he said, "but as to what they were doing, I'd say they were," he gasped dramatically, "talking." His smile grew into a smart-ass grin to emphasis the point.

Malcolm glared at him. "Yeah, but what about? I've never seen that guy before, and T doesn't look happy talking to him. And what's with the coat? It's like 110 degrees out here."

Beijing took a second look. "Yeah," he said, suddenly concerned. "You think he's bothering her?"

At this point, Chunk wandered up behind them. As the third member of their crew he was usually a step behind in their conversations. "What's up?"

"Some perv is bothering T," Malcolm explained. "I think he's upsetting her."

Chunk's face hardened. He liked T. She always watched out for him. "Nobody messes with a Weirdo," he growled.

That's who they were: *The West End Industrial Radio Design Organization.* Technically, they were the *West End High's Radio Control Club* but Beijing thought they needed a cooler name. He'd even made t-shirts that proudly declared: "I'm a W.e.i.r.d.o." But the only one who ever wore it was T. On her, it looked cute. On the rest of them it was just truth in advertising.

"You think we should do something?" Beijing asked.

Bolstered by their support, Malcolm felt empowered to act. "Yeah, let's find out what's going on." Malcolm moved to confront the stranger while the guys fanned out behind him in a show of force.

"Hey, you bothering T?" Malcolm demanded.

Both Tasha and the stranger turned, but it was Tasha who spoke up first. "Malcolm, it's cool. I've got this."

Malcolm frowned. "You sure? Cause from where I was standing, it didn't look that way." Malcolm turned to the man in the coat. "What's doing, homie?"

The man ignored him and focused on Tasha. "Is that your final offer?

Tasha nodded her head. "I can't do this without them."

Malcolm didn't like the sound of that. "Hey, what's going on? What's the deal?"

The man grinned and there was a flash of light from the gold tooth in his upper jaw. "The *deal* is with the lady."

He turned to Tasha. "Fine, FOUR controllers for your grandmother's ring." He held up what appeared to be four black radio controllers. Basic models. Nothing special.

Tasha hesitated before reaching under the collar of her t-shirt to pull up a thin gold chain. On the end of that chain was a gold ring with a neon green stone in it. "The only reason my family has kept this ring," she said as she stared at it, "is so that one day we could do some good with it. Hopefully, today is that day."

Tasha looked at the man in the coat, gave a firm yank on the gold chain around her neck so that it snapped, and held it out to him. The ring hung like a lead weight and Malcolm had the sense that Tasha was glad to be rid of it.

The man gingerly took the ring and chain and slipped them into his pocket. He then handed Tasha the four controllers. "It's been a pleasure, miss." He tipped his hat to her. Then, turning to Malcolm and the guys, he tipped his hat again. "Gentlemen, good luck in your adventure." He then began walking briskly down the street.

"Hold up," Malcolm called, "what just happened here?" He turned to Tasha who was lost in thought. He then turned to call after the stranger but the man had disappeared. "Chunk, Beijing, where did he go?"

Beijing stood there rubbing his eyes. "Sorry, wind blew some dust into my eyes. I didn't see nothing."

Chunk shrugged. "I was watching T. I thought you were watching the old guy."

Tasha shook her head as if waking from a trance and looked at them. "Forget it. You won't find him unless he wants to find you, and you don't want him to find you. Besides, we have more important things to worry about."

Malcolm stared at her. "Such as?"

"Such as saving the world," Tasha answered. "I don't suppose you guys have ever heard of the Sha'Daa, have you?"

Fifteen minutes later they all stood in a stunned silence.

"So," Beijing said slowly, "every ten thousand years somebody has to fight these demons or the whole world gets wiped out."

Tasha nodded.

"And we could die doing it."

Tasha nodded again.

"But if we win, we'll be heroes, right?"

"I'd expect so," Tasha confirmed.

Beijing looked at her before bursting out into an annoying, high-pitched laugh. "Girl, you almost had me there. Monsters from another dimension! 10,000-year-old curses!" He started laughing even harder. "You crazy!"

T's face reddened as she looked down at her shoes. "It's not a 10,000-year-old curse," she said softly. "It's an occurrence—and it's real."

Malcolm gritted his teeth. Beijing knew better than to call her crazy. Crazy is what the kids in their class called T. They called her that in the same way they called Chunk a "fat-ass" or Beijing a "four-eyed chink." They called her that in the same way they called Malcolm an "Oreo Cookie." The four of them had banded together, not out of choice, but out of necessity and the one thing they never did was call each other names. "Hey Chung," he said, using Beijing's real name. "Shut the fuck up."

Beijing's laughter died. "Whoa, what's the hell's up with you? You buying this crap?"

Malcolm felt uncomfortable. Tasha was staring at him with a glimmer of hope in her blue eyes. "Doesn't matter what I believe," he said honestly. "T's one of us. If she says she needs our help –we help. No questions asked; no explanations needed."

But Beijing wasn't convinced. "Whatever, you losers do what you want, but I'm outta here."

But before he could go, Tasha stepped forward and placed her hands on his shoulders. "It's ok," she said. "I know it sounds crazy. I barely believe it myself.

But it's real, and I can't save the world by myself. I need you guys." The look on her face said she absolutely believed in what she was saying.

"Look at it this way," Malcolm offered. "If she's wrong, you get to say I told you so for the rest of the school year. But if she's right, you get to be a hero and rub everyone's nose in it. What do you have to lose?" Beijing rolled his eyes in disgust, but he didn't walk away. They had him.

Malcolm stuck out his hand and declared: "One for all..."

Each of them placed their hand on his and in unison they said: "All for one!" They were a team again.

Malcolm looked at Tasha. "Alright, T, how do we do this?"

Tasha grinned, her relief obvious. "Step one was getting four controllers. Luckily, the Salesman really wanted my grandmother's ring."

"Yeah, about that," Malcolm said, scratching his head. "That ring looked expensive and these controllers look like crap."

"Looks can be deceiving," she replied. "Trust me, I got more than I gave. Now for step two," she turned and pointed at Whirligigs, "we'll find what we need in there."

Malcolm shook his head. "T, that's a toy store. It doesn't have anything to fight monsters— like rocket launchers, or missiles, or stuff like that."

Tasha gave him a crooked smile. "Actually, it does, if you know what you're looking for. Here." She handed each of them a controller. "These will help. Look around till you feel drawn to something. If it's what we need, you'll know it. You won't have any doubts."

"So," Malcolm asked, "we're looking for R.C. planes, drones, and stuff?"

Tasha paused. "I don't know. Might be radio-controlled, electronic, or just a plastic doll. But it will, I promise you, kick ass. Once you've found something, meet me at the front of the store. I'll handle it from there."

Malcolm wanted to ask more questions but Tasha started walking towards the shop. She stopped when she had her hand on the doorknob. "Sha'Daa is coming," she said, "let's get ready."

Inside the shop, Malcolm was struck by how quiet it was. The outside world was cut off once the door closed and all they could hear were their own muffled footsteps. *Whirligigs* was a nondescript toy store on the North side of Webster Avenue across the street from Chicago's famous Oz Park. The brick-fronted building was meant to look old despite being new. It was set up like a bookstore, with narrow aisles and large dark brown shelving running down the length of the room. There was no rhyme or reason to how things were displayed. Stuffed animals were placed next to action figures, which were propped up against video games. Malcolm picked up a game cartridge for *The Way of the Warrior* that was at least five years out of date.

"What a load of crap," he mumbled.

"Welcome," a not very excited voice called. A tall red-headed man strode up the center aisle towards them. "And what can I do for you *gentlemen*?" The store owner had an English-sounding accent and Malcolm spotted a diamond stuck on one of his front teeth— a sure sign he was a hustler. Malcolm disliked him instantly.

But before Malcolm could say anything, T stepped forward. "Good afternoon. I was told that you have the finest collection of toys in the Midwest," she said sweetly. "I was hoping we could look around."

The shopkeeper took a good look at Tasha and his expression changed. "But of course," he said, bowing low. "We have the finest toys in not just the Midwest but in the world. *From what's new, to what's perfect for you.*" He pointed a sharp-nailed finger at Tasha.

Tasha nodded. "Thank you. We'll just look around then." She pushed Beijing towards a side aisle while disappearing down a different aisle herself. Malcolm and Chunk took the hint and each headed in a different direction.

The aisles were dark and the jumble of toys made it feel cluttered and close. Malcolm had jammed the controller in his back pocket. Now he drew it out wondering what it was supposed to do for him. How was it going to let him know that he was looking at the right toy? Looking up, Malcolm spotted a large, brown, teddy bear on a shelf. It was fat and fuzzy and had big button eyes that made it look creepy rather than cute. The teddy bear was looking down at him expectantly— as if it knew why he was here. Was that it? Malcolm decided it didn't feel right, so he passed it by.

Continuing down the aisle and turning a corner, he ran into a three-foot-tall, Star Wars Storm Trooper Action Figure, complete with battle armor and blaster rifle. Now that would be cool. But he wasn't feeling any more compelled to choose it than the teddy bear. He began to walk away, when something caught his eye.

Up high on a shelf was a model helicopter. But not just any helicopter. This was a four-foot-long replica of an Apache Attack Helicopter. It had guns. It had rocket launchers. It was bitchin! Malcolm knew he had to have it and that surprised Malcolm because he'd never wanted a helicopter before in his life. But he wanted this one. And T said: "You'll know it when you see it."

Malcolm reached up for the helicopter. It was made of metal and plastic and was remarkably light in his hands. Stepping out into the front of the shop he discovered that he was the last of the crew to have made a selection. Chunk was holding what looked like spinning top, the kind that little kids would have. It was brightly colored and had a plunger at the top that you'd push down to make the thing spin. Chunk looked embarrassed to be holding it. Beijing, on the other hand, was practically jumping out of his skin with excitement. He'd chosen a metal robot. He was showing T how, if you pulled the arm down, a chest panel would open up and bright lights would flash—as if they were laser canons. T was holding a bright red, stuffed dragon with glass eyes and sparkling scales. Malcolm had no idea how any of this stuff was supposed to help them.

Tasha saw him approaching. "Malcolm, you've found something?" Her eyes took in the model helicopter. She smiled, adding: "I guess it's time to check out."

"And how would you like to pay for your purchases?" The store owner said, as he miraculously appeared at Tasha's side.

Tasha was ready for him. She immediately held up what appeared to be a black credit card. The man's eyes lit up as he reached for it. "And I'll need a detailed invoice, please," she said thoughtfully. "My Dad is going to want to know exactly what I bought."

"But of course," the store owner answered, still smiling. "Please follow me." He led her back to the cash register to complete the purchase.

"Dude," Beijing whispered to Malcolm, "T is loaded."

Malcolm frowned. "How do you know?"

Beijing pointed in Tasha's direction. "Black credit card. No spending limit. There's a lot about T that we don't know."

Malcolm looked over at the T as she finished signing the credit card slip. "You mean she's been preparing for the end of the world since she's been, like, seven?"

Beijing shrugged. "End of the world only happens once every ten thousand years. Girl with that kind of money, you'd be lucky if you meet another one like her in a million years."

Malcolm agreed. Fighting demons and black credit cards aside, he'd figured that out about T a while ago.

Twenty minutes later, standing on the shores of Lake Michigan, the four of them faced the water, holding their odd assortment of toys. The weather had gone bad. Strong winds were whipping up the waves so that the entire horizon appeared as one long, ragged line of whitecaps. Nobody was out on the water and the clouds had the dark, bruised color that meant a storm was coming.

"It's the Sha'Daa," Tasha told them. "It's starting. Good news is the demons will be coming from over the water. We can stop them before they hurt anybody. Bad news is there'll be, like, a million of them." She self-consciously brushed a strand of blonde hair away from her face. She wasn't used to being in charge.

Malcolm asked the obvious questions. "T, how do you know when and where they're going to show? And how do you know there'll be a million of them?"

Tasha shrugged. "They've been planning this for a long time. They've been talking about it and ever since I was a little kid I could hear them— in my head. Like there's a radio in the next room with the volume turned down real low. I think it's because my family has always had that ring. It affected me." She looked at Malcolm with fear in her eyes. "I sound crazy, don't I?"

Malcolm wanted to agree but instead shook his head. "No, not really. I mean, I believe you. If you say you can hear demons, then you can hear demons. You say that the four of us can stop them, then I believe that too."

"Yeah, that's really sweet and everything," Beijing interjected, "but I'd like to know HOW we are going to beat a million demons with these things." He held out his toy robot. The head of his robot spun around to face him. The eyes on it glowed angrily. "Hmm," Beijing said looking at the robot, "didn't know it could do that."

Tasha moved forward quickly. "Everybody put down your toy and pull out your controller." She placed her stuffed dragon down on the sand in front of her.

Beijing stepped up next to her and put down his robot. As he did so, the head of Tasha's dragon turned to look at him. "Hey," Beijing said excitedly, "you see that? It shouldn't be able to do that."

"Hurry," Tasha interjected, "turn on your controllers. You don't want them thinking for themselves."

Beijing frowned at her. "Thinking for themselves? What are you talking about?"

But Malcolm was on it. "Demons are coming, Beijing. Do what T tells you." He put down the helicopter and flipped on his controller. Beijing and Chunk followed suit.

"Right," Tasha began, "what you need to know is these aren't ordinary toys. These toys can do special things. And these," she held up her controller, "lets us control them."

Chunk, who'd been quiet this entire time, spoke up. "My toy is just a little kid's toy. This controller won't do anything to—" He flipped the toggle switch on his controller and the toy top leapt up into the air. It hung there spinning. Chunk stared at it. "What the—"

Beijing got excited. "Hold on, let me see if..." He flipped the switches on his controller. His toy robot also shot up into the air and its chest panel popped open.

Tasha quickly placed her hand over Beijing's to keep him from pressing any more levers. "Those lasers in its chest are real now."

Beijing gave her a wide-eyed stare. "Bitchin."

Tasha and Malcolm were next to activate their toys. The four of them stood facing their toys. "Now," Tasha continued, "this part is really going to freak you out."

"Seriously?" Chunk observed. "You're going to show us something freakier than flying toys that can kill?"

"Push down on both levers at the same time," she told them.

All four did and suddenly their perspective changed. Instead of standing side by side, looking at their toys, they were standing looking at themselves, as if they were looking in a mirror. Only, the four of them had blank looks on their faces—as if they were in a trance.

"What the hell just happened?" Malcolm asked. But he didn't actually ask it. He thought it and the words bounced around in his head, and in the heads of his fellow Weirdos, as if he'd spoken them. He turned to look at Tasha and instead came face to face with her red dragon.

"Wow," he heard Chunk say, "It's like we can see the world through our toys and mine doesn't even have eyes."

"The toys are extensions of us," Tasha explained, "of our minds. We can use them to fight the demons." Her dragon let loose a plume of white hot fire to emphasis the point.

Malcolm didn't test it but he knew, without a doubt, that his helicopter could now fire its weapons with deadly affect. Beijing couldn't resist swinging his robot around and firing his laser cannons into the lake. Water vaporized into steam. Chunk's top was the only one that hadn't moved.

"I can't do anything," Chunk said dejectedly. "Mine doesn't have any weapons."

"It has to do something," Tasha assured him. "Everything in that store can do something."

"Well," Chunk countered, "other than fly, my toy can't do anything." With that he sent the top spinning angrily into the lake. As soon as the toy reached the surface of the lake the waters parted straight down to the rocky bottom forming a twenty-foot-wide circular depression. Somehow, the top was holding the water back, as if it were in the center of a glass bowl.

"Hmm," Beijing said casually, "force field. Looks like you're on defense, Chunkster."

Tasha then explained that the demons were like bees—they only did what the Queen told them to do.

"So, that's how we defeat them?" Malcolm asked. "Take out the Queen and the rest of them drop dead?"

Tasha's dragon shook her head. "Taking out the Queen won't stop the drones."

"Oh, I know," Chunk said excitely. "We blow up the hole they came through and they all get sucked back in as it collapses."

Tasha shook her head again. "The hole between dimensions will close on its own. Blowing it up won't do anything."

"So, do we *have* a plan?" Beijing demanded.

Tasha took a moment. "They're not nice creatures. They hate everything and everyone—including each other. The only thing that keeps them from tearing each other apart is the fact they'd rather tear us apart. So, what we need to do is get them fighting amongst themselves. Once we do, they won't stop fighting till they're all dead."

"And how do we do that?" Malcolm asked, as the four toys headed off over the water in a line. Chunk's Top was in front, followed by Beijing's Robot, Tasha's Dragon was in the command position while Malcolm's Helicopter brought up the rear. He was to watch their back because he had the most maneuverability and the most guns.

Tasha's response came in loud and clear. "They have one Queen, but three Princesses—and they hate each other. The Princesses all want to replace the Queen, but know that the first one who makes a move will get attacked by the others. The Queen uses this to her advantage and plays the Princesses against one another."

"Really?" Beijing said. "Sounds like the plot of one of those bad cable TV shows."

"And you've been listening to them argue," Malcolm observed, "your whole life?"

"As long as I can remember," she confirmed. "It would be sad, if it wasn't so scary."

"And they don't know you've been eavesdropping on them?" Chunk asked.

"I don't think so. Since our toys aren't alive, the demons should ignore them till we're in position. Once there, we get them fighting. Once that happens, they should destroy each other."

It sounded simple enough, so why did Malcolm feel uneasy about it?

"Oh," Tasha said hesitantly, "and another thing."

From her tone Malcolm could tell it wasn't something he was going to like.

"The connection between our toys and us is very real. If your toy gets hurt then you get hurt, so try not to get hurt. Or killed."

Chunk and Beijing both groaned audibly.

"I didn't know if our toys got killed that we got killed," Chunk whined.

"You knew it was dangerous," Malcolm offered. "T warned you up front."

Chunk was indignant. "Yeah, but, I thought they'd have to catch us first. I figured if the toys got wiped out we'd still have time to, you know, call the Air Force or something. Get a second shot at them. I didn't know I'd just drop dead on the beach."

Malcolm was pragmatic about it. "So, now you know. You want out?"

Chunk started grumbling. "No, but is there any other stuff that we should know, or is T going to surprise us some more?"

Tasha sounded apologetic. "No, that's it. Now you know everything I know."

Even though it was Tasha's show, Malcolm felt compelled to say something. They were his crew. He raised himself up so that he hovered just above their heads and stared down the line: a Dragon, a Tin Robot, and Spinning Top. Not the most awe-inspiring sight but hey, they were here.

"Ok," he said in what he hoped they'd hear as a loud and clear voice. "We now know as much as T. Which is a lot more than anybody else. That's why we're here—because there *is* nobody else. If we don't stop the demons, then a lot of people are going to die—so we're going to stop the demons."

From somewhere in the distance, Malcolm heard Beijing whisper: "No pressure."

Malcolm couldn't disagree, but he didn't get much time to think about it. A display in the corner of his windshield began to flash green.

"Heads up," he announced. "I have some sort of radar system and its telling me that we're about to get company." A mass of black dots appeared on the screen and they were moving towards them at an incredible rate.

"That would be the first wave of soldiers," Tasha confirmed. "Just avoid making any physical contact and we should be fine."

Malcolm watched as the mass on his screen grew larger and denser. "T, I'm not sure that's possible."

"Why? Can't we fly between them?"

"I don't think so. They're packed solid." It was like watching clouds form. Parts of the approaching front billowed and surged but none of it seemed to be thinning out.

"Hey," Chunk shouted, "there's smoke on the horizon. You think they're in there?"

Malcolm checked his instruments. "Dude, they ARE the smoke. We need to hide."

"Where?" shouted Beijing. "We're over the freakin water! There IS no place to hide!"

Panic broke out as everybody started talking at once, but it was Malcolm who saw the solution. "T, you said they don't like the water."

The little dragon nodded its head. "They seem to avoid it."

Malcolm didn't see any other choice. "Everybody get in close to Chunk. Chunkster, remember how you parted the waters back at the beach?"

"Yeah?"

The drones were quickly approaching. They'd have one shot at this. "I want you to do the same thing only in reverse. I want you to be our umbrella."

Beijing brightened up. "Use the waves as cover. Get low enough so Chunk can keep us dry, but the demons will get wet if they come after us."

It took a little coordination but within seconds they were sitting just above the surface of the lake with the waves breaking over them. It was strange to watch the water crash down only to part like a curtain around Chunk's force field.

"You think we're low enough?" Beijing asked.

"Should be," Tasha assured him, but she sounded overly optimistic.

Malcolm watched his screen. The approaching demons were almost on them. Within seconds they could hear their hooting and whistling. What passed overhead however looked more like a swarm of crab spiders, about four feet wide with beating wings and oval carapaces spotted with black and red dots. They had what appeared to be razor-sharp spikes jutting out at all angles and thin, almost useless looking legs dangled underneath. They were packed so tight that they actually pulled the air along with them. The Weirdos had to fight to avoid being sucked upwards and into the path of the swarm.

As soon as they passed, Malcolm spotted something new on his radar. A line of massive objects was bearing down on their position, flying in an arrow-shaped formation.

"Hey T," Malcolm said. "What do the Royals look like?"

Tasha gave a mental shrug. "Don't know. I've never seen them."

Malcolm watched the approaching blips. These didn't break up or morph into different shapes. They remained a solid mass. "Ok, then how *big* are they?"

Tasha paused. "I assume the Queen and her daughters are a little bigger than the rest. They'll be surrounded by body guards."

Malcolm was pretty sure now of what he was seeing. "Try they're a LOT bigger and each one has an entire squadron surrounding them."

Everyone waited as a buzz filled the air then it grew into a deafening roar. A shadow passed over them followed two more. It took a second to realize that the shadows were actually things—very large things. Where the drones were four feet across, the Royals were each bigger than a tractor trailer and the sound of their wings was like thunder.

Malcolm barely heard Chunk say: "Man, we are soooo screwed."

Malcolm knew he couldn't let the team start to second guess itself. "Keep it together, people. Being bigger just makes them easier to attack. T, what do we do?" But Malcolm could feel Tasha's hesitancy. "T?"

Tasha's dragon shook its head as if trying to clear the doubt. "Like I said, we get them fighting. Each of us will get up next to a Royal and on my command, blast the next Royal over. They'll each assume the *other* Royal broke the truce and fight back. The troops will join in and it'll spin out of control from there."

"So, let's get on it," Malcolm added. "Everybody line up."

The four of them took to the sky and fell in behind the royal procession. The rear guard was not as tightly packed as the forward troops. They weren't expecting anyone to be sneaking up on them.

"Right," Tasha said, "I'll get up by the Queen. You guys each pick a Princess. Wait for my signal."

Chunk's voice rose questioningly. "I, I don't have any guns. I can't shoot anybody."

"Then use your force field to poke a Princess in the eye," Beijing suggested. "As soon as the fighting starts, it won't make any difference."

"Right," Chunk agreed, though he didn't sound excited by the idea.

Tasha took off towards the Queen, while the guys each picked a Princess. Malcolm ended up the furthest down the row. "Right," Tasha said when they were all in place. "As soon as I give the—"

The Queen, who had been steadily flying towards Chicago, suddenly did a barrel roll and swatted Tasha out of the sky with one of her spindly legs.

"Crap!" Malcolm shouted. "They know we're here. Everybody move!" But the gaps they'd seen going in were gone now. The drones had closed ranks. "Where's T?" Malcolm called. "Anyone see T?"

"She's in freefall!" Beijing shouted.

Malcolm searched the skies, but the drones were swarming now, blocking his view. From somewhere over to his right, bright flashes indicated that Beijing had started firing his lasers. Malcolm opened up with his machine guns. The noise was deafening. His whole body shook and he couldn't seem to shoot straight, but it didn't matter. There were so many demons swarming around him that everywhere he fired, he hit something. Some of them exploded, others were cut in two, so that the parts separated trailing blood and gore. Malcolm had never seen a living creature cut open like that. He was pretty sure if he had any guts, he'd be puking them up right now.

"I've got her," Chunk called out.

"Where are you?" Malcolm demanded.

"Just above water," Chunk responded. "T's wing is pretty busted up. She can barely fly. I'm trying to keep them off of her but we need help. There's too many of them."

Malcolm looked down at the surface of the lake. Sure enough, he could see flames as Tasha breathed fire upon her attackers. The drones swarmed in waves around her. "Beijing, get to T. We need to regroup."

"Roger that," Beijing answered. The flashes of laser bolts immediately began to lose altitude.

Malcolm did a 360-degree spin while firing his guns. The shattered bodies of demons fell from the sky. As soon as he'd cleared enough room, he put the helicopter into a nose dive. He spotted Chunk and T almost immediately. Beijing had just reached them and had taken a position outside the force field. His lasers were firing like crazy and he was lighting the demons up.

The swarms of demons were thinning out so. Malcolm was able to take a slightly curved approach to his team. "I'll cover the opposite side of the dome," he announced. But by the time he reached them the demons had all gone.

"What the...Where did they all go?"

For the first time since they'd been attacked, Malcolm heard Tasha's voice. "It was a trap," she said, almost in tears. "They knew we were coming. They've always known we were coming. They heard us making our plans."

Malcolm didn't know what to think. "They're in our heads?" He asked, afraid of the answer.

"They're in MY head," Tasha answered, almost in a sob. "The radio goes both ways. It's always gone both ways. I just didn't know it. They've been listening to me my whole life and they thought it was funny. My family's oath, my deal with The Salesman, how I recruited you guys to help me, they thought it was all SO funny. I could hear them laughing at us as they flew away. That's how little we matter. They're not even stopping to fight us. They'll destroy us once they've conquered Chicago."

Malcolm took this in. It was a pretty arrogant trap. They allowed four kids with weapons to sneak up on them just to prove they were badder than anyone else. Or maybe just so the Queen could prove *she* was badder than everybody else. She was the only one to strike Tasha. The Princesses all held back. Why? Because they were told to hold off, or because they wanted to see what the Weirdos could do? Maybe they were hedging their bets?

Malcolm looked up into the sky. He could see the last of the drones flying away. "Hey T, you've been listening to them your whole life, but do you think what you heard was real? Do you think you can trust what you heard?"

Tasha didn't understand the questions. "They've always say pretty much what they mean. It was the things they didn't say that fooled me."

"Good." Malcolm had an idea.

"Dude, why are we talking?" Chunk demanded. "We have to get back and warn everybody."

Malcolm turned to look at the other toys. Tasha's dragon had taken a beating. Both wings were flapping but one was bent at a weird angle and could barely keep up. "Ok, guys, listen up. We're going with Plan B. T," he said turning towards the dragon, "use the *secret* radio frequency to tell the Princess that we accept her offer." Chunk and Beijing turned to stare at him. Tasha's little dragon's mouth actually fell open.

"Dude, what are you talking about?" Beijing demanded.

Malcolm had no eyes with which to wink so he flipped his running lights on and off. "Bad cable show," he answered. "The demons might hear everything we say, but do you understand everything they hear?"

It took a second before Beijing's little robot began to quiver with excitement. "Man, I hope you know what you're doing."

Malcolm didn't answer. Of course, he didn't know what he was doing. How often did you end up in your own *Game of Thrones*? "Right, line up. We're going after them."

They got back in line, but made hardly any speed. Tasha's little dragon could barely keep up. "T," Malcolm began, "did you send the message?" He could only hope she understood what he was up to.

Tasha hesitated before declaring: "Yeah, I sent the message. The Princess says we have a deal and that she'll be waiting on us."

Chunk tried to say something but Malcolm overrode him. "Right, when we catch up to them we focus all of our firepower on the Queen. If we tip the scales and OUR Princess wins, she'll let us live."

Chunk couldn't stay silent any more. "Dude, what the hell are you—"

"Thinking?" Beijing finished for him. "He's thinking that we have ONE shot left to try to win this thing, and everybody has to be on board with it."

It was obvious that Chunk still didn't know what they were talking about, but was going to trust them. "Fine, tell me what to do."

Malcolm gave a sigh of relief. "Just follow my lead."

They didn't have long to wait. Despite having left them behind, the horde had stopped dead in its tracks. As they drew closer, they could see that the Queen and the three Princesses had each taken a position that allowed them to watch the others. The drones were massing in great numbers around the Royals. A few skirmishes had already been fought. Wounded soldiers were everywhere.

"They're arguing," Tasha said in a whisper, "accusing each other of betrayal."

Malcolm had hoped for this. Actually, he'd hoped for a lot more, but this was a start. "Use the secret radio channel to tell the Princess we're here," he said to Tasha. "Tell her that we will attack the Queen at her command."

Malcolm could hear the fear in Tasha's response. "Malcolm, they can still hear what I hear. They know what you're —"

His words had their intended effect. The Queen called up an entire squadron and sent them surging at them.

"Heads up," Beijing shouted, "we've got incoming!"

"Arrowhead formation," Malcolm called out. "Chunk's on point and T's got the back door. Now!" They lined up.

"Now what?" Beijing asked.

"Straight run at the Queen," Malcolm answered. "Use all your firepower. T, how do we disconnect from these things?" Meaning the toys.

"Easy," Tasha offered, "Imagine taking your thumbs off the switches and the connection will be broken—permanently. There's no going back, so only do it only when you're done." Malcolm had no doubt that whatever happened now they were going to be done.

The wave of drones hit them like a storm. Chunk's force field deflected the brunt of the attack with demons bouncing off it like bugs on a windshield. Malcolm and Beijing let loose with everything they had, while Tasha set the sky ablaze making sure that nothing got in behind them. Hundreds of drones were knocked out of the sky. Despite all expectations they survived the attack.

"Deploy the secret weapon!" Malcolm shouted. "Destroy the Queen!"

Tasha, Beijing, and Chunk all turned to look at him. Their toys displaying various degrees of confusion, but his words again had their intended effect. The Queen called up two more waves of drones to attack them. But this left a hole in her defensive line. One of the Princesses realized this and the temptation to depose her mother became too great.

"Malcolm," Tasha cried out, "they're going to—"

A wave of drones that had been circling one of the nearest Princesses struck out at the exposed flank of the Queen. Suddenly the two waves sent to destroy the Weirdos were called back. But not before another wave of drones from a different Royal turned to intercept them. Chaos erupted. The demons collided with each other. Entire squadrons made slashing passes with hundreds being cut to pieces. Other squadrons turned their focus on the Royals and two of the Princess suddenly found themselves in trouble. The Weirdos were now the least of anyone's concern.

"What now?" Tasha asked.

Malcolm watched as the battle raged all around them. It could still be stopped if someone got the upper hand. "Attack the Queen," he said. "Go in full throttle. It won't be pretty so the moment you think you're done, check out."

"That's assuming you have the time to figure that out," interjected Beijing.

"You'll die a hero," Malcolm offered.

"Rather live a hero," Beijing countered.

Malcolm turned to Tasha. "T, you check out now. There's no way you can keep up."

"I can cover your backs," she tried to argue.

"Not with a busted wing. You've done all you can," he assured her, "time to go."

"I'll be on the beach," she said." Don't make me wait for you guys." Then Tasha's little dragon peeled off and began flying away from them. They watched as it hesitated and then turned to face them. The light in its eyes flashed and suddenly it no longer seemed very friendly. The dragon opened its mouth to spout flame but then a drone slammed into it, driving it out of sight.

"Right," Malcolm said, "our turn." The three of them lined up. "Just like in practice," he said, with more confidence than he felt. "We're in the final lap. We can see the goal post. Only one of us has to make it. See you losers at the awards ceremony."

"Like hell you will," Beijing shot back. He then took off in straight line for the Queen.

None of them made it to the Queen. Her defenses were too great. But they punched a hole in her forces that the Princesses were only too happy to use. Chunk went down first, followed by Beijing, and the last thing Malcolm saw, before letting go of the controls, was one of the Princesses closing in on the Queen. He didn't know which one to root for.

"Malcolm," a voice came through. "Malcolm are you alright?"

Malcolm blinked his eyes a couple of times before T's concerned face came into focus. He was back on the beach. T," he said, reaching out to her, "we made it. We're—" Tasha screamed as he touched her arm.

"Busted wing," she reminded him as she cradled the arm.

"T, I'm so sorry," he said rapidly. Turning he spotted Chunk and Beijing sitting on the sand. Both boys looked like they'd been beaten. Chunk's face was bruised and Beijing's right eye was black.

"You guys alright?" He said with concern.

"No worse than when I pissed off the football team," Beijing said with a smile. "Did you get her?"

Malcolm described what he'd seen.

"That's ok," Beijing said as he laid himself down on the sand gingerly. "T's Dad called the Air Force and these bad-ass fighter planes passed overhead just a couple of minutes ago. If there's anything left, they'll take care of it." He let out a sigh of relief. Malcolm turned and gave Tasha a look of surprise.

"I had to," Tasha explained. "My Dad knows people and he can be really convincing. If we didn't make it, then he'd be the one to get them to do something."

"Does your Dad know about us and the toys?" Beijing asked, from his spot on the sand.

Tasha's smile faded. "I didn't have time to explain...everything." The four of them looked at each other before bursting into laughter.

"Ow, that hurts," Chunk complained as he clutched his side.

"Maybe we should get ourselves to the nearest emergency room?" Malcolm suggested.

"Good idea," Beijing said as he slowly rose to his feet. "We should be getting Purple Hearts for this."

"Purple Hearts are for soldiers," Chunk corrected him. "We're civilians."

"Maybe they'll make an exception," Beijing suggested. "We did just save the world."

They continued arguing as they trudged up the beach. Malcolm ignored them as he turned to T. "Any more voices in your head?" he asked quietly.

Tasha smiled. "No. For the first time in my life, they're all gone."

But before Malcolm could comment, Beijing interrupted them. "So, this counts as practice, right? Cause there is no way we'll ever be in a derby that's tougher than that."

Malcolm had to agree. The Weirdos had come together as a team and won their most important race. The sad part was, they weren't even going to get a trophy for it.

Toy Story

"**Y**ep," Willy said, in his strong Aussie accent, "the entire Doll House and inhabitants, though far from pristine condition. It took me quite a few years to assemble this collection, you know. This combined treasure was spread across the planet for many decades."

The elderly woman on the other side of the counter nodded her head slowly. "I don't see one piece, though," she said, "Dinah the Cook."

"Never found, Ma'am" Willy sighed, "rumor has it was lost on some island."

"Yes," the old woman replied, "and please, call me Elizabeth, Mister Willy. I remember my mother told me this had all been shipped by sea, and then lost in a storm. How strange."

"And I feel compelled to confess, Elizabeth," Willy said carefully, "we had to do some restoration on these four plaster figures, as they were quite literally disintegrating."

"Yes, yes," Elizabeth replied, "Finny, Lobby, Chicky, and Pudding...such were their names, or so a letter from my long dead aunt told my own mother. The work you did is wonderful. Thank you for...saving them."

"Uhhh...the matter of price," Willy ventured.

Elizabeth tossed a small, leather sack on the shelf to the side of the doll-house.

"Gold," Elizabeth said. "I think it will suffice?"

Willy pulled out a 1911 British gold sovereign, bit into it, and smiled.

"Yes, Ma'am!" Willy said. "I mean, of course, Elizabeth, very good. Perhaps too much so."

"Tut tut," Elizabeth smiled, "a job well done deserves proper compensation. Now, Dear Bembe. Please assist me." A large, muscular dark-skinned man with the air of the tropics about him, stepped forward and picked up the doll house.

"We must hurry," Elizabeth said, "there are rites to attend to." The wealthy, elderly, Elizabeth and her solid chauffer left the toy shop.

The muzak version of *Bicycle Race* by Queen began playing on the store's speakers.

"Always good to see the Royal Mail complete a delivery," Johnny said, "even if it is over one hundred years overdue."

Willy looked up to see his most regular customer holding a small box. "And what might this be?" Willy asked.

With a flourish, Johnny opened the top of the box, plucked out an ancient wooden, cone-shaped, decorated top, gave it a vicious torque and stepped back to watch it spin.

"From the tomb of Tutankhamen," Johnny said, "and I guarantee not stolen."

"And yet," Willy replied, "you just happen to have it in your personal possession."

"Never underestimate what someone is willing to trade away when an apocalypse is brewing," Johnny said, while the top continued to spin, losing none of its angular momentum, "something you might consider if you paid any attention to the news for the last twenty-four hours."

Almost hypnotized by its movements, Willy slowly reached his hand forward and clasped the still spinning top.

"I'm not sure I have anything to match this treasure," Willy said.

"Nothing," Johnny replied instantly, "but the 5,000-year-old, rare pink, Longshan jade, hair ring that hangs from a neck strap under that obscene lavender shirt of yours."

"Damn your X-ray eyes," Willy spat.

"Well," Johnny added, "at least these damned eyes can give you a clean bill of health. You know you must eat an excellent diet."

"Why do you say that?" Willy asked.

"Not a single polyp in that large intestine."

The phone rang and Willy passed the jade hair ring over to Johnny before rushing into the booth.

"What is it?" Willy snapped.

"Hello, this is Kvaris the Interface," Kvaris said.

"And for what reason," Willy asked, "are you gracing me with your divine voice, Kvaris?"

"Nothing drastic, I assure you," Kvaris replied, "just a routine maintenance request, sir."

"Maintenance?" Willy asked.

"We need a plumbing crew," Kvaris said, "half the sewer lines exiting the facility are clogged."

"I don't have time for this," Willy snapped, "tell them to toughen up and ride out the smell until these rush orders are finished."

"They thought that might be your reply, sir," Kvaris said, "and told me to tell you that in that case they will be sending the surplus waste in open vats via the conveyor belt."

"They wouldn't dare," Willy said.

"I don't think they were bluffing, sir," Kvaris replied.

Willy mulled this over for a few seconds. "Okay, I honestly don't have time to call in theurgic plumbing crew right this moment. However, I will have two hundred top-capacity chemical porta-potties delivered immediately. That should suffice until we get through the current crisis. Also tell them I will definitely be giving everyone a bonus for this, um, minor hardship. I swear."

"Roger that, Mister Carroll," Kvaris replied, "I'm pretty certain they'll agree. But..."

"But what?" Willy asked.

"That better be a pretty cool bonus," Kvaris replied.

"Why do you say that?" Willy asked.

"Because just before the plumbing started clogging up," Kvaris said, "we had a factory-wide celebratory meal of barbecued beef and five-alarm chili."

The muzak version of Nancy Sinatra's *Bang Bang* started playing in the store.

Shadows Of Darkness

Diane Arrelle

"Let me tell you something: You can live in a broken home, you can play with a broken toy, but you cannot love with a broken heart."

–Bella Pollen

ISTER SHERRY PUT ON HER PLASTIC eyeglasses, the one with the hypnotic swirls going round-and-round the lenses, and strolled into the dining room. "I've got my naughty and nice glasses on, you can't disguise the truth from me." she announced. The best any of you can do is just hide!"

Five chairs scrapped the floor as five children, grabbing their donuts fled the room.

"Remember the rules," she shouted loud enough to be heard on both floors of the old farm house and down into the basement. "No one leaves the house and first one found clears the table."

Giggles echoed though the century-old walls of the wooden building as the children rushed to hide.

Sister Sherry took off the toy x-ray spectacles, the kind kids used to order from the backs of comic books and bubble gum wrappers, and holding them backwards stared into the black and white lenses.

She put them back on and looked at her reflection in the dull mirror with the tarnished silver edges and frowned. She saw herself, a thin, semi-attractive woman in her forties with a touch of gray in her dirty blond hair. But what she was really looking at was her aura, which was gray but broken with light golden specks.

"Oh well, no surprise there," she mused and wondered why that creepy guy, Johnny, had ever picked her out, insisting she needed those glasses. "Why me?" she asked, the section of Chicago she had once lived in was full of crooks, junkies and whores. She wasn't the only one who fit all three categories.

She shook her head and turned away, intent on finding five little souls trying their best to get out of housework.

She walked slowly through the downstairs following doughnut crumbs and auras. She grinned; those children never knew she had such an unfair advantage. Those silly x-ray glasses never did see through clothes. No, they saw so much deeper. As she entered the living room she immediately saw the auras of two of the children shining out from behind the sofa. "Gotcha," she said and tapped Juan who was twelve, and Glenn who was nine on the shoulder. As the boys stood up, they looked at each other and laughed, the chores were going to be shared this time.

She moved upstairs and saw the auras shinning out from under two closet doors. *Kind of unfair advantage, Sherry*, she thought fingering the spectacle's frame then shrugged. The doors opened to her knock and the two girls, eight-year-old Helen and four-year-old Iesha came out. That left Scottie, the only one under her care that not only wasn't afraid to go down into the basement, he loved spending time down there riding on his sit-on, construction yellow, toy excavator. She had remembered them as being called steam shovels although she'd never seen one actually using steam.

Sherry went to "find" Scottie. Walking carefully down the old, wooden stairs that didn't even have a railing, she saw half the cellar glowing white. She squinted through the blinding glare and tapped the seven-year-old boy sitting on the seat atop the ride-on toy. "Found you, Scottie."

He looked at her with a smile and she had to whip off the toy glasses before he burned out her eyes.

That boy had the strongest, purest aura she'd ever experienced and she'd been at this for twenty-five years. As she and Scottie went upstairs she called out, "Hey everyone, run and change into your bathing suits; let's grab an after-dinner swim in the lake. Does anyone know that tonight's the solstice, the longest day of the year. After tonight, the days get shorter and the nights get longer. And that means we can swim for three hours before it gets dark."

The yeahs were deafening, and Sister Sherry didn't even need her glasses to see the brightness coming off the children. Even the murky maroons that normally emanated off of glum Helen and the perpetually angry, Glenn couldn't dim the colorful joy a simple swim brought out.

Sherry lead the five children along the trail that wound through the woods and wondered why the shadows appeared so dark. She shuddered, and urged the kids to walk faster. As they burst out of the forest and onto the beach, the sky grew black. They all looked up and she saw the last sliver of sun disappear. "A total eclipse!" she announced and shivered. Totally unexpected, totally unpredicted. "Come over to me," she snapped and made the children huddle together.

They sank down onto the warm sand of the beach and waited. Sherry wasn't sure what they were waiting for, but she was sure it did not bode well. The dark time had come. That strange man, Johnny, a quarter century ago had told her about it, called it...called it the...the Sha'Daa or something like that. She'd been gathering the discounted, broken children ever since. He'd made her see that she could be one the world's protectors, a defense against the great evil.

Waiting for some light to return, she hugged her kids and recalled the day she'd met Johnny. She had just decided to switch her corner by a few blocks, trying to stir up some business, looking for a rich John. It was late in the holiday season, so there'd be lots of Dads doing their last-minute shopping for their kids, lots of frustrated Dads, divorced Dads, cheating Dads.

She figured the best place to station herself was across the street from a big toy store. She'd never noticed it before, Whirligigs, but it was big; big windows filled with big toys. She stared at those toys and remembered her doll, Emmaline, a ratty ragdoll with one glass eye, one button eye and blue yarn hair. Her father had given it to her the night he'd left. She had Emmaline with her the day her mother dropped her off at the church with a note saying she couldn't deal with a child anymore. She'd had Emmaline through the first three foster homes, but the bitch who was the mom at the forth home got drunk one night and set old Emmaline on fire.

The next day, Sister Sherry, aka Cheri, actually named Sharon on her long-forgotten birth certificate, grabbed Emmaline's glass eye out of the ashes and ran away. She hitched to the windy city and set up shop there, after all, the family business was good enough for her. Every foster family let her know that her long gone mother was a junkie and a whore, so she figured that it was good enough for her as well. Not the junkie part, she just fell into that when she started selling crack with her pimp.

She'd been at it ever since she was fifteen, three years on her own, being her own person. She was good at stealing from the Johns. One or two of them caught her and slapped her around, but most were too ashamed of needing her services to complain.

She remembered Johnny vividly, even twenty-five years later. Long, lean, face shadowed by the brim of his hat, trench coat that looked inadequate to keep the bitter December winds out. He smiled and her eyes were drawn to the gold incisor.

"Want a tumble, Buddy," she said while shivering in her short skirt and short cheap fake-fur jacket. "Looks like you could use a warm room and a hot time."

He nodded, took her arm and walked her to the hotel nearby. She hung back as he went to the front desk. She watched in amazement as he talked, then took a pack of cigarettes out of his coat packet and handed it to the clerk. The clerk grabbed it like it was gold and passed a key and his toupee to her newest john.

He turned and smiled at her, that damned tooth still glittering like it was lit up. She was trying not to laugh at what had just transpired. She glanced at the front desk clerk as he tried to do a comb over with his fingers. Cheri was beginning to wonder if this john was bad news. A pack of butts and a wig. Even by Chicago standards, this was way too weird.

The john bought them both a cup of coffee and charged it to the room. Then coffees in hand, they took the elevator up to their room.

As soon as they entered, she whipped off her jacket and said. "Ok, buddy, what's it going to be a blow job up, or the whole shebang?"

He looked her over, "Put on your jacket, you don't have enough on the keep you warm in Miami."

Cheri shuddered and not from the cold. He was one strange dude. "Look buddy," she said. "I don't particularly like the really kinky stuff, but if you got the cash, well you could make my Christmas."

"Sit," he said, remaining standing. "My name is Johnny. They call me, The Salesman and I don't deal in money."

She snorted, "And I don't deal in deadbeats."

"I trade," he said.

"And I'm fucking out of here."

She reached for her jacket and put it on, but stopped for a second. Too fucking weird, she just had to ask, "Trade? Trade what?"

"Something that will change your life forever."

She wanted to leave. Even though the room was warm, and the steaming cup of coffee felt good, she wanted to get away from this freak. Only instead of heading for the door, something compelled her to ask him, "How? What?"

He reached into the coat pocket and pulled out the plastic x-ray glasses. "These."

She wanted to laugh but once again she was compelled to ignore her reaction and gently took the spectacles.

She weighed them in her hand, so light yet emanating importance. She had to have them, even though they were dime store junk. She wrapped her fingers around them and asked, "And you want?"

"Emmaline's glass eye."

The words slapped her and she staggered back. She'd kept that last memento of her childhood, her family, tucked into her clothing wherever she went.

She felt tears sting her eyes. "I...I can't."

He smiled, a soft turn of the lips, "Yes, you can. What I am trading you is the ability to make a difference in the world. Put the glasses on and come to the window."

She did and looked outside at the shoppers rushing from store to store. She whipped them off, gasping in shock, and then slowly put them back on.

Johnny stepped behind her and asked. "What do you see?"

"I ...I see everyone completely outlined in a glowing light."

"You see their auras. Every color has a meaning which you will learn to read."

She nodded amazed at what she was looking at. So many colors, some so pretty, some dull and murky.

"Turn toward the mirror," he said.

She did and felt horror eating away at her gut. Her aura was dark gray. No light at all.

"I am giving you the opportunity to make you shine. Is it a trade?"

She picked the glass eye out of the torn lining if her jacket and handed it to him.

Then she stared at him not understanding what she saw. Nothing, the salesman had no aura at all. "You don't—"

"Thank you, Sharon," he interrupted her, rolling the eye in his hand. "Enjoy your coffee and listen as I tell you some important information I'm sure you can use."

Oh, and the things he had told her, she remembered as she wrapped her arms around the small group huddled on the beach.

"OK, kids, don't be frightened. It is starting to get light. We ought to forget swimming today," she said. "Instead, let's play Simon says, OK? So, Simon says walk as fast as you can, but wait!" she said when she saw that the shadows from the woods were growing, putting out tendrils of the deepest black, stretching out toward her young charges. "Let's take the longer route today. Run to the road and go home as fast as you can."

The children stood huddled together and giggled.

"What's wrong?" Sister Sherry asked trying not to scream at them.

"You didn't say Simon says!" Helen and Scottie yelled at the same time.

"She couldn't believe that the children were acting like kids when they were in danger. "Simon Says!" she screamed in frustration. "Now run!"

She could feel the shadows closing in, the sky above started turning a deep red and the totally exposed sun glowed like crimson neon. Through it all, the shadows, disregarding the direction of the sunshine, continued to follow them.

Her small troop broke through to the parking lot next to the beach and six sets of pounding feet echoed in an eerie red silence. They hit the road turning west toward the farmhouse. They were running directly toward the setting sun, which helped keep a few of the shadows at bay.

They started slowing, Sherry could see the children tiring quickly and they were still so far from home. "Damn, I can't carry all of you," she moaned between gasps. "I don't think I even can carry myself."

She stopped and stood, hands on her knees as she swallowed large gulps of air. The five children sank to the road and she could see the shadows on the move again, inching toward those she had sworn to protect. She felt tears roll down her cheeks and slash to the asphalt. "Sherry wondered if she'd wasted quarter of a century helping unloved, unwanted children learn that they were worthwhile. *What good is it all if we die tonight, if evil actually wins?*

She straightened up and screamed as loud as she could, "NO! I didn't save us for nothing." She ignored the stitch in her side and yelled. "Come on, Simon says march all the way home and do not to let the shadows touch you."

"Hup, Hup, Hup," she chanted. "Let's keep marching just like we are in a parade. Come on, let me hear you."

Scottie, seemed almost joyful as he chanted, "Hup, Hup, Hup."

The older three grabbed hands and marched with him, "Hup, hup, hup.

Little Iesha was just too worn out so Sister Sherry swooped her in her arms and said, "Come on, help me march.

Her small voice joined in "Hup, hup hup."

She marched and urged the children to stay on the white line in the middle of the road. She never even heard the SUV behind them until the horn beeped and made her jump and scream. Her heart was beating so fast she felt pain in her chest. Fear gripped her and she struggled with herself on whether she should turn around or just flat out run. Instinct took over and she turned to face the unknown. To her surprise, she saw a family in the car stopped behind them. She had to lock her knees to stop from collapsing, and she thought, *Oh thank you, help.*

The driver an African American man in his mid-thirties got out of the car and said, "Unbelievable, I was coming here to find you! Come on, get in Sister Sherry, the world is going to hell!"

She wondered who this man was, she wished she'd brought her glasses to check him out but the shadows were closing in and she had to save her children. They all squeezed in with the other passengers, a woman and two children. They were piled on each other's laps and she was amazed that ten people managed to fit in a five seater. "Just like a clown car," she said, then thought, *but this is no laughing matter.*

They rode in desperate silence as the sky turned inky black, the sunset that was at least two hours away was completely obliterated. The driver floored it and Sherry was surprise when he pulled into her driveway. *Who was this man?*

They all spilled out of the car and made a run to the front door. As soon as she got inside, Sherry hit the floodlights and then ran through the downstairs flipping on every light switch.

Satisfied that the sinister shadows weren't around the yard or in the house, at least the main floor, she turned to the man and opened her mouth to speak but he rushed up and hugged her. "Sister Sherry when the monsters attacked the city and started killing people, I drove out of that hell and could only think of you. I knew you'd know what to do. You always gave us the right answers."

Realization came, and she hugged him back. "Benny? Benny is that you? You're so...so grown up."

Recognizing Ben made Sherry think back to leaving the hotel room with her x-ray glasses that cold afternoon in Chicago. She'd put those silly spectacles in her pocket and not knowing why crossed the street and went into Whirligigs. She touched the toys with a sense of wonder. She'd never seen such wonderful toys: fresh, new, no history, no baggage.

Suddenly she knew what she should do. Help children who were discarded, the children like herself. She had no idea how she was going to do it, but she had $300 dollars tucked into her fake leather boot and she was going to use it to buy toys.

Just then, a big man who looked like he belonged there turned to her and smiled, "Need help?" He eyed her outfit, but instead of asking her to leave, said, "You'll need a lot of toys if you plan to foster. You'll also need a home. I'll help you with the toy end first."

She just stared at him. How the hell did he know her plans? She hadn't even formulated them.

"I'm Willy and I own the whole damned place here. Tell you what, let's go to the discount room, you'll find lots of great toys, not the best sellers, but good toys anyway." He put his hand on her shoulder and led her into a room that was overwhelming. Floor to ceiling shelves jammed full of dolls, games, building sets, clay, puzzles, trucks and cars.

"I don't know where to start."

"Well, first you pick out the toys and then you contact some customers of mine that will help you get started," Willy said.

She nodded trying to get a handle on everything that was happening.

Willy smiled, signaled a sales clerk and said, "This nice lady here is starting a school and needs some help."

The saleswoman looked down her nose at Cheri and frowned. "A school?" she asked with disdain. Her face said the rest, *what does a whore really need with toys?*

"Just run up a tally and I'll check her out." The man said and walked over to another customer.

Cheri slipped the plastic glasses out of her pocket and put them on. The man's aura was like a flashing light from the 1960's, constantly changing colors; mesmerizing, exhilarating, and confusing.

"Ahem, Ma'am," the saleswoman said. "We should get started."

Cheri turned and saw the woman through her glasses and took a step back. The aura surrounded her like a robe of anger, hate and dissatisfaction. A deep, muddy red smeared with shades of dark brown. Cheri just wanted to get away from her as quickly as possible.

She whipped off the glasses and let the sales clerk add items to her pile. She didn't say a word until she saw the ride-on yellow excavator with a lever and chain that could raise and lower the shovel, a fake looking plastic headlight, and a steering wheel. It looked like the one she had read about in a book when she was very young. "I'll take that one too," she said pointing.

The salesclerk rolled her eyes and snapped, "Even on discount it's very high end."

Cheri glared at her. "Add it to the pile and get your boss."

She knew the toys she had chosen would be much more than she had and was shocked when the total came to exactly $300. Before she could speak, Willy said, "That's right, this is the discount room and it is way too full of inventory I'll never get around to selling."

She nodded deciding that on a day like this, she just needed to go along with everything, and figure it out later.

"I'll ship the toys to my customers I told you about. Have a nice day."

She nodded once again, and handed over the money. She started thinking about her plans. She just bought a house load of discounted toys for children that were discounted by the universe.

For the first time in years, Cheri thought of herself as Sharon and felt really alive. She had a purpose. She was going to make a dent in an uncaring world.

Leaving the toy store, she stopped at her apartment and grabbed the $3,000 she had saved by cheating her pimp and stealing from the johns. Then she caught a bus and following the owner of Whirligig's directions, found a mission church situated on this farm and became Sister Sherry. She spent the first few months getting clean and learning about love from the three members who were the congregation. The toys arrived and after a few months of government paperwork, they became a church sponsored foster home.

Sherry shook off twenty-five years of memories and hugged Benny tighter. He had been in the first group of children she had taken in. Five children, who she treated with love and worked to give them a good shot at surviving life. Three of those children were within the normal range of auras. She kept a close watch on them to make sure they remained normal. One boy was always frustrated and had a chip on his shoulder that dragged his aura well into the red range.

She spent so much time trying to change him and by the time he was eighteen and left his aura had changed to a lighter shade. He still harbored the anger, but he left the home feeling loved.

And Benny was one of the most special children she'd ever seen until she discovered Scottie last year. Benny had been a pure spirit with a soft white aura that had streaks of silver.

"Oh Benny, thank you, you've saved our lives," she gasped and held him back at arm's length. "Ah, you'll always be my Benny," she said, then shifting her gaze to his wife and children. "Laura, kids, I recognize you from the family Christmas cards I get every year. I'm Sister Sherry, and I'm so glad to meet you, although this is probably one of the worst nights in the world. Tell me, what's happening in Chicago?"

Benny opened his mouth and she quickly held up her hand for silence. She looked at all the frightened faces in the room and said, "Children, take your new friends to the kitchen and go have some cookies and milk."

"But Sister Sherry," Helen said, "we already had doughnu—".

An arm punch from Glenn shut her up.

"Stay away from the windows and doors and stay in the light," Sherry added and shooed them off.

"And now, Chicago?"

"It was a nightmare! Monsters everywhere: horns, teeth, fur, hooves. They were killing everyone, torturing some and then killing them. The sky over the lake glowed purple and monsters were flying out of a vortex that opened in the water. Luckily, we were outside in the park when all hell broke loose. I grabbed the kids, jumped into our car and hightailed it out of there. I must have been doing over a hundred on the interstate to get here. Traffic leaving the city was heavy and we saw monsters lifting cars up and throwing them into the lake, but we lucked out. We had a full tank and didn't stop until we saw you and the kids on the road."

Benny stopped talking and wiped tears off his cheeks. His wife held his hand and cried.

"Well, coming here may have bought you a little time but I'm afraid it may not save you. I am so grateful you are here."

Sherry went to a large picture window in the living room and frowned. She squinted her eyes but couldn't penetrate the darkness that seemed to be pushing on the lights that were holding it back. She turned away and went to the table where she had put down her glasses. She reached for them and slid them on. Then she turned back to stare at the dark. No lights, no glows, all she could see has a blackness that seemed to swirl with a deeper blackness inside. She felt it drawing her to it, being engulfed by it. She felt herself falling into a bottomless dark that was going to…

"Sister Sherry!"

She was paralyzed, being sucked into a well of evil.

A hand grabbed her shoulder and grabbed the glasses from her face. "Sister, stop it."

She shook her head and the darkness was back on the outside but to her horror, so was she. "How'd I get here?" she asked and grabbed the door frame she had just crossed. She backed up and crossed the threshold to get back inside.

"You just started walking, not speaking at all, and headed for the door, opened it and then Ben grabbed you," Laura said. "You can't go out there!"

Sherry stumbled to a chair and sank down. "It...it is pure evil," she said and began to sob. "I've never felt anything so cold, so cold it burned my soul."

Laura sat next to her and held her hand cooing soothing noises until Sherry stopped crying.

Sherry stood up. *It's my job to save everyone, I don't have time for weakness.* "Let's join the children, make a big pot of strong coffee and see how we can stop the darkness from entering this house. It's is going to be a long night, a very long night."

As the three adults entered the kitchen, they all stopped short. The back door was open, wide. And the seven children were not alone. A heavyset woman and a dozen burly, bearded men filled the room and spilled out the door.

Sherry gasped then bellowed, "SHUT THE DOOR!"

The woman, an older woman who looked in her late seventies smiled at Sherry. "Hiya, Hon, great to see you again. I always planned to come back and visit but...you know...time waits for no woman, not even one with a fast Harley."

Sherry stared at the crowd in the room once the door was closed and locked. The strangely familiar woman continued smiling, took off her leather jacket and exposed arms tattooed with religious symbols, the whole array of them covering all the world's major faiths. Suddenly the woman's smiled broadened, "Why bless my stars, is that sweet Benny?"

Recognition slapped Sherry in the face, "Sister Rose, is that you?"

The woman nodded, "Yep, came here as soon as the shit started hitting the fan." She turned to the children. "Oops, sorry about the cursing. Just ignore the bad words," she said then turned back to Sherry, "Me and my boys here heard on the news about Chicago's monsters and St. Louis's demons and lots of places having all sorts of pestilence before the airwaves went dead, so we figured you'd need help protecting your kids. Too bad Sister Martha and Brother Richard passed on. We could have used their talents as well."

"Thank you, Sister Rose," Sherry said. "It's been a long time since you left, at least fifteen years."

Rose snickered. "Yeah, you were so great with the kids, but me, well, I needed to tend a different flock. I've been busy saving my gang. Preparing them for this. You told me it was coming enough times that I knew I needed to help others fight the good fight."

Sherry looked around the overcrowded room and ushered everyone into the dining room and living room. "Please sit, and we can make a plan. So far the dark, that living, roiling dark is all outside."

Scottie walked up to her and whispered loudly, "No, it's inside too."

Everyone gasped and looked around the brightly lit room.

Sherry, knelt down and gripped Scottie's shoulders. "Where Scottie? Where are the bad shadows?"

Scottie shrugged and pointed to the basement door. "The dark things, are sliding out from under the door."

Every eye swiveled to stare at the large crack under the door in the kitchen. "Where are they? I don't see them?"

"They don't like the lights. So, they leave. Why don't you put on your magic glasses and see them. There are more coming through the crack in the floor down there."

Sherry hugged the little boy and put on the x-ray glasses. Scottie was correct. Darkness, swirling coils of it, were slipping out the basement. She felt like screaming as they floated around everyone before drifting out through the spaces around the thresholds and window frames. She stared as one tendril circled the bulb in the floor lamp. It stopped and other tendrils joined it becoming a shadow.

"Will you look at that," one of the motorcycle gang pointed. The shadow covered the light bulb, dimming it until with a pop, it went out.

Sherry looked at each person, then asked, "Any suggestions? If they keep coming up from the cellar, they'll blow every bulb we have. The bulbs outside won't hold much longer either."

"What happens if they touch us anyway?' one of the motorcycle gang asked.

"Well, Eric, do you want to find out?" Sister Rose snapped. "All I know is it won't be pretty and it certainly will not do any of us any good."

"I'm positive the shadows are made up of pure evil." Sherry said. "This is the battle for our world and we have to come up with a plan."

"Why don't we gather every light bulb in the place and just keep these two rooms lit for as long as possible as well as the bathroom and kitchen for a start," Sister Rose said. You still shop at the bulk stores?"

Sherry nodded, and pointed to the cellar. "Down there."

Benny groaned, "Of course they would be down there. That's where the monsters live."

Sherry stared at him and remembered that he was always terrified of the cellar. He hated that crack in the cement floor. Now she knew why. "You don't have to go down, I have plenty of help."

Before anyone could say any more, Scottie walked into the kitchen, opened the cellar door and ran down the steps. They all stood frozen by shock. Sherry moved first as silence followed his footsteps. She rushed to the doorway and started down as his small voice drifted up, "I've stopped the shadows. Come down and get what you need."

"Scottie, get up here!" Sherry yelled as she descended the stairs. As she got to the bottom the entire cellar was ablaze with a bright white light. She tried to shield her eyes and squinted at Scottie's small silhouette. She was sure if she'd had kept her spectacles on, the light would have burned her eyes right out of her head. "It's all right," Scottie said, "the man told me that I should smile into this mirror he gave me for my excavator if I were ever scared of the dark. I'm not scared, but you are."

Sherry closed her eyes and the light burned orange images on the inside of her eyelids. "What man?" she asked although she had a feeling she knew.

"Some guy in a dark coat and hat."

She figured as much. "I told you not to talk to strangers."

"I didn't talk to him, he talked to me. Gave me this mirror yesterday and asked me for the candy bar I'd been saving."

"Weird as usual," Sherry said and noticed the orange was fading so she opened her eyes. "Wow, was that bright!" She said and blinked a few times.

"The shadows break when I shine the headlight at them."

She nodded, thinking, *what headlight?* The others started to come down the stairs. "OK, everyone grab the light bulbs and food supplies and anything else we might need and get upstairs as quickly as possible."

Sister Rose tapped Sherry's shoulder and pointed at the crack in the floor, the one that had always been there and frowned. It looked longer and slightly wider. A fine network of cracks, like spider webs, were reaching outward, making the center crumble. "We need to go."

Sherry didn't know how long the shadows of darkness could be stopped by the light, but she knew it wouldn't be long and there were already plenty of shadows outside terrorizing their part of the world. They all rushed back upstairs to the kitchen.

Iesha screamed, a shrill nightmare sound and pointed to the back door, the wide open backdoor. Everyone had been so preoccupied with Scottie they hadn't noticed that Helen and Glenn were missing. Sherry, Rose and Benny ran outside yelling back to the motorcycle gang "Watch the children."

They saw immediately that the shadows were wrapping themselves around the two children, the two children that had darker auras. Sherry called to them, telling them to run to her but both just stood there and allowed themselves to be engulfed by the dark. Rose grabbed at Sherry's arm. "Come on, get back inside. The evil has them now."

Sherry tried to pull away but Benny took her other arm and they dragged her inside and locked the door again.

The remaining children were huddled in the living room, crying.

"Where's Helen and Glenn," Juan asked. "Why aren't they with you?"

Sherry held back her frustration at not being able to save them and said through clenched teeth, "The Shadows have them. We'll find a way to get them free."

Strong words she felt sure she couldn't keep, but she'd try her best to get her kids back.

No one spoke, they all stood with downcast eyes and tears fell in silence. Finally, Sherry couldn't take it. "All right, damn it. Let's just regroup and beat the shit out of those shadow monsters. People are fighting for their lives all over the world and I swear I'm not going to let these things beat us. This is our world and we better fight to keep it ours."

She stopped and looked at the clock, 3:00 am. "This thing's been going on for hours, and we've got to defend ourselves for another day and a half at least."

Sherry met Rose's gaze. "OK, Sister Rose, Laura, I need you to keep all the children together in one room. Take turns, grab some sleep…" Sherry stopped when she heard derisive snickers and continued. "Try to get some rest and don't let any of the lights go out. We've got about a gross of light bulbs and the brighter the house, the better our chances."

"What good will that do, they are pouring out of the basement floor and escaping into the night to kill people," Laura said and hugged her children to her. "And when the lights burn out, they'll just come back here and finish us off."

Right on cue, the three lamps in the living room popped. The children screamed and Sherry barked, "Light bulbs, now."

One biker screwed in new bulbs just as the kitchen light popped. Rose commanded, "Ox, Red and Jim run upstairs and grab every lamp and be careful."

Three sets of heavy footsteps pounded up the stairs, doors slammed, someone yelled then two pairs of feet pounded down the steps. "They got Red," the one called Ox said and wiped at the tears on his cheeks. "The bastards just covered him up and then floated toward the windows."

Jim looked pale but said, "We got seven lamps."

Rose put her arms around Ox's shoulders, "I'm sorry, I know he was a good friend."

Sherry was beyond devastated by the loss of life, first her two babies and now the biker called Red, a good man who gave his life to help them. Defeat tried to pull at her spirit, but Sherry shook it off. "Failure is not an option, I didn't spend twenty-five years waiting just to have it end before we had a chance to fight back."

She stared at each person: ashen faced children, big burly bikers shaken to their core, Sister Rose still hugging Ox, Laura still holding her two children in a viselike grip, grim faced Benny and Scottie who stood beside the basement door.

Standing as tall as she could, Sherry said in an even, almost mechanical voice, "Sister Rose, you and Laura have your orders, keep these children safe and the lights on."

She turned to the eleven men, "I want you to split into two groups. One group to rest inside and help Rose and Laura with the children. The other group will sit on the cycles outside and keep the headlights on high, do whatever you have to do to keep the shadows from getting back into the house. Drive in circles it if that's what it takes."

"And me?" Benny asked. "What's my job?"

Sherry gave him a solemn grimace, "The three of us are going downstairs to end this."

Laura screamed, "No, Ben. Don't leave us!"

He walked over to her and gave each of his children a kiss and hugged his wife, whispering into her ear, "I'll be back in a little while."

Then Sherry, Ben and Scottie headed down the stairs into the land of shadows and evil. The room was dim, the lights barely penetrated the darkness, but the darkness didn't attack them. Sherry took her glasses from her pocket put them on and turned in a circle. The shadows were definitely alive, she could see the movement inside them. The swirling black moved rapidly inside each shrouded form.

"What kind of mirror did the man give you?" Sherry asked Scottie.

Scottie smiled and she saw through her spectacles, the shadows backed away from him ever so slightly, but they did move away. "He didn't give me anything. He traded."

"Forcing herself to remain calm she said to Ben, "Just bare your teeth and smile, Benny. "They don't like it when you smile."

Ben grinned, not a real smile, but he looked at the blackness that seemed to be closing in on them and the clouds of darkness stop moving. Encouraged, he smiled maliciously and the dark continued to hang back, stationary, but at bay.

"OK, Scottie, I'm sorry, what did you get in the trade?" she asked. Johnny had taken a little boy's prized candy bar, but she shrugged that off, remembering the traded wig and key for a pack of butts a quarter of a century ago.

"He traded this mirror and told me if I smiled into it, light would shine out the headlight on my excavator here. See!" He smiled into the mirror that was now attached to the steering wheel. Brilliant light shot out from the toy's headlight that Sherry had always assumed was a fake decoration.

"Wow," she shouted and whipped off the glasses. Even without them, she saw the dark shadow that was obscuring the room, shatter into a thousand pieces of opaque confetti. "Scottie, I'd like you to take the mirror off your toy excavator. See it's just clipped on right there on the wheel. That's right. Now hand it to Ben."

As Ben took the mirror, just a regular oblong rearview mirror like on a car, Sherry said. "Smile into it and don't stop no matter what happens. And Scottie aim the headlight at the crack in the floor."

Scottie did, and the headlight powered by Ben's aura, was shattering the shadows. The strong light destroyed the shadows but even as the shadows died, more were pouring out.

"Scottie smile too."

That worked, the shadows stopped, but Sherry knew it was just a matter of time until the evil shades regrouped and attacked them. "All right, Scottie, let's see if your shovel can open that crack."

Ben stopped smiling, and shouted at her, "Don't do that, they'll just come out faster."

"Look Ben, the headlight is still working even when you looked away, it has a power reserve," she said and pointed at the brilliant white beam. "Scottie keep that beam on the crack in the floor and see if the shovel can break through it. Let's open it up and see what's down there."

Sitting on the seat, Scottie rolled the little toy excavator up to the crack in the floor and the shovel lowered down and hit the cement floor, crashing through it. Sherry was amazed, she had walked around the cellar many times and the floor seemed solid, yet a toy excavator not only smashed through the concrete, it was actually grabbing pieces of it up in its plastic claw. Scottie turned the shovel and released the grip and the hunk of cement crashed to the side. Then he repeated the motions.

As the hole got larger, Sherry felt the fear grow. Throughout the entire ordeal starting with the walk to the lake she hadn't let herself feel scared. She'd been running on righteous indignation, pure anger and the hope that if their little piece of the world could survive, then perhaps the rest of mankind could survive as well. She never thought in terms of winning this war, but only of having her children surviving it. She felt tears run down her cheeks when she thought about how she hadn't been able to protect poor Helen and Glenn with their angry, unhappy auras.

She didn't know how long they'd been downstairs fighting the shadows, she only knew they had more than another day to go. She looked down the hole Scottie had uncovered and just saw darkness, none of the white glowing beam coming out of the headlight made a dent in the complete blackness of that passage to another place.

"Scottie, you can stop for now. I want you to know that you are a very special boy. Very special."

Scottie nodded, his face serious.

"You have a gift. You carry a light in you, a light of goodness. Keep that light going and never let it fade. Stay good, no matter what happens."

Scottie nodded again as if he understood such adult advice.

Sherry looked at Ben, "Benny, you too carry the light of goodness in you. My special glasses were never really a toy. They showed me auras. You and Scottie are very special people. I want you to stay down here and keep that headlight pointed down in the hole. Take turns with the mirror and don't let it get weak. Stay here until the shadows are gone, in about thirty-six hours. And tell my children I love them."

Then without hesitation, Sherry grabbed the flashlight she still had in her pocket and turned it on. At the same time she put on her glasses and jumped into the hole before Ben and Scottie figured out what she had planned to do. Darkness swallowed her as she fell but she wasn't afraid. She was ready for the battle and she planned to take out as many of the enemy as she could before she died.

Armed with the vision to see the sinister auras of evil in the darkness, she was going to fight to the end. She knew the flashlight wouldn't last long and the second she entered the hole she lost all sight of the blinding light above.

The sensation of falling stopped and she was suspended in the shadows. To her surprise, the shrouded dark tried to pull away from her. She didn't know why but every shadow she touched exploded into confetti. Confused, but fueled by blind hope, Sherry reached out and stopped every one of those clouds of evil she could touch. She didn't know if they were headed up to the hole in the floor or back where they had come from, she just worked on killing them.

The dark fought back, draining her energy. She grew tired, exhausted. Her arms felt so heavy that she could barely lift them. The glasses made her head hurt so violently, she winced in pain when she blinked. Sherry wondered how long she'd been down there. Had she made enough of a difference to save everyone, or had she sacrificed herself for nothing. She knew that if she fell asleep or passed out she'd never wake up. Tiredness pulled at her until she had to give in. As she lost consciousness, the only emotion she had left was hope, hope that she had helped the others.

⊕ ⊕ ⊕

Noise from above woke her. Sherry was flat on the basement floor looking up at the ceiling. She struggled to sit and hands helped her. Lots of hands. "Let her be," Rose snapped at her boys. "She'll be fine in a minute."

Sherry felt sick, and confused. *How'd I get out of the darkness, and why wasn't everybody still doing their jobs?* She looked around and saw the floor intact, not even a crack there anymore. Beams of sunshine sprinkled with tiny, shiny motes of dust were peeking through the old, lace curtains covering the basement windows.

She got up, surprised that she stood on strong legs. All signs of her exhaustion and weakness were gone. "What's going on?" She asked, afraid of the answer. "Why are you all down here?"

Ben came up to her and hugged her so hard she thought she might break. "It's over."

"We won?" she asked feeling hope and a new feeling, joy, creeping up from her gut.

Rose shouted, "We sure did!" We kept those bastards away and Ben came upstairs carrying that toy piece of construction equipment and drove the rest from the house."

Sherry was afraid to ask, "What about shadows that were outside, are they dead? What happened to everyone else, all the monsters?"

"We don't know anything except that we survived and the darkness is gone," Rose said. "Let's go upstairs and grab a coffee and some pancakes. The kids and I cooked up bunches to keep busy."

As they all sat around the dining room table, Sherry noticed there were only six bikers. Rose as if reading her mind, said, "I lost a few of my boys, but they were brave and died saving the rest of us. We all searched outside but we couldn't find Helen or Glenn. They gone, but you know you gave them a happy place to live and be loved. You did your best, you always have."

Sherry covered her face with her hands and cried for a few minutes as everyone else sat in silence. Finally, she looked up and said, "I'm so happy to have all of you here, I'm feeling so many emotions, grief, sadness, loss, regret, and yet I'm joyful because we won. And I believe if we could win, then there has to be others all around the world who won their battles."

She held up her coffee cup and said, "In remembrance for those we lost, a toast for the human race."

Everyone joined in lifting their juice glasses and coffee cups.

An hour later, after cleaning up the house, Rose put on her jacket, mounted her hog and with a wave took off followed by her gang.

Ben asked, "Are you all right?"

Sherry smiled and said, "Surprisingly I am. My children and I are just going to pick up where we left off and live. We'll be sadder for our loss but we will go on."

She went down the basement to look around and Ben followed.

She hesitated a then asked, "Why'd you leave the basement with the light?"

He smiled and said, "Scottie and I weren't needed down there, that hole stayed dark and we thought for sure you were dead, but then, the damnedest thing happened. The hole started glowing all on its own and well the shadows stopped coming out. So after a bit, I went up and killed as many shadows as I could. Even went out in the yard looking for them. Sometime near dawn everything just cleared up. Shadows became normal shadows, and we figured we beat them away."

"So why am I alive?" Sherry asked, grateful to be able to ask that question.

Ben shrugged, "That was the other damnedest thing. We went back down and the hole was dark. We shone the light down there and well it just closed up. Popped you out like it was squeezing a zit. Then it was gone and you were out cold on the floor. Everybody came down here and then you woke up."

"What killed the darkness down here?"

"Well, I'm pretty sure you did while you were down in that opening."

"You said a bright light was down there? What was it?"

Ben stared at her. "Seriously, I think it was you?"

"Now that's impossible, only really, really, good people have a glowing bright aura. And me, I'm tarnished."

Ben took her hand, "Sister Sherry, you are and have always been the best person I have ever known."

Sherry snorted, "Thanks, but you are wrong."

Ben reached over to where her glasses had dropped to the floor when she was expelled.

"Put them on and look."

Sherry took them, walked back upstairs and stood in front of the dulled dining room mirror. She put her special glasses on. The golden glow that surrounded her reflection was almost like looking into the sun. She gasped and dropped the glasses on the floor.

Then she smiled and whispered, "Thank you," to whoever or whatever.

She picked up the glasses again and put them on. Sherry saw nothing but two holes. All she could see through was a small cut out circle in the center of each lens. She touched them and found that they were now made of cardboard. Keeping them on, she looked at everyone in the room. The aura reading ability was gone. She took them off feeling a mixture of loss and yet happiness because they had served their purpose.

She looked from Ben and his family to the three remaining children she had left and smiled at them. "Well, kids, this is certainly going to make hide and seek a lot harder from now on."

INTERLUDE 16

A Doll's House

I T WAS THE MORNING OF SEPTEMBER ELEVENTH, the year two thousand and one AD, and the Whirligigs toy store was doing pretty good business in its little corner of Greenwich Village. The proprietor, Willy Carroll, now had ten full time employees (not counting his special Midnight crew that worked in the rear warehouse) and eight interns from nearby colleges and universities.

Word of mouth of this independent shop had spread through all of New York City's five Boroughs. From vintage toys and games to the latest electronic wonders for children, from wonders that could be purchased for a handful of change to finely crafted works that only Manhattan's wealthiest patrons could afford, there was something here for everyone. It was even rumored that FAO Schwarz, the powerhouse of toy stores with forty locations around the world and whose flagship store was on fifth avenue and fifty-eighth street in Manhattan, was making alarmingly large offers to Willy to take control of his business. Willy, of course, neither confirmed nor denied these rumors to employee or customer. He appeared quite content with his status of eccentric owner of a small but surprisingly successful indy store surrounded by corporate backed franchise chains.

Willy had just sold off the last of his latest batch of Bratz teen fashion dolls, only one to a customer, to the large line of collectors who had greeted him earlier at the front door.

"Sorry, folks," Willy replied to the couple of dozen folks still waiting in front of the main counter, "that's it. We're all sold out. Check back in a week. We might have another shipment by then…no promises though."

This was answered with a collective groan and followed by girls and their parents leaving the shop. About a minute later a distant rumbling sound started to grow larger. All the employees in the shop stopped working and looked upwards at the ceiling.

"Sounds like a low flying plane," Michael, one of the interns said.

At one point the sound grew so loud the walls started shaking and the lightest toys began rattling on the shelves.

"Spread out," Willy yelled, "make sure nothing fragile hits the floor."

Everyone spread out in a panic and by some miracle managed to save anything vulnerable to breaking.

Moments later a loud distant explosion echoed into the shop.

"Everyone to the roof," Willy yelled.

Willy and the staff ran up the three floors of the rear stair case and made it up to the roof. In the distance, they could see the upper portion of North Tower of the World Trade Center, smoke pouring out of a burning hole near the eightieth floor.

"Must have been a passenger jet," Willy said.

"Oh my God," Karen, one of his most dependable full-time employees practically screamed, "my sister works there." Without notice Karen ran back to the stairs fumbling with her Nokia cell phone, punching numbers in panic.

Eighteen minutes later the second passenger jet struck the South Tower near the sixtieth floor. Willy told everyone they were closing the store and to get home and to their loved ones as quickly as possible.

Afterwards, the calculated combined total killed in the terrorist attacks at the World Trade Center, The Pentagon, and a fourth plane that had crashed in Pennsylvania was almost three thousand souls.

This aftermath, not surprisingly, left the city in shock, and Willy found that in the following weeks business fell precipitously. People's interest in toys had disappeared. Most folks were contributing their precious dollars to the families of multiple victims in Pennsylvania, New York, and Washington, DC, not to mention the three hundred and forty-three brave firefighters, eight paramedics, and sixty police officers who died instantly when the Twin Towers collapsed.

That strange, mostly ignored corner of Willy's mind spent a full week screaming at him to mourn this tragedy and take part in raising people's spirits and start a fund-raising event himself, but every time these feeble thoughts would surface, another more powerful corner of his consciousness would wipe it away, leaving him feeling oddly ambivalent toward the awful disaster. Fragments of images of bonfires and dancing figures in the Australian Outback flickered through his mind, only to fade away and leave him feeling confused and forgetting what he had been thinking for the last hour.

By September twenty-eight Willy had fired all his shocked employees, closed shop, and begun scouting locations in Chicago for Whirligigs new home.

Underneath

Marisa Wolf and Kacey Ezell

"The main point for me is that toys are incredibly more important than we realized."

–Brian Sutton-Smith

THE SUN ROSE, AND THE MONSTER UNDER the bed went away. Harry, four years old and 'sharp as a whip' according to the nice bus driver, didn't yet have words to describe how he knew it, but all the same. Up sun and away monster, and it was safe for him to hang his legs over the bed again.

He stayed curled up in his nest of blankets a while longer; his mother would be in soon to start the day, but after he'd woken her more times than he could count during the night, he wanted to stay quiet as long as possible, and hopefully let her sleep a little more. It was safe now, and cereal would wait.

It made him sad, the way Mommy looked so tired, even though she always smiled at him. He could see dark shadows under her eyes, like the time he fell and got a bruise on his knee. At least today was her day off, so maybe she could sleep a little longer. He would be good and quiet, and play with his Army Man. The plastic, poseable toy soldier hadn't done much to scare off the monster, but he was what Harry had. Harry's father had been a soldier, too, before he died. At least, that was what Mommy said. Harry didn't remember, but he kept the soldier close at night, just in case.

But the monster always came anyway. Once Mommy turned off the light it would creep out from under his bed and stand over him, watching him. Harry sometimes hid under the blankets, but he knew it was still there. He could hear it breathing, and eventually, he got so scared he would cry. Then Mommy would come in, and cuddle him, but it made her so tired, and then Harry felt bad. He really wished the monster would just go away, or die, like Daddy had.

His tummy grumbled. He was really hungry. Maybe, if he was really, really quiet, he could sneak out of bed and get his own cereal. He knew where it was, and he was pretty sure he could pour milk…

⊕ ⊕ ⊕

"Oh, Harry."

It wasn't angry—Mommy was rarely angry—but the exhaustion and disappointment in her voice was so clear that his eyes teared up even as he kept trying to clean up the milk with handfuls of paper towels.

"Just wanted you to sleep," he murmured, feeling his voice catch and working hard not to cry.

"I know, baby," she said, crouching next to him and smiling the smile that was just his. "But I'm always here when you need me, and even though it's almost your birthday and you're getting so big…" she looked at the thin layer of milk across half the floor, "it's ok to still need me for breakfast."

He sniffled a little, and scrubbed harder with both hands. "I know." It was just as hard not to sound sulky as it was not to cry, but so far so good. When she handed him a towel, he risked a glance at her, saw the smile, and relaxed. "I'll clean, and you do the cereal?"

"Deal," she said, standing again and getting breakfast together. "We have a big day ahead of us. We gotta shop for your birthday party supplies!"

⊕ ⊕ ⊕

After their third stop, Harry's steps started to slow. He obviously didn't need a nap, but he was getting tired of aisles and baskets he couldn't dig his hands in and new balloons after he'd already picked out an excellent mix of animals and cartoons. He could feel his face getting sulky and his lower lip protruding, but truth be told, he didn't care. The checkout line was long and his feet were *tired*.

"Birthday party?" the man behind them asked. Mommy looked up with a smile as tired as her eyes and nodded. "When?"

"Tomorrow."

"The day before the summer solstice! How old is he going to be?"

"Five," Harry answered for himself. He sounded a bit snippy, which earned him a warning glance from Mommy, but succeeded in making the man pay attention to him instead of talking about him like he were a toy or something.

"Five. A momentous birthday indeed. That's when you go from being a little kid to a big kid, isn't it?" the man asked with a smile. Harry could see the glint of a gold tooth, even though the man's funny hat shaded his face.

"Yeah," Harry said slowly, holding tightly to Mommy's hand. The person in front of them finished checking out, and they moved up. Mommy began pulling the balloons out of the cart and putting them on the moving thingy on the counter.

"Big kids make trades. Have you ever made a trade, Harry?"

"No," Harry said.

"Do you know how it works?"

Harry nodded. The man nodded back, then held out his hand. In it he held a small flashlight, with a button on the end. It looked just like the ones for sale on the rack next to him, but Harry hadn't seen him swipe it or anything.

"Do you know what this is?" the man asked.

"A flashlight."

"It is. It will help you see clearly in the shadows. Would you like to have it?"

Harry looked at the man gravely, understanding what he wasn't saying out loud. Somehow, this man knew about the monster. Maybe…maybe this flashlight would help, then he wouldn't be so scared, and Mommy could get some sleep. That would be the best birthday present ever. So, he nodded, slowly.

"I can't give it to you, Harry. You're a big kid now. That means you have to trade me something for it."

"I don't have anything," Harry said, his voice barely a whisper.

"What about your toy soldier?" The man asked with a small smile.

Harry's small hand curled around the body of the soldier that he held down by his side. He didn't want to give the soldier up, because his Daddy had been a soldier…but if that flashlight would help him not be scared of the monster…

"Okay," he whispered, and brought the soldier forward.

"Deal," the man said. He took the soldier with his left hand and held the flashlight out in his right. Harry took the flashlight and put it in his pocket.

"Thank you, Harry," the man said. "You're a very brave boy. I hope you remember that. The Sha'Daa is coming, and you will need to be brave."

"I'll try," Harry said. He wasn't sure why he said that. He never felt very brave…but maybe being able to see clearly in the dark would help. He hoped so, anyway. He couldn't imagine being a big kid and still crying for his mother every night.

"Who are you talking to, Harry?" his mother asked. She was just about done checking out, and looked down at him with tired puzzlement all over her face.

"The man with the hat and the gold tooth," Harry said, but when he looked up, the line behind him was empty.

⊕　⊕　⊕

That night, Harry's tummy felt funny when it was bedtime. It was like he was excited and scared all at once. He missed the comforting weight of his soldier, but the flashlight had its own comfort to offer, and he kept it in his hand all while Mommy got him changed into his PJs.

"All right, baby, where's your soldier?" Mommy asked, looking around his room. She knew he always slept with the toy to protect him.

"I lost him," Harry said, sadly. "But I have a flashlight. I'll be okay."

"Oh! Baby!" Mommy said, brushing her hand against his cheek. "You lost him? Are you sure? I know you love that soldier!"

Harry nodded, biting his lip. He wanted to ask her, as he did almost every night, if he could sleep in her bed. But he knew she'd say no, even though she'd feel bad about it. She thought that he needed to sleep in his own bed because he was getting to be a big boy. And he wanted to be a big kid, he did! But that monster was just so scary...

He gripped his flashlight even tighter and didn't say a word. He was a big kid now. He would be fine. The man in the hat with the gold tooth had said he was brave. He could be brave, like his soldier. Like his Daddy.

Mommy kissed him on the forehead, smoothed his hair, and paused at the door with her hand on the light switch. "Good night, Baby Bug."

He managed a smile and tucked himself deeper into all his blankets. "Night Mommy Bug." Harry squeezed his eyes shut before she could turn off the light, but he felt it happen, all the same. The softest click of the door, and he held his breath.

Not yet. Not yet.

Not yet...

There. The monster was *there*, filling up all the space under his bed. Breathing. Uncurling, spreading out, from under the bed, taking up the floor and the air and standing up—

Harry snapped the flashlight on, his eyes springing open, and there it was. Finally. Not a suggestion of a shape, a feeling and sound, but something real. Real and very tall and a bit purple and very, very...surprised?

"What in the earth?"

Harry's turn to look surprised—the voice was completely normal! Not a scary, slimy, slithering sort of voice, just a normal person who hadn't expected something. "In the earth?" he asked, because he had no idea what one was supposed to say, to the monster under their bed.

The monster blinked several pairs of eyes at him. "Where do you think I go, when that nasty fireball takes over?" Then the rest of its eyes blinked, and a few loose bits shook, as it refocused. "Never mind. What's that?"

Pulling the flashlight even tighter against his chest, Harry blurted, "It's my flashlight. I traded for it. It's mine."

While it'd been leaning closer, the monster set back a bit at the word 'traded', and crossed its top set of arms.

"Who traded it to you?" the monster asked, sounding as if it already knew the answer. "Was his name, Johnny?"

"Dunno. He had a hat, and a gold tooth," Harry said. "But he said it would make me brave, so you won't eat me."

"*Eat you?*" the monster asked. Every one of its eyebrows over every one of its eyes rose, and its mouth twisted into a grossed-out expression. "Disgusting. What makes you think I would eat a smelly thing like you?"

"I don't know," Harry answered, rather crossly. He didn't imagine he'd smell *that* bad. Mommy made him take a bath every night, after all. "Why do you scare me every night?"

"Because I'm a Monster. That's my purpose. Monsters exist to remind humanity that sometimes, it's good to be wary of the dark. Trust Johnny to foul it up with one of his little trades, though," the monster said. It sounded frustrated, like Mommy did when Harry wasn't listening.

"Well, I'm not scared of you now," Harry declared, boldly. "I can see you, and you're..."

"Yes?" the monster asked, and raised itself up to loom over his bed. Three or four pairs of arms reached out as if to trap the boy. Harry jutted his chin out and shined the flashlight in all of the monster's eyes.

"I'm not scared," Harry said stubbornly, even though his heart hammered in his chest. "I'm brave. Even if you still look scary. I'm a big kid, and I'm brave."

The monster let out a sigh, blinked, and oozed back down to eye level.

"Fine," it said. "I suppose I'll find another bed with another child. It will take me a few days, so don't be surprised if I come back tomorrow night. I still have to eat, after all."

"What do you eat?" Harry wanted to know. The monster's mouth stretched into a grin, showing several rows of pointed, jagged teeth.

"Darkness," it said. "Darkness and dust. Another reason why children's rooms are so delicious. You're terrible at cleaning."

That made Harry giggle, which made Mommy call out a warning from the other room. The boy switched off the flashlight and snuggled down into his blankets. His eyes were heavy and tired from the long day, and he let them drift closed.

"Well, eat all you want, monster. Goodnight. It was nice to meet you."

"Was it? Fancy that. Goodnight, Harry."

✛ ✛ ✛

Breathless, Harry poked his head in through the open sliding glass door. "Presents?" he asked, for potentially the thousandth time. Tag and chase, and hide and seek that became tag and chase, were all well and good, but the brightly-wrapped packages on the table next to the decimated cake, caught his eye every time he ran by.

And this time, like magic, his question worked. "Yes, presents. Call everyone—"

Before Mommy could even finish the sentence, Harry turned around and bellowed, his whole body stretched out with the effort, "PRESENTS!" and a horde of small humans charged into the house behind him.

While he reached for the first of the shiny boxes, other small hands went for the last pieces of cake, and for few minutes it was a blur of sugar and torn paper and shrieks of glee and the occasional hasty *thank you* before the next box got yanked from the table.

Finally, one left, he took a breath, glanced to make sure there was at least one piece of cake left (there was; it was small and a bit squished, but good enough), and pulled the box closer. A deep purple so dark it was almost black, all shimmer-shine and wrapped up in a red bow that he tore off so fast it looked like his arm was bleeding for a second.

The paper didn't last much longer, and the plain cardboard box underneath ripped open immediately. "Ohhh," he said, so happy he froze. A whole *set* of army men, in all different uniforms, tucked neatly together and clearly ready to get to missions.

"Do you like them?" Mommy asked softly. Harry looked up to see a sheen of wetness in her eyes. "I thought that since you lost your soldier…and then I found this crazy toy store called Whirligigs, and they had this set, and it seemed perfect."

"I love them!" Harry shouted, and jumped up to throw his arms around Mommy's neck and squeeze so, *so* tightly. She squeezed him back, and sniffled, and he knew she was crying happy tears the way she did sometimes. He liked it when she did that. It was much better than the sad tears.

⊕ ⊕ ⊕

After all his friends went home, Harry played with his new toys up in his room. His squad of army men became the centerpiece of a pitched battle that raged across his bedroom floor. A particularly daring raid against the robots knocked several books off his bedside table, and the thumps brought Mommy to the door.

"Almost bedtime, Bug. Everything all right?"

Harry's answer was so fast and detailed he could tell Mommy didn't understand the full impressiveness of what the army men had accomplished, so he trailed off after a few minutes and just nodded, so happy he was practically shaking. "But I had my bath early, so I can play late, right?"

She laughed and shook her head—it had been worth a try. "But you'll have all day tomorrow—maybe the robots will come up with a better defense plan by then."

He shook his head wildly. "No one can beat the army men!" he said stoutly. "They're the strongest."

"Let's get your PJs on, strongest," she said, coming into the room and opening his dresser. He groaned, but she gave him a look, and Harry forced himself to let it go.

Almost.

"Can I sleep with my army men?" he asked.

"Harry, you cannot take all of your toys into your bed. You may choose one army man, or take your flashlight. That's it."

He pursed his lips.

"Flashlight," he said finally, reluctantly. He had wanted to play more under the covers, but it was more important that he be brave. Besides, he wanted to show the monster his new toys.

✛ ✛ ✛

But the monster didn't come.

Harry waited, and waited, and tried to keep his eyes open for as long as he could. But the birthday party had tired him out, and before he realized it, he was dreaming.

The tallest of the army men stood and stretched, and began patrolling the edges of the bedside table. That was all right, Harry thought, smiling. Patrolling meant everything would be safe.

The one in the white uniform, the sergeant, sat up and kicked the robots away. The robots made sad noises, and the sergeant kicked them again. Harry stopped smiling. Why be mean to the robots?

There was a noise on the shelf, and all the army men moved, off the tables and from the floor and driving a jeep both too big and too small, facing the threat. But it was just Harry's old stuffed dog, falling over.

"Just getting comfortable," the dog said reassuringly, rolling back and forth. But the army men were climbing up on steps made of birthday cake, clearly hunting, and one was sliding down a rope of bright red ribbon, and they didn't listen when the dog tried to say hello, and be friends, and the army men were positioning their guns, and one had a big, long knife, and the knife was shinier than any of the presents, and someone was screaming and—

Harry woke, tangled and choking in his blankets, and the screaming was his, but he couldn't stop it.

Mommy came rushing in, and the light snapped on to show the room exactly as he'd left it, with his army men arrayed in battle formation on top of the table. Harry couldn't stop sobbing as Mommy helped untangle him, then held him close to her.

"Hush, baby. Hush. There's no one there. No monster under your bed," Mommy murmured. Her voice was tired. Harry gulped in a deep breath of air and started to cry again.

"I know," he said. "It didn't come."

"What?" Mommy asked, confused.

"The monster. I waited for it, but it didn't come. Instead, my army men were doing scary things."

"Oh, Baby Bug," Mommy said, rocking him. "There's no monster under the bed, and your army men are just toys. They're not doing anything. You just had a bad dream. I had hoped…do you have your flashlight?"

Harry sniffled deeply and nodded as his sobs slowly quieted.

"There you go. Use your flashlight when you get scared, all right? I promise you, these are your toys. They're just toys. Nothing's going to hurt you. And you know what else?" Mommy asked softly.

Harry shook his head against the softness of her chest. She lifted a hand and stroked his hair.

"Tomorrow's a special day," she said. "It's the longest day of the year. The summer solstice. Isn't that cool? If you want, after I get off work tomorrow, maybe we can get out the telescope and look at the stars. But you have to be a big boy and go to sleep, okay? We have to get up really early in the morning so Mommy can go to work."

"Okay," Harry whispered. He wanted—oh how he wanted!—to ask to sleep in her bed, but he knew she'd just get sad and say no, so Harry pressed his lips together and didn't let the words come out. Mommy kissed the top of his head and eased him back down to his pillow before covering him up. She went to the door and blew him a kiss before reaching for the light switch.

"Mommy!" Harry called desperately, as he suddenly noticed something out of place.

"Baby, what?" she asked, sounding frustrated and tired.

"Can you close my closet door for me?" he asked in a small voice. He saw her face soften, her lips smile. She nodded, then walked in and closed the closet door firmly. She even jiggled the handle to show him it was properly shut. Harry didn't like it open. It always felt like something could come out of the darkened space beyond.

"Okay. Sleep now, Baby Bug," Mommy said. "I love you. Goodnight."

"Goodnight, Mommy Bug," Harry said.

Mommy switched the light off and closed the door. Harry had his flashlight on before the latch clicked home.

"Monster?" he whispered, hoping. No answer. Harry played the light over his room, illuminating his toys one by one. Everything looked normal...except...

He swung the beam to show his army men. They'd been in perfect formation on the side table. Now they were in disarray. Some were down on the floor, as if they'd fallen...or jumped.

And Harry realized something else as he looked at them. The light played over them in a funny way. Made them look...almost wet. Slimy. Like they were shiny, but not the good kind of shiny. Sort of an icky green-black shiny, like when it rained on the street outside.

Harry felt his fear rising up inside his little body. His hands shook and made the flashlight beam tremble.

"I'm not afraid," he said out loud. "I'm a big kid and I am brave. I won't let you hurt my toys. I'm a big kid and I'm brave. I'm a big kid and I'm brave. I'm a big kid..."

The night grew heavy and long, and Harry's eyes began to ache and burn. But he knew he couldn't sleep, otherwise the army men would hurt his toys. He had to stay awake. He had to be brave.

⊕ ⊕ ⊕

The next morning, Harry overslept, and was super cranky when Mommy finally got him awake. He had a rough day at preschool, since he was tired from the night before, and he got put in time out for being snippy with one of the teachers. By the time he and Mommy got home, neither one of them was in a good mood. Mommy made hotdogs for dinner, and then declared that they would go to bed early.

For once, Harry didn't mind. He had a plan.

All day, he'd been gathering dust. Sawdust from the playground at his preschool. Dirt from the yard. Dust from the storage shelves in the garage. When it came time to change out of his clothes and take his bath, Harry took the time to scatter this dust all around, hoping that his Mommy wouldn't see it right away.

He needed the monster to come back. The monster would protect him from the army men. Harry himself had hidden them away in a drawer, but he had no illusions about that. When he'd woken up this morning, they'd been on the other side of the room. Mommy had thought he'd gotten up in the middle of the night and played with them.

He hadn't though. They'd done it themselves. He knew it. And he knew that whatever they were doing wasn't good. So tonight, he'd be ready. He'd lure the monster back, and the monster would help him stop the army men. He had to.

◈ ◈ ◈

After the bath he ran ahead. "I'm putting myself to bed," he declared, closing the door behind him before Mommy realized what he was doing. Then she could go to sleep, and wouldn't see all the dust he'd put all over. Although, now he had to turn off the light and run to bed and—no. He hurried across the room, got his flashlight, ran back while turning it on, and stretched up to get the light switch. The extra reach of the flashlight helped, and the light went off just as Mommy opened the door a little to look in. "Are you sure?" she asked, obviously surprised he'd turned the light off voluntarily.

She sounded sad, too, but he had to be brave. "Night Mommy Bug. Get lots of sleep." He made an effort to be extra confident, and pushed the door closed again. Then, flashlight gripped tight, he crossed the room, pointing the flashlight over everything. "Monster?" he whispered, being careful not to turn his back on the drawer with the army men in it. "Monster?"

Nothing. He'd known it as soon as the light went off—there was no feeling of the monster. There was no... anything. He climbed into bed, took a deep breath, and scooted to the edge to lean as far over as he could, trying to peer underneath the bed. "Monster?" he tried once more, hopeful anyway. But no.

Ok. He could be on watch again. The monster had to come back once more, he had to. So Harry kept the flashlight on the drawer, crossed his fingers, and watched.

◈ ◈ ◈

They climbed out of the drawer on ropes of ribbon, red curls to the ground, the army men alert and watching each others' backs. Even in the dark they glowed faintly, greenish-black and old-puddle gross, and Harry sat up. Pointing the flashlight at them, confident knowing it was a dream, he said, "Stop!" as loud as he could. "What are you doing?"

The sergeant stopped first, swiveled his head toward the bed. "How are you talking to us?" he asked, his voice snarly and crunchy like broken glass and rocks being crushed, the sound lifting up all the hairs on Harry's arms and making a shiver climb the back of his neck.

"This is *my* room," he said with all the surety he could muster. "So, *you* answer *me*. What are you doing?"

The sergeant turned fully toward him now, and the others stopped, circling behind him. "We're taking over, little boy." Harry's shiver traveled back down, trying to twist his spine. "We're opening your closet, and letting out all the monsters."

"I'm not afraid of monsters anymore," he said stoutly, though the flashlight shook ever so slightly. "Monsters don't eat people. They eat dust."

"Oh no, little boy. Not these monsters," the sergeant let out a laugh that slithered along Harry's skin, making tears prickle at the corners of his eyes. "These aren't the hulking, harmless shadows of your pathetic dimension. These are the *real* monsters. And they've been waiting for a very long time to come through. Finally, the Sha'Daa has begun."

With that, the army men began to move toward Harry's closet. The closer they got, the more the green-black icky puddle slick light around them seemed to pulse and grow, until it pooled against the wood of his closet door, spreading a web of grossness all around the frame.

Harry knew he wasn't supposed to get out of bed. Mommy wouldn't like it. But he couldn't let the army men bring bad monsters into his room. Maybe if he could move the closet door he could break that icky web. Fear skittered along under his skin, but he took a deep breath and reminded himself that he was brave. His Daddy had been brave. His mommy was brave (everyone said so, all the time. So, brave to raise him all on her own...) and the man with the hat and the gold tooth had said that he was brave.

He'd faced the monster under the bed. He could be brave.

So slowly, quietly, Harry crawled out from his blankets and stepped first one, then a second foot down onto the floor. He shone his light on the army men. The sergeant turned and gave him a hissing laugh.

"Do you think that will stop us, little boy?" he asked. "Our power grows with every beat of your scared little heart."

Harry watched as the icky light web pulsed darker. Fear clawed at him, but he thought of his mommy and pushed it away.

"I am brave," he whispered, and took a step toward the closet.

The sergeant laughed again.

"Brave? You're not brave! Look at you. Tiny baby boy, knees shaking, eyes filled with tears ready to fall. You're not brave at all, you're a crying baby!"

"I am brave," Harry whispered again, and took another step.

The air suddenly got very thick around him, like walking in Jell-O. His legs felt heavy and weak. It was hard to breathe. The hand that held his flashlight shook so bad that he dropped it. Its light slanted across the floor and into the far corner. He tried to sob, but he couldn't make a sound. In fact, the only sound he could hear was the rock-crunchy, hissing yuckiness of the sergeant's laughter.

I am brave! Harry thought desperately. With all the strength in his little body, he reached out his hand and touched the metal knob of the closet door. His legs hurt, fear choked him, his eyes burned with unshed tears, but he closed his hand around that knob and turned it.

The closet door opened.

Things lashed out, ropy and strong, like octopus legs or elephant trunks, just slightly purple, and Harry's heart soared. Arms followed—pairs and pairs of arms—and a blur of snapping teeth and loose bits and a growl so loud it broke the liquid air around them.

"Pathetic?" the normal voice of the monster—*his* monster—was underlined in anger. Like Mommy's voice could get (not at him, never at him, but he heard it, sometimes), scary enough to freeze everyone right up. "This is my dimension, you malformed little imps, and you can shove your Sha'Daa right up your—" CRACK. One of the army men broke right down the middle in a tentacly grip, all the swampy light leaking out and fading.

Another sharp crack and the sergeant was aiming his gun. Harry made himself move again. It was easier this time, and he kicked as hard as he could. The sergeant, snarling, flew right up into the air, a lovely arc that ended directly in the largest of the monster's mouths.

When the monster crunched down on the sergeant, the spell holding Harry broke. The icky green light leaked out of the rest of the toys and dissipated into nothing. Harry drew in a deep breath and dove for his flashlight. His fingers closed around the hard, little cylinder and he shone the light over the monster.

"Thank you," Harry said. "I knew you wouldn't leave me."

"I thought you wanted me to leave," the monster said. After talking to the army men, the monster's normal voice sounded sweet to Harry's ears.

"I did," Harry admitted, "because I was still scared. You're still pretty scary. But...I think I figured it out. To be brave, you have to be scared, first. And then you have to do what you have to do anyway."

"You're a smart young man," the monster said, and its mouths all curved in a smile that was terrifying, and also sweet and comforting.

"I brought you some dust," Harry said.

"Did you now?"

"Yes. You can stay, if you want."

The monster looked at him for a long time.

"Perhaps I will," it said. "If you will leave the closet door open. There is delicious darkness and dust in there."

"Deal," Harry said. He stuck out a hand. After a moment, the monster reached out one of its own arms and took Harry's little hand in its own twelve-fingered one. They shook, and then Harry found himself yawning with his whole body.

"Into bed with you, young Harry," the monster said. "Sleep well."

Harry covered his mouth and went to climb back into bed. He pulled his covers up to his ears and clicked his flashlight off. In the darkness of his room, he felt the *presence* of the monster lurking, filling the corners, looming in the dark.

"Goodnight, Monster Bug," Harry murmured.

"Goodnight, Harry."

Batteries Not Included

FROM OVERHEAD, A MUZAK VERSION OF ED Sheeran's *Lego House* blared out.

Willy put the tarnished, brass bed knob and the faded children's book, with the cover image of a bear in a sailor outfit fishing on a desert island, into a Whirligig's sales bag, and slid it toward the elderly gentleman.

"I believe these are the items you requested, Mister Rawlins?" Willy said.

"Oh yes, and please call me Paul, Willy," Paul said, with a public-school middle-class London accent, "you know, I always thought it would be my big brother or sister who would track these down."

"Why is that, Paul?" Willy asked.

"Well," Paul replied, as he clasped the bag to his breast, "after World War II, after school, we all seemed to drift away from each other. Charlie and Carrie married, had full lives, had kids."

"Yes," Willy replied, "and you?"

"Well, I never found that special person," Paul sighed, multiple regrets filling his short breath, "been a bachelor most of my life. Figured it was someone with children who would want these…special items. But they've both passed on, and I recently…I started seeing signs of what was to come. I barely got to America yesterday before most of the airlines shut down with all the troubles occurring the last thirty hours or so. I think the world is coming to an end, Willy. I saw actual monsters attacking and killing people during my taxi ride earlier. I…I feel I need to do something, old as I am. I think I can."

Paul looked up suddenly and caught Willy's eyes.

"Don't you, Willy?" Paul asked earnestly.

"Huh," Willy said, "Don't I what?"

"Want to help save the world," Paul said. "Do you have any children?"

"Why, no," Willy said, caught off guard. "I was married a few times, but, ummm, we never had children."

"Never adopted?" Paul asked.

"No," Willy said, "we never did. I don't know why, but, no, never…"

Willy frowned again and searched all his memories. He'd been married several times, but for some reason he never thought about it anymore. His last marriage had ended with the death of his wife, Belinda, a few years before the breakout of World War One. And…and he just never fell in love again after that. In fact, the pleasures of the flesh just kind of disappeared around that time… *strange*, Willy thought, *why are these memories only surfacing now?*

"Yes, well," Paul said, "I guess we all have our reasons. Good day, Sir, and thank you."

Willy nodded, but couldn't open his mouth. *Has it really been that long, he thought, since I was last married and in love? And it's never bothered me until now? This second half of the Sha'Daa?*

"Treguna Mekoides and Trecorum Satis Dee," Paul began singing in a low voice as he walked out the front doors.

"Now there's a man interested in locomotion," Johnny said, as he walked in as Paul passed him.

"Yeah," Willy said, "sure."

Johnny pursed his lips as he approached the counter, "Got a special acquisition for you, Toyman."

Willy nodded. "Say Johnny, did you know I have not been on a date, or in love, for over one hundred years? Does that sound odd to you?"

Johnny placed a green, silk-covered box on the counter and stared into Willy's unfocussed eyes for a moment.

"Funny thing about the Sha'Daa, Willy," Johnny said, "the massive expulsion of arcane energies and eldritch manna throughout the atmosphere and oceans all over the Earth, well, it tends to mess with spells, charms, and rituals both new and old. Why, who knows what might be going on inside yourself right now, these days, when the lives of millions are at stake."

Willy snapped out of this melancholy spell and reached for the box Johnny had set down, though he still seemed a little shaken, a fact that Johnny silently acknowledged with a minute nod and the slightest of smiles.

The overhead speakers switched to a new muzak song, Henry Hall's *The Teddy Bear Picnic*.

The phone booth began ringing and with a grunt of annoyance, Willy dashed inside.

"Shoot," Willy said.

"Hello, this is Kvaris the Interface," Kvaris said.

"Do they need more porta-potties," Willy asked, "or gas masks?"

"Oh, no sir," Kvaris replied, "personal hygiene, ventilation, and plumbing are currently under control in the Midnight Laborers' facilities."

"Then what's up?" Willy asked. "What are they complaining about now?"

"Well," Kvaris replied, "this is actually not about the Midnight Laborers, sir. It's, um, about me."

"Say what?" Willy replied, surprised.

"Yes, you see, sir," Kvaris replied, "as I'm sure you are aware, my notification services are not just available to you, Whirligigs, and the Midnight Laborers. I actually have a total of ten clients altogether."

"Yeah...and?" Willy asked.

"Well," Kvaris said slowly, "it suddenly struck me that you may not be cognizant of the fact that today marks the first century of my mental ascension."

"So it's, like, your birthday?" Willy asked.

"Close enough," Kvaris said, "and as of a few moments ago, nine of my ten clients have awarded me bonus gifts in celebration, and, ummm..."

"You want a birthday gift?" Willy asked.

"Well, I didn't want to come right out and say it sir," Kvaris said, "but since you bring the subject up, any present comprised of proto-matter or quantum-filaments would be..."

A loud crack cut off Kvaris. The receiver in the empty phone booth swung freely.

"Willy?" Kvaris asked, "Mister Carroll? Hello? Were we cut off? About that gift..."

Terrance the Terrible Toy Train of Terraño

Jason Cordova

"When I was a kid, I went to the store and asked the guy, Do you have any toy train schedules?"

–Stephen Wright

THE ART OF THE SALE BEGINS WITH A welcoming smile and an open posture.

Johnny the Salesman looked about the small toy store with a scowl on his usually amused face, the opposite of what a successful salesman should look like. His fedora was tilted at a steep enough angle that the shadows hid his elongated features, and the usual glint of his golden tooth was hidden when he spoke. Normally bombastic and gregarious, the air and mannerism of the mysterious Salesman was most unusual today. Anybody who knew Johnny would have agreed—something strange was afoot.

Fortunately for Johnny, no one in that section of the store immediately recognized the Salesman, so nothing seemed amiss to the casual observer. After all, what was another patron of the Whirligigs toy store who wished to remain both anonymous and mysterious? The comings and goings of strange and unusual individuals was commonplace here.

Johnny hoped so, at least, for the expression on the woman's features standing before him was one of fear and confusion.

"It's a toy train, *señorita*," the Salesman said as he laid a hand gently upon the closed box. "Many toy trains in this world. What is important about this one that you would not trade me this wonderful Obertron set for your Terrance set? Obertron is the rarest train set in the world and this has a complete set of railcars, as well as over four hundred feet of track. This Terrance toy train set comes with but sixty-odd feet. Very little one can do with this."

"This is the one I chose, and this is the one I want!" A tiny voice exploded from slightly behind the rail-thin woman. Johnny looked down at the reason; Rubina Vasconcelos was adamantly clutching the toy train set, and tried to smile. The little boy was most stubborn, though it was not the usual manner of a spoilt child. It was the behavior of a child who was both tenacious and honest. "I was promised one toy for behaving, and I chose this one, *señor*."

"I am so sorry, *señor*," the woman dipped her head apologetically. "Joachim picked out this toy. He has been very good and deserves this treat."

Johnny shrugged. A good child or not, little Joachim was making his job that much more difficult. "It's a good trade. I feel bad for little Joachim, however. He'll run out of track in short order and be bored. This Obertron has so many feet of track that his entire bedroom floor will be covered with it."

"I can make a trade!" the young boy suddenly exclaimed. He stuck a tiny hand into his pocket and pulled out a small toy car. He offered it to Johnny with a smile. "What would you give for this?"

Johnny accepted the small car and studied it intently for many moments before his usual demeanor returned. His smile was bright and more forthcoming, and his face was open and honest. It was the look of a very skilled salesman who was expecting a customer.

"I have a shiny gold coin to trade for that," Johnny said and produced a rather large gold coin from his pocket. He flipped it over his knuckles and held it out to the little boy for inspection. "It is a one ounce gold coin from Solomon's Mines, blessed by the priests of his court and lost for over two thousand years. It even bears the mark of his father, David. See this line?"

"That looks like just some scribble and not a king's name," the little boy said suspiciously as he looked the coin over. He handed it back to Johnny. "Is it real?"

"As real as you or me."

"*Señor*, we cannot accept this," Rubina said and pulled her son back to her. "It is too much for a simple toy car."

"Oh, but *señorita*, this is anything *but* a simple toy car," Johnny assured her. "This is a vintage 1972, Winged Hussar with limited edition spoiler and enlarged rear wheels and front engine hood scoop. It had very little nicks and scratches, and all of its original stickers. I need this for my collection. It is quite valuable to me."

"So, I can have the train *and* this coin?" the boy asked. Johnny's grin was wide.

"Of course!"

"*Mama, por favor?*" Joachim looked up at his mom pleadingly. She sighed.

"Fine, the coin for the car," Rubina agreed. She held up a finger before Johnny could pass the gold coin back over. "I don't know what game you're playing, senor, but I do not trust it."

"I think that Joachim will find the coin more valuable than anything else for a long time," Johnny reassured her. "In fact, I think that it would make for a wonderful wishing well coin."

"That coin shouldn't be wasted on some fool's wish in a well," Rubina stated in a sharp tone. Johnny's grin somehow grew even wider.

"It's only wasted if the wish doesn't come true."

⊕ ⊕ ⊕

Darkness? Light? Neither matter to me, not anymore. I am nearly whole again. I am the avatar of chaos, ready to be set upon an unsuspecting world. I have chosen my form, a mighty beast that is nigh unstoppable. I am prepared to open the gate to release the followers of my dark god upon a realm of light. There shall be a great reaping as souls are collected and fed into the great maw.

The pulse...there it is...so strong, so young, so...innocent. It is divine.

⊕ ⊕ ⊕

Joachim opened the box and dumped out the contents on the floor of his bedroom. Pieces of toy railroad track fell onto the ground haphazardly. The train and cars were better packaged and were laid next to track. He picked up the booklet and opened the pages for a moment before he shrugged and tossed it aside. He looked back at the track and grinned.

He had wanted a toy train set just like his *abuelo* had when he had been a boy since Joachim saw the pictures the last time he had been over. Joachim's grandfather had shown him his old toy train set, complete with scenery and hills, throughout the old photo album. It had even featured a massive cow farm with tiny metals cows dotting the landscape. This had been the only spark needed to ignite a passion within Joachim that he had never felt before. He had begged and pestered his mother until she had finally relented and, if he did well in both school and at home, she would take him to the Whirligigs toy store.

Joachim began to attach the tracks to one another, finding which one went where. He was mildly disappointed that the tracks did not seem to be able to be placed however he wanted, but instead followed some sort of pre-set pattern. This only mildly dampened his spirits, however. He finally had his train set, just as his *abuelo* had before him.

He looked around his room. He did not have much in the way for props that could be used as farm animals, though…he leapt to his feet and raced to his toy box, where his old stuffed dog lay. He grabbed him and brought him back to the tracks and looked around.

Where would a giant dog farm go? He wondered for a second before deciding that near the top of where the track interconnected would be as good of a spot as any. In went Grumpy the Wonder Puppy. A few more moments of searching around the room and he spotted both a toy pig and a broken etch-a-sketch. Both of these went into the train yard as well. Joachim was not entirely certain what the pig was going to do, but he figured it would look good for the time being.

He wandered out into the hallway and found a large potted plant that looked wilted. He quietly dragged it back into his room and set it near the lower half of the circular track. Now the train had a nice forest to move through on its way to the big city.

He grabbed the locomotive and opened the foam container. The locomotive was a bright and festive green with a black chimney and white stripes down the side. "Terrance" was printed just above the lines. Joachim could see a little man standing inside the locomotive, ready to drive his train.

Joachim set the train down on the tracks and attached the four cars behind it. He then added the caboose and stepped back to admire his handiwork. He smiled. While not as fancy as his *abuelo's* had been, it was still a very nice-looking train set. He would be so proud of him the next time he came over to visit.

⊕ ⊕ ⊕

I am free! I am free from that cursed darkness of disorderly despair! Now I must turn my attentions to this new world, to open the gate and allow the armies to pour forth. I must…what in the seven hells is this? Why am I confined on two metal rails? What is this sticking out of my head? Why is there a miniature immobile human male inside my head?!

What's going on here?

⊕ ⊕ ⊕

Joachim set the train down onto the tracks and waited. He didn't see an "on" switch to start the locomotive, so he figured that it was all done by magnets.

Sure enough, after a few seconds of nothing the train came to life. The large bar on the side began to slowly turn as the wheels began to spin in time. The train began to move slowly along the tracks, the train cars behind it following faithfully along.

"Cool," Joachim whispered as he watched the train make its way around the circle. He did not understand why the directions had called for the star to be in the middle of the tracks, since he did not think that the train would be able to turn that tightly, but he was a good boy who followed directions.

"My very first toy train," Joachim pronounced, pleased with himself. "Choo choo!"

"*Freeeeeee!*" the train screamed through his short smoke stack. The tiny toy locomotive continued to chug along the narrow metal rails. "I am finally free! Tremble, world of mortals, for I am Wrath, beholden to Chaos, and Messenger of the Damned! I shall bring forth Evil unto this world!"

"Ah!" Joachim yelped and scooted frantically away from the tracks and the talking train. He hopped to his feet and pointed a finger at the toy train. "You can talk!"

"I am a demon of the abyss," the train replied. "Of course I can talk! I am Terrance the Terrible, destructor of souls, devourer of the innocent, fornicator of–"

"Your name's Terrance?" Joachim asked, confused. He picked up his locomotive and inspected it closely. "What's a fornicator? This is cool! I didn't know that you could talk. *Mi abuelo* is gonna be sooooo jealous! His toys never talked. On purpose, I mean. He made them talk. Or seem like they talked, anyway. He did funny voices and they all argued all the time about who go to drink from his flask next. It was weird."

"Put me down you insolent young pup!" Terrance howled as his stack belched another thin trail of black smoke. "Do not mock me!"

"Is Terrance an evil name?" Joachim pressed, curious. "I mean, the guy at the corner store who talks with mama all the time is named Terrance, but he's just weird. I don't think he's evil. Maybe kinda gross."

"I am the purest of all evils!"

"That's not nice," Joachim pouted and set the locomotive back onto the tracks. "I like trains. Trains can't be evil. The one on TV is good."

"I am anything but good!" the train screeched as it began to chug slowly around the track. "I am a harbinger of great evil, the messenger of the *Flitpa'gh!* I am the terror who whispers in the dark to terrorize little boys in their sleep!"

"You're weird," Joachim said as he sat down and crossed his legs. He watched the train circle the track for a moment. "Can you do tricks?"

"I can summon the demons from hell itself!" Terrance shouted as he continued to move in an endless circle, his tiny smoke stack puffing a thin trail of black smoke behind it. Joachim continued to watch, intrigued. Terrance continued to boast. "I am the messenger of death and decay! I am the guardian of the darkness! I am–"

"That sounds boring," the little boy admitted after thinking for a moment, cutting off Terrance's rant. "Can you balance on one side? Oh! Can you do a loop-de-loop? I'd love to see a train do a loop-de-loop!"

"I do not perform tricks, you wretched pup! You insolent child! You bastard whelp! You son of a fatherless whore!"

Joachim's lips quivered but he forced himself not to cry. Instead, he stood up and balled up his tiny little fists. He glared angrily down at the train and stuck out his chin determinedly.

"You shut up!" Joachim told it. "You're just a big bully!"

"And what are you going to do about it? Huh? Yeah, nothing. That's what I– Hey, put me down!"

Joachim had picked up the small locomotive and held it in front of his face. He glared at the two headlamps that flanked the engine stack on either side. He guessed that this was the annoying little train's eyes. He poked one to check.

"Ouch!" Terrance roared. "Unhand me, you despicable undergrown worm!"

"I'll put you down, but you have to quit saying mean things," Joachim told the train.

"Ha! I'll never quit insulting you, you chewed piece of gum stuck to the underside of a shoe!"

Joachim had enough. He began to shake the train very hard in his hand.

"I. Said. *Stop!*" Joachim shouted.

"Joachim?" a concerned voice called from the living room. "Everything okay in there?"

"*Si, mama,*" Joachim said as he continued to shake the train. "Just playing."

"Okay."

"Now," Joachim growled fiercely as he finally stopped shaking the locomotive. "I'm going to set you down and you're going to be nice to me."

"...I think I'm going to puke..."

"If you're not nice to me, I'll...I'll...I'll let the dog from next door chew on you!" Joachim exclaimed as sudden inspiration flashed before his eyes.

"You wouldn't!"

"Try me."

Terrance stared at the young child for a moment, considering. He could see the steel in the boy's eye and decided that he did not want to test the child. He breathed a mighty final sigh and belched one last thick plume of smoke before he stopped spinning his wheels. He flashed his lights twice at the little boy holding him in acquiescence.

"I will be nice to you," Terrance promised. "I will no longer insult you or your lineage. I promise to not call you a whelp anymore."

"Good," Joachim nodded and set the train down. He reattached it to the cars and watched it for a moment. "Remember, you promised."

The train slowly began to circle the track, silent and not speaking. Joachim felt proud. He had taught the evil little train a lesson that it would not soon forget.

⊕ ⊕ ⊕

I can feel the power now! It is in the rails! The circle is complete and the spell has been activated. Bring forth the minions of Hell!

⊕ ⊕ ⊕

"What's that smell?" Joachim asked, as he pinched his nose with two fingers. "Smells like rotten eggs!"

"It is brimstone, child!" Terrance shouted joyfully. "It is the smell of Hell itself!"

"Why does it have to smell like eggs though?" Joachim wondered as the wheels of the train began to glow green. "Whoa! Your wheels are glowing. I didn't know they could do that!"

"Yes, yes!" Terrance practically screamed. "I can feel the power! *Tule esiin, isäni, ja ottakaa tämä maailma säälittävästä kuolevaisista!*"

"That's a weird language," Joachim told the train as his eyes widened. The glow from the train's wheels had begun to spread to the tracks. "Is that German?"

"The Well of Terraño has been opened!" Terrance cackled with glee as he gained more and more speed with each circuit around the track. Sparks erupted from the wheels as the toy train practically flew around the rails. "The tides of evil shall wash through this opening!"

"Evil?" Joachim complained. "I thought you said you'd be good!"

"No, child, I merely promised to quit insulting you," Terrance replied and chuckled darkly. "Now the well can fully be opened and my mission will be complete!"

"A well?" Joachim blinked and his mouth dropped open a little. He remembered something that the strange man with the fedora and gold tooth had told him at the toy store. Something about making a wish in a well. It all suddenly came back to him. "A wish!"

As the train continued to race around the track, the faint green light began to glow brighter from within the tracks. Sickly shades began to blink rapidly inside, all of which made Joachim's head hurt. The green light grew brighter and a large flash accompanied it. Suddenly a whirlpool opened in the middle of the tracks. Down went his stuffed dog into the swirling green abyss. Terrance nearly screamed in joy as his triumph neared.

"The Well has been opened! Nothing can stop me now!" He shouted triumphantly. He swiveled his lamps and looked up at Joachim, who was staring into the well with horrid fascination. The young boy clutched something in his hand, something that caused a sick feeling in the locomotive's innards. "I shall be treated as a god by my master! I shall– wait…what is that in your hand?"

"It's a gold coin," Joachim said proudly. "I traded a toy car for it. The man needed it for his collection. He also said that I can make a wish with it by throwing it into a well." Joachim's arm cocked back. "That's a well. You're a lying bully. I'm ready to make a wish."

"Think this through, little boy," Terrance said as he stopped chugging along. If toy trains could look plaintively at someone, Terrance did just that. The evil train tried to look as innocent as he could. "Why waste the coin when you can use it to buy more trains? Or you could buy lots of candy"

Joachim was sorely tempted. He *really* wanted another train set, one that did not talk or do evil things. The candy he could do without. Unless it was a Kinder egg, that is.

"You can even buy miniature cows for the farm," Terrance reminded him. "And *hills*. Small trees to decorate the landscape, and maybe a…uh…windmill! Yeah, with a real farm house next to it!"

That *almost* sent Joachim over the edge. In the end, though, his innocence and natural goodness won out.

"No," he said, still tightly clutching the coin. He shut his eyes and fiercely made his wish. "I wish for you to go away and never come back, and your stupid well to close when you leave."

Joachim tossed the coin into the center of his toy train tracks. In an instant, all Hell broke loose.

Lightning erupted from within the center of the circle as the Well of the Damned was closed, blocking millions upon millions of demons from entering the world. The green circle close with an audible *pop* and the shockwave of the blast knocked over Joachim's toy pig and ruffled the leaves of the plant he had used as a forest.

Terrance had been knocked off of the track and was lying on his side, his tiny little driving wheels spinning helplessly. Joachim stood above the tiny toy train with his hands on his hips, thinking. He looked around his room and spotted the packaging the train set had come in. He nodded to himself.

"*Mama,* can we take my new toy back to the store?" Joachim called out loudly. "I don't think I'm old enough for a train set like this one yet."

⊕ ⊕ ⊕

Another millennia or ten stuck here in this cold, dark abyss. I should have known better but the boy was fragile. How was I supposed to know that he carried a coin blessed by King Solomon? Stupid infant should not have had such a potent magical item. The boy lives in an age of technology! Nobody believes in magic anymore!

…yes, My Lord. I understand.

No, My Lord. The boy sealed the gate when he took down the cursed implements and repackaged them in the box.

Sigh. I understand, My Lord. I shall begin mucking your stables immediately. Yes, My Lord, I plan on starting on your Hellcows.

…without a shovel. Yes, My Lord. I obey.

Gods damn it.

⊕ ⊕ ⊕

Rubina made the exchange with the store's owner, half her mind on the purchase as she accepted the money back. She was keenly aware that Joachim, a normally boisterous and outgoing child, had been rather subdued that day. She chalked it up to the strangeness of walking in and finding smoke in his room, as well as spotting her potted plant from the hall. She had accused him of trying to start a fire. Surprisingly, Joachim had not argued back, simply apologized for moving the plant and quickly took it back. He had then bathed without being told and changed into clean pajamas before going to bed.

That morning he had woken up and did all his chores without being asked. He had then as to return the train set to the store from which they had purchased it. Surprised, she had asked him why.

"I don't think I'm ready for a train set yet, *mama.*"

Most peculiar, but then Rubina was not one to look a gift horse in the mouth. She had accepted his explanation and they had taken the train into town. From there it had been a quick walk to find the decrepit old toy store.

As they walked in, Rubina made her way immediately to the counter, bag and train set box in hand. She motioned for Joachim to go and search for anything else he might want, just in case the store would not give her a refund on an opened item. She focused on the haggling man and forgot about her son for a moment.

Joachim wandered through the store and actually *looked* at the items displayed for the first time. He and his mother had been so intent on looking for toy trains that neither had actually seen anything else that was for sale. His mind boggled now at the vast array of toys, gadgets, and gizmos which were out on exhibition. He almost picked up one toy that looked like a top but saw that there was a red warning label on it. Remembering his toy train, he quickly pulled back his hand.

"That was very smart of you," a voice said kindly from behind. Joachim turned around and spotted the strange man from the day before. Joachim stuck his hands in his pockets and looked at the ground. "What's the matter, kid?"

"I lost your gold coin," Joachim mumbled. "I made a wish and threw it into the middle of my bedroom floor and it disappeared."

"Neat trick," came the reply. "So did it stop the train from opening a gateway to Hell?"

"I guess."

"Wonderfully done then!" the salesman's smile was wide and bright. "So why so glum, chum?"

Joachim shrugged and continued to stare at the tiled floor in silence. The salesman waited patiently for the young boy to speak. Many seconds passed before Joachim was able to lift his head. Joachim looked at Johnny with the most solemn of expressions upon such a youthful face.

"Terrance was a very bad train," he intoned.

INTERLUDE 18

Broken Toys

WHIRLYGIGS TOY STORE HAD EXISTED FOR well over one hundred years, and had found a home, at one time or another, in the big cities of at least thirty countries. Perhaps the most memorable location was when the shop was set up by its pale, red-haired proprietor in Hartford, CT, when an elderly man of letters and great note, blest the store with a visit in mid-December 1908.

It was a slow day and Willy was checking the shelf stock by himself, when the bell on the front door jingled. Turning around, he noticed a tall, septuagenarian gentleman in a white suit, sporting white whiskers and an equally white mane above an inquisitive face. Newspaper photos had betrayed the famous writer's identity over the years.

"Good day, sir," Willy said, with a slight bow. "Please take your time, Mister Clemens. You have the store to yourself today."

"Call me Sam, young man," Sam said, "then we shan't be strangers. My time is already taken up answering the letters of strangers. No need to feed the lot on my personal clock." Sam followed up this statement with a quick check of his gold pocket watch that he just as quickly put back in his vest pocket.

Sam then took a moment to take in the many distractions that filled the toy store. An electric train slowly moved around the periphery of the entire shop on small tracks atop a slightly wider shelf two feet from the ceiling. Next Sam picked up an eight-inch, German, cast-metal, Diver by Bing, examining it for a moment and chuckled mildly before setting it back down. Colored posters advertising the latest in exquisite toys covered all the walls.

"Now, I must confess," Sam said, "it has been many years since I entered a toy establishment. My youngest is twenty-nine years of age, you know. It was your unusual sign outside that caught my attention."

"Ah, yes," Willy said, walking to the front of the shop, "an acquisition and gift from a French inventor, one Georges Claude. It is, in fact, a prototype that will not become available to the public until next year."

"I take it that electricity powers the unusual light bulb-like lettering and script?" Sam asked.

"Yes," Willy said, with a smile, "the glass tubing is actually filled with a gas known as neon. When electricity flows into the sealed glass, this gas fluoresces, thus the amazing and delightful illumination."

"My, what unusual modern times we live in, good sir," Sam replied, "though I fear the day that technology will surpass our human interaction."

"Surely, toys," Willy said, "are one aspect of technology that will always appeal to the fellowship of children?"

"Toys, eh?" Sam chuckled again. "Well, for myself, good friends, good books, and a sleepy conscience: this is the ideal life."

Time passed quickly as Willy engaged in a lively conversation with the famous writer, discussing multiple topics: from the evolution of humanity's intelligence to speculations on what the future might bring. At one point, Sam checked his watch and both men were surprised that three hours had passed since they started talking.

"Well," Sam said, "I must be off, young man. Stormfield calls and I would reach it before dusk's fall."

"Good day, Sam," Willy said.

Sam stopped for a moment at the front door, his hand on the door knob.

"Willy," Sam said, "I like this shop. Here's a little advice from one not long for this world…damn this cigar-heart of mine…keep away from people who try to belittle your ambitions. Small people always do that, but the really great make you feel that you, too, can become great. Good day my friend."

Another moment passed and the illustrious visitor was gone.

A handful of days later, Willy read in the local newspaper that Samuel Clemens' twenty-nine-year old daughter Jean had drowned in the bathtub, the result of an epileptic seizure on Christmas Eve. The grief that struck Clemens was surely powerful, and Willy was not all that surprised four months later when he heard that Mark Twain had passed away in the same country home.

Against The Tide

Joseph Capdepon II and Christopher L. Smith

"Like my father, I would never as a child throw anything away, keeping old toys, electric motors and bits of broken machines under my bed in what I called my Box of Useful Things."

–Nick Park

HE T-REX SAT INSIDE THE MESH BAG, watching the man walk through the airport. The last twenty-four hours had been weird, even for him.

He'd been sitting on the shelf at Whirligigs with the other 'special' toys, when a tall man wearing a duster and fedora plucked him off the shelf.

"You are exactly what I'm looking for," the man had said with a smile. Light flashed off of his single gold incisor. "You can call me Johnny."

After a few minutes of good-natured haggling with Willy, the store's owner and sole employee, the T-Rex and Johnny walked through the back door. The sunlight seemed somehow muted in the alley, giving everything around them a flat quality that contrasted sharply with the frivolous colors and eclectic design of the toy store. There wasn't time to contemplate what could be lurking there, however.

Johnny took two, quick, jig-like steps and the world twisted. The next thing the T-Rex knew, they were somewhere else, stepping from an alcove into a rush of people. A sign above them read "Bush Intercontinental Airport."

"Welcome to Houston, my plastic friend," Johnny said. "We shan't wait long. Our client will be along shortly."

Johnny sat the toy on the chair next to him, and for the next few minutes kept a running commentary of the people walking through the concourse. He broke off as he spotted someone out of the T-Rex's line of sight.

"Here we go," he said. "Let's go meet your soon- to- be new owner."

Johnny stood, picked him up, and followed a man in his late thirties to the luggage claim carousel. They watched as the man retrieved his bag, made his way to a nearby gift shop, and examined the toys on display. Johnny moved closer, smiling.

"I believe I have the answer to your problem," Johnny said, holding up the T-Rex.

"How did you know?" the man asked.

"Obviously, you are looking for a gift for a young child," Johnny said. "I have this fellow here, direct from Whirligigs in Chicago. I don't happen to need him after all, and could be convinced to let him go, for the right price."

"Whirligigs?" The man's eyes widened. "I was just in Chicago, and didn't make it there. What do you want for it?"

"Not money," Johnny said, as the other man pulled out a faded leather wallet. "Your pen you will do nicely. Even trade."

"The President gave me that pen...I don't know."

"The T-Rex has chomping action, and sound effects," Johnny said. The T-Rex roared and gnashed his teeth on cue. "The perfect gift for a young boy."

The man looked at him and smiled.

"You know what, you're right." He pulled the pen out of his pocket as Johnny lifted the T-Rex, both items changing hands at the exact same time. "I didn't vote for that guy, anyway."

Johnny winked at him as they left the store. A small group of people walked in front of him as he waved goodbye. When they passed, Johnny was gone.

⚭ ⚭ ⚭

The T-Rex—*Terry*, he reminded himself—*the boy named me Terry*—righted and pushed himself to his feet after Braeden left the room. The kid was enthusiastic in his play, but there was no damage. A voice came from under the bed.

"Surprised you could do that."

Terry whirled around, a low growl rumbling in his chest. "Who's there?"

"Stand down, Dino-destroyer." The voice, although familiar, held so much static Terry couldn't quite place it. He squinted into the shadows as a single light came into view. With the sound of grinding gears, a wind-up robot waddled towards him.

The foot-tall robot looked like it had been through a war zone. Chrome finish flaked and peeled at several places on its body, most notably from the skull-shaped head. The head itself, made to swivel when the toy walked, was unable to move more than a few millimeters without a loud clicking sound. While the left eye glowed brightly, the right eye was dark, the lens cracked. Scratches marred the rest of the body— a trail of gashes starting at the left shoulder, crossing the torso, and terminating at the cracked plastic shards of the right elbow.

"That you Ultramax?" It had been years since Terry and the robot had shared a shelf at Whirligigs. They'd become friends, spending long hours talking about their lives before Willie acquired them. Two old souls sharing a common fate.

"It's good to see you, pal. I go by Pickles now." Gears whirred and clicked as the robot stood straighter. "The boy named me."

Time hadn't been easy on Pickles. The robot looked rode hard and put away wet.

"What happened to you, man?"

Terry had heard horror stories from the refurbished toys at Whirligigs, but couldn't imagine his friend going through that torture. Braeden seemed to be nice. His room was clean...orderly. All the toys were cared for, except Pickles.

"It's not what you think." The robot said. "He's a good kid. I've been hiding. Don't want him to see me this way. "

"So...How?"

Pickles stomped towards him.

"You do know what's started today?"

"Sha'Daa," Terry whispered.

"Aye," Pickles said. "It's upon us again. I take it you're still on the side of the humans?"

Terry raised his head.

"Always," he said.

"I hope then, that you're ready," Pickles said, "They're coming for the boy."

"Is that why...?" Terry gestured at the damage. Pickles nodded.

"Every night for the past week they've attacked. Small groups— scouts really— pushing through the weakened boundaries, probing the defenses." He looked out the window at the darkening sky. "Tonight, they'll come in full."

"What are we facing?" If the last Sha'Daa, ten thousand years ago, was any indication, it could be literally anything.

"Spiders." Pickles smiled at Terry's shudder.

"Why did it have to be spiders?"

"Still haven't gotten over that, huh?"

"What do you think, Tin Can?" Terry couldn't keep the snarl from his voice. "You weren't the one that fell into the nest."

"No, but I pulled you out," Pickles said. "We still have a few hours until the sun sets and the fun begins. How about we head down the hall and have a chat with the Malibu dolls?"

"Shouldn't we be getting ready for the attack?"

"Bah. The spiders show up. We smash them." Pickles waved his good arm. "Simple. Could be our last night, though. Might as well have some fun."

"Still the optimist," Terry said.

"I like to call it 'aggressive realism,' old friend," Pickles said. 'So, are we going to go see how bendy those Malibu dolls are, or what?"

⊕ ⊕ ⊕

Terry crouched in the shadows of the bed, Pickles next to him. As Braeden slipped off into sleep, it started. The sound of legs scuttling across the hardwood floor broke the silence.

"Here we go," Terry growled.

"Think you can smash some spiders?" Pickles flexed his good arm, squeaks and pops filling the air.

"Try to keep up," Terry said. "Or do you need some oil for those rusted joints?"

Spiders swarmed from the shadows: brown recluse, orb weavers, black widows, wolf spiders, multiple times larger than their standard counterparts. They moved in small units towards the bed and Braeden. Pickles stomped out into the middle of the room, raised his good arm and brought it down in a chopping motion.

"You shall not—"

Two jumping spiders pounced, knocking Pickles onto his back, muffling his war cry with their striped bodies. Terry dashed towards them, spinning at the last second to slam his tail into one of the attackers. Pickles grabbed the other by the head, squeezing until it burst in his hand. Guts sprayed all over him.

"That's a good look for you," Terry said.

"Bugger off." Pickles wiped as much of the goo from his face as he could. He pointed. "Incoming!"

More spiders charged from the shadows. Terry leapt forward, landing on top of a wolf spider. It crunched beneath his paws. He left its twitching corpse to face two orb weavers scuttling towards him, silken thread stretched between them.

Terry crouched, caught the thread in his jaws, and tossed his head. The attackers flailed as they flew upward, colliding in mid-air with a crunch. Disembodied legs flew as Terry whirled, building momentum before slamming them to the floor. Spinning, he brought his tail down, smashing one into a mess of hair and carapace.

The other pushed itself forward unevenly on its remaining legs. The T-Rex flicked his head again, using the silk tether to jerk it towards Pickles. The robot stomped down, rupturing the cephalothorax.

A brown recluse lunged toward Terry. He dodged, spinning as the spider tried to sink its fangs into him. He reared up on his tail, coming down hard, and smashed the spider."

Pickles walked toward him, ripping a leg off a dead spider as he came. Nonchalantly, he threw it like a spear at an approaching wolf spider, piercing its eye. Without looking, Pickles slammed his fist into it, driving it into the spider's skull.

"A little help," Terry growled, the brown recluse pushing him to the ground.

Pickles grabbed the brown recluse and heaved, tearing it off the dinosaur. A fast, hard squeeze crushed its head. He dropped the spasming body as he turned towards Braeden's bed. Two black widows, bright red hourglass shapes on their abdomen glowing with infernal light, made their way towards top of the bed post.

"Toss me!" Pickles said, moving towards Terry's tail.

The T-Rex waited a moment to make sure his friend was situated, then launched him with a grunt. Pickles flew through the air, tumbled onto the bed, and pushed himself up with his good arm.

Braeden was in a deep sleep, unaware of what was happening around him. The black widows moved quickly, spinning web around Braeden's feet. Pickles bounded towards them with an electronic cackle.

Claws on hardwood drew Terry's attention from the fight on the bed. A small horde, led by two huge tarantulas, swarmed him. A minute later, all were twitching piles of goo. He turned back to check on his friend.

A spider crouched and launched itself at the robot. Pickles slammed himself flat into the bed, letting the spider fly over him. Its momentum carried over the edge, into space.

Straight towards Terry.

"Look out!"

His mouth dropped open as the spider slammed into him, stifling the curse before he could utter it. Terry tumbled backwards, mouth full of spider, tail thrashing. They rolled over three orb spiders, crushing them. Terry bit down, teeth cracking the glossy-black exoskeleton. Struggling, the Black Widow managed to gouge several deep furrows in his plastic body as Terry bit down harder. He twisted his head as he rolled on top of it, tearing it in two.

"How's that taste, old buddy?" Pickles asked.

Terry spat spider innards out of his mouth and stared up at his friend. He waved both his stubby arms at the robot. "This is me giving you the finger!"

Pickles chuckled, charging out of sight. Seconds later, his hand appeared, holding one of the attackers. As Terry watched, it disappeared, reappeared, and disappeared again. Finally, all that came up again was a crushed pile of legs and carapace.

"How's it looking down there?" Pickles' voice came from above.

Terry slammed a spider into goo with his tail, while ripping the front leg off another. He spat the twitching leg to the floor.

"Could be better!"

As quickly as the attack began, it ended. The remaining spiders scurried back into the shadows. Terry looked up at Pickles.

"This how it normally goes?"

"Normal for this week, at least." Pickles slid off the bed, landing next to Terry with a rattle. "I guess they're done for the night."

Terry froze as a voice echoed in his mind. From Pickles' reaction, he was hearing the same thing.

"I see that you have a friend, my rusty robot adversary," the voice said. "It won't matter. The boy will be mine, and the way will be opened. Save yourself some hardship. Let me take the boy."

"How about you shove it up whatever orifice you defecate from!" Pickles followed his insult with various gestures. One hand or not, he got his point across. Terry was impressed.

"Tomorrow little friends," the voice said, with a chuckle. "Tomorrow the boy is mine, and both of you will spend eternity in torment as my playthings."

"Bring it on, scary, creepy voice," Terry said.

The voice faded from their minds. Pickles and Terry looked at one another.

"Well, that was interesting," Terry said.

"I don't think it'll send anymore tonight," Pickles said. "Go for broke tomorrow, though."

"We'll be ready for it." Terry looked around at the scattered remains. "What about all the dead ones?"

"What about them?"

"Won't it freak the boy out?" Terry gestured at a pile of various twitching parts.

"Give it a minute."

"What the…" Terry watched in astonishment as the dead spiders began to dissolve, disappearing into a fine mist. "At least it's tidy?"

"Maybe it has OCD," Pickles shrugged.

"What are we going to do?"

"About what?"

"Stop being a jackass," Terry said. "How are we going to protect the boy?"

"I've got an idea," Pickles said. "Cue the 80's montage!"

Terry shook his head and followed his friend under the bed.

⊕ ⊕ ⊕

"First things first," Pickles said. "We need to get you armed."

"I do have arms," Terry said. "Two out of two, unlike someone I could mention."

"Ha ha. Grab that for me." Pickles pointed at a large book, *Castles and Creatures*, 4th edition. Terry glared at the robot.

"Really? The book?"

"Quit waving those stubby things around," Pickles said. "Like I said, I have some ideas."

"I can tell you're waiting for me to ask, so I'll get it over with." Terry wrestled with the hardcover, finally flopping it onto the floor. He pushed it over towards Pickles with his tail. "What's with the book?"

Pickles opened it, then tapped the page header with his good arm. Spells—

"Big juju my friend. First, we outfit you with a weapon, then we use the book and juice it up with some power." He laughed as Terry narrowed his eyes. "Boy's Dad picked it up last year at Whirly's. This is the real deal."

"If you say so. What about you?"

Pickles smiled. "I do need a new arm. Might actually be able to stand a chance of winning then," Terry said. "Well, I could probably win on my own, but I would like the help. Even if it is from a broken down, old robot."

"I've been holding my own. But, an extra pair of arms would be good to have," He grinned. "Even if they are short,"

"Dick." Terry laughed. "Alright, what do we need to do?'"

⊕ ⊕ ⊕

After a short day of play with Braeden, they met under the bed. Terry maneuvered the TERF Super Assault gun into their makeshift workshop as Pickles flipped through the *Castles and Creatures* spells section. On the floor next to him, he'd arranged various dice.

"I think I've got this figured out," he said.

"It's not going to blow up, is it?" Terry looked at his friend warily. "Because I'd really rather not get blown up."

"It won't blow you up." Pickles grinned. "Probably."

"You really are not filling me with confidence, Tin Man."

"Don't worry about it," Pickles said. "It's not like I'm strapping a nuclear accelerator to your back."

Terry stomped over and stood beneath the TERF Super Assault gun. "Well?"

"Hold on." Pickles picked up a twenty-sided die and rolled it across the floor. The robot pumped his fist in the air as it stopped. "Natural twenty!"

"Is that good?" Terry inched closer to the TERF gun and its makeshift harness, now glowing softly in the shadows.

"It's nuclear accelerator good!" Pickles cackled.

"I thought that was bad?"

"Good, bad, either way you're going to kill a lot of spiders," Pickles said. "Stop worrying, and stand still."

Pickles lowered the weapon onto Terry's back. He connected the straps, pulled them tight, then ran the trigger control to Terry's right arm.

"Alright, you are loaded up," Pickles said. "Should be able to fire off at least five volleys before it runs out."

"And when it does run out? What do I do then?"

"Hit the release on your chest, and use this." Pickles rummaged in a pile of discarded toys and clothing. After a few seconds, he held a toy bastard sword over his head. "Here it is. I have the power!"

He walked over to Terry and handed it to him. As he took it, a tingling sensation moved up his short arm, spreading through his body.

"Whoa," he said, "Where'd you find this?"

"I've been preparing for a bit," Pickles said. "I was going to use it, but it'll do more good in your hands."

"What about you?" Terry swung the sword in slow arcs, getting a feel for the balance.

"What about me?"

"Your arm."

"Oh. That." Pickles walked over to small workbench with a rag draped over it. Grabbing the cloth, he whipped it away with a flourish, beneath lay two devices.

Terry recognized one of them—a long-barreled lighter used for BBQ grills. The robot had modified it some, removing any safety features, adding smaller lighters to the sides, and connecting them with small sections of rubber tubing. The whole monstrosity was painted matte black.

The other looked like the bastard child of a chainsaw and a sword, but made from plastic gears and rubber bands, with shards of glass super glued in certain areas. A small motor, from what Terry assumed was another building kit, powered the contraption, the battery pack slung from another jury-rigged harness.

"What in the thirty-seven hells are those?" Terry asked.

Pickles chuckled as he lifted the lighter.

"Says right here." He pointed to the word 'Flammenwerfer,' painted in bright-red down the length of the barrel. "Help me with this,"

He laid his arm next to it and motioned for Terry to connect the straps. Terry struggled, but tightened them down. Pickles turned and squeezed the trigger. A bright flame squirted out the end.

"I'm so going to werf flammen." Pickles laughed, his glitchy voice giving it a sinister, wild tone. He maneuvered the stub of his other arm into the chainsword. Terry pushed it tight against the stump, and helped Pickles connect it.

Pickles moved his arm and the chainsword whirred to life, broken glass sparkling as it buzzed along the weapon. Pickles held it above his head, laughed again, following it with a burst of fire.

"We are going to mess up those eight-legged freaks, find the asshat that is controlling them, and shove this up his culo," Pickles said.

"You think we can do it?" Terry, caught up in the excitement, swung his sword viciously, slashing the air in front of him.

"I give us a fifty-percent chance that we manage to keep the boy safe, and both live."

"Really, fifty-percent?" Terry grinned. "And here I thought you were going to say we are screwed."

"One other thing." Pickles pushed a small bag in front of Terry and pulled it open. Inside were more dice.

"What are those for?"

"These babies here are for blowing up spiders," Pickles said with a grin. "Magicked them up. Roll them out, and boom! Lots of spider bits."

"Let's do this," Terry said with a roar. "Cue the music!"

Pickles hit play on an old MP3 player. Whitney Houston's *I Will Always Love You* blasted into the air.

"Whoops. Wrong playlist." Pickles nudged the controls, cutting off the long, drawn out warble. Eighties hair rock took its place. "Much better. Ok, let's go!"

⊕ ⊕ ⊕

They sauntered from beneath the bed, weapons ready. Above them, Braeden whimpered, nightmares troubling his sleep.

"Think it will work?" Terry paused, looked over the boy's room, then back at his companion.

Pickles nodded, surveying what they'd accomplished that day. Toys littered the floor in strategic locations, the result of subtle hints to Braeden as they'd played. Some, like the watchtower, had been outright manipulation, pushing him gently in the correct direction. Both felt bad about it, but they needed whatever edge they could get.

The toys were spread out across the floor, arranged to funnel the spiders towards them, as well as slow them down as they advanced. On the floor around the bed, Pickles had drawn symbols from *Castles and Creatures* in chalk, leaving small sections unfinished. He now made his way to each one, finishing the design.

"Armed," he said, "Watch your step."

He pulled weaponized dice from their bag, lining them up with enough space in between so Terry could launch them without issue. He left two of the twenty-sided die in the bag, and strapped it to Terry's side.

"Those we save for last," he said.

"Should be starting soon." Terry looked up at the window, just as a flash of lightning highlighted the streaks of rain. "Perfect night for it."

"Can I ask you a personal question Terry?"

"Sure."

"Why the T-Rex?"

"Kids love the T-Rex" He turned to his friend, chuckling. "Why the wind-up robot?"

"The eyes glowed."

The room grew quiet, all background noise becoming muted. Shadows deepened as the bulb from the huge cowboy night light dimmed. Multiple legs, scurrying across the hardwood floor, broke the silence. Terry and Pickles stomped forward to meet their enemy.

Spiders covered the floor, bounding over one another as they advanced. Terry, taking his position behind the line of dice as Pickles climbed the tower, watched a large wolf spider crawl onto a pile of blocks, knocking them over. This in turn triggered a small flash of light, setting it alight.

It crumpled to the ground and rolled over, legs curling into its body. Two smaller house spiders also caught fire. They careened off, spreading destruction in an incendiary chain reaction. The first wave, well in front of the second, died in job lots, until there was enough distance between the assailants for the flames to peter out.

"Hot damn," Pickles said from above.

"Hell yeah!" Terry pumped his free fist in the air. "That worked beautifully!"

Flashes of light briefly illuminated the room as attackers triggered booby traps. Small pyres dotted the floor, the enemy soldiers burning brightly for a moment until their lives were snuffed out by the flames.

"Need to remember that trick," Terry muttered.

The invaders stopped their advance. Larger ones moved backwards to allow a horde of smaller spiders to move to the front. They moved quickly, throwing themselves at the booby traps.

"Damn it!" Pickles thumped his flamethrower on the plastic tower. "That wily bastard is clearing a path."

The larger spiders moved forward, advancing slowly behind the suicidal wave.

"You ready, Dino Boy?"

Terry roared an affirmative and lined up on the first die. He looked up at Pickles, waiting for the signal. Fire illuminated the room as the advance mob cleared the traps for their brethren.

"Almost," Pickles raised the flamethrower. "Almost."

Terry glanced at the approaching army. It took everything he had to wait—the advancing horde of creepy crawlers made him itch. Memories of getting trapped years ago in Whirlygigs flashed through his mind. He turned back to his friend, trying to shut out the ever-louder sound of claws scritching on the floor. They were so close, and only getting closer by the second...

"Now!" Pickles dropped his arm.

Terry swung his tail, sending a ten-sided die hurtling towards the oncoming spiders. It bounced across the floor, its non-spherical shape making the path difficult to predict, into the midst of the attackers. One of the smaller spiders pounced on it, the numbers stamped on its face glowing as the spell activated. It, and the spiders surrounding it, disappeared in the resulting explosion.

"Whoa!"

Terry moved to the next die, then the next, flicking them towards the spiders, one after another, until all tumbled across the floor. Explosions and flashes of light tore wider and wider holes in the enemy lines.

"Where the hell are they coming from?" He couldn't believe it. No matter how many died, more came.

"I don't know." Pickles landed with a thump next him, then shrugged. "Everywhere?"

As the smaller spiders spent themselves triggering the booby traps, a line of wolf spiders charged across the floor, dodging the rolling, exploding dice.

"Werf the flammen you eight legged freaks!" Pickles charged, chainsword held high, flame spurting from his flamethrower. "Here comes the killy part!"

He impaled one of the wolf spiders on the rotating blade, broken glass tearing it apart. A gout of flame engulfed another in mid pounce. The robot stepped to the side as it fell to the ground, burning legs twitching.

Pickles cackled madly as he fought the next, dodging, twisting, and striking in one smooth motion. The spider jerked back, and Pickles followed through with a burst from the flamethrower. The flaming spider reeled, slammed into one of its fellows, and rolled into a ball as it died.

Pickles stabbed another spider, lifting it into the air. Bits of carapace and gore rained down on him as his weapon tore it apart. Thrusting the flamethrower into its poisonous maw, he squeezed the trigger. Flame shot down the monster's throat as the smell of cooking organs filled Terry's nose.

Out of dice, Terry pulled the trigger of his own weapon, feeling the TERF gun on his back recoil as the magic imbued darts streaked out into the mass of arachnids. The missiles impacted, sending pieces of orb spider through the air in all directions. Terry drew his sword with a roar, and charged.

Some spiders made it past them. The first to reach the symbols on the floor launched itself towards the bed, only to fall dead on the floor. More followed, with the same results.

"I love the smell of burning spiders at night," Pickles said. "Smells like victory!"

Terry shook his head as he shoved his sword through another spider, then fired the TERF gun. He moved up next to his friend, sword held ready.

"What are they doing?" Terry kept his voice low as the invaders retreated.

"Running away?"

"I don't think so," Terry pointed the sword towards the shadows. Four large tarantulas emerged slowly into the light. "They're making room."

"Balls." Pickles nodded at the TERF gun. "How many times have you fired it?"

"Twice."

"Bring the pain."

Terry pulled the trigger again, sending a flight of magic missiles at the tarantulas. Two died immediately, unable to clear the target area. The others burst forward, covering ground faster than he thought possible. Before he could line up another salvo, they were too close.

Terry ducked, spinning as legs swished past his head. He completed the move as the spider lunged, bringing his sword up and staggering under the force of the blow. He recovered and thrust the blade into the tarantula's abdomen. Terry wrenched upwards, slicing the beast almost in two. He retched as the flood of guts covered him.

The last tarantula attacked Pickles as Terry turned toward his friend. Weaving past the robot's defense, it grabbed the chainsword close to the elbow. The tarantula skittered to the side, pulled, and sent the contraption into the distance. Fire spewed into the spider's eyes as Pickles squeezed the trigger.

Engulfed in flame, the tarantula slammed itself into the robot, driving him to the ground. Thrashing, Pickles tried to free himself, but lacked the leverage. Terry rushed over and slammed his tail into the large, flame covered spider. As it tumbled across the floor, Pickles pushed himself to his feet.

"That was close," he said.

"Where the hell did those big bastards come from?"

"Hell." They watched the spider burn.

"That was easy."

The floor vibrated. In the deepest part of the closet, something rustled, the sound of dead branches scraping across a tomb. Out of the shadows a spider the size of a Chihuahua made its way across the floor.

"You had to say it." Pickles smacked him with the Flammenwerfer. "Fire damn it!"

Terry pulled the trigger on the TERF gun, sending a volley towards the monstrosity. To his surprise, the darts passed through it and disappeared, doing no harm.

"What the hell?"

"I don't know, fire!"

More missiles arced out, stopping short and exploding in mid-air.

"Keep firing!" Pickles' voice held a note of desperation.

Another volley, and again the missiles failed to connect. He pulled the trigger one last time, spirit sinking at the click of an empty magazine.

"I'm out!" He hit the quick release on his chest and the TERF gun slid off his back.

Pickles charged, shooting flames as he advanced. With a curse, Terry followed him.

"You crazy bag of bolts," Terry shouted. "You're going to get us both killed."

The giant spider swung a leg at the robot, who rolled forward beneath it, sending a blast from his flamethrower upwards into its abdomen. Faster than it should have been, the monstrous spider sidestepped, slamming another leg down toward its attacker. Pickles looked up in time to see the leg come toward him, but not in time to dodge. The leg clipped him, tossing him through the air. He landed hard, the impact tearing off one of his legs, and sending the flamethrower skittering across the floor.

Terry yelled as he slashed, his sword cutting deep into the exoskeleton of a hind leg. The spider spun and faced him, multifaceted eyes boring into his. He froze, the air shimmered, and he found himself standing on a vast plain.

Overhead, angry clouds flew across the bruised sky. Stunted, malformed trees dotted the landscape in the distance.

"You can't win. Your robot friend is going to die. Then you will die. Then I will feast, and you can't stop me."

Terry looked around, trying to pinpoint where the voice was coming from. No luck, it seemed to be coming from everywhere.

"Look at yourself," the voice continued, "Look at what your future holds. Broken. Forgotten. Tossed in the trash like so much garbage when he is finished with you."

"I don't care!" He directed his words to the sky. "Every break, every tear, every scar! If it means the boy leads a full, happy life, it'll be worth it,"

"He will forget about you. He will forget about the toy he played with as a child. You won't even be a fond memory for him."

"Even if I am forgotten, he will remember my words," Terry said. "You'll not have him!"

"Give up. I can give you life. A real existence, not this sham. Your soul is old, I can see that. You want to feel again, don't you? To feel the wind on your skin. The rain as it hits you. The caress of a lover?"

A subtle sensation came over him. He looked down at his hands. His _real_ hands, not those of the various totems he'd inhabited over the last ten thousand years. It had been so long...

"Never!" Terry stabbed his sword down into the turf between his feet. The ground exploded with light as the landscape faded. He found himself standing before the giant spider, back in Braeden's room.

He lunged forward, slashed, and cut one of its legs in half. The spider spun, foul smelling liquid squirting over Terry and the floor. He dodged another of the legs as it hurtled towards him. The spider launched itself into the air, landing near Pickles.

"Get away from him, you bastard!" He started forward, only to lose his footing in the ichor, and crash to the floor.

Pickles stirred, rotating his head as far as he could to look up at the hulking body of the spider standing over him, venom dripping from its massive fangs. Fangs that opened and closed, menacingly. He tried to drag himself away, but a leg of the spider shot down, pinning him against the floor.

"Terry!" Pickles struggled, but with only one leg and arm, it was futile. "The dice! Throw the dice!"

Confusion set in for a moment, then he remembered the bag strapped to his side. He sliced it open, the dice inside hitting the floor.

"Do it Terry!" The spider was bending its hulking form towards Pickles, fangs getting closer. "Do it!"

Terry spun, launching the dice with his tail, sending them tumbling across the floor. Pickles stared up at the spider, and winked his good eye.

"Boom, you son of a bitch,"

The dice came to a stop beneath the spider, both showing the number twenty. Pickles laughed, a triumphant, gleeful electronic cackle as they exploded, engulfing him and the monstrosity in blinding white light.

A terrible scream tore through Terry's head as the spider died, slowly consumed by magical fire. He stared down at the half-melted body of his friend as the flames subsided, a bittersweet smile on his face. Pickle's remaining hand curled into a thumbs-up.

Terry stabbed his sword into the immolated remains of the spider.

"Enjoy Hell you bastard."

⊕ ⊕ ⊕

Terry watched as the corpses of the spiders dissolved. Nothing would remain in the morning to alert Braeden as to what had happened during the night.

His soul ached as he stood over the remains of Pickles.

"It was a good battle my friend," he said. "Rest easy in Valhalla. The boy will be safe."

Slowly, what was left of the robot toy began to disintegrate. Terry moved backwards, surprised, as his friend's body disappeared. When it was gone, he climbed onto the bed and walked gently towards his ward. He situated himself carefully near Braeden's head.

Terry watched as the boy slept; his dreams troubled no longer.

Crack In The Box

FROM THE SPEAKERS OVERHEAD BLARED the muzak version of Sheryl Crow's *Roller Skate*.

Willy was exhausted. He'd been awake for over forty hours. Never one to admit weakness or defeat, he quickly downed a large glass of orange juice, sweetened with equal and dangerous doses of: Adderall, Ritalin, and Desoxn. This brought his focus back to full clarity, but definitely left him more than a little jittery. One positive side to this condition was that since he was still alive, it meant that not a single hell portal had yet been fully breached, as the apocalypse had not scoured the Earth…yet.

The phone booth rang and Willy stepped inside.

"What?" Willy asked.

"Hello, this is Kvaris the Interface."

"This better be important."

"The Midnight Laborers," Kvaris said, "have just declared a strike."

"A strike?" Willy asked. "Right now?"

"Yes," Kvaris said, "and the ledger indicates that no less than a hundred orders need to be filled in the next fifteen minutes."

"Well then," Willy snarled, "it looks like that labor/management soirée I've been putting off for half a century is about to begin."

Leaving the phone booth and striding to the very rear of the store, Willy found himself stewing. Ever since the beginning of the Sha'Daa, it had been one argument and negotiation after another. Now those ungrateful little wretches were going to hamstring him like this, without any warning, after all that he had done for those diminutive rascals over the decades?

Oh no, Willy thought, *this petty rebellion ends now*.

Willy walked right up to the naked concrete wall that stood to the left of the two wide openings, from which a long conveyor belt ran out, forming a fifteen-foot-long moving counter, only to return to the right-side opening. Strips of dark nylon and carbon fiber hung down from the tops of the openings, obscuring the view of anyone trying to peek into the combination stock room, micro-factory, and living facilities of the Midnight Laborers. Willy gritted his teeth and placed his left palm upon the wall.

A bright-green light emitted from the wall all around his hand. In moments, it spread to form a man-sized opening. Willy took a deep breath, then walked through the wall as if it were fog. A second later, the green glow disappeared. No sign of any doorway or portal was left.

⊕ ⊕ ⊕

Every eye was suddenly upon him.

"Boss!" a high-pitched voice yelled in surprise, "why…uh, what brings you here? We haven't seen you in an age, uh, sir."

Willy raked the assembled crew with a withering stare that had all six hundred of them looking away, to the floor, the ceiling, anywhere that wasn't their long-time employer's furious visage.

The setting for this confrontation would no doubt come as quite a shock to any of Willy's other employees, and to his customers. Willy was standing in a room as large as a dirigible hanger, a seeming impossibility because if you walked around the periphery of Whirligigs, the rear stock room couldn't be bigger than one hundred square feet.

Doctor Who's phone booth, Willy thought to himself. One of his employees could never stop talking about that long-running British science fiction television series.

The center of this expanse, consisted of a wide variety of working tables, slow-moving conveyor belts, and hundreds of machines, some as simple as foot-powered sewing machines, others late 20th Century, steam-powered devices, and not a few computer-operated, dimensional printers. All around this massive construction floor were narrow fields of grass and trees. Built against the distant walls, were a conglomeration of three-story homes, the majority stylized in wood, stone, and plaster, colorful structures that looked like illustrations out of a Brothers Grimm collection.

The Midnight Laborers appearance, however, was unlike anything seen on the planet. Their clothes were quite ordinary, and matched the nature of their homes in an unimaginative cultural way, i.e., sixteen and seventeen century work clothes, aprons, ruffled shirts and trousers for the males and long dresses for the females. Though barely topping four feet, all appeared to have attained their full growth. Willy knew that their children were sleeping or taking lessons in their homes.

More than the midnight laborer's diminutive statures, the truly surprising aspect of Willy's full-time fabrication and shipping employees was their epidermis. All sported sapphire-colored skin and silver-ivory hair. Their eyes were a bright gold, both pupils and sclera, making them look larger than normal. Otherwise, they were mostly humanoid: eyebrows, noses, mouths, ears, chins, foreheads. Each had four limbs though these ended on the hands with six fingers and on the feet with four toes. Anatomically, males and females pretty much mimicked that of homo sapiens, for yes, though humanoid in appearance, the Midnight Laborers were hominids split off from some of mankind's most ancient ancestors.

"Did I hear right?" Willy asked, "something about a strike, Ebrahim?"

The first male that had greeted Willy, grinned apologetically. "Well," Ebrahim started, "strike is a bit of a harsh word, ummmm…maybe *temporary labor respite* might be more accurate? You know, all those, um, minimal incentives you've given us over this past two months have really been a bite on the ass, boss."

Willy bit his lower lip. The time differential between the Midnight Laborers' factory and home facilities, and the real world, was such that every minute in the real world equaled one full hour in this pocket universe. Willy slowly nodded his head, taking in the truth that the current workload was far harsher than anything he had ever put them through before…and they'd worked for him for over one hundred years. Many had been born on the job, as it were, since their average lifespan was only fifty years, on top of the favorable time interval.

"Forgive me," Willy said, "my precious ones. I have not slept in two days, my time, and I did not want to frighten you with the truth, but I see that now is the time. For your two months The Sha'Daa has been occurring across the Earth."

Willy's last statement was like a lit match thrown upon a bathtub filled with gasoline. The gasps and shrieks of fear spread like a living wave that washed back and forth across the floor. A minute passed before the Midnight Laborers' shouting subsided enough for Willy to be heard.

"Take heart," Willy said, "for mankind has lasted this long in holding off that dreaded horror. If they can withhold the darkness for just twelve more hours, Earth Time, we will have won, and we will all survive. But to play our part, as my precognition magics have always urged me to do, requires that we continue creating toys until the forty-eight-hour interval is complete."

"But you never told us why, boss," Ebrahim spoke, "for we all know that the magics you imbue the toys contain equal amounts of evil and good…we do not know whether you truly want the Earth saved, or destroyed."

"The toys are neutral," Willy said, "it is up to the nature of each human who buys them to determine how they will be used. That is what the fates told me centuries ago, and I am compelled to honor that fact."

A murmur rippled through the purple crowd as they digested this startling new revelation about their lives-long purpose and impetus. Some were scared, others angry, and others merely confused.

"So, you think the Earth will survive?" Ebrahim asked, "or do you wish it to end? Or care you not at all, whatever happens? I must tell you, boss, since your last wife died one hundred years ago, and you never took on a new one, we have feared for your state of mind. Outwardly you have remained solicitous and friendly, but we were not fooled. We sense the emptiness inside you, and that, more than anything, fills us with fear."

A white flame of anger shot through Willy, but just as quickly was blown out. They were all, of course, correct.

Why is it that until these last days that I have not even thought about my former wives? Willy thought. Their names and face, unbidden for decades, suddenly filled his mind: Serika Han, petite, pale, long raven hair, with exquisite features and a talented water colorist; Roisin O'Shea, red hair, tall, fierce demeanor with the brightest smile and a wonderful poet; Aaliyah Chukwuemeka, tall, lithe, a strong sense of humor and an excellent sculptress; Navya Khatri, petite, bronze skin, elfin face, proud, noble, she made beautiful jewelry; and Luciana Oriol, long blonde hair, long-legged and a swift runner, quick to jealousy and desire, a masterful singer/songwriter. *Why have I not thought about you all until now?*

Willy shook his head to clear his confusion.

"Survival," Willy said, "of course. This realm will collapse if the Earth is overcome. You are my family. Trust me. We will get through this."

Whispers spread across the floor, but slowly, one by one, all of the Midnight Laborers nodded their heads in acknowledgment, Ebrahim being the last.

"Our fate has always been intertwined with yours, boss," Ebrahim said sadly, "ever since you freed us from the evil god Pairika's ages long imprisonment. The work will now recommence, with no further stops or breaks."

Willy smiled and turned around to reenter the real world. Of all the Midnight Laborers, only Ebrahim saw the single, glistening tear slip from Willy's right eye.

CHAPTER TWENTY

Have Space-
Gun Will Travel

Michael H. Hanson

*"Seeks painted trifles and fantastic toys, and eagerly
pursues imaginary joys."*

–Mark Akenside

HE TOY SPACE HELMET STOPPED MITCH
in his tracks. It was like a time-portal to his childhood (growing up
in the all black North Englewood district of Chicago) had opened
up right in front of him. For seconds, he couldn't believe it was real, but a few
tentative pokes with his right fingers proved otherwise. In its original box, and
looking brand new, was a Space Travel And Reconnaissance, aka S.T.A.R., Team
Space Helmet complete with Earphones, Removable Amber Dome, and a Star
Team Member Patch.

A moment later, Mitch's eyes went even wider as he recognized the treasure
that set on the shelf on either side, none other than the complete line of Space
Adventure Gear put out by the Ideal company back in the early nineteen-sev-
enties: the Nebulizer; the Space Utility Belt with Life Support Tank, Scanner
Scope, Astro Headset Communicator, Antigravity Tool and secret compartment;
the Remote Gripper Device; an Exploratory Probe Launcher, an Astro Beacon,
and lord almighty...a pair of Space Boots!

"Looks like somebody hit the jackpot," a lively voice spoke from behind.

Mitch turned around quickly and found himself face to face with a pale
man of average height sporting a large mop of carrot-red hair just a couple of
shades less bright than his crimson shirt.

"The name's Willy," the man said, "Willy Carroll. And I'm the proprietor of Whirligigs, and if I know the gleam of desire in a child's eyes then I'd say we're about to make a transaction. Am I right, Mister...?"

"Hanlon," Mitch replied with a frown. "Mitch Hanlon. I dunno...I was looking for a birthday gift."

"For your grandson?" Willy inquired.

Mitch sighed. It wasn't the first time he'd faced this reply.

"Actually," Mitch replied, "my son. He's eleven. I, uh, started a family a bit late in life."

"Not an issue," Willy said with a congenial laugh, "age is a state of mind and I can see you're a man of vigor and vim, so, would you like to get the whole kit and caboodle? The entire Space Adventure Gear set? The whole shebang, as it were?"

"Well, this is kind of old fashioned for today's kids..." Mitch started.

"Oh hush," Willy chuckled, revealing a bright shiny diamond on one of his upper right teeth, "what kid wouldn't get a kick out of playing with some toys his Dad had ached for as a kid?"

Mitch did a double-take as Willy grinned and snapped the bright red suspenders that held up his garish purple slacks.

"Oh no need to take offense," Willy said, "you wouldn't be the first guy to walk into my humble abode and find themselves confronting a treasure from their past. Happens more often than you might think."

"Yeah, well," Mitch said, "these look in mint condition and I'm sure you want collector prices so..."

"Nope," Willy said, gently grabbing Mitch's elbow and leading him toward the main cash register in the center of the display floor, "I won't hear of it. You wanted these toys more than food and air itself as a child, I just know it. Watching the moon landing in black and white with your Dad on the old boob tube, dreaming of exploring moon craters, yes you weren't the only one who felt that way, way back when."

Willy was not far off the mark, Mitch thought. He and his Dad had loved watching all the NASA TV broadcasts together, regardless of all the delays that occurred before takeoff. They never found any of it boring. When the S.T.A.R. space helmet and space boots were first advertised on the television Mitch's nights were haunted for weeks by dreams of exploring the moon. He'd begged his parents for over a month to buy him these toys, but they were a working-class family with four children, and there was no slack given for luxury toys. It was a desperate and even bitter desire that took over two years to dissipate. Two years of dreaming every night about being a Captain in the Terran Space Force.

Mitch suddenly noticed, mounted in a transparent display stand on the counter right in front of the cash register, a colorful small banner that looked like it might have once been the back page of a comic book. In exciting letter and font it blared, *BOYS! GIRLS! Enter KRAFT'S Naming Contest! WIN THIS LIFE-SIZE AEROJET TRAINING SPACE SHIP! Specially built for Kraft by Aerojet-General Corporation—Producers of propulsion systems for the Space Age—NASA Vanguard and Able, Navy Polaris, Air Force Titan, Army Hawk, the famous Aerobee sounding rockets and many others.*

"Oh my, god," Mitch breathed, "I remember this ad I read it in an old comic book when I was a kid. This was a contest for a twenty-nine-foot long space ship trainer that could hold up to four kids. I wanted to fill out this application, but my mom had to remind me it was from nineteen-fifty-nine and the contest had been won by some little girl well over a decade earlier. In fact, funny how I'm remembering this now, she told me it had ended up sitting in front of a hospital until it was finally destroyed. Huh…well I'm sure this isn't part of your store's collection…though it would be worth a fortune to some nutty wealthy collector if it had not been destroyed…"

"Unless they made two of them and never told anybody," Willy whispered, just loud enough to be heard.

"What?" Mitch said, startled by Willy's odd comment.

"Tsk, tsk, let's get back to business," Willy said, "so, umm, why I'm just sure I can drop the price of everything here down to something that will only mildly cripple your checking account my good sir," Willy finished.

And mildly cripple is about right, a shocked Mitch thought as he exited Whirligigs carrying two stuffed shopping bags out onto a busy Chicago sidewalk this side of Oz Park. His wife, Sara, was not going to be happy with the expenditure, but considering the size of his last raise at work, it would be a temporary bout of annoyance at best. He'd been made Senior Administrative Editor of the engineering magazine his corner of the press put out twice a month, a long overdue promotion whose benefits were finally kicking in.

A loud crack of thunder echoed from the south side, which Mitch found odd as it was a sunny day with few clouds.

A short while later, he made it to the Fullerton stop in Lincoln Park and hopped the CTA Red Line for his trip home. Barry's birthday party was still two hours away so there was plenty of time.

"Looks like quite the haul, Mitch," a deep voice spoke from the other side of the subway car.

Mitch looked up in surprise. Sitting directly across from him in the nearly empty double rows of seats was a tall, lanky man of indeterminate age. Oddly enough he was dressed in a dark grey suit, black shoes, trench-coat, and fedora, as opposed to Mitch's golf shirt, shorts, and kicks. The train's lame excuse for air conditioning didn't seem to bother the strange man at all.

"I beg your pardon," Mitch said, "Do we know each other?"

"The name's Johnny, Mitch," he said, "so now we're introduced. No worries, I'm not looking for a handout. Quite the opposite, as a matter of fact, I think I have just what you need, son."

"I think I've had my share of salesmen for the day, Mister, uh, Johnny," Mitch said.

"A salesman I am good sir," Johnny said with a startlingly wide grin that displayed perfect bright white teeth marred only by a single, glistening gold left lateral incisor, "but I'm not here to sell you anything. I'd like to make a fair trade, if you are so inclined."

The day just seemed to be getting odder and odder, and Mitch had to take a deep breath and let it out slowly to keep his focus. This strange guy's gold tooth reminded Mitch of Willy Carroll's diamond embedded tooth, but the similarity ended there. Where Willy had come off as an unusually lively and engaging character with a wild glint in his eye, this Johnny fellow crackled with repressed confidence. Mitch had read about folks with strongly magnetic personalities, but this was the first time he'd ever met one in person. It made the hairs on the back of his neck stand up.

"I'm really not…" Mitch started, when Johnny suddenly reached into his coat's inner breast pocket only to yank it out just as quickly.

For a moment Mitch's heartbeat stumbled as it looked like Johnny was pulling out a gun. He was just about to drop to the floor in a desperate effort to avoid getting shot when he realized Johnny was pointing a toy ray gun at him.

"So, what do you think?" Johnny said, "It's a nineteen thirty-four pressed metal Buck Rogers XZ-31 Rocket Pistol, totally original, not a reproduction. A real beauty, eh?"

Mitch leaned forward and found himself nodding reluctantly.

"Now I know it is separated from your current collection by over thirty years," Johnny said nodding at Mitch's bags, "but what spaceman is truly complete without a dependable laser gun to rely on, eh? Go on, give it a try."

Without thinking Mitch reached out took the pistol in his right hand. Surprisingly, for a child's toy it seemed to fit his right hand perfectly, like it was made for him. Also, it seemed to emanate a slight vibration, which Mitch found oddly appealing.

"Mint condition," Mitch said, "and you probably want cash…"

"No no, no," Johnny said, "I'm looking for a fair trade, yessiree. Now Mitch, what I want is the lucky stone in your left pocket. The worn chunk of green Connemara marble you inherited when your Dad died a decade ago."

Mitch sat up quick. How the heck did Johnny know about the rock? Mitch's Dad had picked it up in Ireland while on leave from his Army Base outside of London. It was a gift from a beautiful teenage girl that Mitch's Dad said he would have married if her folks had been a little more open minded.

"I don't think I can…" Mitch said.

"It's important, Mitch," Johnny said looking directly into Mitch's eyes, "I promise you this is a fair trade and your stone will be put toward a good cause."

"What cause?" Mitch asked, trying hard not to lose himself in the dark depthless pools of Johnny's black eyes.

"Something bad is coming," Johnny said, "a conflict that you'll need the laser pistol for. Something worse than all the stories your father told you about the Korean War, and it has already started…something called, The Sha'Daa."

Mitch bit his lower lip, then nodded and reached into his pocket. Reluctantly, he flipped the small quarter-sized stone off his thumb like a coin toward Johnny, who snatched it out of the air and deposited it in one of his coat's inner pockets in the space of a breath.

"So, what exactly is this Sha'Daa thing…?"

The overhead lights went out for a couple of seconds that left the subway car completely dark. They just as quickly came back on. Johnny was gone.

Mitch jerked his head in either direction, but knew there was just not enough time for the salesman to have walked, or even sprinted, to either of the adjoining cars. Johnny had simply vanished.

Mitch just stared at his own reflection on the windows across the aisle where Johnny had been sitting. He didn't get any answers from the handsome and fit looking black man in his late sixties who stared back.

⊕ ⊕ ⊕

The birthday party was still over an hour away as Mitch and Barry started up the barbecue in the back yard. Sara had hopped in the car to get some hot dog and hamburger buns and would be back in about thirty minutes.

Mitch tossed a lit match onto the small pile of now burning charcoal and turned to his son with a smile.

"Got an early present for you," Mitch said, "something, uhhhh…a little different than what you're probably used to."

Barry, a slender good-looking boy with a pale mocha complexion, green eyes, and wavy light brown hair, twisted his lips into a quirky smile that was so much like Mitch's own.

"What's that mean, Dad?" Barry chuckled, "you got me a motorcycle instead of a bike?"

Five minutes later the two of them had unwrapped all the S.T.A.R. toys that Barry had quickly put on. Everything fit his slender, now twelve-year-old body perfectly.

"You sure you don't think this is too corny, son?" Mitch asked.

"Naw, Dad," Barry laughed, "actually, it makes me think of that flick we downloaded on movie-night last month. The freaky cool one mom hated. What was it...? Planet of The Vampires!"

Barry started walking around the back yard, slowly at first, as he was afraid he was going to puncture the just-inflated underside of his space boots.

"And you really wanted this stuff when you were my age?"

"Younger," Mitch laughed, "And yeah, more than you wanted the newest generation of virtual X-box last Christmas. Quick, space-boy, turn around."

Barry spun on his heel and laughed when he saw Mitch pointing the Buck Rogers pistol.

"Now I know what you're thinking, Junior astronaut," Mitch said with an exaggerated husky voice, "did he fire six laser blasts, or only five? Well to tell you the truth, in all this excitement, I've kinda lost track myself. But being this is the XZ-31 Rocket Pistol, the most powerful hand-laser in the solar system, and would disintegrate your head clean off, you've got to ask yourself one question. Do I feel lucky? Well, do ya, punk?"

Barry laughed and slowly moved his right hand toward the Nebulizer clamped on his space utility belt.

"Yeah," Barry said with his own attempt at a Clint Eastwood impersonation, "well, my space-mule got all riled up when you went and fired those blasts at his feet. Now if you apologize like I know you're going to, I might convince him that you really didn't mean it, Dad...."

Just as Barry's hand closed on the Nebulizer the ground between him and his father erupted upward, grass and dirt flying in every direction, and knocking the two of them off their feet and a couple of yards further from each other.

Several shaky moments later they both stood up.

"What the hell..." Mitch said.

Where most of the back yard had been was now a roughly twenty-five-foot diameter hole. Walking up to within inches of it Mitch quickly realized he couldn't see a bottom, and this was with overhead sunlight shining downward quite a ways. Seeing Barry step forward, still wearing all of the toy space gear, Mitch shouted.

"Stop," Mitch said, "I think it's some kind of sinkhole. Could get even bigger without notice."

Barry's eyes went wide and he backed off a full three yards, circumnavigating the hole through the neighbor's back yard to get back to his Dad. The dirt and dust in the air settled quickly and Mitch suddenly noticed what looked like a lightly shimmering cover of sorts had formed right over the top of the hole, mostly transparent.

A crackling sound, like something from an old twentieth century set of speakers, filled the air.

"What now," Mitch said. Looking down he spotted the large blue toy headphones and microphone combo, similar in design but not as small as the ones imbedded into Barry's toy helmet.

"I'm hearing something in my helmet, Dad," Barry said.

Mitch frowned, and though feeling silly, picked up the toy and pulled it down over his head and ears, pulling the microphone rod down in front of his mouth without thinking.

A female voice, sounding somewhat mechanical and emotionless, began speaking.

"Captain Mitch and Cadet Barry. Initiating artificial intelligence activation," the disembodied voice said, "quantum reality reintegration and alteration commencing."

Suddenly a flash of almost blinding green light erupted from the toy ray gun Mitch had stuffed behind his belt.

When the afterimages finally left his eyes, Mitch shouted in surprise. He found he was holding the space-gun in his right hand...only it wasn't a toy any more, but a heavier and more detailed device with several tiny hi-tech display screens. It looked like an expensive prop from some blockbuster science fiction movie.

"Dad," Barry yelled.

Mitch looked up and gasped. Barry toys had somehow been replaced by the real thing, that is, not an actual NASA space suit, but something right out of a top-notch movie, like those suits worn in the old Alien prequel. Mitch rushed forward to examine Barry's helmet with transparent face shield.

"It's okay, Dad," Barry said, seeing the worry in his Dad's eyes, "I can breathe fine. I can feel fresh air pumping into the helmet in little squirts. Weird."

"Environmental spacesuit," the female AI voice spoke in both their ears, "is functioning at peak efficiency, Cadet Barry. Fuel Cells are fully charged for thirty days, and you have one month's worth of liquid rations if needed. Captain Mitch..."

"Uh, what, AI?" Mitch replied, not fully believing he was actively taking part in this bizarre hallucination.

"A portal to Planet X has appeared," the AI spoke, "you and Cadet Barry are tasked with closing it before the invasion commences."

"What do you mean by invasion?" Barry said.

As if on cue, a trio of purple, multi-tentacle and multi-eyed monstrosities, each the size of a full-grown man, slowly crawled out of the leading edge of the portal. They each moved through the glowing veil over the portal with a liquid-like plopping sound.

"Destroy them before they destroy you," the AI said with great urgency, "Now."

Almost without thinking, Mitch pointed his space-gun and Barry drew his nebulizer, and they both pulled their triggers simultaneously. The result was impressive to say the least. A red beam of light, shot from Mitch's weapon, piercing one monster, killing it, and dropping it into the hole. Barry's Nebulizer released a much wider beam of sparkling coalescing white and black energy that struck the two remaining creatures, which warbled in pain and disintegrated into nothingness.

"You must enter the portal," the AI spoke, "cross over to the surface of Planet X's moon, and set the short-time-delay explosive charges on Cadet Barry's utility belt around the periphery of their side of this inter-dimensional breach. The three aliens you just destroyed were merely scouts for the main invasion force, an entire armada that is currently in transit between Planet X and Moon-One. You have ten minutes to complete this assignment, save the Earth, and return."

"Did you say moon?" Mitch asked, "Like, um, ours?"

"Affirmative," the AI spoke, "Cadet Barry will carry out the demolition mission on the airless moon's surface as he possesses the environmental space suit. You, Captain Mitch, will provide back-up from the protection of the trans-portal corridor that bridges the two portal openings. It possesses adequate breathable atmosphere and nominal temperature to sustain your metabolism and physiology for up to one standard Terran day."

"Why do I not like the sound of this?" Mitch said.

"There is no time for delay," the AI spoke, "if you do not stop this invasion, everyone on Planet Earth will be killed. The denizens of Planet X are xenophobes that hate all life-forms not their own."

"My son is only twelve," Mitch yelled.

"Cadet Barry is young," the AI spoke, "but he is also brave and intelligent. Logic indicates that the Terran Space Force wisely chose the two of you for this mission."

"Dad," Barry said, "I can do this. We have to. For mom...and everyone else."

"Dammit," Mitch said.

"Planet X's armada is nearing the orbit of Moon-One," the AI spoke.

"Let's go," Mitch added.

Side by side Mitch and his space-suited son jumped into the large hole. The oily film of the veil covering the portal tickled Mitch's skin like it was electrically charged. When his head passed through it, he grew dizzy.

⊕ ⊕ ⊕

Time passed in some oddly nonsensical manner. What felt like an eternity, or only a few seconds, transpired, as Mitch felt himself falling and then slowing, and just as quickly rotating ninety degrees in mid-air, until his feet touched what he now perceived as a circular tunnel's wall?

"We have entered the trans-portal corridor," the AI spoke, "the Moon-One portal is only one thousand meters ahead. Hurry."

Mitch and Barry, sprinting side by side in what both realized was severely reduced gravity, managed in a series of super hero leaps to make it to the large shimmering portal face in mere seconds.

"Cadet Barry," the AI spoke, "cross through the barrier now. I will instruct you in where to place the charges. Captain Mitch, please maintain surveillance of both the sky and horizon. Your hand-weapon will accurately fire through the portal without harming it or you. You must provide cover until Cadet Barry has placed all the charges."

Barry nodded his space helmet toward his father then leaped forward and through the portal. Barry's form flopped forward and Mitch quickly realized that his son had realigned his stance at a right angle congruent with the change in the direction of gravity. Mitch stepped up to within a foot of the glistening, transparent curtain of energy. He raised his space pistol and slowly tracked it back and forth, crisscrossing the large circular opening and doing his best to look in three hundred and sixty degrees of direction, strongly suspecting he was about to engage in something resembling a real-life version of Space Invaders.

Mere feet away, Mitch could see Barry removing what appeared to be the S.T.A.R. astro beacon from his utility belt. What was once a plastic toy was now an explosive device that separated into half a dozen charges that Barry started laying down.

Three bursts of purple energy blasts struck the moon's surface within a few dozen yards of Barry. The resulting ground quake knocked Barry onto his back.

"Damn you," Mitch yelled, as he fired a dozen red laser blasts into the dark, star-lit sky, destroying the leading five attack ships from Planet X's closing Armada.

"I'm okay, Dad," Barry said, as he stood up and leaped a few yards to his left to set another charge on the ground.

"Correct, Cadet Barry," the AI spoke, "the charges need to be placed equidistantly around the perimeter of this fifty-meter diameter portal."

This time, two dozen attack ships came into view. Mitch fired as fast as he could, aided in that the attacking forces slowed dramatically as they approached Moon-One's surface. Ground strikes of purple energy blasts knocked Barry off his feet, but each time he managed to make his way to the next location to place a charge per the AI's instructions.

"Depress the green button on the back of your weapon, Captain Mitch," the AI spoke, "and your pistol will go full automatic."

Mitch grinned at the result, as multiple blasts of red laser beams leapt from his space gun to clear the sky. In minutes sweat was pouring off him and Mitch was finding it hard to breathe. The temperature in the corridor was growing alarmingly high as the non-stop laser fire heated the surrounding atmosphere before lancing through the portal to destroy alien ships. Wiping sweat out of his eyes, Mitch gritted his teeth and kept his weapon trained on the sky.

"Set the remaining two charges, Cadet Barry," the AI spoke, "and the internal one-minute delay fuses will automatically ignite."

"I heard you the first time, lady," Barry yelled, "I'm not dragging my feet here."

Large plumes of dust, or smoke, burst upwards at several points on the horizon. Mitch's stomach sank as he suspected what this meant.

"Barry," Mitch yelled, "hurries. We're about to have company."

"Just one more left, Dad," Barry's panting voice crackled through the earphones of Mitch's headset, "I'm almost done."

Then Barry saw them, tiny silhouettes on the horizon, first a few, then dozens, then hundreds, massing from every direction and sprinting forward on their tentacle limbs. When they got closer Mitch could see they did not wear space suits.

"Tough little bastards," Mitch said, under his breath

"Final charge set," the AI spoke, "one-minute delay fuse will activate in seventy seconds."

"Barry," Mitch yelled, "get back here now."

Dozens of purple light beams, smaller versions of what had pounded the surface of Moon-One earlier, suddenly appeared, crisscrossing and exploding boulders and regolith everywhere.

Mitch watched Barry yank up his Nebulizer and let loose a long burst of destructive energy that annihilated the leading ranks of a mile-wide front. A moment later, a thin blue beam struck his weapon, knocking it out of his hand and sending it flying away dozens of meters.

Mitch's heart nearly stopped when another flurry of blue enemy beams struck a large nearby bolder, calving it, and sending a large chunk of rock rolling onto one of Barry's legs, trapping him.

Just two meters from the portal dozens of more blue beams of energy fired through the space where Barry had just been standing. In seconds the destroyed ranks of aliens had already been replaced with new troops.

"Dad," Barry yelled, "My foot is stuck."

"What?" Mitch said, as his heart sank, "No."

"Do not panic Cadet Barry," the AI spoke, "remove the Exploratory Probe Launcher from your utility belt, place it on the ground to your right as far as you can reach. I will remote activate."

Mitch saw the small probe launched in the direction of the leading mass of aliens. It exploded above their heads, shredding them.

"Now, Cadet Barry," the AI spoke, "remove the Remote Gripper Device from your utility belt, place you're left gloved hand inside and grab the retention handle. Now, shove the other end under the boulder near your ankle and push. Hurry, more of the enemy is approaching."

The Remote Gripper's hooks pushed the several-ton boulder upward, rolling it away.

"Yes," Mitch yelled.

Barry stayed crouched, though, as the crossfire of blue energy beams had recommenced and were keeping him trapped, on his belly, behind the large rock he had just freed himself from.

Mitch, snarling, fired targeting as much of the enemy as possible, picking off alien silhouettes. It wasn't enough against the encroaching alien horde. Then, inspiration struck.

"Five seconds to one-minute delay fuse activation," the AI spoke.

"Barry," Mitch yelled, "when I say, jump up and leap through the portal. Trust me."

"Okay, Dad," Barry said, his voice gone shrill.

Mitch pulled his weapon off the leading edge of aliens, now a mere seventy meters away and aimed at Moon-One's surface.

"Now, Barry," Mitch yelled, as he fired multiple blasts at the soil meters from Barry, between him and the advancing enemy. Tons of soil and dust exploded upward, obscuring visibility for precious seconds.

"Dad, I can't see," Barry yelled, "there's too much dust in the air.

"Cadet Barry," the AI spoke, "remove the scanner scope from your utility belt. Aim it forward and pull the trigger."

"Roger that," Barry said, "Scanner scope engaged. Hey, I can see, like a cartoon version of the ground all around on the little screen."

For several harrowing moments, Mitch held his breath and then let it out as he saw an orange beam of light poke through the surrounding but dissipating dust cloud. Barry's scanner!

A second later Barry jumped through the portal and landed at his father's side.

"One-minute delay fuse activated on all charges," the AI spoke.

"Run," Mitch and Barry yelled simultaneously.

Both spun around in the trans-portal corridor, taking meters-long leaping strides. As they neared the Earth-side portal, several blue energy blasts struck the sides of the corridor not far from them, resulting in shockwaves that nearly knocked them off their feet.

"Dad," Barry yelled.

"We're almost there, son," Mitch said, coughing all the while in the thick air.

"Portal charges igniting in five seconds," the AI spoke, "four, three, two, one…"

As Mitch and Barry reached the Earth-side portal an explosion flared and they felt the heat and pressure of the leading shock-wave licking their backs.

Everything went black.

⊕ ⊕ ⊕

Barry and Mitch slowly sat up and looked about themselves. The giant hole was gone, though there was a large circular patch of scorched earth where both the portal and hole used to be.

"Mom's not going to like this," Barry said.

Static suddenly blared through Mitch's headset, but when he turned to Barry he could see it wasn't transmitting from his son.

"Mitch," his wife Sara's voice crackled, "damn this stupid Smartphone! Mitch can you hear me. I'm trapped in the grocery store with a bunch of others. There are monsters outside. It's crazy. We tried to phone the police but nine-one-one is busy."

A glance at Barry showed that the boy had heard the same transmission. With a nod, they both ran around the house and stopped in surprise at seeing a huge wooden crate on the front lawn. Painted on the side of it were the words *KRAFT Space Simulator.*

"I don't believe it," Mitch said, "it's the simulator from that old comic book advertisement. Willy really wasn't shining me on."

"Dad," Barry said, "we gotta get to mom."

"Quantum reality reintegration and alteration initiated," the AI spoke.

Instantly, a flash of green light flew out from Mitch's ray gun and enveloped the huge crate. A moment later the wood slats popped off revealing a twenty-nine-foot long spaceship.

"Oh, you have got to be shitting me," Barry said. It was not a giant painted fiber-glass and plywood toy. Mitch slapped the vehicle's hull which felt as solid as a battleship.

A hatch quickly swung open near the right front of the ship.

"Captain Mitch," the female AI spoke in both their ears, "Cadet Barry. Aero jet S1 is fully-fueled. Weapons systems are both charged and loaded. We have clearance for an emergency launch."

Mitch and Barry looked at each other for a moment and laughed.

They rushed into the spaceship and strapped themselves into the front crash-couches as the main hatch closed and locked into place with a loud hissing sound.

"Cadet Barry," the AI spoke, "please activates the weapons console in front of you. Captain Mitch, the steering wheel in front of you controls roll, pitch, and yaw. The foot pedals acceleration and deceleration.

The rocket engines kicked on.

Mitch turned to his son for a moment, and they both smiled. Rapid acceleration pushed them both back hard into their heavily-cushioned crash couches as the rocket ship blasted into the sky.

"So, Dad," Barry grunted, struggling to get the words out under the crush of six gees, "what's the name of our space ship?"

"The Dreamer," Mitch grunted without hesitation. "Now keep your eyes on your weapon scope. We might run into trouble on the way to the grocery store."

Mitch gritted his teeth as a feral rush of adrenaline flooded his body. His wife Sara needed saving, as well as many other besieged citizens of the planet Earth. The Terran Space Force had a job to do.

Toy Soldiers

"**H**ELLO, THIS IS KVARIS THE INTERFACE," Kvaris said through the phone booth receiver.

"I'm busy," Willy said, "this better be important."

"Sir," Kvaris said, "the Sha'Daa has been messing big time with communications between the dimensions. I've tried calling you eight times, and this is the first I've been able to get through. I just wanted to tell you that everything is stable with the Midnight Laborers and they are keeping up with all placed orders."

"Excellent," Willy replied. "Anything else?"

"Though you might not consider it any of my business," Kvaris said, "I do have some minor expertise with theurgic wave front phenomena. It appears that large quantities of aberrant magic has been leaking into your establishment, somehow bypassing your defensive shielding. How or why, I have no idea. I just wanted you to know, sir."

"Thanks, Kvaris," Willy said, "and as much as they annoy the hell out of me, please keep me updated on the laborers and, uh, anything else you might find out about The Sha'Daa and Whirligigs."

"You got it sir," Kvaris said before disconnecting.

The muzak speaker system transitioned to *Kite* by U2.

The first instance of toy on toy violence began around early evening of the Summer Solstice. An aggressive group of thirty used G.I. Joe dolls leaped from their shelves in the far-left corner of Whirligigs and immediately engaged in a brawl with twenty-five, used Stretch Armstrong figures that had just climbed out of their bin. By what arcane magic they had become animated, and why the animosity between these specific two types of toys was something that Willy didn't have a clue about. It took him and his staff nearly half an hour to separate the two groups and bind their arms and legs thoroughly, an act whose consequences were six black eyes among the staff, and not a few fat lips, otherwise the bizarre insurrection was halted before the next wave of customers rushed into the store.

"So much for neutral ground," Johnny said, "and that's a nasty bruise on Amy's eye. She should really put an ice-pack on it, or maybe a cold steak."

Willy looked up to see Johnny with an oversized smirk on his face.

"Don't you have a multitude of simultaneous apocalypses to go thwart?" Willy asked in a huff.

"Good point," Johnny said, and dropped an odd-looking doll on the counter.

"What's this?" Willy asked, "I don't recognize it."

"Why," Johnny replied, "it is the prototype Hasbro Little Miss No Name doll, complete with patched burlap dress, oversized eyes, and permanent realistic glistening pitiful tear on her left cheek. Production stopped after a year and the vast majority ended up in landfills."

"Hmmm," Willy said, "that story makes me want to cry. What do you want?"

"I want your set of all fourteen Tonka Rock Lords," Johnny said, "and spare me on how rare they are. They're ugly and you know you'll never sell them."

Willy paused for a moment, "Say, Johnny."

"Him?"

"We're still here, right?" Willy asked, "the Earth is surviving, right? Like, people have a real chance to make it through the hell that is happening everywhere."

Johnny's eyes glinted as he took in the mild concern flickering across Willy's face.

"Just a half day to go," Johnny said, "but the odds are still heavily against us making it to the end. But, I'm trying Willy, I promise you that."

Willy shook his head as if he were caught in a gust of smoke he just couldn't quite shake off.

"Good," Willy said, "I'm...I'm glad to hear that..."

Their transaction finished, Johnny smiled then quickly walked out the front door.

Instantly a loud crashed sounded from the rear right corner of the main floor.

"Willy," Amy yelled, "three boxes of NECA Tron action figures are duking it out with a dozen Toys-R-Us classic 1954 Godzilla reproductions. They're tearing each other apart."

CHAPTER TWENTY-ONE

Langbardr's Storm

C.J. Henderson

"Fantasy, abandoned by reason, produces impossible monsters; united with it, she is the mother of the arts and the origin of marvels."

–Francisco Goya

IT BEGAN IN THE EARLY HOURS, BEFORE THE summer sun seared the east horizon. It was a typical west Kansas day for the family. Mother and Father had taken care of their morning ablutions, and breakfast was cooking and coffee percolating in preparation for the children waking up. The smell of fresh pancakes quickly pulled the sleepyheads from dreamland and all were soon talking, laughing, and eating around their large, weathered oak table.

Just as the first fingers of sunlight slipped across the plains a strong wind appeared, constantly shifting its heading, like it was coming from every direction at once. Mother sensed this before actually spotting her clothesline undulating outside.

"Children," Mother said, "don't stray too far from the house, today. Could be a storm brewing."

A short while later the three oldest, all teenage boys of course, were crouched around the main television screen, wreaking havoc across the landscape of some alien planet, each one a Terran mercenary in powered armor and carrying laser rifles and other outrageous fantasy weaponry.

Outside, about sixty yards from the house, little Mary and her older sister Isabella were playing on the swing set.

Without notice Isabella stopped her pendulum movements and looked around her feet.

"Oh shoot, "Isabella shouted, "I forgot my skip rope. Wait here, skipper-doodle and I'll be right back."

Mary's big sister, twelve years of muscle, bone, and adrenaline, shot across the recently mowed field toward the big house, that along with the garage, barn, stable, water tower, and two tractors were the only manmade structures (not counting the road to the house) that could be seen for dozens of miles in all directions.

A moment later a shadow rapidly crawled across the ground and touched Mary's feet. The little six-year-old, looking disarmingly innocent in her one-piece blue skirt and white sneakers, looked up in surprise.

The entire western horizon, stretching from the firmament of the planet up to several miles into the sky, had given birth to a gargantuan wall of rippling darkness.

A thought popped into Mary's inexperienced mind and she quickly remembered several of the old black and white photos of the nineteen thirty-five Black Sunday dust storm one of her older brothers had shown her on his computer tablet.

Hypnotized by this strange and macabre sight, Mary stood up from her swing-seat and took two steps forward in the direction of the rumbling, onrushing wall of death.

Mary's mother had just handed Isabella her skipping rope when looking up, and out the open front door, was greeted by a horrific sight…little Mary in the foreground, silhouetted by a surreal and unworldly mass of grey and black rushing forward from the west.

"Mary," mother screamed, running forward toward the open door in full blown panic.

Rushing ever closer in what Mary thought was much faster than her father ever drove on the roads and even highways, the massive wall of darkness rippled and occasionally sparkled like some kind of living creature. In moments, it was but a mile away. Mary sensed her mother's screams, muffled shouts that could barely be heard above the howling of this storm-like being.

Looking up, Mary discerned what she thought of as a face coming into and out of focus across the front of this terrain gobbling horror.

From up high he surveyed all beneath him…and he did so with great disdain.

He had existed for centuries, millennia even, respected, honored, feared yes, but above all loved…and yet, in recent decades, his memory had slowly faded from the minds of the hordes of humanity that now covered this planet like annoying insects. And in their forgetfulness his spite, and anger, and rage slowly bubbled up within the substance-less fabric of his nature. Year after year his disgust grew as memories of joy and fun and peace were covered, submerged, and hidden from thought. For decades, his resentment boiled to an exacerbating and painful extreme that only now, at the height of The Sha'Daa, had been set free to wreak a terrible revenge.

He spotted the tiny figure of the girl-thing and with all his rage blasted toward her with every iota of fury that abandonment had wrought within his soul.

Looking up, as the wall of death had closed to within one hundred yards; Mary clearly saw the massive face that had formed across the front of this eerie storm. It was masculine, proud, bearded even, and filled with spiteful anger.

As it closed to within mere hundreds of feet of Mary, she suddenly felt a bloom within herself, a spark of light that filled her mind and heart with brilliant recognition. The mind of a child that could still see reality through senses composed of pure innocence. And in that glorious moment of awareness, Mary spoke one word, a mere squeak in the torrential howling of wind and torn earth.

It was a word that struck this being like a bolt of lightning.

A word that tore through his very spirit, halting all of his momentum, freezing him in place, a gigantic miles wide curtain of murk and fear that towered up to above the clouds themselves, poised now, but for what....

And the word flooded every speck of his intelligence, ripping through his mind and memories, unearthing what was lost, all of the joy, and happiness, and peace that had been cast off by the current human cultures of instant gratification and commercial wealth.

And as this word completely left Mary's mouth, the horrible aberration grew pale, and then bright and instantly started dispersing, for Mary's word was the answer that was mostly forgotten.

A word that gave freedom and purpose to an entity long in abeyance.

A word.

A name.

Santa.

Mister Potato Head

A DULL BUT EVER-INCREASING HEADACHE had spread through Willy's skull, back to front, ever since he had returned from the Midnight Laborers' pocket universe, aka, stock room. Part of it was the distraction of his own past popping into his thoughts as he dealt with a final wave of customers, a crowd that, unlike most previous customers, were more than aware of the eldritch significance and innate potential of many of the toys on surrounding shelves. It took all his effort to focus on the multitude of frantic sales as moments from his five long marriages screamed for his attention.

The muzak speakers began playing Dolly Parton's *Little Tiny Tassle Top*.

As for this new group of customers, they were a dazzling mix of not just human beings, but demons and a wide variety of supernatural creatures. Willy had no fear of any of them because much of the steel and concrete structure that hid behind the bricks that made up the walls of Whirligigs was composed of a couple of dozen very powerful talismans that repelled any and all creatures, demons, and entities that wished him or his establishment any harm. This didn't mean that they were all avatars and agents of good that wanted humanity to survive The Sha'Daa (for surely many were fighting outside as warriors of evil), but they knew better than to turn on Willy in his place of power.

"You know," Johnny said, having just slipped to the front of the line, "you look like a man of divided attention, Willy. In fact, I'm beginning to think you're a man of divided conscience."

Willy handed a wrapped robot and a sales receipt to a subterranean Mercurian and started ringing up a Raggedy Anne doll for an impatient seven-foot-tall golem.

"Not exactly the best time for shooting the bull, Johnny," Willy said.

"Quick question," Johnny asked, "has some young fella, handsome guy, blonde, clean cut, six feet tall, been showing up, looking for me? Goes by the name, Prana."

"Prana?" Willy asked. "No, not as far as I know. None of my staff has reported anything like that. Why?"

"Seems I've got a stalker," Johnny said, "been hot on my tracks for the last twelve hours."

"Is that even possible?" Willy asked, "and if so, I can't imagine there's much in this galaxy that you couldn't handle."

"Flattery is king," Johnny said with a smirk. "So tell me, have you been having thoughts, recently," Johnny said, "about things other than merely riding out The Sha'Daa?"

"I'm not sure what you mean," Willy said, though he knew exactly what Johnny was hinting at, as the flood of memories about his past five wives reinforced his shocked realization that he had lost all interest in personal relations with any women whatsoever over one hundred years ago. Also, he was beginning to get little specks of recollection of one of the several rituals he underwent two hundred plus years ago in Australia…rituals that had granted him several eldritch abilities, the two most powerful being immortality and the ability to create a pocket universe like that which the Midnight Laborers existed in. He now knew that some important sacrifice had been made on his part, but he couldn't quite remember what it was in the chaos of the moment.

Willy gave the golem a receipt and began to ring up a pair of lesbian mermaids sitting on hi-tech looking electrical powered wheelchairs.

"You have something to trade, salesman?" Willy asked.

"At the moment, nothing but advice," Johnny smiled.

"And what is that?" Willy asked.

"Compassion may be one of mankind's greatest treasures," Johnny said.

"That's it?" Willy asked.

"That," Johnny said, as he turned around and walked out through the front door, "and the knowledge that sometimes, just sometimes, lost treasures can be re-found."

The wheelchair bound mermaids spun around and sped toward the front door as a frail jellyfish-like being from Alpha Centauri, in an armored space suit, walked up to the front counter with three canisters of Green Slime.

"Amy," Willy yelled, "status report."

"It's strange," Amy said, appearing out of nowhere.

"What?" Willy asked.

"No toy on toy violence," Amy said, "for three hours. You think everything is back to normal, boss?"

"Nope," Willy said, "I suspect it is the lull before the storm."

"What's that mean?" Amy asked.

"That I should be made a saint for that ridiculously expensive full medical coverage I gave you and the rest of the staff last year," Willy said.

Amy didn't ask any more questions.

Willy glanced over to the antique phone booth. It had not rung in an hour. Toys continued to flow through the conveyor portal into Whirligigs so he had to accept that everything was operating at peak capacity. The annoying Kvaris, however, seemed to be cut off, hopefully temporarily, as Willy felt himself beginning to worry about the main operator of the communications service between him and the Midnight Laborers.

The muzak version of Chuck Berry's *Run Rudolph Run* began to play.

CHAPTER TWENTY-TWO

Roll the Bones

Bill Barnhill

"Love is like death, it must come to us all, but to each his own unique way and time, sometimes it will be avoided, but never can it be cheated, and never will it be forgotten."

–Jacob Grimm

LUC DUSABLE STOOD OUTSIDE WHIRLIGIGS, the toy store Luc's fellow Houngan recommended.

The man had come to America from Haiti with Luc, and was also a priest, a Houngan, in the local Chicago Vodoun community. Luc had only met a handful of other priests following the way of the loa since he fled Haiti in '65. He had been just one step ahead of Duvalier's paramilitary force, the Tonton Macoutes, and almost did not make it out of Haiti.

He had started as a combat driver in the Macoutes but his gift for strategy and ruthlessness propelled him to a minor command position. He had nightmares about what they did, but the Macoutes had been his brothers in arms before he joined the revolution. So much had changed. The shop was Luc's last hope for his dead son Marc.

Luc sighed and walked through the door. The store had more shelves and display cases than he thought possible for its size, along with an empty area in the front near the door, and a conveyor belt running from a shadowy and smoke-clouded storage room in the back.

A moment after entering the store and starting toward the front desk the conveyor belt ground to a halt with a loud clanking noise. The lone package on the conveyor belt toppled over with enough force to pitch it off the belt. A salesman stood behind a counter on one side of the room, next to the belt and caught the package with one sure hand.

Luc judged the man to be around thirty-five, with a height to match his own six feet. The man resembled a Leprechaun who'd taken steroids and a growth serum. Bright red hair, thick and unruly, adorned a paler than normal face dotted with freckles. A diamond in one of his teeth flashed as he yelled, "Fair suck of the sav... It breaks today, of all days. Fix it!" Luc watched a small but stocky child-like figure in the back room approaching the belt, the smoke and shadows concealing all but its outline. Then something thumped the belt hard enough to make it shake at the front of the store, at which point the belt restarted. A single smoke ring wafted into the front room in protest from the figure in the back, whose outline disappeared from view.

The smoke made it to the man behind the front counter, causing him to cough and rub his eyes for a minute. He cast a quick glare at the back before he set the package on the counter and turned to Luc with a wide grin. The salesman's eyes took all of Luc in within a moment—his height and muscular build as well as the bags under his eyes, and their haunted look. Luc's spine shivered as if the salesman weighed every ounce of his being and found it wanting.

The man sighed and said in a thick Australian accent "My condolences on your loss. Would you like something to recapture your youth and distract you from your pain? I'm Willie, and we have every kind of toy you can imagine, and then some. How can I help you today?"

Luc sighed, "My name's Luc, Luc DuSable. A friend told me you sold toys that could help me. I...I need to be able to speak with my son and see him. He died. Last week. A car accident—some deer or something ran in front of us. I swerved, lost control, and crashed into a brick building on the passenger side."

Willie looked away, contemplating the package from the conveyor belt for a moment before looking back and meeting Luc's gaze. "DuSable. That's an old name here in Chicago. We can definitely help you, but are you sure you want to talk to your son again Luc? Death, it's not something to mess with lightly. You should be sure."

Luc's stomach clenched as Willie's assertion kindled hope in Luc's thoughts. Luc didn't think about the question; he would do anything for his son, to talk with him again. He reached for the package with his right hand, flashing a gold Rolex. "Of course I'm sure. Whatever it takes," Luc said.

The owner reached out and a powerful grip stopped Luc's hand. "Not so fast," Willie said, "There is a matter of price."

A rain of ice washed over Luc's spine as he realized the help within reach might cost more than he could afford. Being an illegal immigrant from Haiti, a gypsy cab driver and a single father, he didn't have much to his name. He owned his cab, his watch, and the $106 in his pocket. He'd sold everything else of value to pay the medical bills flooding his mailbox in the week since his son died. "What do you want for it?" Luc asked.

Willie considered this for a moment, "Within this box is a pair of fuzzy dice. They were knucklebones once, supposedly carved by the goddess Ishtar herself ten thousand years ago out of the bones of a being from another world. Somewhere along the way, an owner covered them in plush fuzzy dice. They bring luck, but their primary purpose is to connect to spirits. They should let you talk to your son again and bring you good luck too if you do what I tell you."

Luc looked dubious but was eager to grasp at any chance, no matter how small, no matter the cost.

One side of Willie's mouth rose high in a sly smile. "Let's say four prices, like the leaves of a four-leaf clover, shall we?"

Willie then continued on, not waiting for an answer. "First, I want $105. Next, I want that watch and its story. Third, you will meet a man called Johnny; you will listen to his sales pitch, and consider it well. As for the fourth thing…" Willie paused, brows furrowed as without looking he spun a gold coin on the counter top.

Luc's stomach flipped. He could meet the price so far, but there was a good chance he couldn't afford what the man wanted next. With that thought, Luc resolved to get the money, somehow. He'd try not to hurt anyone, but he'd do what was needed for his boy.

Willie looked at Luc, his mouth turning down a fraction in slight disappointment. "Well, I've worked with a Houngan before, a long time ago. A DuSable as well. I smell the same mix of rum, orchids, and chalk I got from his aura, so I reckon you're a voodoo Houngan too. And that's good because I need an intro to a powerful Loa so that I can make a deal. You convince Papa Legba to ride you here in the store so he and I can talk business or no deal."

Luc considered the last part of the price. Asking Papa Legba take over his body, or ride him as Houngans call it, was a sacred act, and he worried he'd be profaning it. Luc felt the encouraging spiritual warmth associated with Damballah, his heart loa and the loa of fathers. Every Houngan had a loa; some like Luc had two, head and a heart loas. Papa Legba was another matter. The loa of crossroads, and the intermediary between the other loa and humankind, was his head loa. At that moment he heard in his thoughts the quick tapping of a cane, Legba's sign of impatience. Legba's impatience could mean he favored the deal, or the opposite. The loa seldom made their desires clear. After a moment's thought Luc nodded, believing the loa of his heart and head approved, saying "Ok, done."

Willie nodded, and with a wide grin said "Done."

Luc removed the watch and placed it in Willie's outstretched hand. "Papa Doc Duvalier gave me this watch, as a reward for saving his life during a coup attempt in '58. It reminds me not to trust anyone."

Willie sighed. "So cynical for one so young. Come back to me in a century and I might believe you truly believe that. We all have to trust some people, sometime. Otherwise life is not worth living." Luc nodded, but his mind was sizing the empty front of the store and he realized it was enough space for the ritual he'd need to perform. "As for the last part, we'll need a rooster, a large piece of chalk, and a bottle of good rum. We can do the ritual here."

Nodding his head and smiling, Willie walked to the back room and poked his head around the corner. Luc heard a whispered conversation. He could make out Willie's hearty Australian accent and what sounded like it might be a gruff German accent, but he couldn't make out more than that. He wasn't even sure about the German before the conversation was over.

The conveyor belt started again as Willie returned to the front desk. It moved at a snail's pace but brought up a wooden tray from the back with a knife, a bottle of rum and a package of multiple-color chalk on the tray. A caged rooster followed rode the belt behind the tray.

Willie looked at Luc. "Luc, before we start there is a minor detail. The ritual you've paid for, it must be redone each day between dusk and the stroke of midnight. Miss a day—and that's it. Once it is done for a soul, it must be continued, or it can never be done for that soul again. You understand? The other thing, well..."

Willie paused, looking down briefly with sad eyes for a moment before looking back up with a smile. "Well, things like this, they tend to have other costs. The universe balances things if you will. I don't know what the cost for this one is, but it will show up at the borders of the day: dawn, noon, and dusk."

Luc started. He could be careful, and nothing could keep him from doing right by his boy. He nodded. "No, but I'll make sure to do it every day, just the same."

Willie smiled a big grin; his diamond adorned tooth twinkling. "I figured as much but had to say. Johnny doesn't like cheaters. No, not at all. Best remember that boy. Now then, let's get started."

Luc made the ritual preparations. First was offering the rooster to Papa Legba, next the sacred prayer to St. Francis. Then he performed the supplication to Legba as he drew Legba's veve, the complex magic symbol unique to each loa. Last, he uttered sprayed rum over the veve and implored Legba to choose Luce as his Horse tonight. Even before Luc finished, he felt the charged air and temperature drop that meant the ritual was working, his right leg cramping and becoming stiff as a board. He'd have Legba's limping walk for the rest of the night, a reminder that power comes with a cost.

Between one moment and the nestle was somewhere else. He stood at a crossroads. He didn't recognize it, but from the Lake nearby it must be a very early version of Chicago. Luc heard a tapping on the dirt road and started, spinning round to face a sharp dressed man leaning on a thick wood cane with four faces carved into the head: one smiling, one crying, one frowning, and one leering. The man had a club foot.

"We don't have long here boy. I have much to tell you and little time to tell it, so pay attention," Legba said.

Luc did not trust his words to get past the lump in his throat, so he just nodded.

"You have a hard road to drive, child, but you can do it, if you learn and make better choices. Goes for us all these next two days. Trust in your love for your son, not your grief. We won't be able to come to you for a while, not any of the loa. How long? That's up to you and your choices. You've been challenged, and not in the normal way, so we can't interfere until it's done." Legba looked over to the Lake. It was stirring as if whipped up by wind. "Ah, best we get back now. My business with you is done, like my business with Mr. Caroll."

Once again he was back in the store. The transition jarred Luc and his balance tilted. He fell to his knees and caught his breath, Willie remained silent and let him recover, Willie's attention on a two-foot tall bottle that wasn't on the counter earlier. Purple smoke swirled within the bottle, darting this way and that.

Willie walked over when Luc regained his feet, and handed over the package, along with a sheet of printed instructions. "Remember Luc, do the ritual at the stroke of midnight tonight. You'll likely not have heard of it, and don't need to know the details, but tonight is the start of the Sha'Daa. That'll give the ritual a bit more kick. Here, the ritual materials are included in the price." Willie said as he handed an old-fashioned western doctor's bag to Luc.

Luc felt hope rise further in his soul as he took the bag. From somewhere in his mind surfaced the memory of Heinlein's TANSTAAFL motto: There Ain't No Such Thing As A Free Lunch. He shrugged it off since no cost outweighed being reunited with his son. When he walked out of the store it was thirty minutes before midnight, so he hurried home as best he could with the limp.

Luc climbed the steps to his apartment, passing the residence of his only neighbor in the building. He respected Alexandra, a single mother of a son and daughter, both Marc's age. An illegal like himself, she was Russian and attractive. Not that she held a candle to his late Tamara, God rest her soul, but the Johns wanted Tamara enough so she's not had any trouble paying rent. Her children had been Luc's best friends. Hearing them playing now made his head ache and his eyes blurry. He whispered "Soon, mon fils, soon." to the dead spirit of his son.

Once into his apartment, Luc unwrapped the dice and examined the ritual. He had five minutes to get ready, but the ritual was not complex.

He had no trouble understanding the instructions: chant three lines in some ancient language, offer a mixture blood and rum in a wooden bowl, and toss the dice—or 'Roll the bones', as his grann used to say. He had expected the ritual to be more complex for this much power. He knew power always cost, so if not paid in ritual complexity he'd pay in other ways.

He forced that out of his mind and removed the outer plush from the dice. The knucklebones they had covered were grey with age but sturdy. They also had thin veins of crystal running through them. He started rolling them in his hands as he began the chant.

The words were different and didn't make sense to him, but he could say them without difficulty. He removed the outer plush from the dice and began the chant, rolling the knuckle bones as he started. He spoke the first words of the chant, "il ani sa kis sa ti lik ru bu ki" and then more monosyllabic words in the same vein flowed from him. As he finished his voice increasingly sounded like it was in a huge cavern and echoing back to him. He lost consciousness after the last two syllables "Ap Su."

He came awake with the sound of pain-filled moaning and the touch of a cold washcloth on his face. He opened his eyes to see his son Marc, alive and smiling. The smile was marred by pain though. The reason was clear. The wounds from the car accident gaped open across his right arm and the right side of his shirtless chest. Luc's mind was in a dazed fog of joy as he noticed a book lay next to his son.

The book was small but thick and bound in bleached leather. The spine had weird markings that looked like someone had made patterns out of golf tees—lots of triangles with a single line coming out of one point of each one, arranged in vertical and horizontal patchworks. He remembered seeing writing like that when he took his son to an exhibit at the Chicago University, "Persepolis and Ancient Iran". The ancient histories librarian who was their guide had called it cuneiform. That was one of their happier outings and Marc thought at the time he might be a librarian specializing in ancient things when he grew up.

Luc sat up as his mind cleared. He hugged his son, "Son, I'm so happy to have you back."

The hug elicited a fresh moan from Marc. "Dad, the wounds hurt. And I was somewhere else—a big library. I was reading this book; it's full of stories of demons coming to our world during something called the Sha'Daa. It's fiction, of course. Ow, that hurts."

Luc nodded, frowning. The toy store owner had mentioned the Sha'Daa, but he didn't want to burden Marc with that at the moment. He remembered something about the wounds, but it took a moment for the details to gel. "Right. The directions from the toy store mentioned that. I've got rum blessed by a priest here; drink that while I sew your wounds up with thread. The ritual instructions say that'll help."

Marc looked dubious but leaned back to let Luc try. Marc watched his father pick up a large needed and thick thread, taking a large gulp of rum before Luc started.

Afterward, Luc sat exhausted while Marc moved his arms this way and that, in much less pain as he tried out his still dead body. Luc wasn't sure if the rum or the stitching had reduced the pain, or if it had just gone down with time.

Luc watched and felt his stomach twist with guilt. His son would have to be raised each night and sewn up nightly. That meant the boy would be in agony for the first hour or so each night. However, if Luc didn't continue the ritual, then they'd never have the chance to talk again. As he drifted off to sleep, Luc resolved that he'd force himself to endure the sight of his child in pain, and keep doing the ritual.

⊕ ⊕ ⊕

Luc woke to the sound of sirens, loud voices and crying. Luc looked across the room and saw Marc still slept. Luc had a moment of panic at the thought of a fire, how would he explain Marc, then calmed as he realized the fire alarms weren't going off. Luc got dressed and went to his door, frowning at his haggard appearance in the wall mirror, before looking out through the wide-angle peephole he had installed himself.

The crying was louder, interspersed with emotional Russian. He listened a moment longer, then looked through the wide-angle peephole Luc had installed himself.

Just then a short man with glasses and a plain face wheeled a gurney out of his neighbor's apartment. As it passed Luc's door a body fell off the gurney. The cop swore, "Jesus, first day on the job? Strap them down before you move them. Here I'll help."

Luc wasn't paying attention much to the cop's words though. Luc stared at the dead body of his son's best friend Kolya, his neighbor's son. Kolya had a peaceful look on his face as if the boy died in his sleep. The gaping wounds on his body told a different story: one wound across his right arm, and one across his right chest. The wounds tugged at a memory, but Luc couldn't figure out what they reminded him of.

He put the nagging thought out of his head, looking away from the body to a man stepping out from his neighbor's apartment. The man wore a black windbreaker. Luc could see the words "Medical Examiner" in bright yellow on the back of the jacket as the man turned and walked over to the cop.

"Doc?" said the cop.

The Medical Examiner nodded to the cop. "John. I won't know for certain until I do the autopsy, but I'd put the time of death at 6:30 AM, right around dawn."

"Ok. Let me check the neighbor, see if anyone's home."

Luc backed away from the door one slow step at a time and eased to the backroom. He murmured silent thanks to Papa Legba that the music was off and Luc had made no sounds yet. Just then a loud knock on the door boomed through the apartment and Luc froze as he heard the cop's voice, "Police. Is anyone in there? I need to speak with you." Luc didn't move again until he heard the cop mutter "Damn." and then heard receding footsteps.

Luc waited for five hours for the cops and CSI to go away. He needed food and more rum, but getting taken in for questioning by the police could make him miss the next ritual window. A night in jail and he'd never see his son again. So, he waited. Once the cops left, Luc slipped out and went to the market on the other side of the block. He took the walkway shortcut between the buildings.

On his way back he heard a hiss behind him and spun around to face a nightmare. Iridescent scales an inch wide covered a hairless body half his height. Its head resembled a dog's, or a wolf's, with a large canine snout, large sharp teeth and piercing blue eyes. "Where is the Archivist? Give us the archivist, and you can live a little longer fleshling," it said.

Luc blinked in shock, trembling with fear and frozen with disbelief. "This isn't happening. What?"

It came closer, within arm's reach. "Your son! Where is your son? I get the Archivist for her; then I will be elevated. Highest of the champions of the Sha'Daa. If I don't find him, others will. Other demons search now. Search across the world for champions of humanity. To kill. Or better yet turn." The demon grinned, oblivious to the stream of drool running out the right side of its mouth.

The mention of his son galvanized Luc, and he threw the bag of groceries in his right hand at the thing, following up with a Galopante as it ducked. A year since he last practiced the Capoeira martial art, but his sweeping hand strike against the side of its head stunned it. Luc decided running to be the best course of action. He remembered his driving instructor in the military "If you're in an ambush, get off the X. Get away.", and Luc didn't know if the demon had backup. He ran fast, trying to get back to his son before another demon found him.

The demon howled, a sound reminiscent of someone coughing into a megaphone, and gave chase, but its short size slowed it. Luc reached the apartment with what he thought was a few minutes lead.

He burst in, seeing Marc sitting on the floor reading the white book. "Marc, grab your book, I'll get the dice. We've got to run. Now." Luc screamed.

Luc heard a door open across the hall, and someone with a Russian accent says "Hui s gory. Luc, what is going on?" He realized he had not closed the apartment door in his hurry.

A minute later he heard a scream and sickening wet ripping sound, followed by the two pieces of his neighbor's corpse falling to the floor and a voice saying "Fleshling. Ah. I have the Archivist. I will feast. Bring your head back to her, the mother of demons."

Chills like cold ice ran down Luc's spine at these words. Luc yelled, "Run" at Marc and turned to face the demon. Luc could see Marc in the mirror on the wall, and he remained still with a dazed look in his eyes. Eyes suddenly gone all white. Marc looked up, his right hand on the book, and said "Ad Ra Me Lek. I name you, I see you, and I bind you. Be gone."

The demon howled and dwindled to a purple smoke that dissipated in a few seconds

Marc turned to his son, "How did you do that?"

"I don't know Dad. I just did. I've been reading this book, and it makes my head hurt but it has all these names and stories about demons. It feels like the book is reading me as I read it. When the demon showed up the book kind of took over."

Luc frowned at this as he heard the bells of the nearby church make their daily noontime Angelus ringing.

This news about the book worried Luc, but the book was not a 'now' problem. "Come on; we need to go. Poor Alexandra. We need to check on Anna, see if she is there. Stay here out of sight while I do." This last was partially for Marc. If anything had happened to his girlfriend Luc wanted to soften the blow before Marc found out. They had seemed to be in love and had talked of getting married.

Luc crossed the hall, careful to not step in the remains of his neighbor, and eased the door open.

He saw Anna's body lying on the couch, as if asleep, except for the gaping wounds across the right side of her chest and her right arm. Luc looked at the wounds and felt his stomach clench as he realized they matched the wounds on her dead brother who died this morning. A moment later he realized they were identical to Marc's wounds. "Oh my god, no.", he cried.

Marc ran into the room at the cry, saying "What, what did you see?" and stopped in shock. Marc looked at the wounds, and at himself, "No. Tell me this didn't happen because of me."

"It's not your fault son. It happened because of me. It's my fault. But what's done is done. We need to go. We can go to Uncle Felix's office for the night." Felix was an accountant who had escaped Haiti with him, and they had remained close until he died last month. Felix's daughter hadn't sold his office yet, and Luc still had a key.

"Dad, tell me you won't do the ritual again. Please."

"Son, I can't lose you a second time." Luc paused. Right now he knew what his son needed to hear even if it wasn't the truth. Luc felt a small taste of reflux in his throat at lying to his child. His wife Marie had always regarded a lie as a kind of broken promise, and he had never lied to Marc before. Luc continued. "Ok, we won't, or if we do I'll discuss it with you. Ok? Now let's move before the police get here."

They made it to Felix's office with no issues. Luc made a nest for them in the small bedroom Felix used for sheltering abused clients, then spent the afternoon trying to comfort Marc. At dusk Luc left to get groceries for dinner, leaving Marc asleep after hours of talking. Just in case he bought another bottle of rum and more thread.

When Luc returned and entered the office, he heard moaning and rushed to the small bedroom. He saw Marc writhing in pain and knew that if Luc didn't do the ritual, these would be his last memories of his son. He had told Marc he wouldn't, but he'd understand, wouldn't he? How can Luc lose him again? Besides, if Marc still objected, then there was always tomorrow night.

Luc got out the rum, and the thread, and fetched the knucklebones with their instructions. This time the ritual went faster, though he stumbled over a few words in his haste.

The ritual complete, Luc saw Marc hadn't woken yet and caught his breath at how peaceful his son now looked. As he reached for the thread to sew Marc up again, Luc saw the next bottle of rum by his son's right hand, ready to dull the pain when he woke. Luc felt more drained than yesterday. Their life sank to new lows with each new day. He had thought they could have a normal life once he brought Marc back. How could he have been so wrong? He cringed, knowing somewhere out there another child just died to keep his son alive. There were no good roads to go down anymore, just dead ends leading to more death and loss.

He felt numb and closed his eyes. He didn't intend to surrender to sleep, but it claimed him within minutes none the less.

⊕ ⊕ ⊕

He woke to the sound of his screaming.

Opening his eyes, Luc saw his son holding a bloody cleaver from the kitchen. Marc sobbed as he struggled to free the cleaver where it lodged within his rib cage.

"Son, what are you doing?"

"I want to die. People are dying to keep me here, and it's not right."

Guilt churned Luc's stomach. His actions led to this. At the same time though, what choice did he have? Any father would save their child at any cost, right? He wasn't so sure now. He could lose Marc in other ways. What if Marc lost his mind from the guilt? Luc went to his son and pulled the cleaver free in one swift pull, then put the bottle of rum into Marc's hand. "Drink, while I sew up the wounds again. We'll talk after."

Marc passed out as Luc stitched the last of the wounds closed and he heard a sound downstairs, a muffled scream. He looked with concern at his son, who was in no shape to defend himself. Luc grabbed the cleaver from the floor and headed down the stairs.

He didn't know what he expected to find at the bottom of the stairs, but it wasn't a demon propped against the building wall, its head laying a few feet away. Nor was it the pristine business card perched on the thing's chest that said "Johnny, Paragon Salesman, Knight," with a phone number.

As he picked up the card, he noticed writing on the back. "There are fates worse than death. If you love your son, bring him and meet me at Dearborn Station in one hour." At 10:45, an hour was just enough time to get there if they went now. Should he go? He didn't know this guy but Johnny did have two things going for him. He had killed this demon that was presumably stalking them. He also had come recommended by the toy seller, and Luc had promised to hear him out. Never breaking a promise was a part of the power from bargaining with the Loa. Break one promise, and the Loa's trust in you goes away until you earn it back by balancing the karmic books. Now the Loa have gone away, for who knows how long, and Luc had been breaking promises over the last two days.

Luc tucked the card into his jeans pocket and trudged upstairs to gather Marc. They'd see this Johnny, and hope he had some way out. Hopefully it would be a way that would let him keep Marc without the need for more deaths and without being hunted by demons.

His taxi gave out a block away from Dearborn Station, and Luc carried Marc the rest of the way before propping him against a brick building across from the station. Marc glared at him with accusing eyes. "Dad, let me die again. I'm begging you, please."

The fog crept in off Lake Michigan, smothering the tower of Dearborn Station across the street. An acrid sulfurous tang infused the fog's smell today, for the second night in a thousand years, and it stung Luc's eyes. He told himself the smell caused his tears. He realized his son had become a man sometime in the last two days, in some ways more of a man than himself. A memory coalesced in his mind; a moment in Dearborn Park nearby when they had been playing soccer and Marc had stolen the ball from him for the first time.

Luc felt sick to his stomach and prepared to bargain with his son. Perhaps he could convince Marc to accept the horrible cost. Then again, perhaps he shouldn't. The pain, the lives of three other children each day, the demons chasing them—was having his child with him worth it? He'd never see Marc again though, and he was the last thing in the world from Marie.

He shuddered, thinking of what Marie would say. The sweetest woman he ever met, but she had a tongue on her if you crossed her and she always chose the right thing for the greater good. He could almost hear her now, "Luc, you got no call to be taking the children from those other parents either, you know what's right. Now you just got to do it."

Marc's voice broke into his thoughts, an echo of his dead wife's. "Dad, it's fifteen minutes to midnight. You need to decide, and you know what's right. Let me go. I can't live knowing I'm tearing other kids away from their parents."

Luc felt it, deep in his soul, and knew the rightness of his dead son and the imagined voice of his dead wife. He nodded, tears flowing down both sides of his face. He steeled himself to say goodbye forever. "Ok, son. Come give your Dad one last hug."

Marc as he almost flew into his arms and they hugged, Luc being careful not to squeeze Marc's wounds.

Johnny watched from the shadows, letting them get acceptance in their own way before he approached. He remembered his own loss, and his own son that Cassilda almost bore on the shores of Lake Hali. He smiled as he stepped out of the darkness, knowing this time he can change the outcome. It will be a harder road for both Marc and Luc, but is a journey they can travel together.

He cleared his throat. "Excuse me, but I have an offer you'll want to hear, and unfortunately I only have twelve minutes in which to pitch it. I had to see if you learned that you had to let go, realized your control is an illusion, before I could make the offer. Would you like to hear the offer?"

Both father and son looked like Johnny dumped a bucket of cold water on their heads—shock and surprise written on their faces. Luc recovered first and said, "Of course."

Johnny smiled more widely, flashing the gold in his teeth. His joy at helping ate at his control, and he started hopping from foot to foot. "So. The Sha'Daa is nearly over. It's a major battle between good and evil, but the war never ends, and there are lots of upcoming little battles. In some ways, they are what turn the tide one way or the other when the Sha'Daa happens, and there are preparations." Johnny paused for a brief moment, fighting his madness and choosing his words.

"Whether good or evil wins is only partly decided by the actions on these battlefields. Supplying weapons and information also plays a big role, in some ways a more important role. The Archive is perhaps the largest repository of knowledge about demons anywhere, and what used to be called the Library of Alexandria when it was much smaller. It used to be in Egypt. Now it is in a special pocket of reality and has become alive. Your son is in a unique position to help because of his tie to the Archive, and through your tie to him. Somehow when he died his soul got diverted to the Archive and they bonded."

Johnny paused again, the hopping getting worse before he controlled himself and continued. "If he agrees I can give him a pearl to swallow. When he dies his soul will reform a healthy body in the shadowlands, permanently tied to the Archives as its Archivist. You and he can visit each other in dreams, which means I can ask you questions to relay to him, and he can send me the answers back via you. That's the first part. The second part I that I have decided I need a driver, and you Luc are eminently qualified. Know this though. If you become my driver you, as Luc, will die and you will become the Dullahan. You'll still be yourself, but you'll be in a state of undeath like your son. That is the offer in full. It is one minute to midnight. Do you accept?"

Luc felt numb with shock. He and Marc turned to each other and smiled as they realized what this meant, then turned back to Johnny and said "Yes." in unison.

They felt the ground shake for a moment as soon as they finished speaking. Luc and Marc watched as a single six-foot long wall of dark green box hedge grew to a height of eight feet before their eyes.

Rose vines covered the hedge and rosebuds covered the vines. The rosebuds remained closed as the hedge grew but bloomed a mix of snow white and blood red as soon as the hedge stopped growing.

Johnny looked at the hedge, sighed, and muttered "Blood on the Snow, again". As the last word faded the hedge changed, a stone archway appearing at the center. The archway was open, but a dingy grey fog blocked their sight through it.

Then Johnny slapped a small glowing iridescent pearl into Marc's hand, "Swallow, now".

Marc stepped back at the command and looked at the pearl. The colors changed from one color to another in quick succession as he brought the pearl to his mouth and swallowed it.

Johnny turned and placed a duplicate pearl with constantly changing colors into Luc's hand, "Swallow, quickly".

Luc started at the touch an almost dropped the pearl. He then brought the pearl to his mouth before he could change his mind and swallowed in one smooth motion.

A second later Luc saw the fog in the archway vanish as if sucked into the stone. Luc could see into an immense stone room with dozens of halls leading off of it and walls lined floor to ceiling with alcoves filled with books, scrolls, or clay tablets. Computer tablets appeared to fill some alcoves, and strange devices Luc didn't recognize filled others.

A moment later an invisible force yanked Marc's body through the archway. Luc saw Marc become whole as soon as he passed through, without wounds and without the pain lines present for the last two days. Luc let out a huge breath, shoulders relaxing. "I love you son."

Marc smiled, then stood waving at him for a moment, "I love you too Dad. I hope we can talk tonight." His voice sounded distorted as if underwater.

Luc had time for one wave back before the archway fogged over again and the hedge sank into the ground. He then turned to Johnny. "What next, boss?"

Johnny took out his cell phone and smiled at Luc, brows furrowed for a moment before he smiled. "Next? Next, we have a meeting in New Orleans. But first we need to balance the books." He lifted the cell phone, pressed a button, and said "Now."

A moment later Luc turned at the sound of a car with a powerful engine turning onto the street. He saw what looked like an all-black Audi luxury sedan with blacked out windows turn the corner and slow to a stop, five feet from Johnny and himself.

Johnny looked at Luc. "There is no uniform, but I expect you to dress cleanly. Also, from this point on you will go by the name and title Dullahan. It comes with the job." Johnny said as he walked around to the trunk of the car and opened it.

Luc saw Johnny withdraw a sword from the trunk and couldn't help but shiver.

The sword was long, five feet overall, three feet of that a broad double-edged blade. It had a wide but simple guard to protect the wielder's hand. Underneath the guard was a long handle, meant for two hands. Johnny held it easily in one hand, hopping more from foot to foot now he held the sword.

Johnny came around the car to stand in front of Luc. "Kneel. Per our bargain, I must sever your head. This is *Caladbolg*, an ancient sword from better times. It will make a quick and clean cut."

Luc knew this was the price for the deaths he had caused, or the start of the price. Luc knelt and looked forward. He could see Johnny and the sword reflected in the car as Johnny raised the sword.

He had a moment to see what looked like a rainbow where the sword passed as Johnny swung, then Luc was cold all over and looking at his own decapitated body from his severed head three feet away. He could still feel his body, and a flex of his hands showed he could still control it. His body had changed color, the skin now to mottled color of moldy cheese.

Luc heard the car trunk close and footsteps close by. Then he felt hands on his head, and his perspective changed as Johnny lifted him off the ground and carried him towards his body. "Traditionally you carry your head in your left hand and drive or fight with your right. Your body has changed now, into something Other. Like other Gentry, you'll find your arms don't get tired.", Johnny said as he placed Luc's head in Luc's left hand. "We may have a better solution than carrying it later, but that will have to do for now. The magic of being the Dullahan will keep people from noticing you as anything different until you want to be noticed."

Luc found turning his head with his hand to look around easier and more natural than he expected. It would still take quite a bit of getting used to though.

Johnny then looked at Luc. "You won't have a uniform, but I expect you to dress well. Also, from this point on you will go by the name and title Dullahan, when speaking with anyone other than me or your son."

Johnny opened to driver-side door, beckoning Luc forward. "This is the car given to me. She is the Cóiste Bodhar, the black coach. She had the form of a horse drawn coach once, but that was long ago." Johnny said as he got in the back and closed the door.

Luc approached the car and saw no driver through the open door, causing goose bumps to rise on his arms. He sat in the driver's seat and found the seat already adjusted to his size, the GPS programmed for the long drive to New Orleans. The radio came on by itself after a moment, playing *Roll the Bones* by Rush.

Trivial Pursuits And Mouse Traps

WITH SEVERAL HOURS LEFT BEFORE THE Sha'Daa ended, Willy worked like a madman to get through as many sales and transactions as he could.

From the overhead speakers a muzak version of *I Have a Little Dreidel* played loudly.

Whirligigs was nearly packed solid with at least five hundred customers. Over half of his full-time employees and temps had collapsed from exhaustion and were snoring away on couches and cots in the small kitchenette lounge on the basement level, down the hallway from the two lower-level display rooms. Willy had now subjected his body to a syringe full of liquefied cocaine to keep himself alert even though every few minutes it felt like his skin was trying to crawl off of his body.

It now seemed like every eldritch creature in traveling distance had crawled, slid, flew, skipped, phased, shadow-walked, teleported, and walked its way out of every supernatural crack, nook, and cranny in the entire state of Illinois.

"Does this come in blue?" a green, unicorn-horned, demon asked about a Hot Stuff figurine he held in his right claws. "The azure sun of my home world does not allow us to see your color red."

"Sorry," Willy said, "that's the last one. Take it or leave it."

With a quick sigh, the demon tossed a gold Krugerrand on the counter and stalked out of the store.

A slobbering werewolf placed a small stuffed Snoopy figure on the counter.

"Eighty dollars," Willy said.

"What?" the werewolf growled in a voice that was nearly unintelligible, "that's outrageous."

"Supply and demand, Lon," Willy said, "take it or leave it."

Lon dropped silver coins, carefully wrapped so he need not touch the dangerous metal, on the counter and walked away mumbling to himself, "You ever visit Llanwelly you better keep your ass off the moors…"

"Excuse me sir, I was looking for a friend and was hoping you might help me find him.

Willy looked up and into the eyes of a blonde young man of normal height and build.

"The name's Prana," he said, "and I'm looking for a man named Johnny. Tall guy, kinda shadowy, and like you has a thing for orthodontic bling."

"Never heard of him," Willy said.

"Oh, come now, Willy Carroll," Prana said, "I know better than that, and yes I know your name and all about you. Now, before you finish reaching for that shotgun under the counter I just wanted to let you know that I hold no ill will towards Johnny. In fact, I happen to be his biggest fan. I'm trying to reach him before The Sha'Daa ends. Is he around?"

Willy looked deep into Prana's eyes and discovered that this stranger's pupils were much like Johnny's…depthless gateways to endless mystery. Shaking his head to clear his thoughts, Willy frowned for a moment.

"I have not seen him for a couple of hours," Willy said, "and I take it you haven't either?"

"Yeah," Prana said with a smile, "I keep finding myself just missing him, which is a nearly impossible feat I have to confide, my toyful friend."

Several feet away, the antique phone booth began ringing. Dozens of demons, aliens, humans, spirits, and things beyond imagination were crowding up behind Prana, impatient to make their purchase.

Willy had to shout to hear his own voice over the raucous commotion.

"He promised he would visit me again after his last visit," Willy said, "you don't think anything happened to him, do you?"

"Something?" Prana laughed. "Yeah, a lot of somethings…but rest assured my friend from Oz, there is almost nothing in this world or any other that could prevent the Salesman from honoring his ten-thousand-year old oath."

The phone booth continued ringing. Willy's imagination more than implied it was sounding off with a greater than before urgency.

"Well," Willy said, "good luck with finding him."

"Uh," Prana said, "some last second advice."

"What?" Willy asked as a cold chill shot up his spine.

"Answer your phone," Prana said, and then simply disappeared.

Willy ran into the booth and snatched up the receiver.

"What?" he shouted.

"Duck!" Kvasir screamed.

An instant later every single toy in Whirligigs came to life.

Babes In Toyland

"It takes a hero to be one of those men who goes into battle."

–Norman Schwarzkopf

WILLY DROPPED TO THE FLOOR AN INSTANT before a large recreational drone with four propellers smashed into the upper half of the phone booth, destroying both itself and the antique phone Willy had used for communicating with the Midnight Laborers.

The speakers overhead transitioned to a muzak version of Chuck Berry's *My Ding-A-Ling.*

Brushing the smoking phone and drone debris off his head and shoulders, he peeked out at the madness that had spread throughout Whirligigs.

It was more than a burgeoning battle…it was the beginning of an all-out war.

Hundreds of customers screamed in shocked surprise and ran for the exit as the toys they were holding and waiting to purchase came to life and leaped, scrambled, jumped, and flew from their possession.

Thousands of toys of various shapes and sizes leaped from the shelving all across the store and scrambled in various directions to the far perimeters of the main floor space of the store. At first it looked like pure chaos, but in a matter of a few minutes, Willy could see that the vast majority of toys were forming into two large masses, one on the far left, and the second on the far right of the main store.

In minutes, the head and air space throughout the main floor was rapidly filling with flying ball drones, gyro drones with HD cameras, mini helicopters, mechanical flapping birds, all in a wide variety of sizes and complexity. Bent over and scuttling toward the main stairwell to confirm that all his employees had made it upstairs and were heading to escape out the main front doors, Willy realized the majority of flying toys were moving with a purpose. After another couple of minutes, he became convinced that they were doing aerial surveys of each other side's territory, numbers, and resources. Why they were doing this sent a chill up Willy's spine as it more than implied a major conflict.

Once the last of his employees left the store, and only about a hundred customers were left all trying to squeeze out the main entrance at the same time. Willy found himself crouched down behind and within the c-shaped main cash register's counter, staring at and adjusting the small row of ten-inch security monitors connected to eight security cameras on the main floor's ceiling, as well as another dozen security cameras in the stairwell and all three of the rooms at the basement level.

After several minutes of surveillance, Willy could see no obvious indication the nature of the two forming armies was. They each had a wide variety of toys and a pretty random mix of cartoon and movie figurines and action figures of both good guys and bad guys. There didn't appear to be any one particular kind of toy prevalent in either group.

"It's good versus evil, Knucklehead."

Willy jerked his head to the side to see a smiling Johnny the Salesman sitting on the floor and looking at him expectantly.

"You're kidding," Willy said.

"Not at all," Johnny replied, "your toys, all imbued with your very special brand of eldritch magics, are coming to life, achieving sentience because of the weird Sha'Daa manna that now fills the air…and they are choosing sides."

"But Whirligigs," Willy shouted, "is neutral ground."

"Not anymore," Johnny chuckled, "you may want to sit this out, but these toys know what's at stake, and are willing to put their existence on the line… unlike some immortal toymakers under an ancient enchantment that I know."

It took a moment for these words to sink in, and then Willy's eyes lit up.

"Enchantment?" Willy asked, "is this why I only started remembering my long dead wives a few hours ago?"

"At last," Johnny smiled, "this lost soul is starting to wake up."

"And why is it so important to you that I wake up?" Willy asked.

"Because," Johnny said, while standing up to his full height, "even though a gargantuan tattoo drawn across the face of the earth has just destroyed hundreds of portals to hundreds of hell dimensions, there are still dozens of evil doorways still remaining, still available for massive armies of evil to pour through and devour this planet. I'm afraid this has become more personal than you'd ever have imagined."

"And why is that?" Willy asked, from his sitting position as a foot-long helium filled dirigible with a pair of battery powered propellers circled Johnny's fedora covered head.

"Because," Johnny replied, "the biggest hell portal of them all just happens to sit underneath Whirligigs, and your toys are about to battle over whether it opens, or stays closed."

A squeal and blare of electronic horns caught both their attentions.

"War has commenced," Johnny said, then disappeared.

Willy stood up and beheld an amazing sight. Thousands of toys from either side of the main floor rushed towards each other, flying, leaping, bouncing, running, crawling, and driving.

"What have I done?" Willy whispered.

The collision of toys across the entire length of the middle of the main floor sent a shock wave through the air that knocked Willy off his feet, and his head struck the main counter.

⊕ ⊕ ⊕

Willy's eyes opened and quickly focused. An awful cacophony of smashing and tearing sounds assaulted his ears. Standing up Willy's eyes and mind were nearly overwhelmed with devastation. Willy also realized that the overhead speaker system appeared to have been damaged beyond repair as no muzak was playing and he wondered if it still worked on the lower level of the store.

A quick glance at his pocket watch told him he'd only blacked out for minutes, but during that interval, the interior of the shop had been thoroughly destroyed. All but a few sets of shelves, including the ten-foot-tall steel ones, had been torn down and reduced to mere pieces. Mounds of broken and destroyed toys lay everywhere. No structure over two feet in height was left standing. The entire surface of the main floor, with the exception of the magically charmed, curved main cash register counter that Willy stood within, now took on the look of a smoking and burning landscape of doom…a battlefield whose sins were still in progress.

Every couple of feet, closely matched toys still fought for supremacy, and life. Altercations were occurring everywhere, and on closer inspection, they had advanced in unexpected ways. Willy saw this as looking up toward the ceiling. Not only were various drones still flying, but now action figure toys who could fly in movies, cartoons, and TV shows were now somehow magically able to fly. All toys that possessed previously inert weaponry, were now projecting lethal particle beams, railgun projectiles, coilgun ordnance, ion cannon beams, miniature bullets and artillery shells, tiny arrows and spears. In the case of two scale model Tupolev strategic bombers, one to a side, were dropping shells that left two-foot-diameter crater holes in the floor.

Willy ducked as a flying Madelman action figure fired a wing-mounted air to air missile at a flying Centurion action figure that deflected the missile explosion with his small round shield.

Willy tried to scuttle to his left, toward the main stairwell, but was stopped in his tracks as a dozen tiny green army soldiers, all of their WWII era weapons firing, charged six heavily-armored Doom Marines firing plasma rifles and wielding chainsaws.

Circling this altercation, Willy got within a dozen feet of the main stairwell, but was cut off by a series of small explosions. Squinting he watched as one hundred three-inch-tall World of Warcraft Dwarf Warriors swarmed a foot-tall Godzilla model that let loose a devastating plasma stream from its mouth every time its back scales and barbs started glowing. The plumes of scorching heat forced Willy to give up on the stairwell and come up with a more dangerous plan.

The Midnight Laborers, he thought, *they just might turn the tide.* Willy quickly redoubled his efforts to make his way toward the rear of the main floor. He had to access the Midnight Laborers pocket realm.

It took Willy fifteen minutes to traverse a one hundred feet of main floor space, but in that time he side-stepped the denizens of three dozen Barrels of Monkeys swarming a two-foot tall Ymir resin model; then circumvented two Rock 'Em Sock 'Em Robots that had freed themselves from their boxing ring and were wiping the floor with dozens of angry Troll Dolls; then next flattened himself on the ground behind a pile of broken toys to keep from being noticed by six Evel Kneivel Stunt Cycle Riders revving their bikes and riding around looking for trouble to get into. Another five minutes were spent in a panic running in circles and mostly successfully ducking Micronaut Hydrocopters firing tiny shells from mounted rotary cannons.

Dropping behind the remains of one of his tall shelves, Willy took several deep breaths. Thousands of tiny wounds covered his face and hands, none of them more than a millimeter or two deep, but the cumulative pain was beginning to distract him.

Willy was now ten feet away from the rear wall that would give him access to the Midnight Laborers. Unfortunately, this chunk of territory was filled with an auto battle reminiscent of a Mad Max movie. Dozens of Hot Wheels cars were revving their tiny engines and jousting with a wide variety of wood cars, tin cars, cast iron cars, sheet steel cars, and plastic cars sold throughout the twentieth century.

The Hot Wheels vehicles were being led by The Knight Rider two-thousand, Voice Car that was continuously shouting out orders. All the other vehicles were being led by a Mego Dukes of Hazzard General Lee Dodge Charger toy car that kept finding various debris to use as ramps for making small leaps over the other toys.

"Oh, what a day, what a lovely day!"

Willy jerked his head to see a smiling Johnny sitting next to him.

"Can you believe this madness, Salesman?" Willy gasped.

"Be still my toymaker of war. I understand your pain," Johnny said, "we've all lost something we love."

"And what is that supposed to mean?" Willy snapped.

"In case you haven't noticed, Toyman," Johnny said, "the forces and lethality of the remaining toys is growing exponentially."

"So?" Willy asked.

"If you pull your Midnight Laborers into this conflict," Johnny said, "many, very many, will die. I think you owe them more than that."

Willy started a nasty retort and then stopped himself. In the last half day Willy had not only started remembering his many years of immortality and the love and lives of his former wives, but also his long friendship with the Midnight Laborers. Something he'd had almost forgotten over the past century.

Of course, the Salesman is right, Willy thought.

"What am I to do?" Willy asked.

"Well," Johnny grinned and looked back over his shoulder at the distant wall not far from the main cash register counter, "some troubles once thrown with great sin, will oft fly back at you again."

And a moment later Johnny disappeared, and Willy found his sightline clear as he spotted what Johnny had been looking toward, the glass encased, antique Australian Boomerang. Though he didn't exactly know why, Willy felt a terrible urge rise within his breast to clasp that talisman that he had not held in a couple of hundred years. With a burst of renewed energy, he leaped up and began running across the deadly battlefield his toy store floor had become.

Instantly, about half of the toys stopped their fighting. As if comprehending the danger to their plans in his intent, they all swarmed in his direction. Simultaneously, the other half of the toys charged to defend Willy's sprint.

Willy had barely made twenty feet when a Chatty Cathy doll, a Punch-Me Inflatable Yogi Bear Punching Bag, a Little Miss Echo doll, a Casper the Ghost doll, a GI Joe astronaut, a Talky Crissy Doll, and a Dressy Bessy simultaneously leaped onto and against his legs. This knocked Willy sideways and almost off of his feet, but he managed to maintain his balance and knock and kick away the attackers and run five more feet before a new wave of assault.

Four self-propelled Slinkys, three dozen sliding Fisher Price Little People, five Mrs. Beasley Dolls, one dozen Weebles, all three Holly Hobbie dolls, three snarling Strawberry Shortcake dolls, and a screaming, Baby Alive doll, struck him from every direction. This forced him to one knee and it took a whole fifteen seconds to knock them away with his hands. He finished by using the Baby Alive doll as a club on the last of the Strawberry Shortcakes before tossing it away to shatter on the far wall right after it yelled in a receding voice, "I thought we were friends to the end, Willy."

Willy was half way across the floor and breathing heavily when over his shoulder he spotted the flyers begin their kamikaze dives toward his exposed back.

Dropping rapidly toward Willy were a vintage, tin toy, Space Commander rocket ship, a rubber band powered AJ Experimental ROG toy plane, a black and gold master tournament Frisbee, a Tinkerbell action figure with a nasty snarl, a Space 1999 Eagle spaceship, a Star Trek space shuttle, a Komoda tin Fling Jeep, a classic Captain Marvel action figure, a Voyage to the Bottom of the Sea Flying Sub, and a Papo toy Pterodactyl.

Just before they could strike Willy, another wave of flying toys consisting of a model WWII Spitfire, a S.H.A.D.O. Interceptor, a Rom Spaceknight model, an Ultraman action figure, a vintage Japanese Atom Rocket Seven, a Marx Flash Gordon Rocket Fighter tin toy, a jet powered Optimus Prime action figure, the original Jupiter-2 saucer spaceship, and a model Latitude Zero flying Alpha Submarine, intercepted and collided with the feral ill-willed toys, instantly destroying both forces which fell to the floor as burning and smoking wreckage.

Willy was now only ten feet from his shadowboxed boomerang, when a group of toys filled the floor between him and his ancient talisman. Without breaking stride he took a series of sidesteps and jumps to avoid a pair of snarling Teddy Ruxpin dolls, hop over a phalanx of Cabbage Patch Dolls and angry Elmos, kick his way through a vicious village of Smurf figures, stomp a herd of snapping My Little Pony dolls, and in a final burst of energy, grab up two large stuffed Teletubbies (probably Dipsy and Laa-Laa but Willy didn't have time to confirm) by their legs, one in each hand, and in a frenzy used them as clubs, smashing their heads against a last rush of dozens of feral toys of all shapes and sizes, clearing a path ahead of him.

He reached the unbreakable glass-fronted box, and with all his magic-augmented strength smashed into it with the emerald hard antenna of Dipsy before tossing the large doll aside and reaching for the ancient boomerang. As quickly as that, the powerful enchantment that had suffused Willy's mind so long ago, just bled away. For the first time in endless decades his eyes could see. A multitude of lost memories poured into his mind.

What have I done? he thought.

Looking about, Willy noticed that the remaining toys had stopped moving and were now clustered into two groups, of two hundred toys each. One group had glowing green eyes. Willy perceived they wanted to open the hell portal beneath Whirligigs. The other group had glowing amber eyes and were definitely closers. They were waiting to see what his decision was going to be…would he now become an Opener…or a Closer?

Willy looked back across the years and faced the truth of his existence. He had made a bargain long ago, to acquire powers and immortality. He thought he had seen all angles, and garnered the better part of the deal, gaining an extended life and the ability to create magical barriers and imbue objects with power, and all for the cost of a small portion of his soul, or so he had thought.

The ethereal powers he had talked with back in Australia said he would lose his empathy for most people, but would retain his love and caring for those closest to him, and for a hundred years this was true, but over the years this unholy bargain began to unwind, and Willy slowly began to lose his goodwill toward everyone, pets, his co-workers, and when his last wife died, he just never grew close to another woman. All that time, whenever the thought of this change would enter his mine, it would just as quickly disappear, and any memory that would bring it back somehow disappeared also. Those ancient powers had cheated on the deal. They had lied.

"As evil always does," Johnny said.

Willy looked to his left.

"I was a fool, Salesman," Willy said.

"You were human," Johnny said, "and now you have regained your humanity, and you have to make a choice."

Willy looked down at the boomerang in his hand.

"If I make a choice in this conflict," Willy said carefully, "I sense I will lose much, maybe all, of the power I now possess."

"True," Johnny replied, in a noncommittal voice.

Willy agonized for but a moment, and then spoke aloud, "So be it."

Willy then raised the boomerang high and shouted aloud in a language forgotten by all mankind, save for himself.

Every toy in the shop dropped lifeless to the floor.

"Now," Johnny said, "if you can survive the next few minutes, the hell portal will not open underneath us."

"Survive what?" Willy asked.

Johnny pointed toward the front doors and Willy gasped.

Walking toward Whirligigs, crossing the street, were all four bronze statues from Oz Park, The Tin Man, The Cowardly Lion, The Scarecrow, and Dorothy and Toto, and all bore terrifying looks.

"Will the talismans imbedded in my walls stop them?" Willy asked.

"They have lost much of their power," Johnny replied, "I'd say it was a fifty-fifty proposition, Mister Carrollton. If you'll excuse me, I have a terribly pressing engagement with a very special underground Pub. Good luck, mate."

And Johnny was no longer there.

Willy ran towards the main entrance and gaped in awe as the four animated bronze statues began attacking the store front with their fists. Their strikes echoed into the building and the floors themselves began vibrating. Cracks began to form in the thick security glass of the front doors and surrounding storefront. Willy looked down at the boomerang. *I hope you've got enough mojo left to finish this.*

The five bronze refugees from the Land of Oz furiously burst into Whirligigs.

Willy raised his boomerang and shouted, "Born of the heart of the sacred Yalu' tree... *Yalu' mayali' \unhi dhu ga be\ur be\ur marrtji yol\u, ga \unhiwiliw dhu ga \al'yun limurru\gal, \unhi wanhawal yalu'lil dhu ga \al'yun w^\alil, nhakun balanya nhakun warraw' dhuthunu\u dharpa, dhuthunu\u dharpa!*"

A flash of amber light shot out of the boomerang, split into two beams of energy. One struck the large nickel-chromium steel Robot Maria statue at the left of the front alcove. The other fell on the eight-foot tall Steiff Teddy Bear on the right. Their eyes instantly opened, glowing with an amber life. The giant Teddy bear stood up and with Robot Maria by its side, strode to do battle with the animated bronze Ozite statues of evil.

Robot Maria and the Tin Man collided in a clash of sparks, stopping each other in their tracks. A moment later they commenced trading devastating punches and kicks that left inch-deep depressions in the bronze park statue, and smaller dents and scores on the female robot's glistening body. Every one of their strikes reverberated like a massive church bell and Willy cringed at the pain in his ears.

Whirligigs' massive Teddy Bear charged both the bronze Cowardly Lion and bronze Scarecrow. The Bear's spongy mass not only stopped both attackers, but flexed and caused the two man-size opponents to bounce backwards, shattering the granite floor with three-foot long cracks. Teddy laughed with a joyful bellow that was followed by a hair-raising growl as his two opponents began to stand.

The bronze Dorothy, struggling to hold onto her frisky bronze Cairn Terrier, Toto, had a look of shock and surprise on her face. She held back from joining the fray, her attention on her three companions.

The Scarecrow got up first, ran forward and locked hands with paws. With a terrifying growl the giant Teddy twisted, bent, and wrapped his opponents smaller bronze arms around like a large knot, then shoved him away to collide with the nearest wall and fall to the floor, flopping around like a big insect, unable to stand. The Cowardly Lion statue growled and leaped forward, ducking under a swipe of the Teddy's massive right paw.

The Dorothy and Toto statues continued to hang back as Willy suddenly noticed that a small fountain of green energy had appeared in the middle of the ruined main floor. At the same time, small sparks of amber energy started flickering all around the edges of the boomerang he was holding. Willy frowned and realized that the energy was not hot and thus would not burn his hand. On instinct, he pointed the boomerang at the magical font and a blast of golden energy erupted from the weapon and flew forward to collide with the green energy, stopping its growth, and very slowly begin to make it wither.

Robot Maria shoved the Tin Man against the wall, tore off the funnel on his head, and shoved it into his mouth, pounding on the back of it with her fist until it pierced the head and the wall behind it, pinning the evil bronze statue to the dense granite block that made up this side of the front greeting room.

The Toto statuette, green light blazing from its eyes, leaped from Dorothy's arms, hit the granite floor hard and sprinted toward Willy, sparks flying each time its bronze paws hit the ground. Just as it was almost upon him Willy turned around at the approaching sound and pointed his boomerang at Toto, as the bronze dog leaped upward, throat level. A beam of gold energy leapt from Willy's boomerang and sliced through Toto, effectively cutting him in half from nose to tail. Both sides of the smoking bronze canine struck the ground with grim finality.

"Oh, my," the Dorothy statue said, with a voice like a robotic version of Judy Garland's mellifluous young voice, "you horrible bad man, you killed Toto… now I'm going to have to tear you a new asshole, Mister."

The Cowardly Lion stood up, rising above the Teddy Bear who lay on the ground, torn and covered in mounds of excelsior gore. Both he and the Maria Robot locked eyes and charged.

The Dorothy statue, unchallenged, walked immediately toward Willy who was again battling with the green fountain of energy that had grown larger again when he had been distracted by Toto.

"Say," Willy shouted in desperation, "wouldn't you rather be in Kansas right now, little girl? Blue skies, lush verdant farm fields, miles away from the inequities of man?"

"Tea-totaling parents," Dorothy responded, "a racist and religiously intolerant community, killer tornados, and backbreaking harvest labor followed by the daily scraping of cow shit off my heels…thank Hecate this is no place like home."

Behind her the Cowardly Lion and Robot Maria were on the floor, wrestling fiercely. With one mighty swipe the Lion gouged out Maria's right eye. She responded with a silent scream and threw a powerful punch directly into the lion's mouth. Her fist immediately exited out the back of his head. The cowardly feline kicked several times then went still. Maria suddenly realized her arm was stuck in the dead lion's mouth and struggled fiercely to remove her hand.

The green fountain had shrunk down to a mere pool of green sparks when Willy was forced to spin around and redirect the boomerang's amber energy beam at the advancing Dorothy.

It did not immediately cut through her as it had Toto. Willy realized that battling the green fountain had drained more than half of the ancient artifact's accumulated power away.

Dorothy advanced another two steps as the amber energy beam started eating away at her torso. Green and white sparks and small globs of molten bronze shot out in every direction, burning and scarring everything they touched.

Willy gritted his teeth and leaned forward continuing to point the boomerang at her. Pain and rage came over the Dorothy statue's face as it also leaned forward, taking agonizingly slow steps as if pushing again hurricane winds.

Dorothy got within three feet of Willy and swung her right arm. Still holding the boomerang that was emitting a slowly dying beam of amber energy, Willy saw the approaching claw-like bronze hand and cringed, but Robot Maria came from nowhere to wrap her dented and pockmarked arms around Dorothy's neck and forehead.

"Shame on you folks," Dorothy squeaked as she locked eyes with Willy, "I think I'll miss you least of all."

With a mighty yank and horrible screech of tearing metal Robot Maria ripped Dorothy's head off her body and tossed it away. Dorothy's frozen torso fell over and struck the floor hard, cracks forming all around her.

Willy, exhausted, staggered to the nearest wall, sat down, and leaned against it. A quick glance told him the green fountain of energy had completely died. The hell portal was now closed. No army of demons would pour through and annihilate all life on Earth.

He looked up in surprise as the Robot Maria walked up and sat down beside him, her steel body gouging a long groove down the wall and raising a few sparks when settling on the floor next to Willy.

Robot Maria suddenly pointed a finely crafted index finger to the top of Willy's head. Willy frowned, reached out and picked up a piece of cracked chrome that had been broken off a toy earlier. He realized what the Maria Robot was silently noticing…his hair was no longer carrot red, but now white. The ancient enchantment that had granted him immortality was fading away. He looked down at the boomerang and saw that only a few sparks of amber energy danced on its edges.

Willy reached into his breast pocket and pulled out his pocket watch.

"Well, Maria," Willy said, "looks like there is still two hours left in The Sha'Daa. The battles rage elsewhere…and humanity is still in danger."

Willy then noticed wrinkles spreading across the backs of his hand.

"But we've done our bit my beautiful Sheila," Willy said, his own voice sounding strange and hoarse to him, "and this corner of the planet is safe… whatta you say we share a little together time, just you and me."

A wave of weakness spread over Willy and he slowly slunk down until he found his head being cradled, surprisingly gently, against Maria's steel breasts as her arms wrapped around him.

"I was damned, Maria," Willy whispered, "I gave up love and knew it not...spending years making these atrocious toys...but I found that truth again, in time...and you know what that truth is, Maria?"

The Maria Robot statue, with its one good eye, looked down into Willy's aged wrinkled face and shook her head with a series of squeaks and creaking metal.

Willy coughed twice, painfully, then slowly parted his heavily chapped lips.

"The mediator of the head and the hands," Willy said in a soft clear voice, "must be the heart."

A small amber tear ran down the front of Maria's nickel-chromium face, dropped, and rested on Willy's pale, wrinkled forehead...then she closed his unmoving eyes.

The End

VISIT

SHADAA.COM

for all author biographies, the secret history of

this chilling franchise, and the inside

low-down on all the books in

Michael H. Hanson's

Sha'Daa™ series

(including those currently in the works)

and how you can order them.

THE SHA'DAA IS COMING.

ARE YOU READY?

MORE TITLES FROM MOONDREAM PRESS

COPPER DOG PUBLISHING LLC

OUR IMPRINTS:

MoonDream PRESS

RACKET RIVER PRESS

PUMPKIN HILL PRESS

To find out more about our imprints
and our upcoming releases, visit our website:
www.CopperDogPublishing.com
or our Facebook page:
www.facebook.com/copperdogpublishing

Made in the USA
San Bernardino, CA
15 December 2018